# Moral Chains

**Book One**
**of the**
**The Absence of Pity Trilogy**

**Also by Richard A. McDonald**

The Flattery of Knaves –Book Two

Love to Justice – Book Three

**Forthcoming**

**The Presence of Hope Trilogy**

The Counsels of the Wise and Good – Book One

Vanity and Presumption – Book Two

Sobriety of Understanding – Book Three

ISBN: 1536837822
ISBN-13: 978-1536837827

"No one who hasn't gone through such a thing, can imagine what the will to live is, what a moment of life is. Every person, without exception, is capable of doing the worst things just to live another minute."

Dov Paisikowic - born 1924 –Velky Rakovec – Czechoslovakia
Prisoner number A-3076 – Slave Labourer – Sonderkommando - Auschwitz-Birkenau Crematoria no.1 – 1944
Died 1988.

# Chapter 1

## Today – 0600 – Northern France - 1940

Teddy's main problem was, he was going to die today. He'd nearly died three times yesterday, but he'd killed instead. He'd kill again today, but even that might not ensure his survival.

If he'd done better at school, he'd be somewhere else, maybe someone else; he hadn't, here he was. That was just another problem; he didn't know where he was.

"Teddy, you little cunt, wake up, wake up!"

A swift kick in his ribs finished the work the words had begun, and he was fully awake.

It was May the 24th 1940, he was somewhere near Calais, he hoped. His company, from the Royal Fusiliers of the British Expeditionary Force, had been heading west towards Boulogne. They hadn't made it, neither had Boulogne he assumed. They'd retreated, heading north and eastward as best they could. He was still in Gaul, and that thought made him smile. There was no pleasure in the smile, just irony, and a good chance he was the last of his company left alive. He needed to ensure he stayed that way.

"I'm not little, I'm six foot," Teddy lied.

"Ha! Well done son, but you're still a cunt and you need to be wide awake, or you'll be a dead one!"

"Yes Corp, my real name's Archie, though."

He'd used his nickname out of habit last night and wished he hadn't. Today would decide who he was.

"Archie? Archibald, my son, is a posh officer's name, you ain't posh, and you ain't no officer, stick with Teddy, you'll live longer, now look lively or I'll shoot you meself!"

Corp, was nondescript, about thirty, Teddy guessed, clean shaven, apart from a thin moustache just above his top lip. Corp had told him his name the previous night, but he wasn't listening. He had a southern accent, London probably. Teddy used a bland English accent, designed to fit whatever company he was in. He could easily do a proper posh officer's voice. He wouldn't need that today.

*'What does 'look lively' mean anyway? Ask me to do something useful. Shall I jump up and down? Have a dance with you? Yeah, let's have a jig then. Jerry might see us and think, Oh Dear, Tommy looks exceedingly lively today, Mein Fuhrer, let's not bother attacking, in fact, let's just go back to Berlin instead!'*

As usual, Teddy didn't give voice to his thoughts. He just listened, watched and kept his head down.

The only other men nearby were *Mad Mike* and *Spotter*. Spotter was a little friendlier than Corp, but that wasn't saying much, he'd called him a wanker instead of a cunt. The swearing didn't bother Teddy, he'd heard and used worse. It just didn't inspire any loyalty towards the men he was expected to stand next to in a fight to the death.

Spotter was Steve Potter, the lookout at the observation post where they sat. His small eyes contained, according to him, anyway, the keenest eyesight in his company. His cheeks also displayed the largest number of spots he'd ever seen in one place. Teddy asked him why the other Private was called Mad Mike.

"Cos his name's Mike, son."

He decided it was a bloody good answer and filed it in his brain for future use. If he had a future.

Mad Mike was a miserable looking, overweight and candle faced abomination who was 'in charge' of a heavy barrelled, belt loading machine gun.

The Vickers; reliable, water cooled and fired up to five hundred rounds a minute. Designed in 1912 and this looked like one of the originals. It weighed a ton and took a six-man crew to work it properly. One fired it, one fed the ammo, then four others carried it, ammunition and spare parts. If it was so reliable why was someone permanently needed to carry spares? The German equivalent fired twice as many rounds per minute and one man could carry and fire it. A skilled operator could even use it to shoot from the hip.

He knew that. He'd read it and remembered it, word for word. He'd chosen to forget a lot lately, but he remembered those details which might save or cost his life. He kept them filed at the front of his mind, every second, ready for immediate use.

Mike looked as rusty as his gun, chain-smoking the Woodbines he'd given him last night. Teddy didn't smoke, although he always accepted his ration to swap for other, rarer goods, like anything remotely decent to eat or a favour. By any standards of army camaraderie, Mike now owed Teddy a favour. Teddy somehow sensed that concept was beyond Mike's limited comprehension. He also sensed Mike hadn't washed in some time. None of them had washed recently or properly, but Mike's crotch smelt of six-month-old classroom Plasticine. Mike had stopped washing before he arrived in France, possibly before he'd left school. Mike looked and smelt like bad luck made flesh.

Teddy was handsome, even in a crummy uniform with dirty dark wavy hair and tired brown eyes. Only twenty, with the lines on his face and gaunt from lack of food and sleep, he looked older. He was five eleven, lean and muscular, he had an engaging smile, but wouldn't be using it today.

He had potential he might never realise. He was a bog-standard Private in a useless army on the losing side in a politician's war. These three men thought he was a nobody, just like them, he wasn't, he was somebody. Somebody they didn't expect.

*'The nation that will insist on drawing a broad line of demarcation between the fighting man and the thinking man is liable to find its fighting done by fools, and it's thinking done by cowards.'*

He'd read those words somewhere too, Lieutenant General William Butler wrote them less than fifty years ago, too soon to have been forgotten. The inexcusably forgotten truth of those words was no use to him now. He pushed them to the back of his mind. Melancholy or self-pity would get him killed today. He needed to become an

3

animal again and concentrated hard on that.

His enforced companions that morning were only the beginning of his impending death. The predawn light was slowly and disturbingly revealing he was in a shell-damaged house, two hundred yards from the town's outskirts. He stood up, trying to loosen the dead muscles which wanted to cramp, give up and sleep again. Above him, what he'd mistaken last night for a roof, was just the remnants of another storey that had leant dangerously over his head all night. It was best not to know some things, he'd already decided that. In his experience, truth was overrated, if not overused.

The next bad news was the view ahead of him, he crouched back down onto his haunches, bouncing on his toes and feigning a measure of calm confidence. He could usually fake that, he'd needed to often enough lately.

The road ahead of the house was a single track country lane, narrow and straight as a die as far as he could see. Well made, tarmacked and somehow undamaged by the now routine mayhem in Northern France. Along that road, half a mile away, a light morning mist was gradually clearing, to show the neat outline of a heavily wooded copse. Jerry would be there, one neat Jerry behind each neat tree, they wouldn't be smoking or having a cuppa, they'd have that when they'd earned it, treats tasted better when you'd earned them.

Jerry would be rolling up his sleeves, carefully. Jerry knew his trade, it was colder now, but would be hot later. He'd roll those sleeves up so they wouldn't slip down until he'd finished his work. While you were adjusting your tunic at noon, he'd blow your head off. Oh yes, Jerry was looking at him right now.

The observation post was so obvious they might as well have put up a sign. A flag of St. George perhaps, or drawn a target on the one wall left standing.

Everything he'd gone through, everything he'd done, and he'd ended up in this dump.

Spotter had a half decent position and a not so decent

pair of binoculars. He kept the right distance back from his improvised spyhole, staying at an angle to the hole to present as small a target as possible. He'd even seen him put some fine dry dust in his pocket. He'd sprinkle a little on the lenses later to reduce their tell-tale glint when the sun was higher. He'd met one good officer at least then, a little tip like that could save your life. Not today though, Spotter would be dead, long before the sun rose fully.

Teddy's frustration grew seamlessly into anger, red-hot anger and animal rage.

Mad Mike didn't seem to have moved since last night. That was good, he smelt worse when he moved; stopping breathing would have helped as well, but that would happen soon. Mike was blowing most of his smoke through the same hole that showed his machine gun barrel to the Germans. If there wasn't a target on the wall already, Mad Mike was blowing smoke signals instead.

Teddy concentrated and stopped gritting his teeth, it was hurting his jaw. He took some slow deep breaths and breathed out fully each time. He couldn't figure out why Jerry hadn't shot Mike already. He must have been watching him all night, the cigarette glow blinking on and off like a Belisha beacon. Jerry must have felt sorry for him, maybe he was just having a laugh? No, Teddy had seen no evidence of sorrow or humour in Jerry. Jerry had quickly worked out if he'd shot the stupid fool, the English might replace him with a less stupid fool. A fool who might do a vaguely competent job, which would inconvenience him on his way to Paris. Even if Jerry's worst sniper, somehow, missed the fat stupid stinking fool. If Mike somehow managed to fire that relic in the right direction, the muzzle flash was so bright, a dozen Jerrys would be shooting at it within two seconds.

The Vickers might have scared the skin off a barefoot Abyssinian native armed with a sharpened stick. Not Jerry, he wasn't going to run straight at us with fixed bayonets, not this war.

Even all that wasn't Teddy's whole problem. His job

today, when it kicked off, was to sit right next to Mike, feeding a belt of bullets carefully and precisely into that gun. Then keep doing it until he was dead; five seconds if he was lucky.

He looked at the three men around him, took another long slow deep breath of fresh morning air and knew they were expendable. As good as dead, like Caesar's legendary, but mythical, criminal shock troops; Chosen Men, chosen to die first, Teddy would make a different choice.

After all the plans he'd made, all the luck he'd worked so hard for, he refused to die today, not this morning, not with these fools, not for nothing.

This observation post would give the main defensive area about one second's warning of Jerry advancing, and would achieve its purpose by exploding apart two hundred yards away from them.

*'Few things are brought to successful issue by impetuous desire, but most by calm and prudent forethought.'*

Thucydides, this time, but he could use those words today.

He badly needed a plan, an excellent plan even, and a fallback plan or another miracle like yesterday. He had about twenty minutes before two or three Panzers came out of the wood, full pelt, half a mile, on that good, straight road. It was Roman; armies had marched along that road before, he could feel it, he knew all the history. For a second, he saw and felt that army in all its glory, and he longed to be with it again. As he had been, in his dreams and imagination.

Those memories, and their voices in his head, all told him to shut up and plan, and he began his mantra.

*'One. I'm wide awake, the air's cold and sharp, it's a good time to think. Survive.*

*Two. The three mugs in front of me, are gonna decide if I live or die today. That's a fact, it won't change so just work with it.*

*Three. These mugs are already dead, they're expendable. It doesn't matter who kills them or when it happens.*

6

*Four. How I live or die, doesn't matter today. Being alive tomorrow matters. I have to survive. Survival of the fittest, that's life. Life's dealt me these cards, all I can do is play them or die.*

*Five. Shoot all three and leg it. I can do that easily and avoid any consequences in the chaos that's gonna start any minute now. I don't know them, I don't like them, and I shouldn't be here anyway.*

*Six. Spotter first, he's right in front of me, looking through his binoculars, easy first meat. Corp second, he's standing up and having a piss behind a wall, he's shielded from Jerry, but not from me. I can't see his rifle, but shock and a handful of pissing dick should slow him down for a couple of seconds, enough for the reload and fire. Corp'll see me and look me in the eye as he dies. I can live with that. Mike last, one hand on a heavy machine gun pointing the wrong way and the other on a fag, piece of cake. There's no time for pity today.*

*Seven. Problem, I'll have to use Mike's rifle, mine's long gone, the Luger's deep in my pack and empty anyway. Mike's rifle's leaning on the wall to his left, two paces from me. I'll have to ask him, casually and quickly, and I'll have to do it, right now.'*

'Yes. Kill them,' one of the voices in his head told him, 'these savages are unworthy of your death. Your value is more than this, much more. Kill them.' He couldn't remember where he'd read those words, but paid attention to them anyway.

He started to rise from his crouch while taking half an important stride towards Mike.

"Mike, you owe me a favour, can I borrow your rifle?" he said.

Mike's answer was irrelevant, Teddy was having it regardless. Mike turned his head towards him while he took the rest of his first stride and the start of the second.

"No. Fuck off!" Mike answered.

Mike's left hand moved unnaturally slowly towards his rifle, like a selfish child reaching for his toy, because it was his, no other reason needed.

The intensity of everything in Teddy's vision flared brightly. No flash, nothing blurred, every single detail as clear and sharp as the brightest daylight. Every colour, as deep and vivid as he could ever remember seeing.

The next half stride and he'd be there first, he knew with an absolute certainty he could move faster than fat, slow Mike. His breath caught in his throat as, astonishingly, his own movements slowed as much as Mike's. A huge surge of Teddy's adrenalin had made time and motion slow down, without affecting speed of thought.

Teddy knew, for what felt like minutes, what would happen, before it did. They'd grab that rifle at precisely the same moment, and they'd fight over it. Even if he won the struggle, the chance would be gone, he was dead.

He grabbed the gun anyway, and, as expected, at the same moment as Mike.

Their eyes met in another stretched slow motion second, just long enough for Mike's left-handed and stronger grip to register in Teddy's mind. He started one final breath, short and deep, to prepare for that last deadly struggle.

That breath never came, a small explosion of blood, flesh and bone punched viciously into his face from Mike's. A sniper's bullet had gone straight through Mike's head, missing Teddy by half an inch, but still spraying parts of Mike's skull and its noxious contents into his face. A tiny part of Teddy's brain registered the resumption of real time for an instant. Then, even that tiny part stopped functioning as two, almost simultaneous, shell explosions hit the ground nearby. The force of the blasts blew his body and Mike's off their haunches and into one motionless, tangled, stinking mess.

The ruined observation post was now an appalling, disgusting, murderous heap. Its four occupants, covered in a fine matt layer of brick, dirt, and plaster with a chaotic litter of half bricks, shards of wood and sods of hard clay. The dull matt effect, occasionally broken by the starkly contrasting wine red of fresh blood collecting in small pools, still fed by trickles and drops from limbs, chests, mouths, and heads. What looked like four bodies, were spread on the ground resembling half clothed offal, around two freshly made shell holes.

Above them, a grey-blue smoke rose slowly and inexorably upwards, like souls breaking their corporal earthly bonds and rising to heaven in the hope of redemption and eternal life.

Not Teddy though, his travels would lead elsewhere and to a very different destination.

## Chapter 2

### Yesterday - 23<sup>rd</sup> May 1940 – Morning – Northern France

Yesterday morning, Private Archibald 'Teddy' Travers Austin and Lieutenant Constantine Brooke Duncan, were in the wide front seat of a Bedford OYD truck. The truck was heading west on a narrow road towards Boulogne at a steady twenty miles an hour. They'd left their former holding area, south of Calais and Dunkirk, early that morning.

Private Micky Preston was driving, he didn't talk much, but Teddy and Lieutenant Duncan's usual private banter had to lessen in front of witnesses. They stuck to discussing what they'd find ahead and how to handle it. Scanning ahead of the truck needed all their attention, so the absence of banter helped them that morning. The silence was occasionally broken by a prompt of *'slow down'*, here and there for Preston's benefit.

It was 1000 hours, and they'd seen no signs of life during the slow four hours they'd been driving so far. Their apprehension increased with each mile. They'd driven north for two hours at first, then taken a left when they'd seen, a hopefully accurate, sign for Boulogne. The sun was behind them as they drove, making their job easier, less tiring on the eyes. Neither thought they could afford a break, so they pressed on.

Lieutenant Duncan was as tall as Teddy, five eleven and similar build, but with poise and elegance Teddy would never match. He had jet-black hair, slicked straight back over a high forehead. Dark-brown eyes under full eyebrows which drooped at each side, slightly hooded eyelids giving him a grave and almost sad appearance. His rank required him to look serious, yet he seemed able to relax and smile more when alone with Teddy, when they chatted, like brothers.

At twenty-two, he was young for an officer and content

that people assumed he was older. He was handsome, with the face of a Major at least, a Lord perhaps, time would tell.

There were ten men in the rear of Teddy's truck, an even mixture of good and bad lads. He already knew that fifty-fifty mix was as much as could be expected in the BEF in France in 1940. The following hours and days would sift that mixture ruthlessly, and identify good men, prepared to be bad. They sat uncomfortably on hard wooden planking that passed for seats. The truck's tarpaulin gave shelter from the wind and sun, but no shelter from their only view, their comrades, well behind them.

The rest of their convoy were keeping a safe distance of a hundred yards away from them on that lonely road. There was precious little conversation either, agitation mixed with silence became the pastime of the day. Some were smart enough to know what surely lay ahead. Some were too dumb to know, and they worried nonetheless. Smart or dumb, they all knew what their Major Feckle was doing that day.

The other eight Bedfords, each filled with ten men, were far behind them in that sorry, nervous, unprepared and even, in places, cowardly convoy. After the Bedfords, came the staff car occupied by Major Raymond Lorde Feckle and his driver, then finally a small armoured scout car.

The scout car was the newly issued Humber Light Reconnaissance Car. Its official name was the *'Ironside'*, but it had become known as the *'Backside'*, or worse in the last two days, thanks to Smudger Smith, who'd rechristened it while unbolting its weaponry.

"For cleaning," he'd said, nobody argued, and he'd not brought it back. "I might need this," he'd explained, "and I don't fit in that fucking Dinky car."

Everyone knew you didn't scout in a truck.

"Jerry's miles away," Major Feckle had said.

*'Why are we reinforcing Boulogne if he's miles away?'* Everyone silently replied.

Still, what could you do? Move fast and keep your eyes

open, they still hadn't been under fire. The weather was pleasantly sunny, the road shaded sporadically by small wooded areas, providing some cover.

"Slow down as these trees end," said Teddy firmly, "stop, stop! What's that?"

"That's Jerry, reverse please, Preston," said Lieutenant Duncan with a remarkably calm air.

By reflex, Micky leant to his right to check the wing mirror. The bullet that nicked his left shoulder would have otherwise gone right through his neck and been fatal. As it was, the wound felt like a small wet burn on the edge of his left shoulder, the arm tingling and temporarily useless.

"Out! Out! Everybody out," Duncan shouted, "get down, find a tree!"

Teddy was the first one on the ground, he'd found the best tree; the nearest one. He was lying prone and ready before Duncan finished shouting. He carefully assessed the scene ahead, Jerry had cheekily just parked at the side of the road, three trucks, it looked like. He'd set guards, who were firing their rifles towards the men on both sides of the Bedford. Two of them, Teddy thought, there's one, shaded by and against a tree, not immediately visible.

He carefully and calmly found a target with the telescopic sight Duncan had fitted to his Lee Enfield rifle. His mantra began; firm position for the barrel, push the barrel down, still firm, butt to the shoulder. Firm and comfortable, take aim, deep breath, let it go slowly, deep breath and hold it, this time, aiming, aiming for the biggest part of the target, torso, squeeze, got him. Breathe again.

"Open fire for fucks sake," he shouted. A few men began shooting, fewer than ought to, but more than he'd hoped.

"Pick a target if you can, chaps," Duncan shouted. He'd somehow just thought they'd open fire, without any orders, it did seem obvious. Teddy had known it instinctively, and he always had a plan ready.

Duncan was crouching, he felt a compelling need to lie flat, to be safer, to be somewhere else, but he also needed to see enough of what might be going on. His lifelong mentor had told him it was doubly important for a leader to be visibly calmer than the men around him. Dead calm, more likely, he mused; he still only crouched, though, just behind Teddy; he might need a plan.

Teddy was gratefully aware of Smudger to his left, setting up his big gun behind what seemed a very small tree. While each man had found a tree by now, some had ensured their particular tree was significantly further from the action. The clamour and gunfire increased, telling him some lads from the second Bedford had moved nearer and were joining the fray.

"Nice of you to join us, you're most welcome," Duncan shouted.

The firing continued intermittently, Teddy had stopped, waiting patiently for a target.

"Cease firing, we're wasting bullets, keep your eyes open, keep your eyes open and don't break cover," Duncan ordered, "someone check on Preston."

Duncan carefully took up a position behind the V shape formed by two limbs in a medium-sized tree. He scanned the scene ahead of him with his binoculars. The nearest vehicles, about half a mile ahead of him, were three service trucks, a fuel tanker, ammunition truck and a plain one. They were half off the road, refuelling. In the far distance ahead, maybe a mile in the clear air that day, were columns of smoke and sounds of serious battle. Jerry was firing heavily into Boulogne, and he couldn't see any sign of return fire.

Duncan half shouted now, ensuring they could all hear and not panic.

"Tanks and artillery, they're busy further up ahead. We're looking at a few support trucks. I think you may have plugged a cook, Austin, or someone guarding the food. We'll settle for that, Fritz might be too hungry to attack us."

"Can you see any food, sir? If you can, me and Nipper could attack right now," Teddy said, deadpan dry.

"Not many," said Nipper from the right, he was under

13

the Bedford wedged against a front tyre with a solid firing position.

"Wait and see," said Duncan.

Nipper, was Freddie Knowles, a cheeky lad, five foot four, skinny as a rake who looked barely sixteen. He must have lied about his age to join up. He looked like his name, a nipper, an ugly one mind. When he said anything, it was for a laugh or a tall story worth hearing. He invariably ate anything put in front of him.

He'd seen a bombed-out house the day before, peeked inside briefly, "lived in worse," he announced. It was typical banter, although Nipper surely meant it. He was in France because he genuinely had nowhere better to go, and he'd stayed with the lead truck.

"He's moving, here he fucking comes!" said an alarmed, familiar melodic Welsh voice from atop the Bedford to their right.

"Pardon my bad language, sir."

"Perfectly okay, whoever you are?" said Duncan, eyes still focussed ahead.

"Eh... Jones, sir," the voice replied in a distinctly posher tone.

"I don't think we have a Jones, do we, Austin?"

"He can call himself what he likes as long as he stays," said Teddy.

"Heh heh," chuckled the familiar voice.

"Everybody down," Duncan shouted, "wait till he gets here, wait till he gets here."

"Down!" he shouted again before resuming his crouch.

"Smith, do what you can with the Elephant Gun, he'll come in fast, Austin, Knowles go for the tyres, we might get lucky."

A small armoured German scout car was maneuvering through the larger stationary enemy vehicles. As soon as the road freed up ahead of him, he went at full speed straight at the Bedford. The driver knew what poor cover the trees would provide close up and could see one plain truck, no scout, and no armour. Quick victories

14

emboldened him, to the point of overconfidence, or so Teddy and Duncan hoped.

The scout moved at about fifty miles an hour, straight at them.

Teddy recognised the Panzer treble two, it was a four-wheel drive reconnaissance vehicle, carrying a two-centimetre cannon and an MG34 heavy machine gun. The MG34 could fire nine hundred rounds a minute and make shreds of trees including anyone hiding behind one. Thirty millimetres of frontal armour and a grenade proof wire mesh over the open turret were useful too. He'd read that and remembered it. He also knew its two man crew could only drive and fire one weapon at a time, and half that mesh was hanging down on his left-hand side. He noted all of that in an instant, before he fully focussed on the tyres. The mantra began, breathe, stay calm.

Smudger managed one hit on its heavily armoured front, the front was all he could see, it skipped harmlessly off the angled armour. Nipper and Teddy fired a couple of shots each.

Nipper shouted, "Gotcha!" but nothing happened, and the Panzer didn't lose speed.

The murderously rapid fire of the MG34 machine gun started soon enough, at a hundred yards distance. Short controlled bursts into the trees to the left and right, just random, but he'd find targets there, even if he couldn't see them properly. He ignored the truck, it was no threat to him.

At thirty yards distance, the burst front tyre finally deflated enough to cause the vehicle to veer slightly to its left and their right. It braked to a stop at an awkward angle, half off the road, the tyre shredded, only about twenty yards ahead of them.

Jerry continued firing, he had no choice, and the now stationary target, received a rattling hail of British bullets in return, mostly bouncing and sparking straight off the armour. Three grenades flew simultaneously towards it, landing nearby or on it. The resulting explosions did no real harm and just added to the general confusion, preventing the enemy gunner from getting off clean shots. He was just firing non-stop now, anywhere he could, then the firing stopped in mid-burst.

Reloading or jammed? You couldn't know for sure. A fifty round magazine, a double magazine or an even larger capacity belt? It must be magazine fed in a small treble two, surely? Teddy thought and planned.

Before he had time to begin any mantra, someone jumped up and ran from his left, grenade in his hand, a dangerous, unwise gamble. The gun opened fire again, sweeping towards the man, but the new angle of the car forced its aim upwards, and it missed. The man leapt up and dropped the grenade into its open top, or tried to anyway. The grenade exploded in his hand, taking the hand and half his face with it. The explosion went directly inside the car and must have hit anything inside the tightly enclosed space.

He'd taken his finger off the catch far too early, or maybe it was just an unlucky dodgy fuse. Dumb, thought Teddy, dumb, but not me. Suddenly there was equal silence and shock, the silence was short, the shock lasted longer.

The silence broke with the rattle of two blasts from a Sten gun. Someone finishing off any surviving Jerrys in the scout car. The Sten then jammed.

"Bleedin' useless thing," Private Potts spat the words at his own gun.

A quick look ahead to confirm the silence was lasting, then Duncan shouted.

"Who's left, who's left? Back in cover, who's down?"

"Jenks and Pick have bought it, sir, I can't even look at that car, who was that?" said Peterson.

"Corporal Price I think, he's not here now any road," added someone from the left.

"Who else?"

"Carter's had it, and I've got a nasty piece of grit in me eye," said Nipper.

"Right, Austin, Smith, Knowles, Peterson, who else?" Lieutenant Duncan took a deep breath, removed the cork and took a swig from the water bottle Teddy had handed up to him, he nearly wiped the top by reflex but chose not to.

"Lee, sir."

"Jordan."

"Tarrian formerly known as Jones... and Wise... and Potts also, sir," said the same Welsh Jones voice. "Potts... he's puking something awful and Wise, I think he's shitting himself."

"Sounds a wise move to me, Wise get over here," said Duncan in a cracked raised voice, he realised he couldn't shout, took another swig of Teddy's water then handed it back down to him.

Wise came over to him, Duncan looked at him kindly, he was shaking like a leaf, but he came anyway.

"Didn't start shaking till it was done, not till it was done," shouted Tarrian, making sure everyone heard.
Duncan took a beautiful silver hip flask from his pocket and handed it to Wise.

"One small sip, son," he said. Wise was four years older than him and said nothing then took one small sip, as directed.

"Thank you, sir, very kind, I'll be all right now."

"I know you will be, thank you Wise."

Aware of the covetous looks towards his small silver flask. Duncan said, "Right, there's not much left at all, I'm afraid, you can all have a sip, you've got to go after Potts, though!"

"No thanks then, sir," said several voices.

"I'll save mine for later," said Teddy.

Duncan went carefully behind the lorry and over to Potts, who was just spitting, rinsing his mouth out.

"Potts?" he asked while offering the flask to him.

"No thanks, sir, it'd come straight back up anyway."

"Later then?"

"As late as you like, much later; in England would be

good."

"Well played, Potts," Duncan said, just touching his shoulder gently.

"Runner, sir!" someone shouted from behind him.

Duncan turned to see a young, out of breath Private, whose name he couldn't recall, and whose scared eyes were flicking from side to side, taking in the bloodshed.

"Major Feckle requests a report, sir, and asks that you return immediately."

Exasperated breaths and sharing of raised eyebrows showed each man knew Feckle should be there personally. Although the brows and breaths returned to normal, when each man realised they didn't want the useless bastard there anyway.

"I'll be right back, chaps, keep your eyes open and don't fire unless you've got a target. Austin, fire one off every count of sixty, just to keep heads down, and change trees as well."

Duncan left.

When Duncan reached the column, every truck had turned around, except this time the staff car was leading the convoy. Feckle's intentions were clear. The armoured column ahead was way beyond their capacity to address, but he hadn't known that until Duncan had given him the details. Four men dead, he told him, Feckle didn't ask the names, Duncan gave them anyway.

A gunshot from up ahead made Feckle flinch.

"Just Austin keeping their heads down," Duncan said.

Feckle was thinking hard, and Duncan decided not to wait until he spoke, he'd say nothing worth a damn anyway.

"That village a few miles back looked defendable, should we retire, regroup and see what we can do from there, sir?"

"Defendable, yes, yes, for a rear-guard action. I entirely agree. Right, everybody, we're moving back. We'll form a rear-guard in that last village we came through," said Feckle as confidently as if it had been his own idea.

"Right, Duncan, you'd better choose ten men and get yourself in the last truck. Look lively, we're leaving now," he said, turning his back and walking to his staff car.

A couple of Sergeants looked at Duncan as if pleading for guidance.

"Mount up and move sharp, come on, there's nothing more the Company can do here," he said.

The Company was a mess, fewer than a hundred men with no support, the men only had what they could carry. Various elements of their original Company were supporting other units across the numerous fronts. All the other officers were elsewhere now, pleased to be away from Feckle, leaving only Duncan and five NCOs to suffer under him. The Colonel had asked Duncan if he wanted to take another role away from Feckle and he'd chosen to stay. He knew these men, he liked some of them well enough, so he'd stayed. He'd stayed, mainly to look after Teddy, maybe so Teddy could look after him.

Duncan had read volumes about leadership and its absence. His upbringing and education had instilled it in him, and he'd thought deeply about it. You could only learn it in practice, though, and there was no time for practice. One small mistake could kill you, or with good fortune, someone else. He'd been hoping for role models that weren't already dead, and he'd had the best mentor, but was having to become a mentor himself before he was ready. He had to learn quickly and on his feet, he already knew people followed the lead they're given.

His Sandhurst officer training had repeatedly provided him with a scathing view of politicians.

*'The best ones look to their own futures rather than that of their country, and the others take their lead from that.'*

He'd soon realised that maxim held in many walks of life, including his own. He'd still do whatever he could, for the men standing next to him.

As he jogged back to his truck, Duncan smiled inwardly, his ten men had all but chosen themselves, just one more willing volunteer needed.

A loud, bright orange explosion, interrupted that thought. A black cloud was rising fast, thick and roiling high into the bright mid-morning sky. He assumed it was the fuel tanker and continued a brisk walk back to a smug set of young men.

"No movement since you left and no shots in reply," Teddy said over his shoulder, still prone, still aiming and looking.

"Smudger said he could hit the fuel truck with the elephant gun, so he did. It went up nicely, sir."

"Good plan, anything that slows him down, anything," Duncan said.

"One poor bastard went up in flames with it an'all," said Smudger, "but it's four each now."

"Well done, Smith," Conner added.

Smudger looked at Teddy and nodded an acknowledgement, he knew he hadn't thought of it himself. It was all Teddy's idea, and he'd told him where to aim, but he'd given Smudger the credit.

Lennard 'Smudger' Smith was a ridiculously tall six foot six inch gentle giant of a man. About thirty years old, an expert shot rather than a big shot. Teddy suspected he'd never had a fist fight in his life, never had to. Two ordinary men could have hidden behind him, but you'd happily stand alongside him. He had a foul mouth and a great sense of humour, he also had a wife and three kids. He got letters and wrote them as well, he shouldn't be in France. Teddy was glad he was, though, and the big man owed him a favour now. That small nod showed Smudger knew that too.

"Right chaps," Duncan said, "I need ten men in this truck. The good news is, we're no longer the scouts. The bad news is, we're the rear-guard. Does anybody know any finer men in this company? I can't think of any, so we'll stick together then." He wasn't waiting for any replies to his questions.

The nods, smiles, jokes and purposeful speed of movement showed he'd chosen well. He knew he'd pick the same names often, picking new names would likely be bad news for one of the originals. He'd do it, though, he'd have no choice.

Teddy knew it too, there was no time to bury the dead either, dead was dead, alive was alive; for as long as possible, please.

"Preston, get that shoulder of yours in the front passenger seat, someone turn the truck around, who can drive? Did anyone collect the discs?" Duncan rattled off the questions as they came to him. "Did anyone collect the discs?"

"Yes, sir, Bennett did it, Price's too, and he can take 'em all back to the Major can't he," said Tarrian.

"Bennett?" Duncan looked around, yes, Bennett was the runner.

"I'd prefer to stay here, sir," said Bennett, "I hid behind a truck when this kicked off, I'll stay with you now if that's okay?"

Every man looked at Bennett, thinking he was too green. Duncan felt it might break the boy if these men told him he wasn't welcome among them. The unspoken thoughts filled the air, then Duncan just looked straight at him.

"Okay, well done, Bennett, you're our driver now."

"You're with me," said Tarrian. "Stay close when it starts again, son."

Duncan nodded briefly at Tarrian.

"Get the truck turned around, and keep your eyes peeled."

There was some banter as they boarded the truck and then some laughter. These men chose to laugh rather than cry, they silently thanked the fate that chose them to live and ignored the other choices. Duncan knew his men had passed the first test of their war. They'd seen friends die, then just got on with their jobs.

"Knowles, are you okay, boy?" Duncan said when he saw the damage above his eye, a lump, a bruise and drying blood down one side of his face.

"It was just a bit of tree, or a stone, or sumfin," he replied. "I've had worse off me dad, and me mum come to think."

"Good lad, anything happening, Austin?"

"No, sir."

They'd already turned the truck around.

"Right, all aboard, come on."

Duncan was last aboard, one behind Teddy, who'd invited him to go first, then realised the Lieutenant needed to be the last man on. They both stayed in the rear of the truck, they needed to see what might be behind them.

Smudger and Nipper sat next to Teddy in the back of the truck. Smudger still held the elephant gun he'd taken from the *'Backside'* earlier, leaving just the Bren light machine gun behind. He'd fired it in anger for the first time today. Anger had helped him, four of his mates killed and four Jerrys dead to even the score. He'd owed Jerry the one who went up in flames, although he was pleased a bullet from Teddy had put an end to his burning misery.

"You should have found a bigger tree, Smudger," said Wise.

"They prob'ly thought he was a fuckin' tree," said Nipper, "I nearly 'id behind him meself."

The laughter rose then subsided.

Lieutenant Duncan waited for that laughter to stop.

"Get this tarpaulin rolled up boys, we need to see what's going on. Check weapons while you can. Potts, sort your Sten out and don't shoot anyone in the truck while you're doing it."

"Not even Nipper?" some wag said.

"Especially not Nipper," said Duncan, using a nickname for the first time, and hoped he was entitled to do that now.

"That's very kind of you, sir," said Nipper, "very kind indeed."

Lieutenant Duncan had just ensured Nipper would run through Hell for him. Watch and listen, copy and act, Teddy repeated silently.

"And Austin, you're the Corporal now," Duncan said, "I'll find you some stripes later."

"Nice one, Teddy," said Smudger.

"Yeah, nice one," said a few voices, and as Teddy looked around him, the nods and smiles were unanimous, Smudger gave his shoulder a huge pat.

"Ouch!" he said, but bloody hell it felt good.

## Chapter 3

### Yesterday – 23rd May 1940 – 1100 – Northern France

The bright sky helped Teddy to scan the road around the truck. It was fresh, almost cold, but he needed to stay alert.

For the last five days, he'd been in the truck, heading for various destinations, none of which they'd reached. Yesterday, the official story had been, heading to Boulogne as reinforcements for the garrison, cruiser tanks to follow, the road ahead was open. To cut the longest story short, no-one knew what was going on. The Romans had more efficient communications two thousand years ago. He knew that too.

He hadn't seen Jerry at close quarters until that morning, although he'd heard him and plenty of his explosions. He'd only seen him from a distance, his superior arms and tactics evident even from a few miles away. His company had habitually been two or three layers away from contact. He'd thought Major Feckle might have been responsible for that safe deployment, more probably, his own commanders knew his limitations, and they'd use him last.

Teddy had read military books and manuals from both sides, Conner had provided them through his unfathomable range of contacts. He could remember them easily, so he already knew this current fight was one they couldn't win. He turned his attention to how he could best lose it and still be alive.

He'd seen Jerry close up that morning alright, he could still see him when he closed his eyes. They'd been bloody lucky, four men dead and lucky it was only four. He'd killed one and finished off another. He'd not killed before, and it hadn't bothered him in the slightest, which intrigued him. He hadn't known he could do it and not care. That would be useful later. Their lives or his? It was the simplest of questions.

It was quiet ahead, noisy behind, beyond that simplicity

he had no real plan.

Ninety-odd men in nine trucks, one staff car, and the scout were all that remained of the full company. They drove back towards the quiet and seemingly deserted village just before eleven in the morning. Feckle had used the scout properly, this time, to recce the village first.

The sign read *'Wacquinghen'.*

"Wanking then?" said Smudger Smith from his position in the back of their Bedford. The *'Back Door Boys'*, as he had christened them.

"Rogered," Smudger said. "Royally Rogered; Roughly Royally Rogered Rear-guard."

"That's enough Rs Smudger," said Teddy. "There's more work to do today, mate."

Feckle told Duncan to lead the rear-guard and pick ten men. He'd picked ten Privates, no NCOs, just Privates who he knew would stand if he asked them to, each would look after the other. Who knew what others might do when it came to it.

*

As they drove, Teddy saw the faces of the dead men, the men who'd died instead of him.

"Remember this," Lieutenant Duncan had said to him back in England. "The infantry comprises 17% of the armed forces, but suffers 90% of the casualties, so be extremely careful when we get there."

"I don't remember that being on the form when I signed it," Teddy said. "So, 17% of the men do 90% of the dying?"

"Yes, so to speak. What's your plan for that?"

"Well, first off, the odds are poor, so I won't be placing any money on it. Gambling's a mugs game. Second, I'd find one of the 90%, a big one, a gambler if I could find one, cos he'd be a mug wouldn't he?"

"Yes, I'm with you so far, what next?"

"Well, I'd stand behind him wouldn't I?"

"And then?"

"I could still look after the man next to me."

"Yes."

"Just not the cunt in front of me, that's all."

"So, he'd have to be a cunt as well?"

"That couldn't hurt could it?"

"No, I'm just not sure you've fully thought this through. At any given crucial moment of impending death, you have to ensure you're in the vicinity of a large, stupid, gambling cunt who's ready to die in a fight. That's got to be a rare breed surely?"

"You've not been in any pubs near Liverpool Docks on a Saturday night have you, sir?"

"No, why?"

"If you don't know, sir, then I can't possibly explain."

"I'm going to have to watch you, Austin, watch and learn, yes, watch and learn."

*

Their truck drew into the empty village, just as it had been earlier, no refugees. They'd seen plenty on the roads before. Refugees consistently knew where Jerry was and stayed away. If they knew where he was, then why didn't the BEF? Teddy decided the BEF didn't know where the BEF was, a fatally bad point from which to start any journey. He'd have to make his own road, now that sounded like a decent plan.

The few houses and one small towered church was hardly a village, the Church must service the surrounding countryside. Teddy noticed its dark wooden door was wide open. Church doors were always open, for prayer, he'd heard. More likely, the French knew Jerry would just blast it open to check inside for stragglers or traps.

The Church was in triangular grounds on their left as they entered the village by the main road. A second road, immediately after the church, again on their left was a smaller country lane, joining their road from the west. The two roads formed the sharp point of a vulgar triangle.

One hundred and fifty yards further down the road it curved to their left where a few buildings congregated tightly on both sides.

"Pull up just after that bend," shouted Teddy, standing

up now and gripping a tarpaulin stanchion tightly. "That's right, swing to the left, stop, this'll do."

Nobody queried the instructions, Lieutenant Duncan just nodded. Like Teddy, he'd also scanned the buildings on either side.

Duncan climbed down from the truck.

"Look around," Duncan ordered, "find anything to make a barricade, just here please, use anything, and don't worry whose property it is!"

"If you see any locals, tell them to bugger off; politely," Teddy said.

"With me, Austin," said Duncan, "not too close, just enough to use those sharp ears."

Major Feckle was waiting for them when they arrived. He was at the far end of the village, his staff car with the door open and engine running. Jesus Christ, thought Teddy, he was such a small man in countless ways.

Feckle had a pale, sand coloured skin, a lifeless expressionless face, if he'd been dead for two weeks, he couldn't have looked less alive than he did now. His thick head of grey hair looked for all the world like a comically bad wig, but wasn't. He had a small beak instead of a nose, you could look him straight in the eyes and see right through his skull to the empty space inside.

He was the first genuine halfwit and idiot Teddy had ever encountered. He'd address the unit regularly, using lots of big words and phrases, exhorting his troops to better and greater achievements, their goals, the regiments wonderful history and equally wonderful future and opportunity. When something went well, he called it fantastic, when something was terrible, he still called it fantastic.

*

Teddy had discussed him discreetly with Lieutenant Duncan, who'd told him to listen carefully to what Feckle had to say and to speak to him again in a week. After a week, he concluded Feckle didn't say anything, he said nothing, used many words, big words, but said nothing, a waste of humanity's precious oxygen.

"How did he get to Major?" he asked.

"On the shoulders of others," Duncan said, "taking credit for the words and deeds of others, imaginary deeds even, a depressingly familiar experience the higher you ascend in the chain of command. There are some excellent ones, and at the highest level, I'm glad to say. Not enough, though, and we can't choose who we work for I'm afraid, so there's not a damn thing we can do about it."

Teddy concluded the only possible worthwhile purpose to Feckle's existence, was as an example to be meticulously avoided. He'd struggled his whole life to find role models. He'd read volumes about Julius Caesar, so he was one and Churchill might be another, he talked a great game, we were yet to see how he played.

Back home, the men had renamed Feckle as Feckless, in France, it became Fuckall or Fuckless.

Smudger had joked with him about plugging Feckle one dark night. Teddy suggested a better plan was to shoot him in the heat of a firefight, he hadn't been joking. Feckle could get them all killed. He was useless, painfully useless, so useless it hurt, it killed.

He researched the word 'fantastic' in the dictionary, it had two distinct meanings, each strangely opposite to the other. Only one could possibly apply to Major Feckle.

\*

Duncan walked towards Feckle, assessing the terrain on either side of the road and behind the barricade spot, he and Teddy had selected without needing words.

"Major," he said to Feckle, who was standing away from the ranks, near his car, arms behind his back, legs firmly apart in an imitation of a military posture. Duncan pictured his hands throttling Feckle's neck, but managed to overcome the impulse. There was no time to waste, so Duncan went straight to it.

"I thought we'd put up a barricade in the road just there," he said, pointing to the spot where his Bedford had parked. "The men will be in the buildings on either side, ready to fall back to the woods over there, depending on what he throws at us. How many men can you let us have?"

"What you have will be sufficient," Feckle said. "Follow us when you can, give me four hours, Duncan, that's an order, after that, I leave to your judgement and initiative."

Teddy heard the conversation clearly, stifling a laugh and his own desire to shoot Feckle in front of ninety-odd witnesses.

Duncan just wanted Feckle gone from his sight, the men were worth saving, best not to think about it too much.

Feckle was swiftly back in his car and off, behind the scout car, followed immediately by the remaining Bedfords.

The ten Chosen Men all looked briefly at the last truck as it started up, they'd made sure Preston was in it and getting bandaged up. An air of resignation, mixed with determination and regret, filled the chosen faces as they looked at that truck. Guilty faces looked back at them, some faces not looking at all.

They watched silently then slightly puzzled, as one man casually chucked his kit out the back of the truck. Then he jumped out too, rolling like a parachutist as he landed on the tarmac still gripping his rifle firmly. Three others followed him, to loud cheers from the ten.

"Nice to have you here, chaps," said Duncan.

"I figured I'd be in the next rear-guard anyway, sir, might as well join the best one," said Private Rigby, smiling proudly.

"Help with the barricade if you'd be so very kind," said Duncan and they moved quickly to help.

Teddy knew of most of the men left behind, without necessarily knowing the person well. If they weren't in his hut, there was no real need, he'd learned all he needed to this morning or when they'd leapt off the truck. You might stand once and be dead, but if you held your ground that first time and lived, you'd do it again. Each Chosen Man could look any other in the eyes and be certain of it. His limited experience already told him that was the rarest of qualities. Later, if he lived long enough, he might learn and respect that each man had his breaking point; not yet, not today at any rate.

As a rule, he didn't ask many questions. If he found someone he wanted to know, he'd ask questions. Until that happened, he reduced the number of questions he answered by not asking any of them. There were aspects of his character that weren't for sharing.

He'd asked plenty questions of Lieutenant Duncan and given many answers in return. He also knew now that Duncan would ask not order, these men had earned that little already, to choose how they died, badly or well but soon enough, he thought. Duncan would ask, and the men would say yes. Teddy was ready to die for that cause, alongside these men, but didn't have the slightest intention of doing so.

"Right, I need one lookout by the church back there. Shout 'Bloody Hell!' and run like it if you see Jerry," said Duncan.

"I feel well qualified for that job, sir," Nipper Knowles said and sprinted up the road without further words.

They continued building the barricade across the narrow part of the road between two sturdy old buildings. The enterprising Chosen Men had found two tractors, without fuel, pushed into place, tyres slashed and deflated. They found three huge and incomprehensible pieces of agricultural machinery, and they were getting similar treatment. Smudger and Tarrian were emptying the nearest house of furniture and piling it on haphazardly.

"That's right, make it look like something a stupid Tommy would hide behind," said Duncan, the puzzled looks he received showed they didn't get the joke.

The barricade wouldn't stop a head on attack or effectively shield anyone daft enough to seek its shelter. It was a distraction target for Jerry to divert some of his considerable attention and deadly firepower away from the better-hidden men.

Teddy drew Duncan aside quietly, away from other

ears.

"We won't be surrendering today, will we?" he asked.

It was a strictly rhetorical question. They knew, in every war across centuries of recorded history, there were times when prisoners were not taken. You could only safely surrender in large numbers and only with senior officers present.

"You're right there, Teddy, not nearly enough officer presence."

"We could just promote ourselves?"

"I do like that thought, but where would we get the uniforms?"

"We need a better plan then, don't we?"

"Yes please."

Their task was to delay Jerry for a few hours, which might just give the Company time to reach Calais safely. Delay was the aim, not defeat, just delay, surviving would be handy too.

Teddy moved position to get a clear view of the Church. It was a drab, dark grey affair, the small tower on the west side facing the advancing German 2nd Army. To its rear, facing away from any impending advance, was a graveyard, raised higher than the two roads, enclosed by an equally drab wall, forming two sides of the triangle.

Duncan took a deep breath.

"Apparently, Brookie said we need a bloody miracle to save the BEF; can you recall any good prayers, Teddy?"

"Well, firstly, I'm sure such a noble gentleman as General Alan Brooke never used such foul language. He fucking should've, though." He breathed out the last words as a sigh.

"Have you got any good prayers or not?"

"No, and my God's deaf, I've prayed for loads of stuff, never got fuck all. No, come to think of it, I did get Fuckall! Only a really shit God would do that."

"Right then, in the regrettable short-term absence of a deity who isn't hard of hearing, we need another plan. Come on Teddy, you told me you always have a plan, you've probably got about ten minutes, no hurry at all."

Teddy silently considered the task, available resources, and options, for what seemed like ten minutes, then said.

"We could just do what Caesar did?"

"Caesar did a lot of things, I need more detail."

"A trap, a feint and a thrust, and we've already set half of it."

"Yes, great, let's get to the rest of it then, we've got about eight minutes."

"Eight minutes?"

"Yes, you've used two of your ten minutes already, you really should get a watch."

"We'd best start now then."

Teddy approached Smudger Smith.

"I need to borrow your elephant gun," he said.

"What do you want it for?"

"I'm taking it down to the Church."

Smudger gave him a knowing look.

"You have it then, my son, I'll swap it for your excellent rifle and a grenade if you don't mind."

"Done."

"You have been, son."

"We all have, Smudger."

The elephant gun was the Boys antitank rifle mark 1, weighing in at a hefty thirty-five pounds and five foot two in length. It could penetrate armour at five hundred yards and fire up to ten rounds of .55 cartridge rounds a minute. The muzzle velocity was 747 miles a second. It was shit.

In theory, its official specification was correct, in practice, it only had a five-round detachable magazine, and the recoil could bruise or break a bone in your shoulder. Its rounds bounced off the front of any German Tank, the rear and maybe the sides of a tank were vulnerable, but you rarely saw them anyway. You could try for a lucky shot on a track or where the turret joined the tank's main body. A lucky penetration would result in an unlucky hole in an occupant, and perhaps a few internal ricochets would cause some random disabling damage. A tank destroying explosion was just not going to happen.

Maybe if you had a plan?

"How many shells you got, Smudge?"

"One clip left."

"How many shells?"

"Three."

"Three!"

"How many bullets in yours then?"

"A full magazine."

"A good swap for me, then."

Duncan could see what Teddy was thinking.

"Right everyone, find suitable spots well away from this mess," he said pointing to the barricade, "then scout out a second spot behind the first one, you'll need it. Stay as long as you dare in each position, shoot from behind or the side if you can, we're not fighting fair today!"

Teddy and Duncan, who'd kept his kitbag, walked casually towards the church. There was no rush, Teddy had his plan. Two minutes left, plenty of time.

The graveyard was small and packed with large headstones, raised sarcophagi and a small memorial stone pillar. There were fresh flowers, the residents of Wacquinghen remembered their war dead, the stonework could still do with a clean. Flowers for God's sake, Teddy thought, affectations for the wealthy dead, what use was such expense after death, what use today?

Among other words on the pillar, that Teddy couldn't read, were *'Morts pour La France 1914-1918'*. Five names were carved in the stone, with room left for more. More names and another war.

"That Church Tower looks good," said Duncan.

"Let's hope so, sir, let's hope so," said Teddy.

They relieved Nipper, told him to join the others. Nipper had nodded knowingly at the Boys but said nothing.

As they made their position comfortable, Duncan produced his cine camera from its case, he'd had it in his kitbag for weeks. It had arrived by special motorbike courier. Originally from the United States, the newest model, and the packaging described it as 'rugged as hell.' Duncan had friends in high places, rumour had it he was the secret son of General Alan Brooke, Commander of the BEF 11 Corps. It wasn't true of course, the shared name was coincidence. It did no harm when he asked for something, though. The camera was a Bell and Howell 70, 16mm motion picture camera, light enough to carry and use with one hand, an ideal camera for war he'd said. He was the appointed intelligence officer for the unit, he'd tested it only briefly, and didn't want to waste precious film on the ordinary.

"You're not filming this are you?" said Teddy.

"I am gathering intelligence, old chap, if this comes off they'll love this film, you'll probably get a medal."

"Blow the medal, can I have some chocolate instead."

They laughed and talked like two brothers playing soldiers in their garden.

"When we get out of here, what next?" Teddy said in an obviously false blasé tone.

"We'll get to Calais or Dunkirk," Duncan said, maintaining the mood, "failing that, we'll swim north or steal a boat."

"We're stuffed here then?"

"Oh yes, definitely, much as you said we would be. The Maginot Line was never long enough, you said Jerry would go north first and then through the Ardennes. It's what Caesar would have done, who would build a square fort with three sides? I hope you're right about the channel too."

"So do I. Caesar conquered all of Gaul with sixty thousand men against three hundred thousand, according to Plutarch, anyway. Although Plutarch may have been an early version of the BBC, a sort of BC BBC, I'd guess."

"You should write a book," said Duncan laughing.

"Anyway, as I was saying, before I was so rudely interrupted. He did all that, and then the rest of the known world in his spare time. However, when he tried to land in

Britain the first time, he hardly got off the beach. The second time, he got as far as Chatham, saw what a shithole it was and went back home empty handed. Hadrian did better, but that took decades, and even he took one look at Scotland and built a fucking great wall. The channel and the Navy will see us right, we can't lose this war."

"Can we win it, though?"

"You know full well we can't, there's not enough of us."

"We need more friends. Perhaps not losing is as useful as winning."

"We'll need to fight dirty, filthy, as dirty as it gets, then dirtier. We'll have to lie, cheat and steal, say and do anything, whatever it takes, murder or be murdered. Honi soit qui mal y pense." Teddy said with great conviction.

"That should be our motto," agreed Duncan.

"That and not getting caught, of course."

"Gentlemen won't win this war."

"Certainly not country gentlemen."

They laughed and talked nonsense mixed with great wisdom as they waited.

Fifty minutes later, Duncan and Teddy heard the sound of armoured tracks on tarmac from their hidden vantage point.

"They're bloody late," said Teddy, looking at Duncan's watch. "Still, it's fifty minutes of our four hours, then we can do whatever the hell we like. Does that sound like Panzer Ones or Twos?"

"Twos, they sound heavy I'd say, shhh," Duncan concentrated, closed his eyes and listened.

"Twos I think, only two of them, from both roads I'd say."

"Two ones is my personal preference, the smaller, the better. And if he doesn't get here soon, I'm going to piss my pants."

At that precise moment, a high explosive five-centimetre shell from a Panzer Three medium tank blasted the church tower to smithereens.

"Or shit myself," said Teddy as debris from the

explosion landed on them like a sprinkling of dust, and small particles of brick and cement rattled his helmet.

He'd looked into the Church briefly to verify the ceiling was typically high with no rafters or roof void.

"Told you that tower looked too good a target for Jerry to miss the chance of a pot-shot," he said, still trying to sound blasé. "I was hoping for lighter tanks, mind you."

Teddy and Duncan crouched between two large, coffin-shaped, stone sarcophagi. Well hidden, giving them at least four feet of cover to the sides and their rear, with a clear view of the intersection of the two roads leading to the barricade. Their raised position in the graveyard would shield them even if the tank commander sat atop his turret, which he wouldn't.

"Fuck off," he said with his most engaging smile as Duncan pointed the camera at him. "Now point that blasted camera up the road and get out of the way, let's do some evil."

The squeaky, clanking metallic rhythm of the Panzers was much closer now.

"Only two I think," said Duncan.

"Great, now start counting slowly."

"One… Two… Three… Four,"

The first tank moved past them on their left.

"Panzer One… Excellent... Seven… Eight,"

The first tank, coming from their left, thankfully a smaller, lighter Panzer One, armed with only heavy machine guns, was twenty yards ahead of them as the next tank drew alongside them on the right.

"Fire!" Teddy said, unnecessarily.

The first tank exploded in a blaze of fire. Bizarrely intact, not blown apart, but with flames shooting from every orifice including the engine vents at the rear. A well-aimed and dead lucky shot had hit the engine, resulting in a flash fire that was choking, burning and, he hoped, killing the two-man crew.

"Reload!" he said.

The second tank coming from their right was a larger,

better armed and armoured Panzer Three. It screeched and scraped to a noisy halt in front of them. Ten yards away, the turret scouting to its right seeking the source of the threat. He fired at point-blank range, aiming for the vulnerable rear and squeezing the trigger slowly and deliberately.

"Bull's-eye," he mouthed.

"Damn," he said as nothing happened.

"Damn," he said again, as he rose from his crouched position and scrambled awkwardly onto the sarcophagus to his left. He strained to raise the heavy weapon to his hip, to fire one last round from a better, higher angle. He searched for a sweet spot on the rear of his target.

The tank turret opened, thick dark smoke came out, then came a head with earphones over an elegant, jaunty angled, tank commander's cap. He was coughing and retching, for one clean breath that never came. A bullet smashed into his cheek and out through the top of his head, killing him instantly.

Then, Teddy saw Smudger Smith using his massive frame to leap and stretch towards the turret, deftly dropping a grenade inside. He slid off the tanks body with a clumsy motion which belied the perfect timing of the explosion which inevitably finished off the remaining tank crew.

Duncan continued filming as he panned the camera across that small corner of Hell.

"Cut," he shouted calmly and replaced the camera in its case, then in his kitbag. He noticed Nipper alongside Smudger.

"Nipper, you and Smudger keep an eye on the road and see what else is coming."

"No need, sir, me and Smudger got a bit bored waiting, so we borrowed your binoculars and sneaked... well, scouted about a bit. This is all that's followed us, these two roads lead back where we came. Jerry's got better maps than us, and Frenchie, God bless him, is keeping him well busy back up the road."

Teddy half listened to this exchange while he put down the Boys, he felt like puking, and if he hadn't been so bursting for a piss, he might have. He jumped off the sarcophagus, clambered over the church wall, walked towards the tank and relieved his bladder against its rear.

"That's disgusting," said Smudger.

"Better than on the graves," said a relieved Teddy, "by the way Smudger."

"What?"

"I love you."

"And I love you, too."

"What about me?" said Nipper.

"All right, you too."

"The Boys is knackered," said Duncan, who was checking it.

"That last shell was stuck in the firing mechanism, you'd have probably lost an eye or a face if you'd pulled the trigger, catch this."

He tossed a scratched and useless cartridge at Teddy. Teddy finished his piss, possibly the best he'd ever had, picked up the round and put it in the top pocket of his tunic. Lucky, he thought.

"Now, back to the barricade chaps, we've used up all our luck for today," said Duncan. He and Teddy started walking to the barricade, suddenly exhausted and out of breath for two men who'd just sat on their arses for nearly an hour.

"We'll just be a minute," said Nipper, who started to search the Panzer Three, the smaller Panzer One was still burning idly ahead of it.

Back at the barricade, Duncan gathered his men.

"Right, no sign of any other tanks or infantry, for now, they're busy behind us. When they work out what's happened to these tanks, they'll be deciding their next move. Could be shelling, more tanks or Stukas, that's the bad news. The good news is, they think we've got effective anti-tank gear here so they won't make their move for a couple of hours at least. We can withdraw, as far as we can, slowly and quietly at first, then put our foot down. My orders, my initiative, my responsibility."

The men started mounting up, a tighter squeeze with the extra men.

"Happy?" he whispered to Teddy.

"Yes, but now, though? There're about three hours left on Feckle's order."

"He said to give him four hours, didn't say we couldn't take some of it for ourselves, didn't say we had to stay here for four hours."

"And you have a reliable witness."

"A very reliable one."

"Right lads, keep that tarp fully off, we won't need it now, eyes peeled, not too much noise and all in an orderly fashion. We are not retreating we are advancing in another direction."

They laughed, they'd heard that one before, and they still laughed and smiled as they gathered their gear.

Teddy looked around briefly, an extra rifle hadn't appeared from somewhere. Smudger and Nipper approached him from the direction of the tanks, carrying the fruits of their scavenging labour.

"We found some food," Smudger said, "not labelled, but Nipper tried some, and he's not dead."

"Pork, I thought," said Nipper. "Lovely!"

"And this is for you," said Smudger, handing him a well-used Luger pistol.

"Think of it as an engagement present," said Nipper.

"The tank commander had no further use for it, no bullets in it, an empty clip and it's been used recently, couldn't find any spares in that mess either. You've earned the right, might be lucky for you," said Smudger.

"Wasn't for 'im, mind you," added Nipper.

"I'll take it anyway," said Teddy.

"And you look like shit," added Smudger. "Give your face a wash in that trough over there, boy," Teddy moved to do it, "and wash your bollocks while you're there, you never know do ya?"

## Chapter 4

### Yesterday - 23<sup>rd</sup> May 1940 - Afternoon – Northern France

The Chosen Men climbed into the Bedford.

This time, Duncan took a position in the front seat next to Rigby alongside Bennett, who was still driving. Teddy stood upright, just behind the passenger side of the cab, holding on to a stanchion for balance again. Duncan had left the cab window open in case they needed to talk. Teddy, like Duncan, scanned the road ahead keenly.

They'd only gone about half a mile when Duncan directed them to take a left turn northwards. They knew the road that lay straight ahead turned south, towards the advancing German forces. They'd driven that route this morning and wouldn't return that way. They needed to head north and east, towards Calais, Duncan assumed Feckle would do the same.

Boulogne to Calais was twenty miles as the crow flies, Duncan had told Bennett to do a steady twenty if he could, to conserve petrol. They were running low, and he knew the spare fuel was in another truck. Teddy knew he ought to have thought about fuel.

Smudger passed him a small open tin of German '*Iron Rations*'. He took one big mouthful and passed it into the cab. Yes, that was tasty, but eating one bite just made him miss the second bite. Teddy found it easier to abstain than eat a small amount.

He carefully placed his Luger at the bottom of his kitbag, he was keeping that. A souvenir or to sell, he wasn't sure yet, but he'd earned it. He patted the top right pocket of his tunic, it contained one useless 'lucky' Boys shell and two medium squares of Cadbury's Dairy Milk chocolate he was saving, the wrapping would keep it fresh. He wasn't sure why he was saving it, or what for? Something big was happening, he wasn't sure what, but he felt certain he'd know when it was time to eat it.

The surrounding countryside held few houses, was flat as a pancake with some small hedgerows and trees occasionally lining the roads. It was mostly flat farmers' fields with the start of healthy crop growth. No cover worth the name, though, Teddy thought and hoped Boulogne, Calais and Dunkirk made better targets than a small country lane.

The truck was quiet, Smudger and Nipper were keeping a watchful eye behind them. The men were rechecking weapons, helmets remained on, food was being eaten, one handed, while they had a chance, rifles still half ready.

"Keep your kitbag strapped to you, we might need to get off this truck sharpish," Teddy said when he saw a couple of men lazily making themselves comfortable for the journey.

They drove on northwards past signs for Connincthun and La Communette, two small hamlets, they saw a few civilians watching them warily, they didn't stop.

"Cunning then," and "the Communist," Smudger had said.

"Three out of ten," Nipper said, "try harder next time."

"Shall I tell you all a story?" said Tarrian.

"Go on then," said Smudger, who'd heard many of Tarrian's stories.

Tarrian, as was evident from his accent, was Welsh. He'd moved to London to play amateur rugby, getting a job in the club owner's factory to provide his income. He'd admitted doing no work at all in the factory, so clearly some fiddle, Teddy didn't yet understand, had taken place.

He wasn't tall, an inch shorter than Teddy, but he was wide, all beef, and fast for a big man. Only over short distances, though, he'd go through a wall for you if you were his teammate.

He was tanned, permanently, with jet-black hair, short and tightly curled, his full lips were usually smiling. People liked Tarrian, he was a right laugh, he too had a wife, no kids yet, still, he was married and shouldn't be here.

That morning, he'd left the safety of the second

Bedford. He'd run up to help and chosen to do so.

"Have I told you one of my ancestors was at Rorke's Drift?" he asked.

"No." "Yes." "Bollocks." and "Whose drift?" came the replies as Teddy scanned ahead. He'd not heard this particular story, but he knew what Rorke's Drift meant.

"Well, let me tell you then," he began, ignoring the answers.

"Rorke's Drift was a famous battle in January 1879, in South Africa. One hundred and forty brave and true Welshmen of the 24th Regiment of Foot stood behind a few carts and sacks of grain. They fought off no less than four thousand screaming, well-armed, native Zulu warriors, over the course of a two-day battle. One thousand Zulus dead and wounded. Less than 20 Welshmen dead. Eleven Victoria Crosses awarded, mostly to Welshmen, you know. The greatest against the odds victory of all fucking time."

"Bollocks," said several voices.

"No, tis true, every word," Tarrian said.

"That's got to be bollocks," another voice said.

"So if that's true and your great, great, fucking whatever, was there, what did he do then?"

"Oh, fuck all, he was skiving on light duties in the hospital building when it got burnt to the ground, lazy bastard he was, famous for it."

Much and genuine laughter followed all around, even those who'd heard it before.

"The moral of the story is, if there's a fight going, you might as well join in, see," he concluded.

Teddy smiled too, and half listened to the tension relieving, lying and swearing contest between the men that naturally followed Tarrian's joke. He knew Rorke's Drift was different from Tarrian's abridged version, but that didn't matter, it was such a good lie, he'd file and use it later.

They drove on until they reached a T junction, at Beuvrequen, where some locals gave them wary looks from houses. Left would take them back towards Boulogne and right would take them East. They turned right but soon realised this road curved south and towards Jerry. All the left and northward turns took them to low-lying waterlogged dead ends, so back East towards Boulogne it was. They were wasting time and petrol, a couple of hours on those wasted northward dead ends.

"Beaver Queen," said Smudger.

"Five," answered Nipper.

They passed another church on their right, with a larger cemetery and more elaborate stones. It was still a dirty, depressing, grey colour like a black-and-white photograph rather than reality.

They were wasting time they might not have, and Duncan's frustration grew, until after a few miles, they saw a wider better road heading north. They took that right turn at La Ronville where they saw a few more locals, yet still no sign of enemy or allied action.

"La Ronson," Smudger said.

"Two," said Nipper.

"Put your foot down on this better bit of road," Duncan said to Bennett, who was proving to be a calm and competent driver. Duncan looked at Bennett. He was Gregory Bennett, 22 years old, he recalled now, not too big, not too small, unremarkable. He would do what he was told to, needed some mates around him and a sense of belonging. A hundred of him and some competent officers would make a worthwhile Company. Cannon fodder? Probably? He hoped not, but suspected so, many Bennetts would live, and many would die, he couldn't look after them all, maybe this one, he thought.

They continued driving north until the road split again, the wider road going left, and right was a smaller road going dead north. They stopped, Teddy leant down to the open cab window, "straight north?" he said.

"Yes, straight north now, Bennett," said Duncan.

This was frustrating, they were guessing, albeit guessing well so far, still just guessing, the absence of a plan needled Teddy and Duncan.

"Last Luck," said Smudger as they crossed a small bridge over a river marked La Slack.

"Six, but I don't like it," said Nipper.

They continued on the straight narrow road going due north. A slow puncture on the driver's side front tyre dashed their hopes of a shortcut. They had a spare, but the poor road surface and inadequate tools available meant it took a long two hours to make the change.

"I told you I didn't like Last Luck," said Nipper, "that's your fault now, Smudger."

The day was proving to be a dangerous mixture of fortunes. After a spell of going northward on that narrow road, they reached a better road leading to their left, still leading north at Onglevert, they took it, they must be near Calais now surely. There was still no sign of allied or enemy activity.

"Uncle Bert," said Smudger.

"Seven," said Nipper.

On their left, about a mile further ahead, they found a wider road on a right turn going north and east, towards Audingen and Tardingen.

"Audaciously then," said Smudger.

"What?" said Nipper.

"Tardy then."

"Two out of ten."

Increasingly, they could smell the salty sea air on their left and came to a fair sized town called Wissant, which had what were obviously seaside holiday hotels.

"Piss Ant," said a smug Smudger.

"Nine out of ten and can we stop for a quick pint?"

They did stop, only for Duncan to ask a sole local how far Calais was.

"Nearly there, keep an eye out ahead, there explosions and gunfire a couple of hours ago, nothing since then," he said.

They drove through the rest of the small town, Margate, thought Teddy.

It was quarter past eight when they left the town,

nights drew in earlier in France, and, the now dark cloud, made it as dull as dusk. The trees lining the road on either side continued and sank between two banks, providing welcome cover for them.

"Slow down!" said Duncan suddenly.

A smaller side road joined the main road from the right, the trees on the right gave way to the typical flat fields. The trees on the left continued, forming a thicker wooded area. The road curved left, trees on one side and open to the right then straightened.

"Stop!" shouted Teddy, slamming his hand on the cab top.

Before them, they saw a scene of brutal, shocking murder. Teddy and Duncan saw the rear truck first, blasted apart by a shell then gunfire, still smoking slightly, the smoke only visible from a few yards in the failing daylight. There were bodies still in the back, mangled metal, shattered windscreen, and windows with smoke blackened frames. Teddy saw more bodies just below the rear tailgate and others on the sides.

"Fucking Hell," said Tarrian. "I was in that truck."

"Me too," said Rigby echoing the thought.

Further ahead, they could see another truck, still smoking, having apparently received similar treatment. They climbed out of their truck, shocked, dazed even, not thinking and doing nothing but thinking as they walked forward.

Teddy froze in his spot behind the cab, he could see most of it from his vantage point.

"Bennett, stay in the truck, keep the engine running, Tarrian you stay with him and keep an eye out behind us."

Bennett didn't want to see this, Tarrian didn't need to.

Teddy left the truck, sleepwalking on to the road towards the carnage. He felt an intense need to be next to Duncan, he couldn't handle the sight and thought of this, alone.

Duncan managed to uphold a false appearance of calm as he walked forward. Examining the scene of the crime, taking it in, measuring it, working out what had happened.

Was this massacre my fault, should this be me lying dead, should I have stayed alongside Feckle, could I have stopped this? As he fired the questions at his mind, he wasn't aware of others walking and taking in the scene. This morning was bad, midday was fun, this was the worst, where was Teddy? What did he think? Would he blame me?

Teddy reached him about halfway down the convoy, he saw no sign of the staff or scout car. He needed someone to blame, Feckle would do, he probably couldn't have stopped this, but he deserved to die for it anyway. He deserved to die, some of these didn't, some he couldn't care less about.

*'A nation can survive its fools but a company can't.'*

It wasn't you, concentrate on that, not ancient words, a small part of his mind told him.

As Teddy took in the sight, he saw this had been pure bloody murder, efficient, effective, and battle winning murder. He admired the accomplishment, Jerry would have taken great pride in this achievement. Nearly a hundred enemy dead and not a scratch on him in return. If Jerry had this ability within him, then we needed it too, unless we just wanted to lose. This was going to be a dirty war, a stinking dirty war, executed without mercy, ruthlessly and brutally.

"Jerry took out the first and last truck with high explosive shells," Teddy said, "then hit the rest with heavy machine guns and maybe another couple of rounds from a tank. There were a couple of half-tracks too," he said pointing out track marks leading from wheat fields to their right. "I doubt we even scratched him. Some might've got lucky and scarpered through the trees, doesn't look like many, we could count them and…"

"Have you seen that?" said Duncan, pointing to his left with the palm of his hand without looking.

Teddy looked at four bodies, neatly fallen in a line, between a truck and the wood. They'd clearly been shot at close range, face down, one still half on his knees, wounds to the back.

"Bloody hell," he said, "not enough officer presence?"

"We won't... Christ!" said Duncan as the Bedford containing Tarrian and Bennett exploded. It was deafening, blinding and stomach churning. Bursts of heavy machine gun fire filled the air. Three or maybe four men to Teddy's left hit the ground, quick thinking or quickly dead, he couldn't tell, couldn't care. He'd leapt headlong into a small depression between the trees.

Duncan crouched behind the cab and front wheel of the nearest Bedford wreck, and shouted as loud as he could, knowing the firing might drown out his words.

"Everybody, into the trees, run like hell, hit the beach, turn right, keep going, don't stop, don't surrender or you're dead. NOW! GO! GO! NOW! That's an ORDER!"

He scrambled awkwardly towards Teddy.

"We need to go, now!" Teddy almost screamed. "Come on!"

They moved as fast as they could, crouching and dodging branches of small tightly packed trees, progress was slow and painful.

*'Damn it, we should have turned tail as soon as we saw those trucks. We should have thought, planned, what were we doing? We examined one ambush and walked into another, stupid, stupid, stupid.'* Teddy repeated that again and again as they ran.

Those men were dead, there was nothing he could do about it, he owed Jerry some death in return, but you had to be alive to deliver vengeance. Live, survive, was all he could think.

It was him who'd told Tarrian and Bennett to stay in the truck, they'd stood no chance, he'd done that.

As he ran, Duncan felt numb. He'd won a couple of lucky encounters thanks to Teddy. He'd saved some men so they could be killed later, now he'd told them all to run, exactly what he was doing.

Thankfully, it was still cloudy and the full darkness of night was drawing closer. The time they'd wasted on the journey there meant they hadn't caught up with the rest of their convoy earlier.

They reached the edge of the trees, "Stop, down, listen," said Teddy, breathing heavily now.

Ahead of them were undulating sand dunes, well covered with tall grass in some places. Beyond that, was a narrow line of flat beach, the nearest half was soft, nearly dry sand and they'd make poor time. The farther half was flat and solid, dampened down by tides, they'd make better time, but they'd be a clearer target. Jerry's attention would remain on what came along that road rather than chasing two men along a beach. They'd still have to keep moving fast and make a poorer target.

"A plan, Teddy?" said Duncan.

"Fast up that flat bit of beach. You've got a pistol, and I've got a Luger and no bullets, we're not going to give any help or do any harm here. You've already done everything you could."

Duncan nodded reluctantly.

"Right, we go now, follow me, you can feel bad later if there's time. We are *not* Fuckless!" Teddy said.

They worked their way straight down to the flat sand, turned right and started running at a steady pace. Teddy had strong legs, made more powerful by running and climbing, the legs of a middle distance runner with a sprint finish. Those legs had made him the regimental 800 yards champion, and if he went steadily, he could go for a long time.

They went on for about twenty minutes, a couple of miles thought Teddy, what with full clothing, a kitbag, and army boots, that should be about right. They went slightly inland to rest in the dunes and took off their helmets which were cumbersome and chafing on the run.

"Just for five," said Teddy, out of breath and sinking to his knees.

It was nearly dusk now, they took some water to wet their throats and listened, it remained quiet.

"I think I saw four go down at least, didn't see who it

was, not Nipper, too big and not Smudger, too small. Some are bound to get away, somehow? They won't shoot Nipper, they'll think he's a schoolboy," said Teddy.

"A bloody ugly one, though, I'm slowing you down," said Duncan sharply changing the subject. "You can go faster than this, I've seen you run. You're slowing down to let me keep up."

"Bollocks, you've seen me run on turf and track with proper gear and hot meals inside me."

"Yes, you go ahead, I can wait and see if any others get this far."

"Wait for Jerry more like, and he's not taking prisoners today, come on, we can afford to go a bit slower now."

"Don't make me say it's an order."

"And don't make me tell you to fuck off."

Teddy, ready to brook no argument, began to stand then immediately resumed his crouch.

"Truck lights, not ours," he said, "come on, stay low, through the dunes this time."

Neither wasted any time, moving quietly, they resumed their journey up and down the dunes. It was heavy going even on their grassy tops, it was darker, silent and confusing, difficult to go in a straight line or keep your bearings.

After ten minutes, Teddy stopped and listened. He didn't hear any sound of pursuit, nor could he see any lights.

"We're okay now," he whispered.

Hearing no reply, he then said, "where are you?" as loudly as he dared, but he still heard no response. He retraced some of his steps and spoke again, louder this time, dangerously loud, there was still no reply.

He mouthed silent curses then paused, took a deep breath and just moved down to the hard flat area of the beach; resuming a slow jog north in what was now becoming full darkness. No moonlight was showing through the cloud cover, but his eyes had adjusted to the dark, and he could see well enough to find his way.

Teddy tried to empty his mind, concentrate on the steps, keep up a steady pace. You'll last longer, keep looking straight ahead, keep listening, don't look back, it's not safe ahead, and it's bloody dangerous back there. Get to Calais, then plan, survive, he repeated that thought, times without number as he ran.

He stopped a few times, listening carefully, hearing only the waves lapping to his left. He passed a small trickle of a stream running from his right, it tasted fresh, so he filled his water bottle and drank deeply. He cleaned his face and hands, it was bitter cold and refreshed him, sharpening his wits. He was exhausted, any adrenaline burst had long gone, he still couldn't afford to rest, not friendless in the night, not alone, not yet.

He kept going, walking slowly now, he was tiring badly and on the point of taking a sleep he couldn't afford when he heard a shout.

"Halt, who goes there!"

"Fuck off," he shouted, "it's Tommy Pongo Atkins, so don't shoot me."

"Corp, it's another straggler," an unknown voice said.

"Get him in here then," said a different voice.

Teddy shuffled past an inadequate barrier of barbed wire and a couple of poles painted red and white, nestling on top of two small piles of sandbags. A shortage of sandbags on a beach, he thought, only the BEF! A short footpath led from the beach to a narrow road.

"Let's have a look at you," said the Corporal. "You look bloody awful, son, walk up this road, head to the next junction, they'll tell you where to go."

"No chance of some food and a rifle?"

"You're right, son, no chance!"

He walked two hundred yards to the next barrier, beginning to plan when he heard a shout.

"In you get, see the Sergeant," said the guard, indicating a ramshackle hut with one light outside its door, its walls painted an unlikely bright blue.

"Watch out, he's a right one."

He approached the Sergeant, standing as square as he could, he wasn't a Corporal here.

"Private Austin, Royal Fusiliers, Sarge. We were heading to… "

"Not interested, son, take the weight off your feet over there while I find you a job. I don't suppose you've got a rifle? No, thought not."

Teddy sat down on a deckchair outside the hut, it felt like a feather bed.

Sarge, whoever he was, went off, clearly busy.

Teddy considered just falling asleep, then spotted another Private approaching him with a tin mug. He squatted down next to him.

"Sorry, it's only coffee, mate," he said, handing him the mug, "and there's no milk or sugar. It's strong as hell, French stuff."

"Ta," he said, "call me Teddy."

"Vinnie."

Teddy took a sip, it was alright, but hot tar would have been welcome that night. Vinnie gave him a couple of dog biscuits, he stuck one in his top pocket and soaked the other one in his coffee.

"What the hell's goin' on, mate, any idea?" Teddy said.

"We got here two days ago, Queen Victoria's Rifles, and we're leaving tomorrow or the next day, that's the word. They're leaving Boulogne and Dunkirk an' all. It's a complete balls up, the boat what brought us here left without dropping off any vehicles so we can't go anywhere, anyway. Loads of us ain't even got rifles. We 'aven't seen any armour and they've got no radios anyway. There's some forts here we're defending to keep the harbour safe for ships. There's loads of auxiliaries in town, fully trained in repairing the vehicles we ain't got, untrained for combat with no weapons anyway, just useless mouths. Ow long have you been here?"

"Six months, this is Calais then?"

"No, this is Sand gate or sumthin, Calais's a mile back there. We are guarding an important road junction here.

You'll be trained then. Sarge'll find you a shit job."

"If I'm lucky," said Teddy swallowing his softer biscuit, it was disgusting.

"Keep your head down, here he comes."

"Right, you with your no rifle and no helmet, head down that road, 200 yards on your left, damaged building, there's three lads up there in the forward observation post. You can help man the machine gun. You'll get some kip there." ordered the Sergeant, who did a neat about-turn and left.

"Shit job?" said Teddy.

"Oh Yes!" said Vinnie, "No other fucker would touch them lads with someone else's bargepole!"

## Chapter 5

### 24ᵗʰ May 1940 – Dawn – Northern France

Duncan woke from a troubled sleep at twenty past five according to his watch, the luminous hands of his Rolex Solar Aqua not entirely hidden by the darkness of predawn. He'd dreamt, but couldn't remember what, all that remained on waking was the lingering feeling of deep unease. Something he'd done wrong, something was going to go wrong, something wrong in the dream or in the waking world, he couldn't tell. You're in France in May 1940, you're bound to have a feeling of impending doom, he said to himself, now move, no time to waste.

He was cold and stiff, yet still alive and fresher than if he'd carried on his slow walk along the beach the night before. From his sandy bed sheltered in a hollow by the grassy dunes, he could hear nothing except the sea, no abnormal noises. His throat was dry and sore, he'd drank from a stream he'd crossed over the night before, but had no water bottle with him. He'd lost his helmet too, they'd taken them off when resting, and carelessly left them in the dunes somewhere.

He had to resume his walk along the beach towards Calais, he was sure Teddy would have gone ahead, as he'd intended him to. He rose carefully and warily, then stiffly walked on for about half an hour, when the increasing dawn light showed a hastily erected makeshift barrier across the beach. He shouted his presence ahead, hoping his English voice would be enough to stop any trigger-happy or tired guard.

"Who goes there?"

"Lieutenant Duncan, Royal Fusiliers."

"This way, and slowly please, sir, Jerry's about. Corp, it's an officer!"

The Corporal hurried and directed him to the gaudily painted blue beach hut a little way behind him.

Duncan reached the hut, the Sergeant was at the door.

"Sergeant Fowler, sir, Queen Victoria's Rifles, we're manning an outer perimeter here."

"Lieutenant Duncan, Royal Fusiliers, we were heading to Boulogne, we've taken heavy casualties, and I'm hoping some made it here?"

"Oh yes, sir, your Major and three men in a staff car, got here about six yesterday, sounds like they gave Jerry what for before they had to scarper."

"About six, you say, anyone else since?" said Duncan, suppressing a puzzled frown.

"A couple, sir, one tall fellow, Smith, had sights on his rifle, I sent him into Calais and told him to join up with the Rifles if he could shoot straight. One other boy, can't recall his name, no rifle, not even a helmet. I sent him to the forward observation post to help man the Vickers," he said, pointing to the lone half building further up the road.

"He misplaced his helmet saving lives, including mine, he's my Corporal now, and I'd like him back if you please," said Duncan without any hint of rebuke, the Sergeant was just doing his best.

"Of course, sir, Leach!" he shouted to the nearest Private.

"Get to the observation post, relieve the new lad and tell him to get back here pronto. Blake, get the officer a hot drink."

"Thank you Sergeant." said Duncan, taking a deep, relieved breath and accepting the tin mug of 'tar' offered by Blake.

He drank the lukewarm coffee, Christ that tasted marvellous and would keep him awake for a week, he thought, draining the last of it.

Duncan began to take in the developing scene around him. Three wooden barriers, on the beach, on the roads from Boulogne and the south, were no more than checkpoints. They weren't remotely defensible and only contained a few men and the Sergeant. Three had rifles, three only had side-arms. He knew the Queen Vics were a reconnaissance battalion, and they should have motorcycles, but he could see no vehicles at all. The nearest defensible position was about half a mile further towards Calais, where the buildings could provide some better cover. Did anyone know what they were doing? As for the observation post, it was…

Duncan saw the observation post blasted apart by two almost simultaneous explosions. Debris flew then fell everywhere, momentary flame turned to smoke and dust and then to nothing at all. He felt instantly that anyone there was dead or mortally wounded. Only a miracle could have saved anyone, and surely they'd exhausted their miracle quota yesterday. Duncan saw Leach duck and start running back towards the barrier. He froze, stunned, staring at the wrecked house as the debris settled. There was no sign of movement, he felt the blood drain from his head, a ring of darkness zoomed into his vision. He thought he might be fainting, but he couldn't afford to, he was an officer, he had to-

"Sir, sir!" shouted the Sergeant.

"Yes?"

"What do we do now?" He said as two Panzers approached their useless barrier at high speed.

Without looking, Duncan said calmly.

"Get all your men up the road towards Calais, fast as you can, stop at the first line of buildings. Get in positions to cover any infantry following the tanks. Not the buildings right next to the road, use the next nearest. Wait for me there."

"Yes, sir! Come on lads, carry what you can, with me," said Sergeant Fowler, already moving and shouting now.

Duncan waited, stone still, counting and identifying the advancing armour, as Leach regained his ground at the checkpoint, out of breath.

"With me, son," said Duncan and sprinted to the cover provided by the buildings and the rest of his new group of men, not chosen, just found.

*

*'Memento, homo, quia pulvis es, et in pulverem*

*reverteris.'*

*'Remember man that thou art dust and unto dust, thou shalt return.'*

*'Not today, not yet.'*

Teddy lay deadly still, breathing through his nose as deeply as he dared, he kept this mouth and eyes firmly shut. He listened as well as he could with his ears still ringing from the explosions.

He kept his eyes closed because dead men don't wipe dust or grit from their eyes.

He kept his mouth shut because Mike's blood and brains were dripping onto his face, and in turn, dripping from his lips down the sides of his face and neck. That was useful, he needed it to look convincing, he needed to be dead.

He could hear the sound of Panzers approaching on the road, at speed, more than one he knew, sounded heavy, Panzer Threes probably. One, two, went straight past the building on the road to his left. One more tank, slowed down stopping briefly. It raked the rubble of the building with its machine gun, which of course drew no response or movement. It then resumed its headlong charge towards Sarge and those other poor mugs, and their garden shed. There was no helping them now, they'd gained no advantage from these three deaths.

*'Survive and plan, that's all you can do. Do it.'*

He had a minute at best. He pushed Mike's body off him and rolled over to his right. The effort caused him to inhale something wet and slimy, he spat it out, furiously retching, but not stopping as he assessed the scene. Mike's front was the best part of him, his back was oozing out from underneath his corpse. The opened pack of Woodbines in the front pocket of his tunic was still usable. Teddy took it then grabbed his own kit.

*'If Mike had let me have that rifle, that bullet would be in my head not his. Still, the bastard did owe me a favour.'*

Spotter was in bits, he ignored him and crawled away, scraping his knees through his trousers, towards Corp.

Corp's head was almost blown off, and Teddy took his eyes away from it. He saw Corp's rifle next to a piece of wall and looking okay, he took it and what bullets he could find from his webbing. Corp's torso was mostly intact, his cock was still out and his trousers wet; Teddy had heard you shat yourself when you died, it looked like he'd pissed his pants too.

*'Dulce et Decorum est? No fucking chance.'*

He pulled aside Corp's open tunic, taking his wallet and stuffing it inside his own tunic.

*'You won't need that now, will you? Cunt.'*

Another explosion further down the road, to his left still, told him the Panzers were reaching the road junction. He turned and glanced towards the trees, confirming that infantry was advancing towards him.

*'Thirty seconds.'*

He saw Corp's dusty pack at his feet, slung it over his shoulder and ran to his right, leaping across a small ditch and away from the road. The line of the ditch, parallel to the road, concealed a lower lying field behind it, which still held a thin layer of morning mist. He ran fast over the soft earth, keeping low, heading instinctively east, away from the Panzers. He still heard firing behind him which soon stopped, there was no heroic last stand going on there either.

He reached the end of the soft earth field, it was turnips he'd decided as he'd trodden on them like cobblestones. He felt it best to keep going east through firmer fields, with the beginnings of wheat, which were easier going for him. He heard no more firing and figured the Panzers were just completing an encirclement, cutting off the coast road, not starting a full-blown attack.

He went on through more fields without incident, then found another ditch where he used its trickle of clear water to wash his face and mouth. When he was sure there was no further trace of Mike in his mouth, he took a deep swig of his own water and started to plan.

He checked Corp's rifle, seeing it was in excellent

condition, if not fired in anger any time recently. Damn, he should have taken a helmet, he was a step up from last night, though. He took out Corp's wallet, finding rubbish, a raffle ticket and photos he didn't look at. He unzipped one large pocket, to reveal a folded sheet of stiff brown paper, containing forty-eight, dirty, well used, one pound notes. This was a fortune to Teddy, more than five months wages, Corp wouldn't need it now, and Jerry had no use for pound notes, he thought as he justified the theft. I've earned that, I just need to earn the time to spend it.

He searched Corp's pack eagerly now, still popping his head up gingerly to make sure no one was near. It contained stockings, condoms, eleven bars of Cadbury's Dairy Milk chocolate, 10 packs of cigarettes and eight bottles of pills, wake ups he assumed. A small drawstring money bag held another five notes and much loose change. Corp was a wide boy then, a spiv, you could prosper in war, Teddy knew that, he intended to. Somehow, he possessed the knowledge that countless armies across time had someone who knew someone in supplies, who could get you anything, for a price. Some *'rear-ender'* probably, his own nickname for rear echelon personnel.

He dumped the pills, they were for mugs, he kept the fags and chocolate in his own bag. He opened one bar and stuffed four squares in his mouth, letting them melt without chewing. He dumped the stockings and condoms, who the hell was buying or using them in Calais? Corp was an optimist as well as a crooked chancer?

In spite of all that had happened, all who'd died, all those he'd killed, untroubled by his murderous intent of that morning, he felt great.

*'I need to get home and spend this.'*

Then, just before he discarded Corp's pack, he lifted the thick card inside it, that formed its base and gave it shape. He'd never know why he did it, but underneath the card, he found an envelope with four postcard sized photographs of a topless woman. This wasn't some common tart, though, this was a beautiful, intelligent woman. She looked like an aristocrat and was the most beautiful woman he'd ever seen. Her short blonde hair slicked back, her breasts were astonishing, small and firm with exquisite erect nipples. One photograph had the words 'Man Ray' on the bottom. He felt the start of a poorly timed erection. He put the photos back in the envelope and placed them just as safely in his own pack.

*'Later maybe? No, definitely!'*

He checked carefully around him again, the day was clearer now, and he could see the line of a railway embankment ahead of him.

"If I go left next to that, heading north then I'm in Calais, must be," he said, confidently now. He knew where he was, another improvement since earlier.

The area remained quiet, and he walked crouching and unseen to the railway line, crossing it carefully, so his outline wasn't visible against the sky.

He walked straight north, passing a small empty pillbox, not much more than bricks with a slit and a collapsed corrugated roof. Further ahead, about fifty yards, he saw the start of a wider railway siding and buildings which must be a line of defence. He could see barricades and empty or dummy positions in the open.

"In here mate!" came a shout from a small, bomb damaged warehouse to the right.

He jogged in, pleased to see some friendly faces and perhaps find a measure of safety and order. He saw about twenty men, in three separate groups, each manning a workable defensive position within the building, with properly laid out sandbags, some newer looking Bren Guns pointing through some improvised murder holes. He could tell from the empty casings around that they'd seen use recently. He smelt strong tea, and one group were having a break, eating something hot. Christ, someone knows what he's doing.

"Who are you then?" said a Corporal, who was taking charge.

"Teddy Austin, Royal Fusiliers, we were heading to

Boulogne and had to turn back after a couple of fights with Jerry, got ambushed on the way back, lost a lot of men, maybe all of them. Jerry wasn't takin' prisoners. When I stopped running, I started walking and here I am."

"You certainly look like you've been in a fight, mate, you any good with that?" he said nodding at Teddy's Lee Enfield Rifle.

"Yeah, fourth best in the regiment, Corp."

"Okay, we can use you, get yourself a cuppa and something hot. I'm Jezz, don't call me Corp, we've no use for rank here, just how good you are and whether you'll stand or not. Nothing else matters today. Hammie, get this man some grub."

"Who are you lot then?" Teddy asked when he'd sat down in the group who were resting and eating.

"We're mostly the First Searchlight Regiment," said a friendly looking face. "Only we ain't got any lights and we ain't searching for anything. Jezz, the Corporal arrived last night, he's from some rifle brigade, and he knows what he's about. Organized us into better positions and told us what to do, threatened an officer until he got us more ammo and food. Told us where Jerry would come from and got it dead right. Sneaky, late last night and we was ready, gave Jerry some, and he fell back. There's even some Frenchie's over there, reserves they say, they stood last night, don't like Jerry, oh no, and they hate our food, which is handy."

"Here have this," said Hammie.

He handed him some fried bully beef, mixed with a little scrambled egg, it was gorgeous, and the best food he'd eaten for days. He wolfed it down and then swallowed a warm mug of tea with powdered milk and sugar! It felt like a banquet. I'll stand with these he thought, yes, I will. He took two packets of fags and two bars of chocolate from his kitbag.

"Share that out lads, no point saving it," he said.

"Very nice thanks, chum."

"No problem. This is like the bloody Ritz after last

night."

"You've never been in the Ritz, mate."

"No, but if I get out of this, I swear I'm going to walk right in there, ask for a pint of best and I'll shoot any bugger who tries to throw me out."

"Ain't that the truth. I'm Spud by the way, yes Murphy, these boys 'ave no imagination, none at all."

"Teddy, Teddy Austin."

He closed his eyes, the food had made him sleepy, he should have kept the wake ups.

"What's happening in there?" Teddy said pointing to a small, office-like room at the rear, where he heard raised voices.

"That's a Jerry prisoner. After he fell back last night, Jezz and one of his oppos went out to see what was what. He said Jerry sometimes leaves a sniper behind, and there he was, an officer to boot. He don't speak English, they figure he might if they hit him hard enough. The Frenchies wanted to shoot him on the spot, but Jezz wants him to talk first. I ain't sure what's what, we've heard Jerry don't take prisoners, there's a lot of useless mouths in Calais, and we can't spare men with guns to guard him."

"I can speak a bit of German, from school," lied Teddy.

*

He'd learned from books, library books, where he'd first met Lieutenant Duncan. He'd read a 'teach yourself' book, so his pronunciation had been incomprehensible until Duncan taught him the rudiments. It was basic at best, so he could ask a few questions and maybe understand the answers.

He'd met Duncan in The British Library in Central London, and he'd spent countless hours reading there. All knowledge across aeons was available free inside, although you had to seek it out. Books cost money, he hadn't been poor, he'd done two jobs to make sure he wasn't, but he still couldn't afford to buy the books he needed and wanted.

The Library was near Holborn, where he'd worked as a

clerk when he first arrived in London. He'd trained as a Territorial first, then later as a full-timer in the Royal Fusiliers near the Tower of London.

Duncan had gone in looking for a copy of 'Achtung-Panzer!' by Generalleutnant Heinz Guderian. Duncan was astonished to find an ordinary Private reading it. It was the single, rare English translation, which had to remain inside the Library. They'd talked about it in detail and its relevance, for 1939.

Teddy wasn't an ordinary private. He had a talent for books, reading and remembering what he read, and heard, too. That was why he knew every specification he could possibly find about German and Allied armament, from a pistol to a tank. That was why he knew the Allies couldn't win this fight.

His primary skill was copying, not cheating, just copying behaviour and actions, what you did and how you did it. Teddy's difficulty was working out what to copy, the absence of better people to copy was a serious drawback, meeting Duncan had begun changing that.

He'd read Caesar's Gallic Wars in Latin when he was thirteen, but that was another, longer story. He didn't have time to think about it today.

He and Duncan had talked endlessly about 'Achtung-Panzer!' and the classics, then also about God, Science, Cosmology, Einstein, German and French. Duncan had been everywhere and seen everything yet seemed to need Teddy to help him apply his knowledge in a practical way. It was a partnership, brothers in arms, I hope he gets out of this, I need him to.

*

The sound of a punch hitting a chin roused him. It wasn't like in films, a thwack, an onomatopoeia. In practice, it was a sickening sound, a mixture of crunching, thudding and something indefinably wet involved. Saliva, blood and brains sloshing around inside a skull. He didn't like it, he'd seen it, but never suffered or inflicted it. He had killed now, easily, not close up, though.

"I'll see if I can help," he said and walked over to the room taking all his kit with him, over his shoulders. He was in a half decent place, he still couldn't afford to relax, he might have to leave any second.

"Knock-Knock," he said as he touched an imaginary pane of glass on the non-existent door.

"Come in," said Jezz, "d'you want a go, you owe him one?"

"No thanks, I can speak a bit of Jerry if you need?"

"Be my guest, mate, any bit of info could help, he's a posh officer cunt, and I hate posh cunts."

Teddy looked at the prisoner who was sitting awkwardly in a wooden chair, his wrists tied to the broken armrests. He wore a pristine Lieutenant's uniform underneath a grey and brown camouflage coverall, which someone had ripped open; probably during a search, with matching trousers over a lovely pair of jackboots. He had no headgear, his hair was closely shaven on each side, with a carefully styled side parting on top. He'd taken a blow to his left eye, which had left an egg and a bruise, his lip was fat and bleeding. He was dusty, dirty and tired, yet somehow still managed to look superior and aristocratic, exuding a calm and noble bearing, he even smiled at Teddy.

"Morgen," said Teddy.

"Morgen," came the reply and a nod of what he thought was recognition, what was this man recognising? What could he see?

"He had this," said Jezz, showing him a sniper's rifle, possibly the most beautiful weapon he'd ever seen.

"A thing of great beauty," he said, "I'd kill for one of those."

"Would you now?" said Jezz.

Teddy turned his attention to the prisoner.

"Diese Mensch möchte, dass Sie sie, wo Sie Ihre Männer bint und wann sie angreifen?" Teddy said.

The German smiled as he replied, "Natürlich sie tun und wenn ich ihnen sage, dass sie mich erschießen. Und sie werden dich erschießen, wenn Sie nicht zu tun. So ich tot bin, werde ich in Ehren sterben."

"Genau so, wie ich sage, verstehen. You bastard!" Teddy added.

The prisoner just nodded slightly.

"He says he's not going to tell us anything, he knows we'll kill him if he does and kill him if he doesn't, he'd rather die with honour," Teddy told Jezz.

"Well, we can arrange that, right now, he's not much less than a spy," said Jezz.

"Hold on," said Teddy, "hold on, those men in there, how many of them do you know?"

"All of them."

"All of them? As well as a brother, as well as your best mate?"

"No."

"Didn't think so, some things need to be done quietly and privately," said Teddy pulling the Luger from his pack, "and what could be more honourable than this?"

"I like you, Teddy, we're going to get on just fine."

"Untie his hands and leave this with me."

Jezz used a bayonet to cut the ties, none too gently.

"Raus," Teddy gestured toward the rear of the warehouse.

The German walked slowly in front of him, he held the Luger in his right hand and Corp's Lee Enfield over his shoulder.

"Links."

"Links."

"Voerwarts," he said directing the German back up the railway towards the useless pillbox.

"I bet your English is better than my German," said Teddy casually.

"Of course, it is, I studied in London for more than two years, my English accent needed to be perfect, like a native, when necessary. Your German is quite proficient too, although your accent is terrible."

"Keep your hands where I can see them."

"Certainly."

"Thank you."

"How did you know I could speak English?"

"You knew I wasn't going to hit you."

"Perhaps you just have a nice face?"

"This isn't my nice face."

"Why won't you kill me?"

"You remind me of a friend."

"Is your friend alive still?"

"I hope so."

"You have killed, have you not?

"Yes."

"But you want to choose who you kill?"

"Not particularly, just not someone tied to a chair."

"Yes, I agree, it's not what you English call, cricket."

"We won't win by playing cricket, will we? We'll have to play as hard as you, even harder. Right, in there please," Teddy said, gesturing to the pillbox, and they went in.

"Face the wall and place your hands on it."

Teddy moved the German's legs apart and away from the wall while he searched him correctly. He reached under his jacket, removing the hidden gun strapped to his back, which had made him sit so strangely when he was tied to the chair.

Teddy took a step away from the German.

"Okay, you can sit down and relax now. Thank you. Very nice, and a silencer too, I can use that," he said seeing a Luger in excellent condition.

"You are very good, Tommy," said the German, as he sat down.

"Now take your boots off, and don't think about using the knife you've got hidden in one of them. That's it, now toss the knife over here, one finger and a thumb only, carefully please."

"Anything else?" said the still smiling German.

"Yes, I haven't got a watch."

"You know the price of a life, Tommy," he said after undoing his watch strap and handing it over carefully.

"Stay sitting please and don't put your boots on till I'm gone."

He carefully unscrewed the silencer of the Luger and put it in his pack with the watch and knife.

"You'll like this bit," said Teddy holding his own Luger in his right hand, he pointed it at the ground, pulling the trigger to produce only the sound of a click.

"No bullets," he said and tossed the empty Luger at the German.

"Oh yes, Tommy, I do like that."

Teddy then fired one real shot from the better Luger into the earth next to him.

"That's you dead then."

"You should go back now, your friends will be worried, and my friends will be here at ten o'clock precisely, quite soon I think. They'll have Panzers this time, and you don't wish to be here."

"I'm searching your dead body now, I have a few seconds, my name's Archie, Archie Travers Austin, remember that if you win."

"My name is Dolf, Rodolf von Rundstedt, a distant relative of the great Colonel-General, remember that if you win."

Archie took one bullet from the Luger's magazine, tossing it to Dolf who caught it one handed.

He took a bar of chocolate and a packet of cigarettes from his pack and left them on the ground next to Dolf.

"Remember that too," said Teddy and then put a piece of corrugated roof over him, "and stay down till your friends arrive."

"We shall meet again, Archie Austin."

"Not today, shhh."

Teddy took a long, careful look into the distance before he left the shelter of the pill box. Then he ran, fast and keeping low, entering the rear of the warehouse where Jezz was waiting.

"Took your time," Jezz said.

"Cried like a fucking baby at the end, I never had to lay

a finger on him, he says they'll be back with tanks at ten, we won't hold here for five minutes against armour."

"You're dead right there, my son, we'll pull back now, and our friend Fritz?"

"Tried to escape, sir, made a grab for my gun while I was taking him for a leak, I had to plug him. No choice."

"Yeah, that's what's happened all right, tried to run. You had no choice."

"I can make use of that rifle, you know?"

"Take it, use it well, he had quite a few clips with him. Right, listen up everybody," he shouted. "We're pulling back to the town walls, gather up all the kit you can, we ain't got long."

He then turned quietly to Teddy.

"Stick with us at the walls, son. The Rifles are reliable men, we watch each other's backs, and we'll do Fritz some harm before we're done."

"Suits me," said Teddy.

*

Teddy walked towards the town walls with Spud, a decent sort, he wanted to ask about the Jerry and had the sense not to.

"Some of my lot bought it before they even left the harbour, bloody Stukas," Spud said, "there's no rules here, that's what Jezz says."

"He's not wrong, mate."

"We only got here yesterday, it's a proper shambles. Jezz saved lives last night by bein' on the ball. I certainly ain't got nowhere better to go. There's forts in the town and old town walls we can defend better on a shorter line, according to Jezz. The new Brigadier's a good un, Nicholson, fought in the last war, rose from Private, I heard. He came across here just as everyone else is buggerin' off, doin' is best in a bad job, I think. There's talk of evacuation here as well as Boulogne and Dunkirk. We've got to stay alive till then, though."

They walked on along the railway, past outlying houses and railway sheds towards the city walls, looking over their shoulders regularly. Jezz took the rear position, walking backwards some of the time.

When Teddy first saw the city walls, vaguely, in the distance, they were much less than he'd expected. The railway line and some roads went right through them, and several houses had been built just outside them, some overlooking the walls. Another square fort with three walls, he thought. He could still see a few suitable locations for a marksman with the best German rifle.

*'I just might escape this mess, I just might.'*

## Chapter 6

### 24th May 1940 – Dawn – Calais - Outskirts

Duncan had seen all he needed to of the approaching Panzers. He ran without looking back, alongside Private Leach, directly to the cover he'd suggested to Sergeant Fowler's men. They heard their previous positions being raked by heavy machine gun fire. The Panzers didn't know how few, poorly armed men they faced. The wooden barriers and beach hut, shattered, splintered and clattered around noisily on the road's hard surface. The firing had stopped before they reached the rest of the men. Fowler had put them into decent cover.

"Leach, get in there with Briggs," said Fowler pointing out a suitable position on the third storey of a nearby house.

"What's the plan now, sir?" he continued, stepping into a nearby house which gave a clear view of the road towards the now stationary Panzers; Duncan followed him.

"We'll wait and see, he might be just completing the encirclement here, preventing us getting out or any help getting in. I don't think there's much help out there anyway. See, they're moving down the road now with trucks and more armour, but those nearest Panzers are just digging in, I'd say."

"We'll stay here and try and pick off the infantry that comes after the armour if you ask us to, sir," he said sincerely. Duncan had no real confidence in the words, though.

"We're okay for the moment, what's the situation in Calais as a whole. As far as you know, anyway?"

"I don't know a lot, to be honest, sir, but I'll tell you what I know for a fact and then what I've heard. We're the Queen Victoria's Rifles, we arrived on the twenty-second, two days ago now, under fire from them Stukas. The ship was damaged and left pronto without offloading any of our transport, so we've got no trucks or motorcycles. There

69

aren't enough rifles to go round, so some have just got side-arms. We sent men scouting on foot and in some commandeered French stuff, and none have come back. I reckon we know where Jerry is now anyway.

"The 60th Rifles got here yesterday, and their brigadier, Nicholson is in overall charge, there's some French reservists around, eager to fight, just not many of them is all.

"There's supposed to be tanks, cruisers, somewhere. I haven't seen any. They say we've got some anti-aircraft gear, but I haven't seen or heard any of that either. I've seen plenty of useless mouths, pardon the expression. For every man who's ready to fight, there's two who aren't, sir. That's why I sent your boy to the Observation Post, at least he was fighting trained, and didn't hesitate when I sent him, and some would have. Sorry about that, sir.

"What I've heard is, Boulogne's fallen and we left a lot of French behind when we evacuated, so they won't be best pleased. We're supposed to be evacuating from Dunkirk and Calais too, and we've only just got here ourselves, so I don't know. The trouble is, if you tell a man he might pull out, that's all he wants to do. If you tell him to stay then tell him why, he'll do it better."

"Wise words, Fowler, we can only do what we can, concentrate on looking after your six men. What's immediately behind us then?" said Duncan sadly, still trying to see if there was any movement around the observation post.

"Well, there's old town walls and forts we're using in bits, they don't stop Stukas, and the town's taken a lot of hits. We ain't seen any of our flyboys. There's a big Fort called Newlay a couple of miles back, and there's some sort of HQ there. Near the docks, there's waterways and canals that'll make stronger defensive lines."

"Okay, Sergeant, we'll sit here for a bit, see what Jerry's up to, not longer than two hours. Then we'll pull back to that fort, and at least we can tell them what's happening on the coast road. Go and let your chaps know what we're doing."

"Yes, sir," said Fowler.

Duncan resumed his observation of the German movements as best he could without his binoculars, he couldn't remember how he'd lost them, it wasn't his biggest problem. He took the time to check his side-arm, he hadn't fired it, too busy telling other people how or where to die.

For the next hour, they saw Jerry digging in around the road junction.

They're not massing for any attack, Duncan thought, maybe for a feint or quick thrust, they'll attack later.

"Sergeant, it's half eight now, we'll fall back carefully and get to the fort, if there's going to be a fight we'll join in there. We won't take on 3 Panzers with side-arms, and we've seen all we can. Get the men together, stay close to the buildings, stay off the roads."

They set off straight away, seeing a few civilians weighed down by baggage, they said nothing, just heading from one poor hiding place to another. They continued along the road, following the coast before turning south towards the fort. As they walked, the actual nature of the town walls and Fort Nieulay became apparent to Duncan. The walls were medieval bastions, demolished in parts to make way for more modern development, roads, and rail. The fort looked like something Napoleon built, it wouldn't hold for long, they could only delay the enemy, not hold or beat him.

Anything that slows him down, then a boat, any boat. It was hardly worth calling a plan, Teddy would have produced better.

From ground level, he couldn't see the full shape of the fort. Its dark grey walls looked thick, seemingly bolstered by broad earthen ramparts behind the set stones. A couple of 2-pounder antitank guns sat atop vantage points facing south and across a large empty space. There was a broad section of open firing ground if the enemy came at you headlong.

They walked past the small forward positions of the Queen Vics without stopping. In places, they saw a few poorly armed French reservists, who appeared resolute enough. This was their home, at least they knew what they were defending.

An officer approached him, after introductions and explanations he placed the seven extra men among the rest, and Duncan went into the fort to report to local headquarters. Fowler nodded an acknowledgement towards Duncan, he nodded back. Duncan didn't think he'd done much, at least he hadn't got any of them killed, yet. Maybe that was praiseworthy on a day like today.

He found a Captain at one entrance, which seemed the main one, he ushered him inside "for deployment," he said.

Another, friendlier Captain, Jennings told him he was welcome and listened to his account of the previous day, and what detail he could give of enemy movement that morning. Jennings was silent for a full minute, thinking.

Jennings looked preoccupied, he was quite short, five six, about thirty but with more lines on his forehead than seemed normal. Duncan saw a flash of anger which turned to a half smile on his lips, stretching his obligatory officer's pencil moustache wider.

"Listen," Jennings said, "it's best you stick with me for the time being and don't repeat what you've told me about yesterday. Your Major was here giving his report, and, let us say, he emphasised other aspects of the day's events. He's at the Brigadier's headquarters, and it's going to blow up here soon. We're to hold this position as long as we dare, then retire to the enceinte, the town walls, and reinforce the Rifles there. We can man a smaller perimeter better, we've got about 3,000 men in total, but not all trained or armed. We can worry about your Major back in England."

"Surviving today is enough of a worry for me anyway, sir," said Duncan.

"Duncan, I won't lie to you, I don't think we'll see England again. A few small boats are taking wounded away. I don't believe there will be any evacuation from Calais. The French will be up in arms about us leaving Boulogne if that's what we've done. There're hundreds of thousands of men in Dunkirk, I don't think there's enough of us here to warrant much attention. I think we'll stay here for quite some time."

"That's what I'd do if I were top brass," said Duncan.

"Right, follow me, I'll show you round," Jennings said, then took him up a broad ramp which gently inclined from ground level to reach the top ramparts.

"The fort itself is held by the French Reservists, sound men, but lightly armed. I'm supporting the fort with the 2-pounders you can see on the ramparts, I'm coordinating these, and the machine gun positions spread out in front of the fort. The central railway station and the Citadel are back there," he said pointing to the main town east of the fort.

"There's a tunnel leading to a small postern gate at the rear of the fort, we'll use that later when we need to. We won't occupy the buildings in the middle of the fort, they're just easy targets from the air. We're expecting the main attack from the east, so we're spread thin here on this side of the town. We expect the 69th Schutzen from the east and the 86th from the west. Here we go!" he said, as he saw smoke rising in the east and the dull thumping sound of distant explosions.

"The Rifles are first class men, they'll give Jerry a hard time. Right, Duncan, here come our German guests for the day!"

The German 86th Rifle Regiment began their attack from the south-west as Duncan had expected. They also attacked from the road junction he'd just left. There was nothing worth attacking there, but discovering that would cost the enemy time and resources he couldn't use elsewhere.

Heavy Calibre German guns fired from a distance, the massive fort was an easy target for a bombardment to hit regularly if randomly. The more mobile individual German tanks were a small target, impossible to zero in on, so the British 2-Pounders stayed silent while shells blasted the fort walls and inner ramparts.

High explosive shells were killing and injuring men in the body of the fort as well as the ramparts, French and British. Those dug in outside fared no better, they had new Bren guns behind firm and deep sandbag barricades about 50 yards to the front, they just wouldn't last against Panzers.

"Where are our cruiser tanks?" asked Duncan.

"Some were sent north-east to Dunkirk with a convoy and some went south, I expect they met some more of what we can see here, I don't know for certain," said Jennings.

"Shall we just give them a few blasts from the twos anyway?" said Duncan. "Keep their heads down and raise our morale?"

"Worth a try, we can't just wait to get hit, be my guest."

Duncan ordered the 2-pounders to fire at the area where the greatest concentration of enemy fire was originating.

"And cross your fingers!" he shouted as he drew back to avoid being deafened.

The 2-pounders fired as best they could, mainly missing their mark. The infantry behind those tanks was suffering casualties and taking down a few would help if they got lucky. They did get lucky, though, as one shell made a direct hit on the turret of a Panzer One. It rose from its mounting and tumbled off, bouncing twice before coming to rest on top of a few Grenadiers.

A loud cheer from the ramparts followed that. Duncan didn't cheer, he feared what might happen next, and he was right to do so. German return fire concentrated on the locations of the 2-pounders, destroying one, including its crew, with a direct, high explosive, hit. The gun was a mangled heap, and mercifully the three-man crew had died instantly. They were in pieces, and he didn't look closely or for long.

Duncan and Jennings crouched.

"Dear God, I made them a target for that," said Duncan, feeling sick again, growing familiar with the feeling and learning to ignore it.

"We're all targets today, and we'll kill more before we're done, that shell could have been you or me just as easily," Jennings said.

The shelling carried on for several minutes before stopping, the other 2-pounder crew had bravely carried on firing, doing some damage and discouraging any head on charge so far.

"They're moving back a little," said Jennings, "that'll mean Stukas soon, shall we get the men under better cover and move the gun, it's making too easy a target where it is," said Jennings.

"You get the men, I'll get the gun."

"Good man, I'll speak to the French."

Jennings sent a runner to the forward machine gun positions telling them to stay down until the Stukas had finished then withdraw immediately into the fort.

Duncan helped the three-man 2-pounder crew to coast their gun down the gentle ramp to ground level, and positioned it to the inside left of the main fort entrance. The entrance was open, ungated, partly blocked by a small, ineffective barricade. A tank would only take a few seconds to push it aside.

"We'll give him a nasty surprise when he comes through there, then withdraw, double quick," he said.

"We'll be happy to do both," said the gunner Sergeant. They said nothing of their mates blasted apart only minutes before.

Duncan ran to the entrance and stood where he estimated the more vulnerable side armour of a tank would be after smashing the barrier.

"Get the gun aimed right at my stomach, please," he said and waited.

"Ready, sir."

"Right," he said and ran back to the 2-pounder, "have

this loaded and ready for immediate firing. I think we'll only get one shot, so it needs to be perfect, dead centre, moving the barricade should slow him down nicely."

They waited patiently for the attack they knew would come. Half an hour later, they heard the Stuka Dive-Bombers before they saw them, coming from the east as usual. Duncan heard some token anti-aircraft fire from their own side. The drone of the Stukas engines changed to the loud shrieking wail of their sirens as they dived towards the fort.

"I can see three!" shouted Jennings from the top of the ramparts near the gate.

The Stukas descended one by one, like dull metal pterodactyls, each dropping five bombs, one medium and four smaller ones. The effect was devastating inside the fort, the small buildings and shelters within fell victim to direct hits. Blast and shrapnel damage left many wounded. When the Stukas had finished their task, the patiently waiting Panzers and Armoured Personnel Carriers started toward the fort. A single Sturmpanzer, self-propelled artillery piece continued to lob shells towards and inside the walls.

Duncan saw two medics spring smartly out of their cover and start work, some wounded would stay where they lay, and some would die there. The walking wounded might make it through the small, one man wide, rear entrance which dipped under then up and out of the rear curtain wall. Each stretcher would use two men to carry it, those men needed guns in their hands, not a stretcher. The medics might stay if the rest ran, he wasn't sure what the protocol was in practice, perhaps they should be allowed to make their own choices.

Jennings used a whistle, to loudly recall his Bren gunners from their prepared positions in front of the fort. They had no trouble hearing the whistle, it was the only sound their ears wanted to hear.

They scrambled quickly into the fort via the front entrance, each man carrying all he could. Just as quickly,

Jennings ran down the ramp and off the ramparts, ordering his men to take up positions in the shell holes obligingly prepared by the earlier Stuka bombs.

He'd seen what Duncan had done and placed his men in the corners of the fort's rear walls. Ensuring there was no direct line of sight of them from outside the fort, he told them to hold their fire until his command. A couple of extra hands moved the barricade fully into place.

"Good Luck Duncan!" he shouted, above the noise of the advancing armour, Duncan didn't hear what he said and just gave a wave and a thumbs up, hoping it looked better than he felt.

The Panzers advanced steadily along the uneven and soft ground in front of the fort, blasting as they went, wasting shells on the unmanned ramparts, there was no return fire. The lobbing of shells from the self-propelled gun had stopped, he'd be wary of hitting his own men.

Panzers would usually advance in the shape of a V, with a Panzer Three at the point and Panzer Grenadiers, well-armed infantry, a little way behind them, Duncan hoped they'd follow that routine.

The rumbling and firing moved closer, and Duncan felt relief at seeing a Panzer Three, easily yet slowly pushing aside the barricade at the main gate and moving into the fort.

"Fire!" he shouted as the tank's weaker side armour was at exactly the right point where he's stood earlier. A side shot at close range destroyed the tank, it shuddered to a halt turning itself into an effective barricade for the entrance.

"Go, go!" he shouted at his gun crew.

They knew they only had seconds, and they sprinted to the rear of the fort, hugging the wall to their left.

"Down," shouted Duncan as they reached the rear.

As they'd expected, the other tanks couldn't immediately enter the fort, but Panzer Grenadiers clambered around the wreck regardless. They found no cover inside the fort and were mown down by concentrated Bren gun crossfire from two sides. From his side, Duncan saw six hit the ground before they stopped trying to get in. A second Panzer would take time to push the wrecked tank out of the way, and that would give them a few valuable minutes head start.

Christ that felt good thought Duncan. Anything that slows him down, anything.

"Come on, out you get, anyone who can walk. Come on! Out the back now!" shouted Jennings to anyone who could listen, Frenchman and British alike knew what he was crying.

Duncan watched the two different sets of men politely allowing others through ahead of them, men queuing patiently to flee for their lives.

*'God, if we'd led these men better what might we have done.'*

Jennings told two big lads with Brens to wait with him until those who could walk got through the small, well-lit tunnel. They held their guns at their hips ready to fire if necessary. He saw no further movement so he let those last two go through ahead of him, Duncan went next, and Jennings went last.

"At least we're learning how to retreat!" said Duncan.

They emerged into daylight at the end of the tunnel, men were already making their way in a line across open fields towards a raised railway embankment.

"That'll take us into the station and headquarters, and give us some cover while we do it," said Jennings, pointing ahead and then to the right.

"We haven't got any explosives have we?" Duncan asked.

"Not an ounce in the whole town I'm afraid, come on let's go. Follow me."

Jennings asked the Bren Gunners to chuck a couple of grenades into the tunnel then they ran too.

"Maybe one'll trip in the dark, or a loose brick'll hit some bugger on the bonce," he said.

They ran across the fields then ducked behind the

railway embankment. They could hear exchanges of fire from inside the fort.

"Good lads," said one idiot.

Not that good, thought Duncan, whoever had opened fire had just ensured few English wounded would leave the fort alive. Maybe Jerry would have finished them regardless, maybe Duncan would have if he was in their position. Half a dozen of your mates have just been killed, and you give the man who did it a cigarette and chocolate instead of a bullet, just because he's waving a white flag? Duncan was learning war quickly, in practice, and learning about himself too.

He looked at his watch, it was 1135. They walked briskly towards Calais old town, sheltered by the embankment.

Duncan heard the sound of tanks firing further west and more firing near the coast, at least they were heading in the right direction.

Only then did Duncan focus on what he'd done. He'd copied Teddy, stolen one of his plans, set a trap then kill, straightforward and efficient. Teddy had saved his life again, from beyond the grave, this time.

So many dead, so soon and he was already getting used to it, in just over twenty-four hours. But his chest was full of a deep life-affirming breath of fresh air, and he held his head high. Thanks, Teddy.

## Chapter 7

### 24th May 1940 - Morning – Midday - Calais

As Teddy and his new comrades reached the outskirts of Calais, Jezz asked his men to rest behind the line of defence they'd just crossed. Jezz went to speak to the two officers in charge, or who were present at any rate.

This section of the perimeter defence straddled a three-track railway line and a narrow road running alongside it. The track and road took a straight route into Calais, the road to the left side as Teddy looked ahead at it. Small houses, some bomb damaged, lined the road on the left with a small church about 300 yards ahead. The defending troops had arranged six strong points across the rail and road, sandbags, wood, bricks and makeshift roofing making effective cover against small arms. There was one 2-pounder in a well-camouflaged position and several Bren Guns, but he could see no Boys rifles. The men looked in proper order and ready to stand firm, though.

Teddy sat on a sandbag barrier behind the strong points, took the weight off his feet and waited for Jezz. He closed his eyes, took a long deep breath then breathed out slowly, it didn't immediately calm him. He cupped his hands tightly over his nose and mouth and breathed the same air in and out for a few seconds, and it did calm him. He didn't know why he did that, his subconscious somehow told him to. Perhaps he'd make it part of his mantra now?

He took a drink from his water bottle and examined his new rifle. The Mauser Karabiner KAR 98Kurtz bolt-action rifle. It was a thing of exquisite beauty, the highly polished wood was almost a cherry red finish, with a silver looking metal butt at the rear. There was an extra wooden cheek rest seamlessly joined onto the left side of the butt, which had the word 'Flesch' ornately carved into it. He'd not seen anything like that before, yet it made perfect sense to him, like a chin rest for a violinist. He took out the clip and tried the chin rest and the sights out, nearly set for his liking already. The bolt-action was silky smooth no matter how fast he pulled and pushed. The gunmetal was dark matt, untarnished; somehow the polish repelled dust and dirt. They'd used some special type of wax. The telescopic sight looked new, its cool dark glass was perfect, custom fitted with 8 times magnification, marked 'Gustloff Werke'. The butt had a serial number of 2015 carved into it, and even the leather strap was perfect, thick and still supple. The bullets came in five round stripper clips, he had a hundred rounds from Dolf's pack and knew he could make most of them count with this.

Dolf was either fabulously wealthy or the best shot in the Reich, maybe both. Dolf had class, thought Teddy, he didn't know why he'd used his real name with him, it just seemed right. He wished he'd asked Dolf why he'd looked at him so strangely. He wished he knew why Dolf looked familiar. He wished he knew why he wanted to be Dolf. There was no time to think about that now, though.

He took the watch out of his pack, it was equally impressive, he strapped it firmly to his wrist and looked at its face, it said 'Rolex Oyster' and read ten o'clock precisely.

The sound of heavy guns opening fire broke the silence. The timing of the explosions and location of the rising smoke told Teddy that Dolf had been truthful and precise. The safety of the warehouse had changed into a death trap, not for me, mate. I trap people, nobody traps me.

He remained unsure how he should feel about Dolf, he might have to kill or be killed by him in the next few hours.

No, he knew there were about twenty men next to him whose lives he'd saved, and they knew it now, they were good men, and they owed him. He could use that.

Jezz left the officers and walked back to his men, the Panzers would reach this position soon, Archie expected Jezz would have a plan, he relaxed.

"The brass asked me to find spaces for you lot in their lines. I told them I was putting you in those houses further into Calais to cover them when they have to fall back," Jezz announced. He looked at Teddy and smiled. "They weren't impressed by our falling back without orders, but those warehouses being blown to fuck, right on cue, settled any argument. We're moving further back about 400 yards into Calais along the rails, then the first spot I choose."

Jezz started walking, and everyone just followed his lead.

"Jezz, can I hang around in that old church for a bit? I need to practice with the Mauser," said Teddy.

"Course you can, in fact, *you* can do whatever *you* like, mate."

"Can I take Spud with me to watch my back?"

"Good plan."

"I'll join you later then. Spud, you okay with that?"

"Yes, mate," said an eager Spud.

"Come on then, grab a sandbag will you."

"One last thing," said Jezz quietly to Teddy, "that pair'll wave a white flag as soon as they can, don't expect any help from them. Posh cunts, they've never had to fight for anything in their lives, how are they going to learn now. Fuck them, I'll look after me and mine. Come on."

Teddy liked Jezz, a lot, although he scared him a little too, he'd have to think that through properly, he could learn from him. Jezz would make a good caveman.

*'Watch and listen, copy and act.'*

Within 30 minutes, Teddy and Spud were in position in the Church tower he'd seen earlier. Teddy had found a horizontal slit in the wooden wall facing the front, he left it intact and placed the sandbag on the internal brick wall immediately below the slit. From a crouched position he could maintain a solid frame for a steady shot.

Spud had smashed a man-sized hole in the wooden rear panelling of the tower, to watch where Jezz went, and also in case they needed a quick escape. He'd then found a way into the roof space and smashed tiles from the roof to the front, right and left covering any approaches Jerry might make. He'd also put a pew against the main door.

"It won't keep them out for long, but we'll hear them

okay," Spud said out of breath.

"Have a drink mate," said Teddy handing his water bottle to Spud. "How the hell did you know to do all that?"

"It's only common sense," came the reply.

"Only it ain't that common."

"Now you mention it, no, it ain't."

"Hang on, there's movement," Teddy said.

"I'll be moving between holes, shout if you need anything, cup o' tea, sarnie, arse wiping," said Spud as he left.

"Will do," said Teddy and prepared to begin his mantra.

Teddy looked at his watch, it was ten thirty, and he could see movement on the railway and road, probably a mile from his position. Tanks and armoured cars were moving towards the defensive positions ahead of them.

He focussed his sights just behind the advancing vehicles, waited and adjusted the scope as they came closer. He waited just a little longer. They were a thousand yards away now he estimated, and he could see individual Panzer Grenadiers within his sights as they walked, bunched together behind the tanks.

He began his mantra, firm position for the barrel, push the barrel down on the sandbag, still firm. Butt to the shoulder, cheek rest even better, firm and comfortable. Take aim at the group, deep breath, let it go slowly, deep breath and hold it this time. Aiming, aiming for the biggest part of the target, torso, squeeze, fire. Breathe.

Even with slight recoil kickback, the quality of his own eyes and the sights he couldn't be 100% sure he'd hit, but his stomach felt he had.

*'Bloody hell, this is the best rifle I have ever seen or heard of, I am keeping this forever!'*

Another deep breath and he resumed the mantra another four times. He concentrated harder on keeping the gun steady after the recoil and his right eye not blinking after pulling the trigger. He'd definitely shot at least four.

Reload. His second clip slid in, every pull and push of the bolt were fingertip smooth movement, effortless.

The second clip was empty, the Grenadiers were close enough to watch each target fall, he still aimed for torsos, on the move, that was the best chance of a hit. He was certain now, all ten of his bullets had hit a mark.

He stopped briefly and moved away from his slot to rest his eyes and fingers, stretch his legs and have a swig of water.

From his first rifle training in the Territorials, aged 16, and then full-time in the Fusiliers, he knew he could shoot well. He was never the best marksman in target competitions, just one of them, which had felt like enough at the time. He knew now what he could do when he was tired, when adrenaline flowed, under pressure, and when someone was firing back. He knew, when needed most, he could kill a live target without thought or pity.

He took a deep breath ready to resume the mantra again. He heard Spud before he saw him.

"Come on we're off!" Spud said and climbed through the hole he'd made earlier, on to a sloping roof before an eight-foot drop onto soft earth. He didn't pause for Teddy, he didn't need to, he was two seconds behind him.

"They'll be through on the right in two minutes, here in five, we'll go straight to Jezz," said Spud, leading the way down the straight pavement, hugging the buildings to avoid making an easy target. The noise behind was enough to motivate the helter-skelter speed they made, they didn't look back, they'd done their bit. Spud could run bloody fast when he needed to.

Teddy followed Spud, who led him into a larger than usual house on the left, a frantic three hundred yards further into Calais.

"Afternoon lads," said Jezz as they entered the double door of the building.

"We're upstairs here and in that red-brick place across the railway track. Looks like a few dead and a lot in the bag down there, if they'd pulled back properly and made another line, they'd have lasted longer and done more damage. At least Jerry's taking prisoners today, so that'll slow him down a bit and waste some useful men to guard them. I'm not sure whether to stick here for a little bit longer or pull further back now, what did you see Spud?"

"There's two Panzer threes and armoured support coming up this road and the railway line. They're attacking further west as well, in at least two places, judging by the smoke. Not sure what that means."

"A slow encirclement," said Teddy, "they can't use Blitzkrieg in a town, they'll crowd us into a smaller area then call in the Stukas when they can't miss."

"Let's keep a close watch for now, but be ready to move back," Jezz said, "you two take a break while you can, any luck with that?" he asked, nodding at the Mauser.

"Two or three," Teddy lied.

"Well done, mate."

It was nearly eleven o'clock and Teddy could hear the distant sound of shelling to the west and east, thankfully nothing more from the south. Jezz had organised a brew up while they waited, only the British could do that, was it like fiddling while Rome burned, Teddy couldn't decide what to think. He drank the tea and felt better, confident his oppos would provide an early warning if needed.

Teddy flexed his fingers, the tension from the earlier firing still in his knuckles.

Spud was silent, he was thinking about what might come next.

\*

Teddy looked closely at Spud for the first time. He was mid-twenties, about five nine, strong looking, a bit overweight, a curly mop of hair under his helmet, fully strapped under his chin, he'd leave that on until he didn't need it. He hadn't shaved for a bit, nor slept well for a while, and had deep bags under his brown eyes. Although Spud didn't strike him as well educated, he clearly had heaps of nouse, common sense and practicality about him, a good man in a team. A good mate. He'd watched and waited at the Church until precisely the right moment, then moved quickly and without hesitation. He'd keep

Spud watching his back.

Teddy had talked this through with Duncan, how could so many well-educated, intelligent people, Government, Heads of the Army, be so stupid, make so many stupid decisions. Intelligent, well-educated people, had put Spud and Jezz where they were, they'd be ten times dead by now, without their own common sense and survival instinct. No one had taught them what they knew.

Look at Chamberlain, what use would he be as a caveman, would he negotiate with a woolly mammoth and ask him nicely if we could eat him, please? Would he come back from a meeting with a sabre-toothed tiger, waving a piece of paper and announce peace for our time? Churchill, now he'd have been a real caveman, although even he couldn't add up, he'd been an incapable Chancellor, useless with money, especially someone else's.

Teddy had told Duncan about the words he'd read.

*'The law of natural selection, the rule of the jungle. Men dispossess one another, and one perceives that at the end of it all, it is always the stronger who triumphs. The stronger asserts his will, it's the law of nature.'*

"Who said that?" Duncan had asked.

"Hitler."

"So Hitler's right?"

"No, no, the words are right, Hitler's the wrong man to say it. He's a liar, he can't do it himself, it's all bluff."

"Who decides who the right man is then?"

"I do, of course."

\*

Teddy's attention drew him to the present, and he focussed on planning and thinking. The practical application of intelligence, the process whereby that happened, making it happen regularly, routinely, survival of the fittest.

That was war.

That was life.

"How come you told Jezz you got two or three," asked Spud, "I saw you get five, and you fired off what? Ten shots?" asked Spud.

"He might have thought it was bullshit, and you don't risk bullshitting somebody like Jezz."

"Maybe, how many did you get?"

"Ten. I was lucky, they were bunched and moving slow."

"I'll still stay on your back if that's okay."

"It is, mate."

Teddy checked his watch again, it was eleven thirty, he took another chocolate bar from his bag, sharing it with Spud, breathed deeply and waited.

*

Duncan was trudging as quickly as he could, through the softer earth of fields, along another railway line into Calais. He could still hear sounds of fighting to the west and south-west. Then, as he walked, he became more aware of further fighting to the south-east and east. The enemy was encircling the town, giving the defenders no choice except to fight on a smaller perimeter, only making them a more compact target for his bombers and artillery.

He was alongside Jennings and had seen Fowler, Leach, and the 2-pounder crew, but recognised no one else. The Frenchmen moved on in utter silence, he could understand that silence and hoped he'd never experience it. He never wanted to see Panzers rolling through the streets of Dover.

He tried to plan ahead, but could only think back, rather than forward. Sometimes the past can help you plan the future, they were definitely not learning the lessons of history, so he just let his mind wander back. He wondered who and what he was, and why?

*

He was born on the Twentieth of March 1918, in Bagnères-de-Bigorre, France. A small town in the Pyrenees near the Spanish border. He lived in a mansion set in private parkland and woods to the west of the town. He'd never known his parents, they'd died in a climbing accident when he was eighteen months old. Raised by a nanny and a guardian, he had no relatives. His nanny had been wonderful, and his guardian had attended to his every need. His parents had been wealthy, and his upbringing privileged beyond belief, he experienced the best of everything; except a family.

A succession of mentors and teachers had privately educated him at home, learning Languages, History, Classical History, Physics, Chemistry, Biology, Logic, Philosophy, Astronomy, Cosmology, everything except Religion.

He'd travelled to England, the United States, Canada, Germany, Italy, Greece, and Russia.

Money was limitless, but he was never spoilt, knowledge and learning were his purpose, for all his life. That and discipline, always discipline, well nearly always, he remembered fondly.

He spent all his teens studying military history, strategy, tactics, leadership, management, logistics, all theory and no practice.

Yes, he'd attended Eton briefly, and then Sandhurst aged eighteen, passed every exam and physical test. Alex, his guardian, and principal mentor had crammed his head full of every piece of knowledge he could squeeze inside, getting it out was his problem. How did you use that knowledge in the right way, in the right place, at the right time? Even then, you still needed to get lucky, phenomenally lucky and live long enough to do it when it mattered.

"The practical application of intelligence," Teddy called it, "necessitated by survival of the fittest by the fittest for the fittest."

Duncan felt a perfect melding of selfishness, selflessness, thoughtfulness and thoughtlessness pulling at him. The synchronicity of time and space. A growing sense of certainty that all his learning and training were meant for these moments. He was where he was supposed to be. Teddy had undergone no such training, he'd just been born for this. They had met, they must have been meant to meet, but Teddy was dead, had he taught him enough, had he learned enough from him?

No, wait, somehow he knew it then, beyond any doubt, Teddy wasn't dead, and he couldn't be dead. If this Universe held real meaning, Teddy was alive, and Duncan needed to stay alive so they could meet again, and it needed to be soon. If this Universe meant nothing then nothing in it mattered, he'd just wait for another to come along. Was that profound or pretentious, he wondered, feeling gently bemused by his own logic, but he now knew beyond the slightest doubt, he was right. He'd have to survive to make those thoughts matter, so he focussed on them, took a deep breath and walked on.

*

They came to where the railway line crossed a canal. They didn't cross there and turned south toward some concrete blockhouses standing behind a small road bridge. He could see other troops erecting a defensive barricade across the bridge. With the deepest irony that none of them were aware of, they were disabling their last few trucks to bolster the barricade. Duncan felt they could only hold that position for hours, not days.

Jennings and his remaining men squeezed through the only tight space left for stragglers in the barricade.

Jennings reported to the Major in charge, Johnstone from the Queen Vics. They had orders to hold firmly here and on several narrow bridges across the canals which circled the old town and Citadel. The Rifles were defending the east resolutely, the same held for the south by French reservists. The main British headquarters remained in the Gare Maritime, but might move to the Citadel later, and there was still hopeless talk of an evacuation. Boulogne, in fact, hadn't fallen, an organised evacuation was under way, although its imminent loss was inevitable. Dunkirk had up to half a million men surrounded, Johnstone didn't think Calais was a priority. They knew they couldn't win this particular battle, but their orders were to hold the ready-made defensive position behind the line of the canal.

Having explained the situation, he turned to Duncan.

"Your Major Feckle's down by the docks on this side of the port, organising the movement of the wounded and rear echelon, there are still some small boats daring it, mostly at night. You can join him if you wish?" he said.

"I can be more use here, sir," Duncan answered.

"Certainly, stay with Jennings," he said with a knowing smile.

Duncan didn't speculate about what Johnstone and Jennings knew, he'd save those thoughts for later.

"Jennings," said Johnstone, "get your French off to the railway station, they're congregating there to form their own last stand unit, should that prove necessary, of course."

The positions immediately next to the bridge were well-manned, so Jennings placed his group of 75 men further south beside the canal bank. That position gave a side view of the approach to the barricade, making a clear field of fire for his Brens. He ordered his men to dig in then scout the rear for fall-back positions. Two men checked further down the canal for risks, and a couple found some food.

Only when Jennings was satisfied that had been done, did they give their legs a rest. They didn't ask for any food, but a Corporal brought them a tin of bully beef and two tin mugs of tea.

"One tin between two I'm afraid, and there's no sugar or milk," he said.

"Has everyone else got something?" Jennings said.

"Yes, sir, they're all sorted."

They settled down breathlessly for a rest, Duncan looked at his watch, it was one o'clock.

*

Teddy and Spud talked and rested until nearly two o'clock, Teddy slept for an hour.

"Christ knows how you do that, mate?" said Spud.

"It's a gift."

"What did you do before this lot then?"

"I was in the Territorials part-time, that's where I

learned to shoot so well."

"No, what job did you do?"

"You don't want to know."

"Yes I do; okay, I was a baker, in Holloway, white bread only, up all night to have tons of it ready and fresh in the morning. I slept all day and worked all night for four years, nothing but bloody white bread, it can't be worse than that."

"Alright then, I was an apprenticed office clerk, in Holborn. I put pieces of paper in alphabetical order and filed them. I wrote down stuff that was already in one book, into another book, I'd rather have made bread, my writing was a thing of great beauty, though."

"Who did you work for?"

"Marley and Marley."

"Who?"

"Oh, Spud! So what's your real name then?"

"Jeremiah. This ain't a great time to be called Jerry, believe me. Who goes there? It's only Jerry, don't worry. Bang," he laughed.

"Spud ain't so bad then?"

"No, so is your real name Edward then?"

"No, it's Archie."

"How d'you get Teddy from that?"

"At school, one kid found out I had this big teddy bear, I didn't play with it or anything, I just hadn't thrown it out, you don't throw things out where I come from. He told everyone, so they started calling me *'Teddy Bear'* for a while, then it came down to *'Teddy,'* it stuck that's all."

"You ain't been at school for a while, though."

"It stuck at work too. Then me and another lad moved down to London for work at the same time, figured we'd make our fortunes. We didn't. He signed up as a territorial, same time as me, the name stuck."

"And your mate?"

"He didn't stick it."

Jezz interrupted them, "Teddy, Spud, I've got a little job for you."

"That's good, we was getting a bit bored like," said Spud.

They followed Jezz upstairs to the third floor of the larger house his men were hiding in. They passed others coming down, they were packing up their gear, ready to fall back Teddy assumed. They followed Jezz up some much smaller stairs to the attic space, where he'd dislodged a couple of tiles next to a brick chimney stack.

Teddy looked out warily at first, then, as he expected, saw the position which had become the German front line. Some tanks were in position already, poised to move forward.

"Who d'you want then?" Teddy asked Jezz.

"Behind the tanks, there's a command vehicle, plug as senior a man as you can, then we're off to the town walls."

"I hope it's a Major," said Teddy casually, "I've always wanted to kill a Major."

"When you're ready, the lads'll be moving soon."

"A bit of quiet please," Teddy said, leaning his shoulder against the brickwork for support, and fed the Mauser's barrel carefully through the hole in the tile roof.

He lined up his sights around the target area, near the enemy armour, then beyond it. He saw the radio masts signalling a command vehicle then searched around for the best target, breathing slowly, using only tiny movements in his grip of the weapon.

There would only be time for one shot.

The number of people milling around was distracting him. Then he focussed on one man, pointing and directing, among a group of officers. He was crouching sensibly, then stood to give directions, presenting a clearer target. There was no question of any fancy target shooting, aiming between the eyes or the like. He started the mantra, finished it and fired, at this short distance he saw the man go down, and others scatter like ants when you stood on a nest.

"Got some bastard anyway," he said.

"Right let's go," said Jezz.

They hurried down the flight of stairs and into the alleyway behind the house, following Jezz, who clearly knew where he was heading. I like a man who knows where he's going, thought Teddy.

I like the way I got that Major too.

## Chapter 8

### 24th May 1940 – Afternoon - Calais

Teddy, Spud, and Jezz brought up the rear of their small group of men. They crossed the open space of the railway line cautiously, then gathered near a larger building along the Rue des Fontinettes, one of the straight main roads heading into Calais.

Having seen no sign of any other line of defenders who might delay the German armour, Jezz chose to head straight back to the old town itself. He knew there was the line of a canal, railway line and station ahead, which were defensible in strength, he'd seen them when moving forward from the docks.

After another twenty minutes steady walking, they reached a wide open space, a park on their left and a large building on their right, just beyond that were the railway station and the canal.

Here, at least and at last, Teddy identified some significant order and discipline. A Major had set up a local command post, a plan was in place for defence with men and equipment placed in sensible positions along the approaches to the old town.

A young Lieutenant from the 60th Rifles approached Jezz and his men as they passed through the line of sandbags and disabled vehicles barring the road. He was skinny, tall, about six foot three or four, with a spotlessly clean uniform and no chin.

Oh Fuck! I hope he's not posh, thought Teddy. He was.

"I'm Duvall," he said in a distinctly upper-class voice, "gather your men in, Corporal and I'll tell you what's going on and what we're doing about it."

That sounded helpful.

"Have you got any wounded?" he continued. "No, well done, and you are Corporal?"

"Hastings, sir," said Jezz.

"Have your boys come from that excuse for a defence of

the railway?"

"Eh…Yes, sir."

"Well you've come in better order than that last lot, two scruffs without a rifle between them, they'd have run into the channel if I hadn't stopped them. What did you see down there?"

Jezz explained what they'd done last night and that morning, missing out the captured German sniper and his opinion of the officers involved.

"Well, we're going to stand firm here, fight house by house and delay the enemy for as long as possible. Your French should join the rest of their reserves in the station."

Duvall then said something in French; the Frenchmen looked surprised, nodded at Jezz and the rest of their comrades, then headed towards the railway station.

"This way, I'll show you what we've got," Duvall continued and led them to the right-hand side, behind the large building, he called the Town Hall. "Beautiful isn't it, it'll be blown to buggery by tomorrow, I'll warrant."

Behind the building, he showed them a straight narrow road, leading south out of Calais, Rue du Pont Lottin.

Duvall raised his voice so they could all hear.

"This is our road then, I've got thirty men, including your lot that's forty. The outline plan is that we defend this thoroughfare, house by house or every other house if things go badly, if it's worse we scarper back to the canal behind us. I'll put ten on each side, Brens and rifles, we'll fire, do some damage then move back bit by bit."

This sounded promising, thought Teddy, and he's explaining it to the men too. He was posh, though.

"The next bit is the best bit," Duvall said, "I've scrounged three 2-pounder mortar teams. They're in position just in front of the canal behind us. They've paced out the range, so I think we can give Fritz a nasty surprise or two as he comes up the road. One bright spark back there found some white paint, and he's marked out lines on the road five hundred, four hundred and three hundred yards. Getting the timing right won't be easy, but it's better than firing blind."

"And where will you be, sir?" said Jezz sceptically.

"I'll take the right-hand side with ten men, you'll take the left with ten, the rest will be in reserve by the mortar teams. If you're up for it, old chap?"

"It'll be my pleasure, sir!" said Jezz.

Teddy overcame his surprise to offer a small plan.

"Sir, if you like," he said holding up his Mauser, "I can get in a building behind your fall-back line and give some cover with this. That looks a likely one just there, fourth floor probably. I can see right down that street and find a lot of easy targets. I should be able to see the white lines, I could signal the mortars somehow to get the timing right. Have you got a field phone and a long line?"

"There's one from the mortar teams to local HQ, I'll get a sapper to move it. Excellent idea, Private," Duvall said.

"Can I have Spud again, for the phone and to watch my back?" he asked.

"Keep coming up with the ideas and you can have my stripes!" said Jezz smiling.

*

Teddy looked at his watch; it was three o'clock in the afternoon. Spud sat behind him manning the field phone and waiting. They'd eaten a lot of Teddy's chocolate in the absence of any choice, there was certainly no point saving it. Untypically, neither of them smoked, so they ate the chocolate, they were sick of bloody chocolate.

"I'd give my right arm for a bag of fish and chips," he said.

"And a pint," answered Spud.

"Oh yes, a lovely cold one."

The building Teddy had chosen sat on the corner of the Rue Du Pont Lattin and Rue Dutertre, giving him a view straight ahead to where Jezz and his men were. It also had views to the left and right and even of the mortar position, providing Spud stuck his head out of the window and looked behind them. Spud also found a back door into a small yard leading to the canal, albeit by a roundabout route through alleys and buildings. He'd even found forty foot of tough knotted rope just in case they had to leave by a window. Spud turned out to be the bloke who did what you wanted before you asked him, Teddy could use that.

Teddy had spoken to the mortar crews, handing out some fags, chocolate and instructions not to hit his hiding place.

Jezz and Duvall had taken some men and positioned them well in buildings, doorways and flat roofs along the narrow street. Each had left some men to cover the mortar crews.

Duvall's plan was as good as Teddy could have made. They were brave men, they had plenty of grenades, and the roofing of the tightly terraced houses would give a good line of defence, and retreat. Teddy still had a bad feeling, though.

Jezz had spoken to Teddy just before he'd left to join the others in the houses.

"Watch out for me, mate, I won't be first back, but I won't be last, not if there's an officer who should be. This Duvall talks a good game, we'll see how he plays. So, don't shoot me and don't fucking mortar me either or any of my lads. I'll make sure mine stay ahead of Jerry and away from those white lines, you do your bit, and I'll see you later."

Teddy looked carefully at Jezz and just nodded. He wasn't sure what to say, he didn't say anything because he didn't want to lie to him, and couldn't think of anything positive that wasn't a lie.

Jezz was about thirty, handsome, blue eyes, well-built and looked like he knew how to live life. He just looked like he'd have been with lots of girls, he was a caveman, a winner, nobody's fool.

"What's his first name, Spud?" Teddy asked when he'd gone.

"Gerald," said Spud. "I spoke to Terry, who knows him. He's got kids you know, he don't talk about it, but he writes letters. The nicest quietest bloke you could meet till he got here. He knows he shouldn't be here, he's angry as anythin', hates officers, wants to get home and scares me a bit."

"Me too, more than a bit."

"I know this ain't the time to ask, but why the hell are we here?" Spud said.

"I don't know, mate. Sometimes, I think I know then something happens, and I don't know again. Sometimes, I think I know what I'm doing, then the next minute I haven't got a bleedin' clue. I know I'm getting out of here if I can, though, that I do know," he said checking his watch then looking back through his sights.

"So do I, that's why I'm on your back."

"You got me out of that church okay," he said without looking back at Spud.

"I was lucky."

"You make your own luck in this world," said Teddy thinking hard. Trying to work out why he knew this wasn't going to work, and why he was still going to do it.

"Listen, Spud, when it comes to it and the Brass throw in the towel, you wait till there's a load of you, and make sure you stand right next to an officer. A senior one preferably, and as many of 'em as possible. Pretend you're some posh twit's batman, anything at all. Try and get to an Oflag with the officers, they need orderlies to work for them there."

Spud remained silent, they didn't say a word, they felt sick, something had been right earlier, now something just wasn't right.

Spud and Teddy heard the attack before they saw it. It was coming from their south as they expected, but Teddy couldn't see any movement down his straight road. He saw smoke rising from explosions on the main line of defence, in front of the park and town hall to his right.

He looked at Spud, who said, "I think I can hear it from the east and west as well, they've just been getting ready to attack from three sides at once."

Teddy couldn't see the defence on his right, the Town Hall was shielding it from his view. He could hear their mortar cover begin to fire, the mortars behind him remained silent.

He used his sniper sights to look down his road; he could see at least a mile in a straight line, but could see no sign of the enemy. He checked his watch again nervously then finally saw one tank, a Panzer Three, then before he could think, the tank fired straight up the road. He flinched involuntarily, thinking it was shooting straight at him, then he saw the round fired, releasing only smoke, then it fired two more. He was relieved to see just smoke, then, as it spread in the narrow confines of the street he started to panic. He couldn't see a thing down the street, tanks or infantry, friend or foe, the plan was gone, useless, the best they could do was fire the mortars blind!

"I'll count to sixty then fire at 300 yards?" Teddy said, half asking.

"Wait till you see some of ours clear the smoke?" suggested Spud.

"That'll be too late."

"What firing distance then?"

"Oh shit, I don't know."

"Just wait."

"Okay, I'll hold on, tell the mortars we're waiting," Teddy decided.

They heard gunfire exchanges clearly and the blast of explosions, big and small, he could only guess what was happening. The high explosive shellfire must be reducing some buildings to rubble, although they couldn't tell which buildings or who was inside.

"Tank!" shouted Spud.

A single tank emerged from the smokescreen, one hundred yards in front of them and two hundred from their mortars. It stopped and turned half left apparently intending to fire at the flank of the main defence.

"Tell the mortars, fire dead ahead two hundred," Teddy said.

Spud did that without hesitation, and ten seconds later three mortar rounds landed just ten yards in front of the

Panzer. The tanks commander didn't even notice the small irrelevant events, as he blasted a high explosive shell towards the main defence.

"Ten more yards, ten more yards," Teddy shouted in full panic now, and Spud relayed the message.

Two of the next three mortar shells hit the top of the tank doing some superficial damage only, nothing fatal. The shells distracted the tank commander, and his turret moved to its right, searching for the best target.

"That's it, more, more," shouted Teddy.

Spud relayed the message again. Three more mortar shells hit their target, this time, a hit on the engine grill doing some damage and starting a small fire.

"More, more," said Teddy, trying to remain calm, aiming his sights at the turret and beginning his mantra.

The turret came open slightly and Teddy, at that short range, easily put a bullet straight through the head of the tank commander.

Two of the next three mortar rounds hit the tank, the fire spread into the tank itself, and an internal explosion overwhelmed the rest of the crew.

"Cease fire," said Teddy.

Spud relayed the message.

Two figures stumbled from the smoke behind the tank, only to walk underneath the next volley of three mortar rounds Teddy hadn't asked for or had he? They fell to the ground motionless before he and Spud realised they were wearing khaki.

"Oh, bloody, fucking hell," said Spud.

"Okay, okay what do we do now?" said Teddy, asking himself, as much as Spud. "What do we do now? I can't see the lines anyway," he tried to breathe deeply and calmly, "tell them one volley at five hundred. We'll see what happens."

They didn't hear the mortars firing or see the explosions.

"Another volley at five hundred," said Teddy.

"Now two at four hundred, our lot won't be there, I'm

sure, I think I'm sure."

"You hope not," said Spud, who relayed the order nonetheless.

"Okay, let's wait now," although the panic had gone from Teddy's voice, it was still in his chest, waiting to return at a second's notice. "What else is goin' on, can you see anything?"

"We had to take that Panzer, we had to, mate, no choice!" Spud said. "We're holding in the middle, their mortars are still firing, not all the time, they'll be saving ammo. Bugger it, I never even asked about ammo."

"Neither of us did, mate, we can only do our best, that's all we can do today."

Neither felt any less sick or guilty, any attempt at reassurance wasn't working.

The smoke began to clear, unveiling damaged buildings on both sides of the street. One German Armoured Personnel Carrier was motionless at roughly 350 yards from the mortars, corpses lying in and around it.

"I can see khaki and grey in there," said Spud.

"Yeah, me too. Keep an eye out, I'll see if I can bag anything," Teddy said getting into a comfortable firing position for extended range.

"Where are you?" he asked absently of no one who could hear.

Through his sights he saw German grey movement towards him, flashing from door to door, from one piece of cover to another, not nearly long enough to aim accurately. He decided to fire off a couple of shots anyway, just to keep them wary and slow them down.

*'Anything that slows them down, anything at all.'*

He couldn't see his own men, but knew some were in the destroyed houses. He spotted movement far down the road, another Panzer, and an Armoured Personnel Carrier were moving forward.

"Mortars ready for five hundred," he said.

Spud relayed the message.

"Fire two volleys," he said at exactly the right moment,

and the two armoured vehicles rumbled slowly into a concentrated, dangerous barrage. This time, they reversed and waited, beyond accurate mortar range. Although Teddy could still see cautious fleeting grey shapes moving, he could do no real damage to them. He couldn't hear individual sounds from that distance, among the cacophony around him. He could see bursts of gunfire flashing and evidence of grenade explosions, telling him that some building to building, even hand-to-hand fighting was taking place.

"Why don't they move back, they should be moving back, they're standing too firm," he pleaded with Spud, who couldn't say anything in reply.

It looked like the line of defence was holding, but he couldn't see the other positions well enough. He couldn't control events, he could only call on some mortar fire using his best guess about where and when. He wasn't in control, he couldn't plan, and he was out of his depth. How did any commander control anything beyond the few men around them, how did Jerry do it? His mind was bursting with questions he had no answers to, he needed a better plan, he needed time to plan, and he had neither today. You needed to take the initiative, to attack first, or to prepare a defence and spring a trap, that just wasn't happening, not today.

Gradually, the firing decreased ahead of him and to his immediate left and right. Without that noise demanding his full attention, he could now hear the distant sounds of battle from the east and west. He looked at his watch, it was five o'clock.

"Christ, that's been two hours!" he said.

"How the hell have they stood this?" Spud said.

"No idea, none at all, mate. I was under fire for sixty seconds, and that was enough. Ask the mortars how many rounds they've got left?"

"They say they don't know, they're going to count them."

"Oh, for fuck's sake!"

"They say, another twenty-four."

"Tell 'em to find some more."

"He says fuck off, he's not leaving his cover."

"Can't blame him."

"We waiting?"

"Yes, we are."

The next attack began about an hour later, the tanks fired smoke again, even more, this time.

"It's guesswork again," said Spud.

"D'you want a go then?"

"No, you carry on."

"Sorry mate, I didn't mean to have a go. I'm just going to guess they'll slow down near the wrecked armour to push it aside and fire two volleys at that spot. I'm guessing it's three hundred and fifty yards, and then I'll guess when they'll get there. Tell the mortars to set for three fifty."

"Will do, mate."

"Quiet, I'm counting." Teddy counted to twelve, then continued.

"Fire two volleys."

"Change to three hundred and fire two volleys."

"Change to two eighty and fire two volleys."

"Stop and wait."

He rattled off the orders, and Spud relayed them.

The attack on their road stopped, the smoke slowly cleared, Teddy's heart beating faster as it did. The scene now showed fire, ashes and smoke rising from bodies. Four vehicles were disabled, one more Panzer and two Personnel Carriers. Behind and alongside them were many grey dead. In front of them, Teddy and Spud could see about ten khaki bodies lying among holes made by mortar shells, Teddy's mortar shells.

"What a mess. What a fucking god-awful mess," said Spud.

"What's that moving?" said Teddy, already aiming his sights at whatever it was.

"Bloody hell, it's Jezz, it's Jezz, and he's got that Duvall with him, he's half carryin' 'im," Spud said.

A short and fatal burst of machine gun fire rang out from behind them. Blood flew out of Jezz's midriff in half a dozen places as he fell to the ground with his arm still around Duvall. Duvall tried to crawl away before he died, but Teddy never saw that, as he began his mantra. He found the target he was seeking and caught him full in the head. The Jerry back shooter was dead before he hit the ground then Teddy put another round into him anyway, just to make sure.

"What have we just done?" said Spud.

"I think we've just done our jobs, just like Jezz, and the others have done theirs, and Jerry's done his. It's dirty, shitty, murder and it'll never be a good thing, but it had to be done. It's just our bad luck we had to do it, and it's our good luck we're still here to see it done. If we're lucky, we'll still feel like shit tomorrow morning."

"You're right, I know, but fucking hell."

"I know, I know. It's done, it's gone, it's done, and we need to get out of here."

"What?"

"Jerry won't attack again tonight, not after that, but when he does reach here is he gonna take any prisoners? Men who've just done that to his mates. Would you? Come on, we're out of here." Teddy said as mildly as he could, trying to talk to Spud like he was a younger brother.

"Listen, Spud, if you've got anything to say, say it now, cos when we leave that door we never talk about it again."

"Not ever?"

"Not ever."

"Suits me."

"Tell the mortar crew, we're on our way back. We'll take the phone with us, wouldn't want them to think we're scarpering."

*'In battle, the men you fight alongside must ever be worthy of the risk taken.'*

Teddy thought Caesar had said that, but couldn't be sure. Maybe he'd read too many books?

Teddy followed Spud through the back door, alleyways

and somebody's kitchen to reach the mortar teams, who were preparing to move back.

When they got there, one bantamweight Corporal from the 60th Rifles had taken charge, he looked like George Formby's little brother, even had the squeaky voice to go with it.

"We're all moving back behind the canal," he said, "we want that water between Jerry and us by the time it's dark. We are to fight to the last man, Churchill says, or Eden or some other bastard who ain't here."

"That's kind of them, have they told Jerry? He might surrender!" said Spud.

"The eyes of the British Empire are upon us, it says here," the Corporal announced pompously while holding an imaginary piece of paper in his hand as if reading it.

"That's just great, Corp," said Teddy, "I was brought up a Roman Catholic. God's been watching me my whole life; in case I do anything wrong. Now it's the entire fucking Empire as well."

"Yeah, can't a man get any privacy around here?" said Spud joining in.

"Yeah, well I need a shit," said another joker, "and I'm having one as soon as I find a private spot to do it, they can fucking watch that if they like."

"Well I've got some news then," George the Corporal broke in, "God is officially absent without leave from Calais. Hasn't been seen for days, and we'd better cross that canal bridge unless anyone's in a hurry to meet him."

"Well if I meet him, I'm telling him he's a complete cunt," said Teddy as dry as a bone.

"Well, I'm going to Hell anyway... it'll be warm, and I'll know people," said the joker.

If you'd bottled and sold the laughter that followed, you could sell it for a quid a time and make a million. Teddy made a mental note to steal that last remark and walked the short distance to the barricaded road and rail bridge which crossed the canal at a sharp angle.

No one asked who was left behind, no one asked who

would follow them, they were falling back. It was done, done was done, dead was dead. They'd learned that much in less than two days, and they still knew nothing.

I'm hellishly tired thought Teddy, making his way past some barricaded wreckage that formed the next line of defence around the old town.

"Spud, do you see any officers telling us where to go?"

"No, mate, not a single one."

"Well I'm tired, and I'm hungry, I'm ordering us to find something hot to eat and somewhere safe to sleep. We need to find some high-ranking officers as well, tomorrow won't be as easy as today."

"Easy? I'm with you anyway, mate."

## Chapter 9

### 24th May 1940 – Afternoon - Calais

Duncan looked at his watch, it was three o'clock, and he'd spent the last hour watching the German Army assemble in the distance. It stayed well out of range of any British small arms fire. The single 2-pounder antitank gun, hidden behind their lines would need to remain so until it could be used effectively at close quarters. They had two Boys anti-tank rifles with skilled men behind them, they'd still need to get lucky.

The German medium artillery opened fire, not finding its range straight away, the first shells fell short of the canal. The second salvo was more accurate, hitting their side of the canal, some shots still landing in it. The third salvo found better range, hitting the bridge and the area behind it. Duncan's hopes that they might blow up the bridge itself faded when the line of fire moved further forward, hitting the rear portion of their defensive position.

The solid concrete blockhouses and pillboxes alongside the bridge stood up to the barrage, and the canal bank earthworks provided extra cover. The Maginot Line would have proved useful here. Instead, its line of immense concrete fortifications and heavy artillery sat idle, four hundred miles away. Its guns aiming at Germany just not at the German army. Duncan's own position, south of the canal bridge, was far enough away to avoid any chance of a direct hit although small debris rattled his helmet in sporadic showers.

After firing intermittently for thirty minutes, the barrage ceased, and the line of Panzers advanced in characteristic V formation towards the canal bridge. Duncan saw one Panzer Two and four Panzer Threes, followed by three armoured half-tracks, small groups of well-armed Panzer Grenadiers came last. They expected to overwhelm any line of resistance, they had already swept through Holland, Belgium and northern France in exactly that way within two weeks.

The Panzers advanced across flat open fields with occasional shallow dips. The fields held the start of crop growth which might conceal a man if he lay flat. Fortunately for Duncan they still presented a sharp picture of the attackers to the defenders, who had dug into well-planned cover.

Looking across to his right towards the bridge, Duncan could see men scrambling from cover to more exposed firing positions. The barrels of heavy machine guns resumed their positions, poking through the slits in the pillboxes. They looked like mostly Brens and some older ones that had seen the last war which would still do some serious damage to men at medium range.

The British guns held their fire, and the gunners held their nerve, waiting until they would be most effective, fifty yards, perilously close range.

The arrowhead of the German Panzer line moved noisily and menacingly forward, like an impossibly huge, slow bomb, descending from a Stuka in some nightmare. The lead tank reached the far side of the bridge, firing dead ahead at the large barricade. It held surprisingly well, the Panzer Three fired again then advanced at speed apparently intending to crush the barrier and push it aside just as Johnstone had expected. As soon as it touched the barricade, the 2-pounder opened fire from its masked position north of the bridge. A direct hit from an armour piercing shell on its weaker side armour disabled the tank. Three seconds later a second round, high explosive, this time, blasted out of the gun and into the tank destroying the interior.

Before the second shell had left the 2-pounder, machine guns opened fire from north and south of the bridge. Jennings' men joined in, catching the Panzer Grenadiers with a savage crossfire into their exposed flanks.

That slaughter made the lighter Panzers acutely aware of the machine-gunner's positions on the canal bank. They started raking their well-protected positions with heavy machine gun fire, but it was too late, about twenty of their supporting Grenadiers lay dead or wounded.

The two Boys rifles zeroed in at close range on the sides of the next furthest forward tank. Distracted by the minor and ineffective hits, the tank commander didn't see the 2-pounder shell that struck him from the side and mangled one of his caterpillar tracks and a drive sprocket. Unable to move forward or back, he was a sitting duck for the two Boys guns whose shells found the weaker parts of the armour unerringly, setting off fires inside the tanks. The crew had perhaps three seconds to get out alive, and they didn't.

Duncan was aware of the 2-pounder moving backwards into full cover with its five-man crew, no doubt Johnstone had another position in mind. The other Panzers and armoured half-tracks then reversed. The Grenadiers scattered and took further hits as they did.

Duncan watched them, reversing over their own dead and wounded. He knew he'd have to be prepared to do the same to beat them.

On open ground, the British and French had no answer to the Panzers, in closer contact in towns and pinch points they could fall prey to the wily use of the limited anti-tank equipment. Trickery had worked three times, but surely it wouldn't work twice in the same place.

Panzer Grenadiers fell to the ground, hidden in hollows and half grown crops. Some would crawl back to better cover, others would stay, lying flat, hoping to do sly damage to the defenders when they least expected it.

Johnstone was smarter than that, he'd prepared his best throwing arms to lob grenades randomly across the canal into the crops and hollows. The small explosions were inaccurate yet effective in causing the brave, crafty Grenadiers to retreat.

A hail of well-thrown missiles continued and hastened their progress. The remaining Grenadiers scuttled back the way they came, running, swerving side to side, often flinging themselves to the ground. The well-positioned sharpshooters, set by Johnstone, continued firing at those running away. Duncan saw only one go down as they sprinted and swerved.

Slow fuses and cricket fielding throws from the boundary, Duncan thought wryly. Jennings told him most of the second wave of grenades were rocks, if you were Jerry you wouldn't wait to see whether it was a rock, he'd said.

As Duncan watched that happening, he was uncertain if he wanted the retreating men to escape or not. Jennings saw him watching.

"We haven't actually got that many grenades you know, the chaps doing the throwing are keen cricketers too. I'm afraid we won't win this by playing cricket will we?"

"No, we won't, will we."

Duncan took a long deep breath of great relief at being alive and also at seeing so little damage done to his comrades. He could see no losses from his crouch. He started to rise from that position to check on the men, Jennings grabbed his shoulder firmly.

"Not yet, let Johnstone check for snipers first," he said.

Duncan saw more rocks thrown from behind a bunker, they won't fall for that again will they, he thought, but they did, several bursts of automatic fire signalled movement, followed by death.

Johnstone knew how to defend a position. He was aware that, even when outnumbered and outgunned, a solid defensive position could stand against a force many times as powerful. Provided you had the balls to stand firm that was.

*'Watch and listen, copy and do.'*

Jennings and Duncan waited and watched carefully for about thirty minutes. A short barrage of shellfire breached the silence. No more than half a dozen shells. Duncan could see no casualties near his position. A break of half an hour followed this then another short barrage began.

"They could just be making sure we keep our heads

down," said Jennings.

"Making certain we stay on edge," said Duncan.

The second short barrage ended and shortly after that a runner arrived at their position.

"Message from Major Johnstone for Lieutenant Duncan."

"Yes that's me," said Duncan.

"Major Johnstone wants to see you immediately, sir."

"What for?"

"Don't know, sir, something about you being intelligent I heard, no offence."

"You better just go, old boy," said Jennings with a laugh.

Duncan adopted what he'd heard the men call the Calais crouch. He moved from one point of cover to another, trying to move his legs as fast as he could while keeping his head down and not falling over. He discovered it wasn't easy, doubly so when carrying kit and a pack. It was a wise precaution, though, and he did it successfully. He moved back from the forward lines to a large open-ended concrete bunker. It could have held a bus, although somewhat incongruously it contained a desk, various tables, and chairs.

Johnstone sat at the far end, well protected as was proper, three officers stood next to him, and he seemed deep in thought.

He was a Sandhurst man, Conner knew, about five nine, slim and handsome, with the ubiquitous officer's moustache, in his case a miniature handlebar, unremarkable, sharp features and intense brown eyes. He looked up at Duncan as if assessing his worth then gestured the others to leave.

"Give us five minutes," he said and asked Duncan to take a nearby seat.

"Good afternoon Duncan," he said with the polite air of a man without a care in the world, "you didn't tell me you were an Intel man. Apparently, they've been looking for you for days."

"It didn't seem important, sir."

"No? Well, it's even more important now. This battle's lost, we need to learn from it and win the war. We're doing okay today, as you saw, it's trial, error and hoping for luck. Tomorrow, they can bomb us to hell and just sit and watch. Painful lessons are being learned in Calais, those lessons must be relayed to the chain of command. You've been ordered back to headquarters, and then to return to Blighty. You need to go to the Citadel straight away, take one man with you, just one; report to Brigadier Nicholson and take direction from him."

"Sir."

"Tell him what's worked here so far. I've worked on a fallback plan, it's the best we can do. I'll try to hold this line for as long as possible, once this line is breached the Citadel's wide open to direct attack."

"Sir?" said Duncan, puzzled, trying to take in what he heard and knew it was a lifeline he had to take.

"You need to know. We've been told to fight to the last man. The eyes of the Empire are on us and all that bull. I know if old Churchill were here he'd have a gun and stand beside me, God knows there's few enough in suits who would. There are people who just cannot be allowed to continue command, and you know at least one instance of what I mean. Take this," he said handing him a letter to his family. "A few just might get lucky, I've heard you'll be one. Get back home and by God, you'd better deserve it when you do."

He paused, took a long breath in and out sounding like a sigh then continued softly.

"I can take decisions that risk these men's lives, I can weigh the odds. I can't just stand here, look them in the eye and tell them they're all dead, no man has the right to do that, no matter what the cause. Nonetheless, I think some of us will have to do it, God damn it."

He then turned to Duncan and added, "I'll tell Jennings what's been done, don't look back, and take your chance. I mean that, Duncan. Go on, off you get."

"Yes, sir," he said, still thinking.

112

Duncan had caught the eye of Sergeant Fowler on the way to Johnstone, and he returned to his position.

"Fowler, with me. Take all your kit. We're off to HQ."

Duncan began his walk along a broad thoroughfare to the Citadel, Fowler alongside him. He could see it ahead of him, and the road led directly to its high, imposing looking walls, it was taller, wider and stronger than Fort Nieulay but it still looked Napoleonic.

As they walked across the characteristically flat Calais landscape, eastward on a straight road, they could see railway lines and the outline of the central town station to their right. To their left were the outer wall, the moat and the small towered entrance just wide enough for a medium truck. The Citadel was a basic rectangle with arrowhead ramparts in each corner. The initial design principle was medieval, to provide an open field of fire with bow and arrow onto any men scaling the battlements. Against Panzers, medium artillery, and Stukas, they just represented an obvious target, easy to hit, impossible to miss.

The Citadel was a historical relic, one more anachronism, just like the BEF and French tactics.

*'They came on in the same old way, and we defeated them in the same old way.'*

Where was Wellington when you needed him? Where was Caesar? Where was the miracle? We'll just have to make our own miracle, again.

Unusually, Duncan became angry, gritted teeth and clenched fist angry. The required knowledge, information, intelligence and willpower existed, but no factor was being applied correctly, or powerfully, or ruthlessly enough. History dictated that you fought a war like you meant it, without mercy, without pity, winning above all else.

Rising smoke and sounds far ahead of them, due east then nearer, behind the station to the south-east, spoke of continuing battle there too.

Fowler seemed lost in his own private thoughts as they walked. He looked about Thirty-five, medium height and everyday looks. He had sandy grey hair and freckles that linger with age. A bachelor who had joined up long before the war, he'd told Duncan. He knew about the army, but knew nothing about war, other than he'd learned in the last two days. He acted reliably for Duncan, his guilt about Teddy was genuine, and that might be useful later. Yes, he could use that. Fowler held only his regulation Lee Enfield rifle, Duncan had seen him use it well and organise proper positions for the Brens at the canal.

As they approached the Citadel entrance, they heard the beginning of another attack on the canal bridge.

"Don't look back, Fowler," said Duncan, "it won't do any good, they'll hold that position for a while yet, they know what they're doing. Now if I can just figure out what I'm doing, we can start to plan how I'm going to do it."

The Citadel fort looked in proper order, the stonework was, so far, unscathed by battle, the moat was extensive and full of deep water.

The walls showed ample evidence of guards, sandbag layers, and heavy machine guns, there was no artillery he could see. Duncan doubted tanks alone could take the fort, he hoped there were some real air raid shelters inside and some anti-aircraft kit.

Duncan spoke to the gate guards, they were a mixture of French and British troops. The guards waved him inside, and he met the Captain in charge of the British contingent, Jamieson, a gruff Scotsman with a thick, yet understandable accent.

"No, Nicholson's not here yet," he said, "his headquarters were in the middle of the newer part of town to the south. That's wide open to Jerry attack so he was going to move here anyway. Right now he's at the railway station on the waterfront." He shrugged his shoulders and continued. "He tried to break out of Calais with some tanks and establish a road link to Dunkirk. Our few tanks can't match Jerry's, so he was beaten back. Before he could retire to his Headquarters Jerry was there waiting for him, so he set up a new HQ. I know it was bold action, but he should have picked a secure permanent position, and bloody well stayed there. People are being ordered to go to HQ, and they don't know where the devil it is. I swear if anyone writes the history of this it'll be a work of bloody fiction."

"I've been ordered to HQ to see Nicholson."

"That's all very well my friend, but by the time you get there it'll be gone, I have a feeling it'll be easier if you just wait here."

"This is a damn stupid question, sir, where are we?" asked Duncan.

"You're in a 16th Century French built strong point, it's called the Citadelle, and it sits behind a moat which separates it from the old town of Calais which has its own walls. It's confusing because we Brits sometimes call the old town itself the Citadel. It's causing the same confusion in Boulogne apparently. We started buggering off from Boulogne before we told the French, bad form, very bad form indeed. I only know this because I speak a bit of French, and I've talked to the locals who've been listening to the radio. The French Commandant Le Tellier is here too, with some keen men, we're just not armed well enough. We need one HQ not two and better communications, and it's too ruddy late now."

"What about the Navy?"

"The Navy's doing its best, and we've asked for some fire to support us. Where the blazes do we tell them to aim that helps and isn't going to hit us as well? Christ what a mess. When did you last eat a decent meal?"

"I can't honestly remember."

"Look, there's a British mess tent here, let's get some food inside you as we talk and decide what to do." He looked at Fowler, who was aghast at seeing such honest talk from an officer.

"Relax, Sergeant, I've had three different sets of orders since midday, I can only follow one of them, and that's to stand here. Being on a charge for insubordination is the least of my worries. Meanwhile, I'm ordering you to eat

115

before things get too hot."

They sat at a trestle table with men eating in shifts. The meal was fried bully beef and mashed potato, the cooks were men without guns or combat training. There were useless mouths aplenty in Calais.

In a ridiculous twist of fate, the boiled sweets and liquorice had been unloaded before the vehicles and ammunition, so several large boxes lay open near the cooking area.

"We'll run out of bullets before we run out of sweets!" said the dry Jamieson. Duncan could have wept. He still took a packet of each variety on offer.

"Fowler, you stay here and rest up, Captain Jamieson can show me round," Duncan said when they'd finished.

"Yes, I should do that shouldn't I," said Jamieson.

Duncan walked with Jamieson to the ramparts.

"I'm sorry if I'm not coming across well, it's just such a complete mess. We've gone to great lengths to actively send real fighting men into this trap, it was never going to work, anyone could see that, now here I am, in charge of a bloody kitchen."

"Have you any idea why Nicholson wants me?"

"Oh yes; you're the intelligence man aren't you, you're wanted back in Blighty seemingly, don't know what you've done, but you're essential to the war effort."

"What?"

"Don't argue for God's sake, you've got a winning ticket in the raffle, use it."

"But there's no evacuation?"

"There are still small boats coming in, taking away the wounded, and useless mouths, your friend Feckle has decided he's in charge of it, characteristically heroic of him I thought. Look, if someone somewhere thinks you're some kind of intelligence genius then go and be that man, Christ knows we need one. Now I need a drink," he said, making his way back to what passed for his quarters, apparently intending to remain topped up with his own private courage, Duncan now realised.

## Chapter 10

### 24th May 1940 - Afternoon and Evening - Calais

Teddy and Spud walked north into Calais old town for a mile or so. They kept the docks and warehouse buildings to their right and the houses to their left. Teddy reasoned Calais must be like Dover or other seaside towns and have seafront cafes or restaurants that might just have some food left. A restaurant couldn't run out of food in two days surely? They passed a few likely spots which were all obviously shut and deserted. He considered breaking and entering, but thought the owners would probably be hiding in cellars, and he might get a shotgun blast for his trouble. They saw few enough civilians anyway, and they stayed well away from the two Tommies. He guessed that no soldier, regardless of uniform, would be popular in Calais.

Eventually, they reached a broad street opposite a quayside on their right, intended for smaller vessels. It looked and smelt like a fish quay and men were loading stretchers gingerly onto small craft. The craft had naval markings and looked like converted civilian vessels. It was no general evacuation and the time wasn't ripe for that part of any plan, so he resumed his search for something to eat.

"Hang on," said Spud, "this way," and led them down a small side street. Only then did Teddy smell the unmistakable aroma of fresh bread baking. Then he spotted two men placing planks and boards against the windows of a small shop and nailing them into place.

"Bonjour," said Teddy and began to introduce himself and Spud in acceptable French, the accent poor, but he was very polite. He explained his friend was a baker in England, and it would be a privilege to sample his methods, and wares, they would pay, of course.

The two French looked like father and son aged about fifty and fifteen. They eyed Teddy and Spud warily then invited them in nonetheless. The son who spoke English showed Spud what they were baking and how. Spud looked genuinely interested and was asking questions. Clearly, there was a difference between mass production and a small work of art.

Teddy had a more serious talk with the father, who offered sticks of bread, butter, cheese and wrinkled apples to Teddy and Spud. He wouldn't accept money, English money was no use to him, but he gladly took a packet of smokes and chocolate. The family was sleeping in the cellar, Teddy advised him to stay there tomorrow as well. He told him the allies were putting up a fight and wouldn't surrender yet. That meant the Germans would bomb and shell the old town, rather than lose too many men on a frontal attack.

He asked about somewhere to sleep, hoping for an invitation into the cellar, but the Baker said he'd show them to a shed with straw. Teddy saw the photograph of his wife, son and two daughters on the wall, he wouldn't have let two strangers into his cellar either. Nor would the baker want two Englishmen in his house when the Germans arrived.

Teddy asked about British Headquarters and air raid shelters, he knew nothing of that, head for the Citadelle, was his only advice.

The father wrapped the food in a cloth and put it in a basket for them, he opened his back door leading to a yard and pointed at a solid brick shed. Just before they left, he gave them a large stonework bottle with a well-used cork stopper. He said *'merci'* and *'bon chance'* then when he shut the door behind them, Teddy heard it being locked, barred and what sounded like a table being pushed against it.

Teddy and Spud just shrugged their shoulders, they were better off than half an hour ago.

They went to the shed, the door was open, and it smelt strongly of damp animal. The hayloft was drier, and some sacks and tarpaulins made rough blankets. It wasn't easy cutting the bread with a bayonet so Teddy used the

German jack-knife which proved much better.

The blade folded out neatly from a beautifully carved wooden handle, shaped to fit a fist, now he looked at it more closely he saw it was identical wood to the Mauser. Its stainless steel blade was shaving razor sharp on one edge and with a matching fine tip, it could kill a man with a thrust or a slash. The words *'Meine Ehre heist Treue'* in Gothic script were expertly carved into it. Teddy knew this was the motto of the SS and meant *'My honour is called loyalty'*. Dolf hadn't been wearing SS uniform when Teddy had seen him, so that was a puzzle to file away for later. The knife was another thing of great beauty albeit lethal, and that thought troubled Teddy somehow. Today, he used it to cut and butter his bread, carefully.

The fresh crusty French bread combined with strong cheese and apple was as welcome a meal as Teddy had ever eaten. Spud was amazed at how the French made bread taste so different with virtually the same ingredients. They filled a mess tin with red wine and drank it down like two condemned men enjoying the last supper. It was strong, rough vinegar and went straight to their heads as they needed and wanted.

"Gall from Gaul," said Teddy, but it was lost on Spud.

Half an hour later, Teddy ate another apple, finished off the last of the wine, said goodnight to Spud, who was already fast asleep, closed his eyes and sank into a welcome oblivion.

You shouldn't drink wine as quickly as beer. Teddy and Spud didn't know that, they'd never drank wine before.

*

### 25th May 1940 - Morning

Teddy woke up with a start, no dreams, no noise, no reason to wake except perhaps the small chinks of sunlight falling on his face from the roof above him. He looked at his watch, it was seven o'clock, nearly full daylight outside, but no sounds of battle came. Yesterday was a bad day, neither side was remotely eager to start another.

He woke Spud up.

"Christ, have I out slept you?" he said.

"Yes mate, you all right?"

"Never felt better, what are we doing today then?"

"Today, we are finding the right officers and sticking with them. After yesterday, Jerry won't be in a hurry to charge at us again, he'll call in the bombers and artillery now we're nicely bunched up for him. Like those lads behind the half-tracks on the railway lines, he can't miss. We're going to need a proper solid air raid shelter today."

They left the loft and had a piss in separate corners.

"I don't think we're the first to have a piss in here," sniffed Spud.

"Thank God for that. I thought it was you?" said Teddy.

"Cheeky bastard!"

They left the hiding place quietly, not intending to disturb their hosts from the previous day. When they saw a standpipe in the yard they used it to drink, clean and wake up. They filled their water bottles, and Teddy looked up at the cloudless blue sky.

"It'll be a hot one today," he said.

"Is that good or bad?" said Spud.

"Both."

Teddy and Spud left the narrow side street and went into the wider road leading east to west along the quayside.

"Hold up, here we go," said Teddy, seeing a group of officers walking from east to west towards them.

"Bloody hell that's Nicholson, we'd better leg it," said Spud.

"No, that's exactly who we want. Smarten yourself up, we're following him."

"Smarten meself up, you are joking aren't you, we look like shit."

"Not at all, we look heroic, come on."

The group of a dozen men, mostly officers, paid them no heed as they approached, nor when they joined them. It wasn't much of a stretch to include themselves in the purposeful striding group of men vainly trying to look like they knew what they were doing. Teddy could do that all day and Spud was a quick learner.

Teddy recognised a couple of Royal Marines green berets and uniforms behind the group. One of them was admiring the Mauser he carried ready in his hands.

"That's a lovely piece, where did you get that then?"

"Just got it yesterday, a Jerry gave it to me."

"Can you use it, though?" the Marine asked.

"There's about a dozen Jerrys who know he can," said Spud annoyed at the tone of the question.

"Sorry, I'm only asking, mate, no offence meant, I know you've had it rough. We only got here late last night from Chatham."

"What are they sending more men here for?"

"We're supposed to be protecting some Navy demolition teams, it seems like Jerry might do the demolition for us anyway. At present, we are guarding officers."

"Well they do need it," said Spud.

"Yes, they do, heh heh," laughed the second Marine.

"Is that any use then?" said Spud pointing to the Thompson sub-machine guns they carried.

"It'll be good at close quarters with short bursts, better than the Sten. Mind you, if the fighting gets that close we'll be in serious bother," the second Marine replied.

"Ain't that the truth, mate."

"What are you two here for?" asked the first Marine.

"We are stragglers who've lost our units, hoping to be usefully redeployed, and fed," said Teddy.

"Lost?"

"Yeah, lost forever I'm afraid."

"Sorry about that, mate."

The group walked onwards to the massive fort which lay ahead. They turned left at its first arrow headed corner and found a small entrance facing east crossing the moat by a small bridge, only wide enough for one small truck. Air raid shelters, thought Teddy.

As soon as they entered the Citadelle, the officers

rushed off to a bunker. Another officer told the Marines to find something to eat while they set up the HQ. That was the first decent order Teddy and Spud had heard for a couple of days so they decided to follow it. The two other Privates in the group were unarmed, laden with other gear, followed the officers, typists probably.

They found the mess tent from the aroma of fried corned beef and now fried potatoes. They found a queue, joined it, collected their food, found a table with a bench and ate their full.

"I bloody hate bully beef," said Spud, wolfing it down.

Then a tin mug of strong hot tea each, with as much sugar as they wanted, four in Spud's case.

"They're not rationing anything," said Teddy, "that's alright for today, it means tomorrow's going to be bad if they're not worried about it."

"What? Oh right," said Spud, getting the point.

A tired medical orderly joined them at their table, he looked no more than a boy. "Where did you Marines come from then?"

"Royal Marines," they said simultaneously correcting him before they explained what they were doing, apart from being precious about their exact title that was.

The orderly proved a well-informed source of information.

"Things have been quiet since last night," he said, "no new casualties here since then, the lines along the canals are holding well, the officers reckon Jerry will ask us to surrender today."

"And if we don't, they'll bomb us to buggery now we're all pinned down in a small area," said Teddy.

"That's what they said too."

"The trouble is, there's loads of civilians still around. They'll be mainly hiding in cellars, and if we choose to fight on, loads of them'll die, the eyes of the Empire need to be on that."

"You think we should just pack it in then?" said the second Marine.

"No, well not yet anyway, Christ I don't know, you have to balance what you might gain against what you might lose. You have to think carefully before you start a fight you can't win," said Teddy.

"That's what the officers were saying, and they didn't know the answer either," said the orderly.

"What else is happening, sorry what's your name?" said Teddy.

"Christopher, well, there's definitely no evacuation other than the wounded in small vessels, some idiot Major's in charge of that, no use for anything else. The Brigadier thinks he's alright."

"His name's Feckle?" Archie asked.

"Yes mate, d'you know him?"

"Yeah, he's my idiot, we tried to lose him in a village, but the Frenchies said they had one already."

"Ain't that the truth," said Spud.

*

Duncan waited patiently while the officers briefed the Brigadier. Nicholson asked the right questions and said the right words. His team were competent and had adapted well to the always changing position. The lines along the waterways were holding determinedly, many brave men from the Rifle Brigade were fighting house by house to the east. The French were holding the railway line, the station to the south, the beach area and some were still in Fort Risban, and they were thinly spread. The enemy was losing more men than us, he was paying in blood for Calais.

Jerry would use bombers today, without question, we'd have to ride that storm. At least he wouldn't attack on the ground while he was raiding by air. He was using snipers from high positions to the south overlooking the old town. Nicholson had issued orders that no allied man be captured with a sniper rifle. The Germans were particularly upset by what they called the murder of one of their Majors the previous day, by a British sniper.

Nicholson knew they couldn't win and had genuine concerns about the inevitable civilian casualties.

Duncan knew he was just trying to work out when he could surrender with as much honour as possible without killing too many of his men and civilians. He was welcome to that decision. If you couldn't win, then you should choose how to lose as well as possible.

At the end of the briefing, Jamieson, who was sober and serious, asked, "the reply to General Schaal, sir?"

"No, I shall not surrender. Tell the Germans if they want Calais they'll have to bally well fight for it. Issue orders, every position must be held."

The officers smiled and made positive noises, but inwardly they knew what was to come, and it was nothing to smile about.

By midday, the Germans subjected the old town to a vicious, deadly indiscriminate artillery bombardment. They were under attack and had no possible defence other than hiding and waiting for it to stop or a direct hit to blow them apart. When it did stop briefly, the siren wail of Stuka dive-bombers ended the short silence. Devilishly accurate, they pounded the canal defences and the Citadelle with clusters of five bombs, unerringly hitting their mark.

Duncan spent the afternoon in the command bunker, Teddy spent the afternoon in a general air raid shelter which housed the hospital. Christopher told him and Spud that this was the best place under fire; the two Marines had sought out the well-sheltered command post to see if any officers needed guarding.

*

By four o'clock the shellfire and air raids had stopped long enough that people felt confident to leave their cover. Teddy and Spud went to walk around the ramparts to see what they could.

"Jeez, look at all those high points," said Spud pointing out the number of towers and tall buildings in the outer part of the town that overlooked the inner part of the old town.

"We're sitting ducks for their snipers in the old town, we're okay here, though."

"That's why we're staying here, for the time being, there's no fights we can win out there," said Teddy.

*

Duncan took advantage of a lull in the bombardment to approach the Brigadier.

"Sir, I'm Duncan, you wanted me?"

"Oh yes, well you took your blessed time."

"Not a good time to travel, sir, and I didn't quite know where I was going."

"Well that's true enough, and you're here now."

"My orders are, you're to return, you're needed, something to do with a report you wrote on all this. Churchill read it and wants you back in England. This sealed envelope has your orders and is for your eyes only. Every able bodied man in Calais is to fight to the death, except you! You're to go with the wounded, your Major Feckle is in charge of that at the Fish Quay. Move there immediately, who knows when it'll be too dangerous for the small ships to keep coming? After dusk is the best time to leave, report to Feckle straight away, there's nothing more you can do here."

"I can't go yet, sir? I haven't finished here, I'm waiting for someone."

"Look, Duncan, I don't care who you are or what or who you know, I've been given an order, I've given you an order, follow it, I don't have time for anything else."

"Yes, sir."

Duncan left the command bunker, he didn't want to leave, but he had no choice now, he'd pushed the boundaries with Nicholson, and had to leave the Citadelle. He went back to Jamieson's quarters, to collect his kit such as it was.

Jamieson was there and still sober, he saw Duncan gather his kit.

"You're off now then?" he asked.

"Yes, I've been ordered to go," Duncan said.

"And you're not happy about it?"

"No, I'm not ready to pack it in yet."

"Move slowly then."

"What?"

"There'll be small boats leaving for another 24 hours or so, they'll take the wounded away till then, don't leave it any longer than that, mind. Head down to the Fish Quay and help with the wounded if you want to do something useful while you're deciding what to do."

"That's as good a plan as I can think of," said Duncan as he rose to leave.

"Take your Sergeant with you if you like, no one knows he's here anyway, give him his chance too. Nicholson's refused another offer to surrender you know."

Duncan nodded and left, in silence.

He collected Fowler on his way out of the Citadelle and headed to the Fish Quay, it wasn't difficult to find by sight or smell.

As they reached the Quay they could hear the sounds of renewed attack, east, west, and south, only the seaward side was calm. He could see a huge degree of bomb damage to his right, civilian houses, dock buildings and probably some defensive positions as well, the war was getting very dirty, very early.

To his left, warehouses and dock buildings had also suffered considerable damage.

Ahead was a small nearly fully enclosed dock area, empty of all vessels and with no sign of life. Thinking he could be in the wrong area, he turned left and headed across a small bridge to another fort to his north, Fort Risban said the signpost.

Duncan headed there with Fowler, reasoning the Fort must have air raid shelters too. It was a convenient staging post for the wounded to wait for vessels taking them to safety. It was a smaller version of Nieulay, there might be some big guns facing the sea, he could see nothing facing the landward side.

There were no British guards, just one unarmed Pioneer Corps Private, who didn't challenge them, only saying.

"The Major's inside if you want him."

Two French Reservists guarded the main door, and he could see more positioned on the ramparts but only with small arms.

Duncan took a deep breath and went inside, he could see a large collection of useless mouths and wounded, mostly British and some French as well. Duncan noticed hardly any weapons in sight, Jerry was going to capture a lot of mechanics and drivers. That wasn't their fault, but it was a shambles and he'd already resolved to wash his hands of it without hesitation when the chance came. He'd take some guilt with him, though.

He sought out Major Feckle and found him in a small office room in the deepest part of the bunker, where he sat, with a cup of tea, in a cup and saucer. Not the best china, Duncan thought, but a cup and saucer for goodness sake.

"Ah, there you are," said Feckle, "I heard you were about, there should be a few small pickups tonight if you're ready to leave."

"I don't think we're done here yet, sir."

"That's the spirit, come and see me when you're ready."

"Yes, sir."

Duncan was glad to leave Feckle, he remained a depressing, frustrating, enraging sight. He hadn't asked how Duncan and his men had fared nor told him how he'd survived while so many of his men had died. Duncan hadn't asked any questions or given those answers, he knew if he talked about it, he'd lose his temper so he kept his own counsel.

Duncan had deliberately not asked anyone about Feckle's account of his journey to Calais, he was certain enough of its nature, a tissue of self-serving lies. The specifics weren't important. Feckle didn't know that and had simply put on a brazen face. He was the kind of liar who believed his own lies.

Feckle might still be of some use to him, he was definitely up to something. Duncan could use that.

*

Teddy and Spud looked out from the Citadelle ramparts, studying what they could of the battle around them. They saw columns of smoke rising in the east, looking like they were from the far side of the main harbour. The firing to the south and west still sounded like the lines across the canal were holding.

They went to the extreme south-east tip of the arrowhead ramparts. That gave them an unimpeded view eastwards along the line of a canal where three well-defended bridges crossed north to south. The furthest bridge was the one they'd crossed to the old town the previous day. They'd come nearly full circle round the old town then. They could see the railway lines running parallel to the canal going into the railway station, next to the nearest bridge.

"I think I'll have a go from here," Teddy said.

"Watch your back?" said Spud.

"Yes please, mate."

Teddy settled into as high a position as possible, secure behind sandbags and began scanning for targets.

Spud took a pair of binoculars from his pack.

"Where did you get them?"

"At breakfast, they were just lying around so I thought they must be mine."

"I'll have to watch you."

They looked carefully and closely.

"The Frenchies are holding the station and the railway line," said Spud. "We're holding three bridges, the one we came across yesterday and another two nearer us. Any target between the furthest two bridges and on the far side of the water is fair game. I think we're still south of the nearest bridge."

Teddy scanned that particular area closely, selected an open doorway and aimed. He aimed, breathed deeply and held it, no luck, nothing appeared so he breathed out. Again, he aimed at the doorway and held his breath. The fourth time, he was lucky, he saw the slightest movement in the doorway and fired just as a German came into view.

"Gotcha!"

"Find me some doorways a Jerry might be in. If I'm patient, one'll pop his head out, and I can do some damage."

Spud was a dab hand at this game, he knew where he'd be if he were a Jerry and where he'd be trying to go. He picked out several likely spots and with patience and good fortune they took six Germans down over a two-hour period.

At one stage, German sappers tried to cross the canal in a dinghy, Teddy took one man in his stomach and the raft with one shot. Spud had a chuckle at the heavily laden men trying to swim clear as the boat sank. Teddy didn't laugh, he took advantage of their slow progress to pick them off, adding another four to his total.

The light was fading when Teddy felt the need to stop and rest his eyes and hands. They just wouldn't work as fast or for as long as his mind wanted.

Something had changed since that night in the O. P. The day before that, he'd been happy to kill one Jerry then when he'd killed two he was content. The height of his ambition had always been to take two down and still be alive himself, he would have done more than his bit for the BEF. If every Tommy did that, then we'd win.

Now, he'd done a lot more than his share, more than he'd ever dreamed of, and it wasn't enough. His mind was pushing him further than his body could take him, though, he had to rest.

"Jerry should pull back for the night if he's got any sense," he said.

Neither would ever know the initiative and skill of two ordinary Privates had held up the German advance by many crucial minutes, meaning it wouldn't succeed that night.

"Anything that slows him down, anything at all," said Teddy.

Spud and Teddy moved well back from the sandbag ramparts before they stood up and stretched properly.

They turned round to see a Captain watching them.

"Sir," they said.

I've been watching you. You were doing so well I didn't want to interrupt," said Captain Jamieson, "you should take a break. They're pulling back a bit now, that means the Stukas will pay us another visit before bedtime."

"Yes, sir," they said.

"Before you go," he said to Teddy, "when things get tight, lose the Mauser. Jerry's looking for a sniper who plugged one of their Majors, it's bad form apparently. He won't be extending any hospitality to you pair if he sees that."

"Thanks for the advice, sir," said Teddy.

"And you can keep the binoculars," the Captain said, before walking away.

## Chapter 11

### 26th May 1940 - Morning - 0500 - Calais

*"Der Feind kämpft mit einer bis dahin nie da gewesenen Eigensinn. Sie werden Englisch, sehr mutig und zäh."*

General Ferdinand Friedrich Schaal, the Commander of the 10th Panzer Division, read aloud the words he'd dictated the previous night for the war diary. It was 0500 on the 26th of May 1940.

After much thought and without hesitation he said: *"Lassen Sie es beginnen."*

*"The Enemy fights with a hitherto unheard of obstinacy. They are English, extremely brave and tenacious."*

*"Let it begin."*

\*

Teddy and Spud woke to the sound of artillery shells exploding above their heads. Safe in the shelter of the small ammunition bunker they'd secured overnight, a light sprinkling of dust fell on them. The shelling had stopped overnight, incoming casualties hadn't; the hospital filled up gradually. The medics were helping some, making others comfortable when they couldn't help them. Medical supplies and expertise were running low.

Ammunition was low too, hence, the empty space in the bunker that Teddy, Spud, and others had taken advantage of. They'd slept well, it was surprising how quickly sheer cursed tiredness overcame the ever present fear of harm.

They were fully awake now and knew they wouldn't sleep again today, but there was no point in leaving the shelter yet. The fresh artillery bombardment would continue, and there'd be no ground attack while it lasted.

\*

Duncan watched the artillery barrage begin from the ramparts of Fort Risban. He'd spent the night helping evacuate the wounded from the Fish Quay. The last small vessel had left about 0300, well before first light made the harbour entrance too dangerous for flight.

Surprisingly, Feckle attended the scene of the casualty evacuation, he only spoke to the vessel commanders and gave no real help. He *was* up to something, his sort never did anything without a reason, and the reason was invariably selfish.

*'Watch and listen.'*

Many brave Frenchmen had helped overnight when they should have been trying to catch some sleep. Not only were the French poorly armed, ammunition was getting critically low. Their Commandant at the fort was a frail old man with the heart of a lion, Carlos De Lambertye. Duncan heard he'd asked his men to prepare to fight to the death, and they were willing to do so alongside him, like a French Churchill perhaps. Was there only honour in death or glorious failure? Duncan hoped not.

The shellfire was unerringly finding targets on the eastern side of the old town, and the firing was from closer range than yesterday. The whole eastern docks would likely fall today ending any chance of evacuation from there.

He could see and hear the same thing happening to the south and western canal sections, the Citadelle made an easy target too. They'd bombed and shelled Fort Risban heavily the previous day, they'd be next today, he thought and sought cover down below again.

*

At 0700, just when Teddy was thinking of scouting around outside, the bombing started.

"Stone me! Jerry likes to stick to a timetable, 0500 exactly, shelling starts, 0700 exactly, the bombing starts," he said looking at his watch. "No wonder Hitler got the trains to run on time."

"Probably shot any bugger who was late, though," said Spud.

"Oh, I can't see Ernie Bevin standing for that."

"Who'd win then? A fight between Bevin and Hitler?"

"A draw I'd say, they'd shout each other to death."

"Churchill and Hitler then?"

"Oh, Churchill without a doubt, I bet he's got a blade in that walking stick and a couple of grenades in his hat. He'd start before the bell went, mind you, or on the way to the ring, or even in the dressing room while Hitler was still putting his gloves on. That's the best way to win a fight, start one when the other bloke ain't ready. That's how we'll win this, not by waiting to see what Jerry does next, let him worry about what we'll do next. We need to act not react."

"That's deep, you'll go far you will."

"I know, it's how far that worries me."

"That's even deeper, I'll still watch your back, mate."

*

When the shelling stopped, Duncan left his shelter only to hear and see the bombers arriving overhead, there were dozens, fifty perhaps, he'd never seen anything like it. He could only guess at the danger from that many bombers, at low level and facing no effective flak capability, there was no way to miss. He returned to the fort to ensure everyone was well under cover, they would target Risban again.

*

At 0900 it had been quiet for half an hour, Teddy shook Spud and said, "Right we're off up now, we need to see what's happening."

"Got a plan?" said Spud.

"Working on one."

The Citadelle was a wreck, the bombing had destroyed any surface buildings and tents. The walls still stood, but were severely damaged on the inside, there were shell holes everywhere."

"No breakfast then," said Spud.

They climbed on to the ramparts using a wide ramp that led up to the north-east corner of the Fort.

"Oh Jesus Christ," said Spud when he looked at the damage done to the houses of the old town, some areas were just piles of rubble. "Would you look at that. We should pack this in right now, Teddy, right now."

"Nicholson'll wait a bit yet, besides how's he supposed

to tell anyone anything in this mess. Come on, there's something useful we *can* do," said Teddy as he led Spud, down a collapsed section of the outer wall and towards the Fish Quay.

*

Duncan left his shelter at 0900, feeling the ground attack would start at exactly that time if Jerry was sticking to a timetable. It came a little late, but he felt they'd planned even the 0915 start to the last second just to make them sweat a bit more. He heard the distant sound of small arms fire and knew that was the beginning.

All he could do now was wait; unsure what for or how long.

Something big was coming, he knew it.

He had the strangest feeling of impending fate or, more accurately, foreordination.

All his life had been for this moment.

*

Teddy and Spud progressed cautiously to the Fish Quay, making quick movements from cover to more cover and they heard the sounds of the ground attack starting as they moved.

"Shouldn't we be helping out somewhere?" said Spud.

"I don't think we can make a difference anywhere except where we're going."

"Where's that?"

"The Bakers."

"Okay, right."

They kept the shattered old town on their right and the quayside on their left as they walked, retracing the way to the Bakers. The damage was so widespread they had difficulty finding which narrow street they were looking for, never mind which building. It took until ten thirty before Teddy found a wrecked doorway and the remnants of a solid table nearby.

"Here we go," he said to Spud, "I think I can remember where the cellar entrance should be."

Teddy and Spud didn't talk as they pulled at the debris,

134

stopping only sporadically for a breather. They heard sounds of battle on three of their four sides, it wasn't close enough to worry about. They worked as fast as they could. There were large pieces of debris that took two to move using shattered beams as levers, and it was slow work.

At nearly two in the afternoon, they finally unearthed the cellar entrance. They could make out a wooden door frame and a pile of rubble filling the top of a stairwell. They pulled at the loose brick, smaller pieces of stonework and plaster that blocked the entrance. They heard sounds of scrambling from below and the bricks began to move downwards into the cellar.

A young girl came up first, dusty and gasping for fresh air, her sister followed, then her mother, brother and the baker last. They all spent a full five minutes just breathing, coughing and taking some water from the offered bottles. They were all in shock, their bodies alive, but their oxygen starved minds, not in control of them.

Teddy and Spud exchanged glances, listened for the noise of battle and started gathering their kit.

When he finally did talk, the baker was still only half conscious, he came towards Teddy and Spud and shook their hands. He only said, "Dix minutes de plus, il n'y avait pas d'air, dix minutes de plus."

"We have to go now," said Teddy, "stay here and keep your heads down, I can hear Panzers."

They began running north at the same time. There was no talk, no decisions to make, no plan. Jerry was east, west and south, they needed to go north.

A small bridge to their north crossed the line of the Fish Quay and another small harbour. They ran like hell towards the Fort they could see, the sign read Fort Risban.

*

Duncan stayed patiently on the ramparts of Fort Risban, waiting and watching. Rumours abounded of surrender, defeat, and evacuation. He could hear and see signs of furious defence all around, Jerry was attacking along the shoreline to the west. A stern defence was underway from trench positions, manned by French reservists and civilian volunteers. He was painfully conscious that he now stood mainly with the useless mouths and wounded. He knew he'd played a part in the fighting, but felt he should have done more; did you have to die before you felt you'd done enough, he wondered. He knew he was doing what he had to do, he had to survive, it still tasted like cowardice.

Sergeant Fowler joined him on the ramparts.

"Here come another couple of stragglers," he said pointing to two Tommies careering across the bridge to the fort. One was running elegantly and effortlessly, but not outpacing the man next to him, he was slowing down so his mate could keep up with him. He knew that man!

*

Teddy and Spud reached the Fort entrance, despite the mayhem, only one nervous unarmed Pioneer Corps Private was guarding the door.

They bent double and panted with exhaustion, the work on the rubble had taxed them as well as the run.

"You aven't got a brew on 'ave you?" said Spud.

"Not sure, shall I check, sir?" said the guard.

"Yes please and see if you've got a bacon sarnie an' all," said Spud as the lad ran inside, "I'd kill for a cuppa."

"If he comes back with a bacon sarnie, I'll propose," said Teddy.

They were still bent double and breathing heavily when they heard a calm, dignified voice.

"Where on earth have you been, Private Austin, you should have been here ages ago," said a smiling Duncan with the tone of a schoolmaster admonishing a pupil five minutes late for a lesson.

"Why what happened?" came the cheeky answer from Teddy. "I have been rather busy, sir; things didn't quite go to plan. Have you met my friend Private Murphy, of the First Searchlight Regiment, he's looking for a searchlight, you haven't seen one have you?"

Spud saluted tentatively.

"Don't bother with that bull," Duncan said, "get in here before a sniper sees you."

They went deep inside the fort, there was tea, there was always a bucket of tea ready.

"There're no bacon sandwiches I'm afraid," Duncan said to Spud. Spud and Fowler drew apart from Teddy and Duncan and sat separately.

"I hope you've got a plan," said Teddy.

"I'm working on one."

"That's good, cos right now I haven't got a clue," said Teddy.

When Duncan didn't say anything, Teddy asked, "and what is this plan then?"

"It involves going north."

"When?"

"Not yet?"

"That's good."

"Why?"

"Cos I can't swim, and I might have time to learn."

They laughed.

"Feckle's here."

Teddy stopped laughing.

"Can I shoot him now?"

"No, he's part of the plan."

"Okay, we can talk later. Is there anything we need to do now?"

"Yes, we need to get up to the ramparts."

"What are we waiting for then?"

Spud and Fowler followed them to the ramparts, Spud instantly went to work with his binoculars.

"The line along the beach is holding well but no targets there yet," he said.

"What about the Fish Quay, behind it and to the left?" said Teddy.

"Left by the big warehouses looks okay first, then to the right, then behind the quay. Have you seen that blooming great lighthouse thing? They'll have someone there as soon as they can. I'll keep an eye on it."

"I need more sandbags and a plank."

Fowler and Duncan did the fetch and carry job and soon had a passable protected position with a couple of narrow, deep slits to fire through. Waiting for a target took roughly half an hour and when it came it was a big one, an Armoured Personnel Carrier with a tightly packed group of Grenadiers behind it. Teddy finished his mantra and brought down two men before the half-track reversed and while it was doing that he took another.

That went on for nearly an hour. Although Teddy had some success, with each shot the Germans advanced, building by building, yard by yard. They were aware of house-to-house fighting on the other side of the quay and the sounds of Panzers coming nearer then just blasting houses apart. I hope they have the sense to fight and move, Teddy thought, not like Jezz.

"Bugger me," said Fowler, who'd been taking pot-shots as the enemy drew closer. They looked where he was pointing, the Citadelle was aflame, fire and smoke spiralling up from its centre.

"Jack it in, for God's sake," he said, "you can't do any more."

At three thirty, Teddy only had two bullets left, Fowler had none.

Half an hour later, they saw a Swastika Flag unfurling above the Citadelle. At the same time, they saw troops gathering on the far side of the quay, preparing an attack on their fort.

The troops gathered and waited, but didn't move forward and stayed under sensible cover.

"What are they waiting for?" said Fowler.

"Down," Spud shouted, "everybody right down and crawl back sharpish, that lighthouse window just smashed, they've got a sniper in there now."

They went back into the body of the fort, Duncan asked them to wait while he spoke with Feckle.

Feckle came out of his office as they approached.

"Gentlemen, Brigadier Nicholson has officially

surrendered, the signal 'Every man for himself' has been issued. The men are leaving now by the front entrance, for an organised surrender. I shall be hanging on until the last moment, of course," he said, stone-faced.

Every man for himself, when was it ever anything else? Teddy thought. What *is* he up to?

"And we shall stay with you, of course, sir," said Duncan.

Teddy waited, knowing Jerry would be kept busy with prisoners all around Calais as well as still fighting those who didn't know it was over. Feckle should be there with the men arranging the surrender, even he could do that, those men would be safer with him there, this time. He'd be safe, what was he up to?

The muffled sounds of battle were still around them, we'd surrendered alright, but who knew? Someone was getting killed for nothing?

Fowler spoke, breaking the silence.

"Well son, last time I saw you, you had no gun, now you've got two and one is the best I've ever seen, you've done well. How the hell did you get out of that observation post alive?" he asked Teddy, who only now registered who Fowler was.

"I was lucky, a sniper took out Mike, and he fell on me just as the shells took out the other two, never had a chance any of them. I played dead until the tanks went past then legged it as fast as I could, nothing to it."

"Well, I'm glad to see you, son, although I think there's more to it than that, or you wouldn't have made it this far, and that rifle's got a tale to tell, I'll bet."

"Some tales are better left untold," said Teddy.

"And I won't ask then, son."

Duncan gave Teddy a knowing look.

Teddy just gave the slightest shrug.

After half an hour, Feckle left his office, it was about six, the sounds of fighting had died down a bit. Immediately outside to the west, the French were seemingly still fighting on sporadically. Teddy held on to his pack,

139

checked his weapons, found a helmet and adjusted it to fit. He watched Duncan remaining calm, so he did too. Spud and Fowler were fidgeting like a couple of ten-year-olds waiting outside the headmaster's office.

"I think we'll use the back door for this, chaps," said Feckle expressionless.

He led them down a short, red-brick arched tunnel, it was dim, and it took their eyes a time to adjust to the darkness. It was a confusing route, changing directions several times then they reached a door. Teddy instinctively felt it would open out eastward on to the harbour entrance. Feckle paused, and Teddy knew why.

Teddy eased past him and eyed the large heavy wooden door and the light that found its way around the edge. He was ready to risk the door when Fowler pushed it slightly ajar.

"I'll do this one, son, it's my turn."

The door would open left to right, effectively shielding whoever was behind it from enemy sight inland. Fowler moved forward, fully opened the door, stepped out, and a heavy calibre sniper bullet came straight through the wood bursting through his chest right to left. Blood and chest splattered the wall on Teddy's left, and Fowler fell dead to the floor.

They froze in position.

"It's that sniper in the bloody lighthouse," said Spud, "he sighted on that door and waited for it to open, he's fired chest high when he knew someone was there. Here, let me have a look."

Spud lay flat, keeping as much brick wall between him and the sniper as possible, and crawled forward. He poked his head out at ground level looking at the stone path that led north to their left.

"Okay, the path veers to the left after about twenty yards. With the door in the way, I don't think he can see us well enough from his angle for a good shot at this distance. If we move fast and veer side to side, we should be okay."

"Give that door a shove with your rifle," said Teddy.

140

Nothing happened.

"And again."

Nothing happened.

"What would you be doing Teddy?" asked Spud.

"I'd have moved on to another door."

\*

Dolf Von Rundstedt had cursed his fellow sniper for smashing the window of the lighthouse like an amateur, signalling their presence. The enemy had abandoned his position on the fort walls leaving the bridge clearer for an attack. He'd dearly wanted that shot. Sniper to sniper, a true test, and he'd lost that chance now.

He'd waited patiently, though, finding other targets and his job was still to take down anyone not actively surrendering or trying to escape. He'd nearly decided to find another target when he'd seen the door move. Just testing him, a quick-witted prey he thought, not enough, though. The motion teased and tempted him, but he chose to resist, then time and again when the door moved slightly. No, he thought, I have just enough time for one shot, maybe even two. When they left the shelter of the door, they would be in his sights for a few dangerous seconds before they reached the safety of the curve in the path.

Dolf waited again.

\*

"I'll go first," said Spud.

"No I'll do it," said Teddy, "you've had my back, I'll have yours, besides I'm faster than you and when I reach the curve I might get a shot at the lighthouse."

Teddy bashed the door one last time for luck and then ran as fast as he could, using a wide gait which he intended to swerve his body side to side as he moved.

\*

Dolf easily focussed his sights on the man who ran from the door's shelter, took a breath, held it and then let it go.

"Archie?" he said to the man who was carrying his best rifle and running away, then he laughed, placing his left

141

palm firmly on the barrel of the rifle in his fellow snipers hands.

"Nein, nein," he said putting his second-best rifle down and laughing while shaking his head. His fellow sniper thought he'd gone mad.

Dolf relaxed fully, he had more than enough kills already to secure the battle status he craved so he might fulfil the next part of his plan.

*

Two minutes later, Teddy, Duncan, Spud, and Feckle were all behind the relative safety of the curve in the concrete shoreside path. They could still hear intermittent sounds of fighting around them.

"This way," said Feckle continuing along the pathway.

Teddy and Duncan looked at each other, Teddy looked at his gun and raised his eyebrows, Duncan shook his head, Teddy breathed out and shrugged again.

They followed Feckle until they reached the end of the fortifications that ran along the shoreline.

"We wait here for dark," said Feckle.

They watched and waited until well after dark, some small light still provided by distant fires across the docks and old town.

The firing had stopped, and they couldn't see or hear anything that might suggest organised enemy activity. They'd be busy with prisoners, the battle was over, they wouldn't take any more risks tonight. Anyone remotely sensible would grab whatever sleep or food they could find, and Jerry had sense in abundance.

At 2330 precisely Feckle spoke.

"Right, we head to the end of the old jetty, if anything happens it'll happen there."

He remained stony faced, still having said almost nothing for hours.

They moved warily across flat land between the fortifications and the beach. The old jetty was just that, a long wooden structure on top of rocks that formed a breakwater for the main harbour. It looked half a mile long

142

and ten feet wide, there was a small white, shattered lighthouse at its far end, not a spark of light came from it.

They reached it and waited, there was no noise or movement near them.

Spud had a look around. "There's no timetable," he said, "I bet we wait all night, and three come along at once."

"There's a rusty ladder leading down to the water. It's seen better days, looks like Jerry machine gunned it from the air," said Teddy, "if anything comes alongside, I reckon we can get on it okay."

Teddy sat silently, the tension increased, he fingered his jack-knife, and they waited. If nothing came tonight, they'd be in the bag, prisoners of war for years, if they were lucky. He had two bullets left and only reluctantly decided the precious Mauser would go in the water if Jerry got anywhere near them. The Luger and knife would have to go too, he still had his Lee-Enfield, and the money would do him no good. The chocolate and fags were long gone, they had two officers though and one a Major, that should get them safely bagged at least, he thought. No, he meant to profit from war, to flourish, not languish.

Spud scanned the darkness with his binoculars looking for any sign of light, a boat, a ship, a submarine, he'd settle for a rowing boat, anything.

Feckle remained utterly silent, Teddy searched his face for some trace of humanity, but could see no life behind those eyes. He was saying nothing, Teddy pondered whether he preferred Feckle not to speak, or to speak and say nothing, or whether he should just shoot him.

Teddy amused himself by imagining the various different ways he might kill Feckle, something fitting and well deserved obviously, and then how he might get away with it. Then, just for fun, he made a mental list of others who deserved death.

He suddenly panicked, certain he was about to be captured or killed.

Cicero calmed him.

*'While there's life there's hope.'*

Then puzzled him.

*'The life of the dead is placed in the memory of the living.'*

*'What the fuck is that supposed to mean?'* He asked himself, but no answer came. Sometimes, the Classical quotations appeared helpfully at the front of his mind, sometimes they just confused him. He returned to his list.

Duncan appeared serenely calm, he needed a long talk with Teddy. That could wait, having found him he just needed another miracle. He wasn't praying for one, though, he was just patiently waiting for it to happen.

It was one long and agonising hour later when Spud spoke.

"Hush."

They all stood up and listened intently.

"That's an engine."

"Is it one of ours?" said Teddy.

"It's definitely one of ours," said Feckle, pulling a torch from his tunic and starting to signal.

The small vessel moved closer, reducing its speed and noise until it was silent and coasted to the jetty. The Captain was brave and knew his craft. The sea was calm with a slight swell that moved the vessel higher and lower then nearer and further from the western side of the jetty.

"I reckon if we go down that ladder, wait for the right moment and jump, we'll be okay," said Spud.

"You go first," said Feckle.

Spud nodded and began to clamber down, when he got to what he thought was the right level, he turned round on the ladder to face the vessel, holding the ladder one-handed. He waited until the right sway was happening, then sprang outwards onto the boat deck. Several pairs of hands grabbed him, and Teddy could just make out the deck being full of a ragbag of army men. At least some others had made it too, he thought, and his spirits rose. Someone on board decided to risk lights to help the rescue, the light revealed the name Gulzar on the side. It looked like a civilian vessel to Teddy.

A loud cracking of timber and a scream drew his

attention sharply back to the ladder. He couldn't immediately see Feckle or Duncan, so he moved sharply to lean over the side of the jetty.

He could see Duncan nearest to him hanging onto the metal ladder which had come loose from the shattered timber. Duncan was holding on to the now overhanging ladder with his right arm locked around it, his left arm held Feckle by the leather webbing of his uniform. Feckle dangled precariously over the sea and the rocks. They risked more lights on the boat, and Teddy could clearly see Duncan struggling to keep his grip on Feckle, his left hand holding, straining and stretching to breaking point.

*'Just let the bastard go.'*

A starburst shell from the shoreline flashed overhead, dangerously lighting up the vessel.

When Teddy looked back to Duncan, he could see Feckle fall straight down onto the rocks below. He landed with a sickening thud like a dozen punches all landed simultaneously, forming a tangle of limbs that were immediately motionless and dead. His head was twisted around, looking away from his back as if someone had wrung his neck. Teddy could see Duncan still holding firm with his right hand although his left hand was bloody and one of his fingers was bent back and dislocated. The ladder had loosened further from the Jetty's ancient timbers, hanging over the vessel at the nearest point of the sway. Duncan let go with perfect timing and fell securely into the waiting hands of those on deck.

Teddy looked over the edge of the jetty, the ladder wasn't an option for him now, he'd have to jump, he'd never make it. The light of the star shell floated above them while Teddy tried to think of a plan when a bass, loud and familiar voice came bellowing from the deck.

"Fucking jump, Teddy, we ain't got all night."

It was Smudger, and Teddy could see his huge frame outlined clearly on the edge of the deck.

A plan came. He discarded his Lee Enfield, strapped the Mauser to his back, took six long strides backwards then

145

sprinted in long-jump fashion off the jetty and into the air. He knew he'd land somewhere near the deck, he couldn't possibly know where.

He needn't have worried, he flew straight into the wide waiting arms of Lennard Smudger Smith, who stood as firmly as if he'd been nailed to the deck. He caught Teddy as easily, and as carefully as he would have cradled one of his own children. He swung him round and set him down gently and looked into his eyes with a smile and more warmth than Teddy had seen in his life.

"I fucking love you, Smudger," he said with a smile and collapsed onto the deck.

## Chapter 12

### 27th May 1940 - 0030 - HM Yacht Gulzar

Teddy was awake. He could remember jumping, falling and knew he was safe. He was aware that Smudger had caught him, he knew Duncan and Spud were safe, he knew he had the Mauser, the Luger, the knife and the money. Best of all, he knew Feckle was dead, and he'd survived.

Teddy was better than he'd been three days ago, he was a better man than when he'd arrived in France. He'd been nobody, now he was somebody, he just wasn't sure he was Teddy anymore.

"Drink this," said Duncan handing him his small silver flask, "there're two sips left."

"One each," said Teddy and took his sip, it was dark navy rum and perfect.

"Here, have one of these," he said handing Duncan one of his last two chunks of Cadbury's, taking the last one himself. He let it melt in his mouth and savoured it as he swallowed then washed it down with water from his bottle, far from fresh but good enough.

"Are you all right, Archie?" said Duncan.

"I didn't faint, I was conscious, everything stopped working for a minute or so. I think I got a bit overexcited there. Are you okay? Your hand?"

"The finger's back in, but the nail's gone, looked worse than it felt, honestly. There's a medic somewhere, a jack tar just snapped it back into place, happens all the time with ropes, he said."

"Where's Spud? Is he okay?"

"He's fine, he's over there with Smudger, he's probably being taught how to swear properly."

Teddy raised a weary hand to them, they were too tired to move.

A Medic arrived, from the Royal Army Medical Corps, squeezing past the men slumped on the deck.

"Let's have a look at that hand," he said.

He washed the blood gently from the hand, probing the finger, bandaging the end and securing it tightly to the other fingers. It'll bruise up, and the nail'll grow back, keep it covered and clean, you wouldn't want a nasty infection would you, sir?"

"Where are we, mate?" asked Teddy.

"Call me Spence, Spencer Ward, mate means something else in the Navy. You are on Her Majesty's Yacht Gulzar," he answered.

Duncan laughed out loud.

"You've heard of it, sir," he said then looked at Teddy.

"This is the luxury yacht the Duke and Duchess of Windsor used for their Mediterranean holiday in 1938. It's a bit posh innit?"

"Can I have the bed?" asked Teddy.

"Listen, I've been on this tub for a week now, there's twenty of us using ten bunks in that cabin! We're officially a danlayer now assisting minesweepers. We've been in Calais a few times, and the Captain decided to come back in the harbour one last time. We took a bit of machine gun fire, he made this lot jump aboard as he went past the east dock, then he got a radio message to come to the jetty as well."

"Radio message?" said Duncan scratching the nape of his neck the way he always did when puzzled.

"Yeah, bloody lucky for you eh! We'll be back in Dover by dawn then we're straight off to Dunkirk, but that's a secret."

"From who?"

"Yeah I know," he laughed and left.

"So, what have you been up to then Archie?"

"No, you go first."

They talked for an hour, exchanging frank accounts of their last two days and three nights. Neither knew how to rationalise the events they'd experienced, they knew this was just the beginning of their war. Neither told the whole truth, but they knew that, so there were no lies told. The full truth would come later. Everything had changed

148

forever.

"Why have you started calling me Archie?"

"Because that's your name; a new name for a new life."

"What?"

"Do you know what Travers means in French?"

"Across or something."

"Crossroads."

"Yes?"

"You are at a crossroads in your life, and you can choose a new direction."

"It feels like a U-turn at the moment, we are heading back to Dover you realise."

"You're missing the point, it's the same road, it's you who is a different person now, and so am I. Our road can take us anywhere we want it to?"

"Did you bang your head when you landed?"

"No, the back of my neck just aches a little sometimes, like an itch you can't scratch."

"That's not what I meant."

"Are you taking the mickey?"

"No, well yes."

"Okay, just focus your mind and listen."

"Okay, I'm listening."

"When I get back, I've been summoned to see the Top Brass for some sort of unique intelligence role."

"If you say so."

"I'll need first class men with me, are you in?"

"Well, I don't have anything else in my social diary for this war."

"We can talk details later."

"Okay."

"We'll need some good men with us too."

"I've already trusted Spud and Smudger with my life."

"That's settled then, when we get back, take a week's leave and then call this number," he said handing him a card with his name, rank and contact details.

"Where did you get these?"

"Never mind, just show that card if anyone asks you

anything?"

"Okay, are you sure I didn't bang my head?"

"Yes, quite sure. I'll be happy to bang you on the head if it would help?"

"No, that's okay thanks."

"Okay, just remember, one week, no longer, I'm going to need you."

"My country needs me?"

"Your world."

"Now you're taking the piss, big time."

"We'll sort it all out later, I can't think clearly right now."

"Okay. Okay, Spud, Smudger over here!" Archie shouted, then asked Duncan, "have you got two more of those cards?"

Spud and Smudger jostled over to see Duncan and Archie.

"Listen up," said Archie, "when we get back, you're wounded and need a week's leave. Take one of these cards, if anyone asks why you're on leave, show them the card. Then ring this number after a week, that's the 3rd of June, no later, we're going to need you for special duties, are you up for that?"

He opened his kit bag, pulled out his money and handed them each ten pounds.

"Use it wisely, Smudger, go and see your wife and kids, Spud, go and see your... "

"Mum, I'll go and see me mum if that's okay?"

"That's fine, mate," he then thought carefully before continuing.

"Listen, have a break, there's more work to be done, but if we need a week's break for every two days' work, it's gonna be a long bloody war. Make the most of it, you deserve it just for makin' it this far. Okay?"

"Okay, Archie."

"Why is everybody calling me Archie?"

"It's your name," they said simultaneously.

"You can still call me Smudger."

"And I still ain't ready to be called Jerry."

"Okay, that's sorted then, what have you been up to Smudge?"

"Pretty much the same as you, Archie, I came into Calais along the road and ended up on the eastern docks with them Rifles. You gave me a bloody great gun and them Rifles blokes were bloody top men, Jesus, they stood and stood then stood again. We can beat Jerry given half a fair chance with men like that. They had decent officers too, Mr Duncan, sir, no offence, and a good Major too. I didn't chuck your rifle either Archie, can I keep it?"

"Yes, you can, mate. You've earned it twice over."

"And you've got yourself a better one an' all."

"I have that, now listen up, try and get a couple of hour's kip and make sure you do what you've been told this morning. There's no more evil to be done today, there'll be plenty to do later, take a break."

"Okay," they said and went to find another place to slump.

"Before I drop dead with exhaustion, one last thing," Archie said to Duncan, "what do I call you now?"

"You'll never have to call me sir again, my fellow officers and friends call me Conner, short for Constantine."

"Not Con then?"

"No, not that, Con is French for Country Gentleman!"

"Conner it is then?"

"Yes please."

"My pleasure, Conner."

Archie fell dead asleep for less than half an hour and woke to find a blanket wrapped around him. The changes of direction, in engine noise and vibration, had woken him, they were pulling into a dock. Conner was standing up, talking to Smudger and Spud, who were nodding and smiling, their smiles were somehow serious. He hadn't seen that particular look on their faces before, but it made sense Calais had changed them too.

Their boat pulled into Dover, Western Docks, where trains were waiting. Desks and clerks were waiting in rows in an empty warehouse to register those leaving the ships. The trains were empty, but every desk had a clerk.

As each man left the ship, they shook hands with the Captain, Lieutenant Commander Cedric Victor Brammall, who stood by the gangplank.

Conner and his three men disembarked, climbing wearily up a flight of stone stairs to the main quayside, the Gulzar was smaller traffic than was usual for the large quay.

"Stay with me," said Conner, who was the only officer going ashore, as such he took precedence at the first available desk. They watched him talk to the clerk, giving their details as well as his.

"I swear I can smell bacon," said Spud.

"You're hallucinating," said Archie.

"No, I can smell it too," said Smudger.

An officer came across to Conner, shook his hand and took him to a side desk. The officer directed a typist who typed out several documents, then prising apart the carbon papers and passing them to another man who sorted them and handed copies to Conner. He spoke a little more to the Captain and borrowed his desk phone to make a short call, then shook the officer's hand again and left.

"More typists, that's what we need," said Spud.

Conner returned to them.

"Christ, what a mess, let's get in that bacon sandwich queue, then we can talk."

They wolfed down their sandwiches, thick white bread, not full of bacon but sorely needed. They washed it down with strong hot tea.

"Right," Conner said, "you're all officially on leave and have travel warrants to London. Not sure which station, this train leaves in ten minutes, it's got to collect more clerks to bring down to the coast!"

He handed out the papers.

"There's been some small evacuations so far, there's a big flap on now and it'll be more chaos everywhere quite soon. There's talk of fifth columns and desertions so don't say anything about where you've come from and what happened. Keep those papers handy and ring that number on the 3rd of June, that's next Monday, and be ready to move as soon as you call. Keep your rifles with you, if you hand them in you'll never get them back, the papers cover that if you're asked. Right, on the train chaps."

"Where are you going, sir?" asked Smudger.

"I'm off to the castle, they've sent a car for me."

"Make sure you get a break too," said Smudger almost indignant.

"I will, don't worry."

Smudger and Spud left to board the train, leaving Archie and Conner to talk.

"Archie, you don't have anywhere to go in London do you."

"I'll be okay. I've got a few quid."

"No, hang on a minute, listen, go to this hotel," he wrote the name on another card and handed it to Archie.

"They'll be expecting you, and it's all paid for, show the card anyway, rest, sleep, eat, I'll see you in seven days, and we'll be busy enough then, don't worry."

"Okay, I'll be fine, after the last few days, I'll never worry about anything other than certain death."

"I'll see you in a week," said Conner.

"A week."

Archie joined Spud and Smudger on the train, and they sat in their own first-class carriage.

"Nice innit?" said Spud.

"Very nice, I could get used to this," echoed Smudger.

The train started its slow journey into London, moving from the docks to the main line west then north.

"Are you okay with the plan?" Archie said to them both.

"We've had a chat, and we'll get on just fine Archie, don't worry," said Smudger.

Archie looked at Spud, who just nodded his agreement.

"It's just, Smudger," he looked at Spud too, though, "it's just I, well, we've had to do some real dirty work in the last few days. I've done stuff I'll never talk about, and I'll do

153

some more before this is done, and I don't mean bad, I mean pure bloody evil, are you sure-"

"Listen, Archie, I'm a big lad, have you ever seen me bully anyone?" said Smudger.

"No, of course not."

"That's because, when you're my size you don't need to, right?"

"Right."

"Well, when that Gulzar boat went past, there was men pushing and shoving to get closer. I thought about my missus and kids for half a second and made sure I was at the front of any queue. I had to lamp two of 'em then the rest stayed well away from me. I'd do it again, in a heartbeat."

Archie nodded.

"And another thing, we didn't say anything cos it's your business, but some of us knew you were big mates with Lieutenant Duncan. We knew you was a lot smarter than you make out, and you could talk posh. Nipper thought you was a spy, but he couldn't say who for. We watched you a lot and copied what you did, if anything happened to Duncan, we'd decided to follow you instead. Tarrian was running a book on which of you would kill Feckle, the smart money was on you."

"I'm sorry I didn't kill the bastard now," said Archie.

"Remember old Sweeney from Third Platoon?"

"Yeah, the idiot who broke his nose falling downstairs."

"Well it was Tarrian's fist what done it, Sweeney called you Duncan's bumboy. I ain't never seen anything move so fast as that fist. We thought he'd fucking killed him at first, but a bucket of water woke him up. Even then, Tarrian picked him up by the collar and said he would kill him if he said it again."

"Well, he's fucking dead now, in a ditch, next to a truck near Wissant. Bullet in the back of his head."

"He won't be missed. Now if you don't mind I'll get some kip, the missus'll have a list of jobs for me to do as soon as I get in the door, Calais or no Calais." He stretched his long legs out placing them deliberately on the opposite seat. "You don't think the guard'll mind do you?"

"I don't think he'll dare," said Archie.

Smudger closed his eyes contentedly, Spud looked at Archie, nodded in silent agreement and closed his eyes too.

Archie had a lot of thinking to do, his mind racing, he wasn't Teddy anymore, had he ever been Teddy? He was definitely Archie, but who was Archie?

He felt safe and relaxed now, he felt he had time to think and plan. He stared out of the window, the regular noise and motion of a train always relaxed him, he looked out at the quiet green fields and hedges. After a time, he stopped seeing them and saw his own past instead.

*

He thought back to that morning, years before, when he'd woken up late after the school holidays. He was thirteen. He'd forgotten it was the first day back, until too late to prepare properly. He liked to plan even then, it gave him confidence, but he'd read that book until late. He'd read the whole book, the book his favourite teacher had asked him to read over the holidays. Caesar's Gallic Wars in Latin! They'd be reading it this year, the last before Grammar, he'd be ahead of the rest.

He'd always had a gift for Latin. The Latin spoken and repeated endlessly during Sunday Mass. The Latin, Mr Heywood inspired him to learn, he'd even given him his old Latin-English Dictionary. Mr Heywood had given him a book, his own book, his only book.

His naïve excitement returned with butterflies in his stomach even now.

He'd read it, alongside playing, daydreaming or just wasting time. He was adept at wasting time, like in church or praying. He'd prayed a lot, not necessarily for a lot, just toys, and money, he'd wasted a lot of time waiting for answers. Daydreaming was better, imagined conversations with people he'd never met; like Caesar, he'd given Caesar some sage advice.

Another year at Catholic school then Grammar, that

was his proudly crafted plan.

For now, he was in the two bedroomed house, he shared with two brothers, two sisters and mum and dad. He was in Watling Street, Wallingford; a small town in Shropshire.

He would get into the Grammar now, Mr Heywood would make certain of it, he'd show the Latin class boys. They weren't bad boys they just did bad deeds sometimes, sometimes without thinking, sometimes with, they were all rich, posh boys, though.

He had read that book, he had made it to school well on time. He'd gone to Assembly as always, then his heart missed a beat when the Headmaster announced that Mr Heywood had left the school, and his replacement was a Mr Kline.

That had shocked him to his insecure soul, now he was panicking, all his plans had lost their foundation. Heywood was gone, he'd have to deal with Kline instead. Would Kline help him like Heywood? How could he make Kline help him? That was easy, he just had to tell him how he'd read the book, in Latin. The achievement was certain to impress Kline, the rest of the plan would progress seamlessly. He hoped Mr Heywood was okay, wherever he was.

The morning had gone as normal. A new timetable to write out, some reunions and what did you do in the holidays talk. Some uneventful first lessons, a couple of new boys, a good dinner and then Latin after that.

He went into the Latin room after lunch, early, of course, he needed to be first in, to impress. One of the new boys was in Latin, he ignored him, he didn't need him. Mr Kline sat impassively as they entered, he looked unusual, Teddy couldn't put his finger on it. Mr Heywood had looked quintessentially English, Kline didn't look English, he looked foreign, when he spoke it was with a hint of an Irish accent, maybe that was it.

Kline took the register, the new boy's name was Kline too, and he had a stronger Irish accent, he couldn't be his son, must be, surely?

Kline went round the class asking each of the seven what work they'd done during the holidays. He should have asked Teddy first. He'd sat at the front, right in front of the teacher; eventually, he came to him, last.

Great, Teddy thought as he proudly told Kline and the others of his achievement. He had read the book, in Latin.

"Oh, we have a joker in this class do we?" Kline said.

"No, sir."

"Don't be ridiculous, boy, I couldn't do that at your age so you certainly can't, can anyone else do that?" he asked the other boys.

"No, sir," they all said at once, smugly.

"So what is it, boy? Are you a joker or a liar?"

"I'm not joking, sir," Teddy said.

"That's settled then, you're a liar, now be quiet and we'll start the lesson."

Teddy was dumbstruck, he couldn't think what to say or do.

The story spread quickly through the whole year, Teddy was a liar and a cheat, of course, he couldn't be trusted, everyone knew that now. A good bit of bad news always did that; particularly when it wasn't about you. That form of playground teasing almost always blew over, always another story, a different victim, this time, it stuck, permanently. Even Teddy's closest friends eventually shunned him in the playground, his nickname became Liar Teddy then Liarbility. No one wanted to associate with him.

Teddy tried to ignore it all and work hard to prove he wasn't a liar, but it was just too late. Inside the ruthless, cruel arena of the children's playground, if everyone thought you were something then that's what you were.

He worked especially hard at Latin, although Kline would always stand behind him and watch him carefully, for cheating everyone knew. He stood behind him during exams, putting him off, flustering his replies to questions. He never gave him a chance.

He became excluded from games and play or was the last pick. He was increasingly isolated. He had to become friendly with 'Sailor' Seabury, who was the smallest boy in the year, he suffered from asthma, couldn't play games and never spoke to anybody. They spent playtimes and lunchtimes in the small school library, reading voraciously and talking too. Seabury knew about the Greeks.

Even before school finished, he knew he'd never make the Grammar, he didn't want to go now anyway. A menial job or face torture at school, it became an easy choice. Teddy also became a liar, he might as well, he had nothing to lose.

He left school at 14, getting a job readily enough as a junior warehouseman at the local Army Depot, he put boxes on shelves then took them off. He was good at it, at organising, working methodically and fast, he'd probably get a promotion if he worked hard and well. They still called him Liarbility.

*

All these years later, his chest still burned with anger, injustice and shame.

*'No, you're somebody now, that boy's gone.'*

He was someone else, he took a deep breath, let it out and became Archie, he'd never be Teddy again. He needed to enjoy being Archie, whoever he was.

*'Look forward, never look back.'*

So, people called him names at school, they'd been trying to shoot him yesterday, which problem was worth worrying about?

He became calm, bit by bit, and he thought of the money in his pocket and the life in front of him.

The train pulled into Victoria station at 0830, they stepped out to receive astonished looks from other waiting passengers. As they walked along the platform and saw the engine that had carried them, they fully recognised the grandeur of their transport, they were alighting from the Pullman Flesch d'Or.

"The Golden Arrow," said Archie, "very suitable for our

new-found status, gentlemen," shaking hands with Spud and Smudger, firmly and at length.

"In a week," he said.

They nodded and walked off, wearily, yet with a spring in their step.

Archie was alone, he suddenly felt lonely, he hadn't been alone for such a long time, not since he'd left England. At least he was safe, and he had a future now, bury that past. You'll be back with your mates soon enough.

He left the grand main entrance of the station. He knew parts of London well, not the grander parts, of course, except the Libraries and the Tower, he'd not taken time for the rest. The rest cost money and for the first time, he had some.

He took Conner's card from his tunic pocket and approached a taxi, he'd never used one before, today he deserved it.

"I'm going to this hotel please," he said showing the card to the driver.

"Are you sure?" the driver asked.

"Yes, I've got a room booked."

"Okay, hop in then."

The journey took ten minutes, towards then past the Palace of Westminster, Big Ben then along the riverbank to the Savoy Hotel on the left. Oh, Christ, thought Archie.

"D'you want me to wait?" said the driver.

"No, this is me," he said handing over coins, "keep the change old boy," he said in his poshest voice.

He left the cab, wearing the scruffiest, filthy and bloody Private's uniform and not having shaved or washed properly for days. He had no luggage apart from what he'd stolen in France and a German Mauser he hadn't quite stolen, over his shoulder. The doorman gave him an astonished look, unsure what to do or say. Archie fixed him straight in the eyes, stood upright, shoulders back, brushed his hair elegantly back away from his forehead and swept it across his head. He then handed him his rifle and kitbag.

"Take these, old bean, I seem to have misplaced the rest

159

of my luggage in France."

He then walked past him, entered the door and moved confidently towards the reception desk.

*'Stay in character Archie.'*

A liveried receptionist at the desk greeted him.

"Ah, you must be Mr Duncan's brother, I never knew he had a brother, I can see the likeness now you are here."

"Yes, we lost contact, and the war brought us together."

*'Make each lie as close to the truth as possible.'*

"Everything is ready for you, sir, you are in room 120, it is the best we have at short notice. Only a courtyard view, I am afraid."

"I'm sure it'll be excellent, thank you so much."

"Mr Duncan has asked us to provide anything you need."

He looked Archie up and down and appeared to be trying not to inhale.

"It seems as if you might need quite a few things, sir, some toiletries perhaps?"

"Yes, indeed." *'What the hell are toiletries?'* "I think a bath would be very welcome, is there one I can use?"

"You are joking with me, sir, of course, there is one in your room."

"Ha, of course, there is, I have grown unaccustomed to luxury in France." *'I think I got away with that.'*

"Would you like breakfast, sir?"

"Yes, that would be perfect."

"I'll have it brought up to your room."

"Of course."

"William," he called out, snapping his fingers at a bellboy who was about fifty, standing, slim, smart and upright in his uniform.

"Show Mr Travers to his room," he said, handing him the key.

"Ask William for anything you need, sir. Welcome to the Savoy."

Archie was expecting to be called Mr Duncan or Mr Austin and had signed the book as Travers without

160

thinking, okay, it's Travers. Brothers could have different surnames, couldn't they?

William took the key from the receptionist and then the kitbag and rifle from the doorman, still bemused by Archie's appearance belied by his welcome.

The receptionist added hesitantly.

"Mr Travers, how can I ask, the rifle, could you keep it in your room, please. Our other guests are unaccustomed to such things, Mr Churchill is a frequent visitor, his policeman will take exception."

"Yes, I quite understand. I don't have much ammo left anyway."

William led Archie to the lift, opening the doors for him and pressing the right button.

*'Watch and copy.'*

He opened the room door for Archie, the room was how Archie imagined Buckingham Palace to look like. An enormous double bed, sofa, table, chairs, radio and its own bathroom with a bath, sink and toilet, this wasn't a room it was a small house.

"Bloody Hell!" said Archie as he flopped down on the sofa.

William carefully placed the kitbag and the rifle on a small stool at the bottom of the bed. Why was there a stool at the bottom of the bed? William shut the room door and sat down at the table.

"The breakfast will be here in about thirty minutes, sir. They'll knock on the door, and you let them in. You don't need to tip them, Mr Duncan always leaves a generous gratuity at the end of a stay.

"The hotel will provide anything you need, might I suggest some civilian clothing, a razor, and a comb as a first step. Some luggage and a case for that gun would be best too... I can procure some ammunition for you if you wish, it's a Mauser isn't it?"

"Yes, it is."

"And recently fired too, unless my sense of smell has gone, it's on your hands too, isn't it? You never forget that smell, it takes a hell of a washing to get rid of. You can't get the smell out of your nose either, it's like blood, shit and tears all mixed up with gunpowder. You'll get used to it."

"You were in the last one weren't you?" Archie said, recognising something in the old man.

"I was, I don't usually talk about it."

"And I won't ask then, William."

"Look, we'll talk later, I know when a man needs to be left on his own. When I'm gone, take your kit off, there's a dressing gown in the wardrobe, use it, have your breakfast and a bath. You'll feel like sleeping forever, but that's not good for you. I'll wake you at teatime, four o'clock, with a meal and some clothes, you should go out tonight, walk and breathe, feel alive. There's a look in your eyes, son, and you need to get rid of it."

"I think we're going to get on just fine, William."

"Billy, please."

"Billy then, and I'm Archie."

"I'll see you later, Archie."

\*

Billy Perry stood outside the room door for a minute. When he'd seen that Mauser and the look in that young man's eyes, he'd wanted to ask how many? He hadn't asked, he already knew what the answer would be.

\*

Archie did as asked and changed into the gown, the elderly maid politely left the food and took the clothes for washing with nothing more than a respectful nod. Archie ate a full English breakfast, four slices of toast with real butter and a whole pot of tea. He tried the orange juice that came with the food, it was the juice squeezed from an orange. It must have taken about six oranges to make so much juice, he'd never imagined such extravagance.

He had a bath, hot water up to his neck, with soap that came out of a bottle! He used the razor, shaving soap and brush, the maid had brought, there was also some aftershave which stung like fury, Christ he wasn't expecting that. At first, he thought it smelt a bit female, but as it faded it smelt, well, it smelt posh.

He looked at his eyes in the mirror, he looked deeply into his eyes and still only saw what he usually saw.

He pulled the curtains, climbed into the bed, naked and clean, the cotton sheets were like nothing he'd ever felt before. He emptied his kitbag and looked at the photographs of the beautiful woman. Half naked and looking intelligent, classy, anything less like a tart, he couldn't imagine. He'd not seen the like before, it was erotic, classical, a Venus De Milo with a modern face and better nipples too. There was a whole world out there he just didn't comprehend. He decided not to sully the image in his mind and, exhausted, with a full belly, he lay back.

"I am somebody now," he said and fell into a deep, dreamless sleep.

## Chapter 13

## Monday 27th May 1940 – Afternoon – The Savoy - London

Archie woke up at half three in the afternoon, unable to sleep more, he somehow couldn't settle, his body tired, but his mind still fully active. He felt an urge not to waste a second of his life, his new life, so he got out of bed and put on his gown. He turned on the radio and listened to the BBC, somehow still drawn to Northern France and what was happening there. The news was bland, we were still fighting bravely in Boulogne, Calais and Dunkirk apparently, and he resolved never again to believe a word he heard on the BBC. Norway was still putting up a fight, it still sounded like another bad, desperate idea coming to its deserved end.

He opened the wardrobe, there was another gown, extra pillows, and blankets, there were slippers too, perhaps the previous guest had left them there. He opened some of the drawers finding a bag for laundry, menus for something called room service as well as the restaurant menu and a guide to London. He opened one set of drawers to find it wasn't a drawer, it was a small refrigerator, with drinks in it. Another drawer had a kettle, tea, coffee, milk powder, and cups. He'd never stayed in a hotel before, but he knew this wasn't normal, Christ, how rich was Conner and if he was this rich why on this earth was he in the army?

The phone rang, the phone? It was in the drawer of the bedside table. He answered, it was Billy, he had new clothes for him and was it okay to come up with them?

Billy arrived, with two others each carrying various suits and shirts, socks, shoes, underwear and ties.

"These are off the shelf for the time being," said Billy. "Mr Evans here will measure you for various items. You might want to put these on first," he said handing him a pair of shorts.

Archie put them on discreetly and loosened the gown to let Mr Evans measure him in places he'd never been measured before. Mr Evans was camp, Archie wasn't familiar with camp, unsure whether it was scary or harmless? Harmless, he decided confidently, if he were going to bluff his way through this week he'd have to work on nonchalance. He made a mental note to copy nonchalance when he saw it.

The tailors left Archie alone with Billy, the clothes laid on the bed.

"It's the sort of thing that Mr Duncan would wear. If they don't fit, don't worry they'll take it back tomorrow. It's the same size as your army gear, but if that fits you properly, it'll be a first."

"I know what you mean."

"Would you like a meal brought up to the room, you might not be ready for the restaurant tonight, I can recommend the steak and chips."

"That sounds great."

"How do you like your steak?"

"I have no idea."

"Well done, is what we'll try then."

"Okay."

Billy got up to leave, taking the breakfast dishes Archie had tidied onto the tray.

"When you're finished with a meal, you can just leave the tray outside your door, and someone'll take it away without disturbing you."

"Billy?" said Archie.

"Yes, sir."

"Thank you."

*

Archie ate the meal, steak was caveman food he decided. He put on one of the lounge suits with a shirt and tie, he ignored the evening suit, he'd never need that. As far as he could feel, everything was a perfect fit for him, even the shoes. Six months of wearing army boots non-stop had toughened up his feet, so the soft, supple leather and thin

165

socks made him feel a stone lighter.

He needed to leave the room, he'd heard anything useful the BBC had to say, and it was a beautiful summer evening. Billy was right, he needed some air. He put the tray outside the door, locked the room and put the key in his pocket. In films, he'd seen hotel guests handing in their keys as they left a hotel, which seemed a bit strange and unnecessary, so he decided not to.

He went down the stairs, it didn't occur to him to use the lift. He looked around the main reception area then into the restaurants and bars of the Savoy, Billy was right again, he wasn't ready for that. He left the hotel, turned right and walked alongside the river towards Parliament, tasting the air, breathing, savouring the blue sky above his head. He noticed people watching him and was self-conscious about it, not understanding why. Could they see he was a killer, a murderer, what was it they could see and he couldn't?

He walked as far as Big Ben, turned right at the bridge and then again up Whitehall past Downing Street towards Trafalgar Square. He knew there were pubs there where he wouldn't stand out.

He found 'The Clarence' in Whitehall, the prices were steep, but they had bottles of the Stella beer he'd sampled in France, and it was ice cold. He looked at his beer, its perfect golden colour, the fizz of tiny bubbles rising, even the glass was perfect. He took one short sip, savoured it, then drained the rest, he asked for another and drained that too. He asked for a third, then found a seat in the fresh air by an open door. Even after the best meal he'd ever eaten, the beer was going straight to his head, which was a welcome relief. He needed to learn how to relax now, although that still conflicted with his need to always remain in control. Teddy had dropped his guard and made mistakes, Archie couldn't afford any mistakes.

He finished the beer, placed his empty glass on the bar, nodded confidently at the barman and walked casually back to the hotel thinking carefully, developing a plan. On

166

his return to the hotel, he spoke to reception, asked them for a pen and paper, then gave them a list of items he needed and went to bed.

*

## Tuesday 28<sup>th</sup> May 1940 – Morning - The Savoy – London

The following day, Archie was up at six o'clock, bathed, dressed and downstairs for breakfast at 0730. He watched the other patrons and copied what they did. After breakfast, he sat on the easy chairs in reception and read the newspaper they'd given him. He read from cover to cover, drinking in whatever information about the war he could. A lot had changed since he'd left London, the war was no longer phoney.

He'd noticed one of the waitresses watching him, she probably knows I shouldn't be here, he thought. She was very good-looking, not a chance, though. She saw him watching her and came over.

"Is there anything I can get you, sir," she said.

"Sorry?"

"A cup of tea perhaps, sir?"

"Oh yes, that would be kind, thank you."

As she left, he noticed Billy and nodded to him, choosing a safe spot for a quiet talk.

"I need a few items which probably aren't available through the hotel," he said.

"I should be in a position to help," said Billy.

"I have a short list," he said passing him a note.

"None of that'll be a problem, things are getting tighter, but London can still fulfil most requirements, at a price."

"Will this be enough?" he said passing him an envelope containing ten pounds.

"More than enough, sir. Will tomorrow be okay?"

"Yes please, and keep the change, Billy."

"One more thing, sir, now that we understand each other, I can get you most items you might need, perhaps even some company if you have that need?"

"No, that's fine, no need."

Billy left, Archie sat back in his chair. He knew what Billy had meant or thought he did. God, he wanted to say yes, needed to but didn't want to admit that willingness to pay, to any other man. No, Archie couldn't afford to show weakness, Teddy had been weak, and he wasn't Teddy anymore. The trouble was, Teddy had been a virgin; Archie still was, he yearned for sexual experience, a desperate, instinctive need to be a proper man.

Archie recalled Teddy's attempts to lose his virginity, a few kisses or an unsuccessful fumble. He'd saved his money for months and headed for the East End just before they were due to leave for France. He was nervous, feeling a mixture of nausea and excitement, when he sought out the street he'd heard about. He'd decided to do it, to pay for it, Christ, he might die in France.

He'd found the street easily enough, down by St. Katherine's docks and walked down it for some way before he saw one. Middle-aged and slim, he walked past, chickening out; then she'd called after him.

"Come on soldier, you won't find better tonight," she said.

He turned round, embarrassed and still determined to do the deed, he just needed to know what it was like, so if he did it for real, he might not be so nervous.

"How much?" he asked; no idea what to expect.

"A pound," she said

He agreed.

"Money up front, Dearie," she said.

He handed it over.

"Now, listen, the Rozzers are out tonight so I 'ave to be careful, I've got a room, clean and warm. We'll have to walk separately so we don't get seen. I give you a key to the door, you go that way, turn left into Dock Street, then carry on under the railway bridge and its number 74, remember number 74."

"Okay?" he said, confused.

"Now, before I give you the key, you have to give me two pounds key money. I can't just give my key to anyone you understand, you get the two pound back when we're in the room."

"Okay?" he handed over the money.

"Now, you walk, Dearie, and I'll be behind you."

Teddy walked on, turned left into Dock Street, checking she was still behind him. He waited for a moment, a short way round the corner, and she did follow him, so he relaxed and walked on under the railway bridge. He checked again, she was still there. He walked past a pub on his right, the Brown Bear.

He walked on a little more, even numbers on the left, he counted the numbers then saw a six-storey building with a grand, well-lit entrance. It was number 74, it was Leman Street Police Station!

He looked around and saw no one.

"Oh great, just great, you idiot, you thieving bitch, that's great, that's just fucking great."

No! That was Teddy, that wasn't Archie, he was somebody now.

The waitress interrupted his thoughts, bringing him a pot of tea and some biscuits, tiny ones, hardly a bite in each. She smiled sweetly at him, he ached at the sight, wait till she sees that Private's uniform, he sighed.

"Thank you," was all he managed to say, not daring to stare or make real eye contact, ashamed of who he'd been.

Several parcels and an envelope arrived for him that day, he had someone carry them up to his room, he was learning how to behave. The envelope was addressed to him care of the hotel and inside were one hundred pound notes. He was beginning to expect pleasant surprises. He put on the running gear he'd asked for and went for a run along the embankment. He needed to stay fit not get soft; although they made him leave and enter through the kitchen area.

He ran along the Thames embankment, wondering how much money Conner actually had. He thought vaguely about the price he'd have to pay for what he'd been given, taken or stolen. Was that just Catholic guilt nagging at him, perhaps, there was always a price, a few Hail Marys wouldn't absolve him of his mortal sins.

As he dressed for dinner, he looked at his Private's uniform in the wardrobe, it was disgusting, how would he ever wear it again?

That evening he had a meal downstairs in the restaurant and, guided in advance by Billy, managed a passable debut in eating and behaving correctly.

The next morning, he was up at six, for a run followed by breakfast and reading the paper, cover to cover. Later he had tea and biscuits brought by the same waitress. He managed eye contact and a smile this time, with luck and a fair wind he might manage a conversation in about a month.

His routine carried on for four of the seven days he had to wait, he'd never had so much rest and hospitality in his life. His body and mind were as fresh as they'd ever felt, each morning he woke with a feeling of exhilaration in his chest, he'd never been more alive, never less dead.

*

**Friday 31st May 1940 – Morning – The Savoy – London**

The bad news he read and heard nagged at the edges of his exhilaration. It wasn't dampening it, though, it was increasing it. The urge to act overwhelmed him, he somehow felt responsible, and he had to do something.

He sat on the bed next to the phone, it was early on Friday morning, and he took out the card and rang the number. It was a switchboard operator who only said *'War Office,'* he asked to speak to Lieutenant Duncan.

"Putting you through to Captain Duncan," she said.

"Captain Duncan speaking."

"Conner, it's Archie, I'm bored."

"Are you sure?"

"Yes."

"I'll be right there, everything's ready for you, I'm only round the corner."

Conner was there in thirty minutes carrying a large suitcase, Archie met him in the foyer, and they gave each other a huge lingering hug as if they'd just won the FA Cup.

"Brothers," said Conner.

"Brothers," agreed Archie, "Captain?"

"Yes, I have a surprise for you too," said Conner. "We'll have to go and try it on."

They went up to his room, Archie hoping it was a Corporal's uniform, he just couldn't wear that stinking Private's kit again.

In the room, Conner opened the case and produced a new, made-to-measure, Lieutenant's uniform, shirts, ties, and shoes.

"You are joking!" Archie said.

"No, No, put it on, man, for goodness sake."

Archie put it on, self-consciously, the very feel of the material was enticing and satisfying, a new skin for a new life. He looked at his reflection intently in the full-length mirror.

"It fits," he said.

"Very fitting indeed, do you, or do you not, look like an officer?"

"I may look like an officer, I don't feel like one."

"You will, and you should."

"Conner, what the hell's going on?"

"It's perfectly simple, we are in Military Intelligence, an Auxiliary Unit, our operational role is not yet fully defined, we are almost a blank sheet of paper, and we don't exist, officially anyway."

"Okay, that's you, who am I?"

"No, it's definitely you, let me explain. You recall reading 'Achtung-Panzer!' obviously, we discussed it for hours, days even."

"Yes."

"Well, you told me exactly how you would attack if you were Guderian. Right down to which units he'd use and where. Even how long each step would take, you even got the start date nearly right."

"Yeah, that was just a game I played in my head, I even had to use an adding machine to work out the fuel consumption and mileages. I was pretending to be him, like Caesar if he were a German."

"The point is you got it exactly right, well almost, you underestimated quite how bad we'd be, I'm afraid."

"Yes, but that knowledge is no use to us now?"

"Well, that's where you are very wrong. Now this bit is a little embarrassing so you must promise not to shoot me."

"What?"

"Promise."

"I promise not to shoot you then."

"Well, I wrote a report on all we discussed, gave it a fancy heading, called it an Intelligence Threat Assessment, they love that kind of thing don't they. That was about ten months ago, never heard any more about it until this week, and now the entire high command thinks I'm a bone fide genius."

"You are, though."

"No, it's just like you called it; the practical application of intelligence, together you and I are geniuses, genii, clever bastards; whatever."

"They must have loads of clever bastards already?"

"No, there's nobody anywhere who's any more capable than you. There are people, excellent at mathematics who can't make a cup of tea. They can break a code, but couldn't crack an egg in a fist fight. There are vast numbers of people out there who are merely bluffing like crazy. Believe me, separately, there's no one out there who is any smarter than you or I. Together, combined we are even better!"

"Okay, so what do we do now?" said Archie and sat down on the bed.

"Well, you deserve that uniform, you've earned it, with those ideas and those actions in France, and you've earned it twice over." Then, slowly and deliberately he enunciated the words.

"You have already paid the price for it, and it is your due, nothing more."

"Okay. What else?"

"You were very accurate in predicting when Jerrys' supply lines would get too stretched, and he'd have to slow down the advance no matter how bad we were."

"Yeah. We ran away so fast he couldn't keep up."

"Well, I recommended a contingency plan be drawn up for evacuating the BEF from the three channel ports by the navy and using small boats off the beaches. Some clever bastard did just that, and they've put that plan into practice for the last week in Dunkirk. Churchill read our papers, we are to define our role and report back as quickly as we can."

"Can we kill Hitler then?"

"No, someone else got in first, the old bastard asked for that even before he met the King."

"Jesus, let me think this through for a minute."

"We have time, we have time to think, time to plan."

"And we can do whatever we like?"

"More or less. Anything we can get away with, I'd say, anything that wins the war."

"No, listen, before we start anything. You think you know me, right?"

"Yes; and very well too."

"Well, you don't, and you need to know before we take the first step together. In France, Calais, I would have done anything to survive. I lost sight of everything except that, I did some evil, some real evil and I would have done more if I'd needed to. You need to know I'll do it again if I need to, I am not a nice person."

"We won't need nice people, Archie."

"No you don't understand," said Archie and he told Conner the real story. The exact story, of what had happened with Mad Mike, including stealing the money and postcards.

"That's what I'm capable of, and it scares me a bit because doing it didn't scare me if you see what I'm getting at."

"You were only doing what you had to," Conner said

gently. "We all did, and you didn't lie to me about it because I knew you weren't telling me the whole truth. I was just waiting for you to find the right moment to tell me."

"Okay, what have you done then?"

"Well for a start, Feckle didn't fall off that ladder, I stood on his hand on the way down, I just grabbed his webbing to make it look realistic."

"You held on to him for so long? You dislocated your finger and the nail?"

"Well, I couldn't just let him fall any old time, the devious bastard might have dropped onto the deck of the ship, I had to make sure he fell on those rocks. That's why I couldn't let you shoot him, I knew the little shit had some plan to get away."

"Blow me, that's the truth isn't it? You did it didn't you?"

"And I'll tell you something else, I bloody enjoyed it, I'm glad I did it, and I'd do it again, in fact, I mean to. I expect to have to."

Archie said nothing for a few minutes, and Conner allowed him to.

Conner turned the radio on.

"You know something? I find silence difficult to deal with now, I need some noise in the background. Oh, yes, you have new papers now, here they are," he said producing a set of army identification cards and handing them to Archie.

Archie took them and looked at them, eager to see the rank in writing.

"It says Archibald Austin Travers and the date of birth is two years too old?"

"Well, Archibald Travers Austin, known as Teddy, never left France you see, he can be reported as missing in action and his family informed if that's what you want?"

"It is, you know I don't contact them."

"And twenty is too young for a Lieutenant of your experience, besides Travers is posh, don't you think?"

"I can fake that."

"Don't we all?"

"So, what do we do now?"

"We should have a meal, a talk, and a drink."

"Well, that all sounds good."

"You haven't still got those postcards have you?"

\*

Conner took the lead that night, he said he was due a night off. They had a small meal with one glass of wine each, a dry white, Sauvignon Blanc, fittingly French, and they talked work, the war and ideas for winning it. It was only seven o'clock when Conner said they could finish work talk and suggested going out to a club. Archie had no idea what to expect, and they were still wearing their best uniforms so he just shrugged his shoulders and agreed.

Conner took him by taxi to what he called an exclusive venue. He paid the entrance fee and smiled warmly at the doormen who knew him.

On entering the club Archie couldn't believe his eyes, this was another world. The club was smoky and full of well-dressed men, young and old, a few uniforms and as many attractive young females as Archie had ever seen in his life.

"They charge the gentlemen to enter, but ladies are free, it does seem to be a novel and splendid idea, the Americans thought of it."

"I do like the Americans."

Conner ordered some drinks and advised him it was best to stand by the bar, which they did.

Somehow, in a way Archie didn't fully understand yet, they found themselves talking to several young ladies at once. They were laughing and joking in an uninhibited way, Conner made sure the ladies were never without a drink. Although he made sure Archie didn't drink too much, just the right amount.

Archie relaxed, more relaxed than he'd been in his whole life, this was great, it was easy, it was natural, he was somebody. Would they have looked twice at Teddy, in

175

a Private's uniform? These ladies listened to what he had to say, and he liked them, all of them. It helped that he had something worthwhile to say, and he dared to ask the question "if only." The answer came from an attractive dark-haired lady, who was not quite the prettiest girl there, who squeezed his bottom. She was talkative and friendly, fixing him with her eyes. Eyes which held a promise, not one of death or murder but one of life. He chose life and life chose him, she put her arm gently into the crook of his and looked up at him.

"I'm quite tired, I wonder if you could see me safely home, Archie," she said.

What else could he do?

"See you tomorrow," said Conner, his own attention taken up by another young lady who held him firmly by the arm in a territorial fashion.

Archie found a taxi and asked, "Where is home then?"

"I meant *your* home silly," she said, "I'm Victoria, by the way, you forgot to ask."

They went back to his room in the Savoy, by way of the kitchen and back stairs.

Victoria was infinitely more experienced than Archie and the first time was quick. She gave him no time to reflect on that and soon made him ready again, the second time was much better for her and the third time was excellent for both of them.

She told him he was 'gifted.' He wasn't sure what she meant by that. It sounded positive, though, and he was pleased anyway.

After that she went to sleep, cradled in his arms, he liked that too, almost as much as the sex, he felt like somebody important.

She woke him halfway through the night, with her mouth around his cock, which aroused her as much as him, so he made her come again when she climbed on top of him. Then she showed him what to do to her with his tongue and fingers, and he enjoyed that too.

Archie would see Victoria again, several times, always

176

meeting at the club but never going back to her home. He always enjoyed her company, as well as the sex, volume, and quality, it just fizzled out after a time. Neither talked about their work, she stopped going to the club, maybe she'd been posted away. He found, like many others, the war was breaking down inhibitions, and people were finding temporary pleasure where they could, whenever they could. She was an excellent tutor, and he was an eager learner.

# Chapter 14

## Saturday 1st June 1940 – Morning - Whitehall – London

On the morning of Saturday 1<sup>st</sup> June 1940, Archie didn't go for a run, the previous night's sexual exertions had provided enough exercise for several morning runs.

Victoria left early, Archie had made her a cup of tea, it seemed like good manners, he hadn't dared ask for breakfast in the room. It appeared this wasn't the first time she'd sneaked out of a bed or a hotel room, she possessed such confidence and poise, he'd copy it and seek it elsewhere. Teddy was gone, and yet Archie still had much to learn; at least now he had personal experience on which to base questions about women. Conner would know the answers, he was sure.

Now he'd done the deed, he'd work on heightening his partner's enjoyment, Victoria had been instructive and responsive. He needed to improve the before, and after, Victoria was excellent at both, touching, stroking, hugging and talking; he needed to be that considerate too.

Conner had gone back to his flat near Victoria Station, Hevlyn Mansions in Carlisle Place, an exclusive residence. He owned two flats on the penthouse top floor, both facing the street, he lived in the corner one and kept the other one free and furnished for guests. He decided Archie would live in the second one, he needed him close, but they would need some time and space for themselves.

Conner had needed space last night, he'd spent the night with two lovely young ladies, spoiling them with champagne and his shrewdly divided attention. He'd not done that before. He'd come close to death in France and worked his socks off since he'd been back, he deserved it. He wasn't sure he'd do it again, it was enjoyable and unique, it just wasn't that one on one intensity he so enjoyed seeing in a woman's eyes. Nevertheless, having two pairs of lips working on different parts of him simultaneously was an experience to savour. Any official government prescribed list of things to do before you died, surely needed that on it. Conner needed a balance in his life and felt he'd taken back some of what was owed to him for Calais. A modicum of debauchery was hardly harmful. Saving the world wasn't going to be easy, even God took one day off, so the fairy tales said anyway.

He made breakfast for the ladies and paid for taxis, that was balance too, he hoped Archie had given Victoria a cup of tea. He liked Victoria, a lot, she could be all things to all men, she was what Archie needed, he knew he'd chosen well. Archie would recognise the arrangement later, he'd tell him if he asked, not yet, though, not while the spell lasted. He hoped Archie wouldn't fall in love with Victoria, it was possible, but she was too smart to allow that to happen, or maybe not; he loved her a little too.

Conner called at the hotel to collect Archie just as he was finishing his breakfast, it was still only nine o'clock. Neither had slept much, they hardly noticed, they were young, alive and full of energy.

They walked the few yards to their building in the War Office in Whitehall. Conner led the way to the top floor, they had two small rooms, one outer office with a desk and a temporary secretary. Miss Battle, Conner had explained, only short term and be nice to her, she got us the desks, we only had chairs until she threatened someone. The second room held two desks, four chairs, pen and paper, a typewriter and two phones.

Conner chose a desk, Archie sat at the other.

"Do we wait for Spud and Smudger to call?"

"They called on Thursday, bored they said. They're Sergeants now and are tracking down some reliable men for us. No more than ten, when we've got enough, we'll get them and us, some specialist training. We'll be doing lots of thinking and planning, and we'll be obliged to get our hands dirty occasionally."

"On our own terms this time."

"Precisely."

"So what do we do now?" asked Archie.

"We brainstorm."

"We what?"

*

### Monday 3rd June 1940 – Morning - Whitehall – London

Forty-eight hours later, the morning of Monday 3rd of June, they'd finished thinking, talking, writing and typing. Conner had done all the typing, another of his hidden talents, even with a dodgy finger. They stayed up all night to finish their report, finished and polished, Conner called it. Archie called it their letter to Father Christmas, suggesting they burn it in their fireplace as the quickest means of delivery.

"Why do adults stop believing in Father Christmas then continue to believe in God? I mean, the message delivery mechanism for them is strangely similar after all, and neither ever write back, it's just plain bloody rude. At least with Santa, you sometimes get what you've asked for."

"You should be a philosopher."

"I don't think so, there's more chance of me becoming God."

Conner suggested they go for a stroll and hand the report in personally. To Archie's surprise, they entered the Houses of Parliament. Conner took the envelope to an inner room to deliver personally, returning five minutes later.

"We have two passes for the Strangers Gallery."

"Strangers? Stranger than what?"

"Guests, visitors then."

They approached a gentleman in full crown livery, the Serjeant-at-Arms, Archie assumed.

"Ah, Mr Bracken's special guests. You're early, but you should go up now it'll get crowded later. Gentlemen of the press, pacifists, and other undesirables, try not to shoot any of them," he said, eyeing their side-arms.

Archie followed Conner upstairs to the farthest end of the public gallery overlooking the Chamber of the Commons.

At twenty to four in the afternoon, a yawning Archie watched the house, now full, sit and listen to a speech by Winston Churchill.

The speech started off solemnly, and Archie could hear a hint of Churchill's slight speech impediment. In another context, he'd have sounded drunk. He could see some MPs, Tory, Liberal and Labour looking disgruntled, making remarks as asides while not listening. He half expected someone to cry out Bah Humbug! Why can't they just shut up and listen? The lowest, thickest Private would behave better than this bunch! He decided they were just unruly schoolboys in assembly.

He listened, as Churchill described the war in France, then became more interested when he mentioned Boulogne and Calais. He heard the Rifle Brigade, 60th Rifles and the Queen Vics mentioned. He spoke of only thirty unwounded survivors out of four thousand brought back by the Navy, and Archie knew that was an accident.

He praised their fight, though, they deserved that.

*"Their sacrifice, however, was not in vain."*

He wasn't sure about that, but he might make it so, given time.

Churchill mentioned the Brigadier, he should have said his name, Nicholson, people should know his name, it couldn't be a secret, surely Jerry knew his name by now.

Then he just rambled a little, making events sound a bit better than they were, more planned than they had been.

He alluded to the *"Knights of the Round Table"* and *"The Crusaders"*, that wasn't what he felt like.

*"Every morn brought forth a noble chance and every chance brought forth a noble knight."*

At that point, Conner dug him in the ribs and pointed to Archie then himself, mouthing, *"That's us that is."* They managed to suppress the schoolboy giggles they felt coming. They weren't much more than schoolboys, and at least they managed to suppress the urge.

Eventually, at ten past four, he got to the best bit.

*"We shall not flag or fail. We shall go on to the end, we*

*shall fight in France, we shall fight on the seas and oceans, we shall fight with growing confidence and growing strength in the air, we shall defend our Island, whatever the cost may be, we shall fight on the beaches, we shall fight on the landing grounds, we shall fight in the fields and in the streets, we shall fight in the hills; we shall never surrender, and even if, which I do not for a moment believe, this Island or a large part of it were subjugated and starving, then our Empire beyond the seas, armed and guarded by the British Fleet, would carry on the struggle, until, in God's good time, the New World, with all its power and might, steps forth to the rescue and the liberation of the old."*

The speech finished at fourteen minutes past four according to Archie's stolen watch.

Right, I get it now, Archie thought, with half a tear in his eye and a lump in his throat.

The gallery cleared, and Conner asked Archie what he thought the house and the public would make of it?

"He wasn't talking to the House, they're irrelevant, he was talking to Hitler; and the Americans as well. Listen, Adolf, don't bother even trying to land here, we'll never pack it in. Then telling the Americans if they don't help out they'll be next. Brilliant, possibly the biggest bluff in history and when the public hears those final words repeated in the papers and on the radio they'll know we can't lose, and now, well we can't can we? Winning is the challenge now, a draw's no use."

"A bluff or a lie?"

"It's not a lie because old Churchill means it, every word, give him a gun or a broken bottle even, and he'd go over there himself."

"And the other Honourable Members of the House?"

"Is there a collective noun for charlatans?"

"You know, I don't believe there is."

"We'll have to invent one then?"

"That would be fitting."

"A chamber?"

"A chamber pot surely?"

"A gazunder of charlatans?"

"I think you're on to something there."

*

## Wednesday 5th June 1940 – Daytime – London

Smudger and Spud had done their jobs well and by Wednesday, the 5th of June they'd found eight good men.

Spud had three of his mates from North London. One Searchlight's Private, Joe Dempsey, who'd made it to Dunkirk and escaped luckily from a beach, on one of the last small boats ashore. He had a younger brother Ben who'd just finished training and was sound and reliable. He also had an old schoolmate Francis Begley, who wasn't sound or reliable. The recruitment office had declared him mentally unfit to serve. He was useful in a fight and had other valuable skills such as breaking, entering and blowing stuff up, like safes.

"A sort of family business you understand," Spud had explained.

"We'll have a look at him then," said Archie, "anyone who doesn't fit in, is out, okay?" Spud nodded his agreement.

Smudger had done well, three Rifles lads, who'd been on the Gulzar and were willing to row back to France the next day if asked. David Stubbs, Stuart Buddy and Joseph Mowles. He'd also found two Fusiliers, Tarrian had made it back from Wissant, with Nipper who'd stolen a rowing boat! Nipper had knocked out a Frenchman, who wouldn't hand over his boat.

Nipper had another, bigger problem now, he was in the glasshouse at Colchester Barracks, charged with desertion and assaulting an officer. Captain Duncan's verbal authorisation alone had secured the release of the others from their units, but Nipper had hit a Major and broken his nose.

"Hitting a Major, can you imagine such a thing?" said Conner, looking at Archie, "I'll go up there in person tomorrow."

"We also have a medic," Archie said, "Spencer Ward

from the Gulzar has agreed to join us, he's done a vast amount of running repairs in the last few weeks, just what we need. He'll be with us when the evacuations are finished, end of June probably. I have the strangest feeling you chaps are going to need one, probably before we leave England."

"You'll all get movement orders to report for training, the location is a secret. It'll last 8 weeks, you *can* fail the course, so work hard, and you have to stay sober for the whole course!" said Conner.

"They'll pass, don't worry, sir," said Smudger, Spud nodded too.

Smudger and Spud left, they'd become firm friends, Spud had been round to his house for tea!

"If you tell anyone how soft I am with my missus and kiddies I'll have to kill you, you know that," Smudger had said. "Don't swear, do call me Lennard and you've never, ever, heard me swear."

Spud showed Mrs Smith how to make bread, French style.

"Good news about Tarrian," Archie said, "I thought I'd killed him and Nipper. Can you fix the glasshouse, Conner?"

"Should be able to."

"What now?" Archie asked.

"We've got our shock troops now we need some boffins. You start on that, and I'll get Nipper."

*

## Thursday 6th June 1940 – Morning - Bletchley Park, Buckinghamshire

Archie drove to Bletchley Park, where he was to meet a Major-General who'd just returned from the Norway Campaign and been put on special duties, Auxiliary Services, ordinary words describing extraordinary actions. The army in England was chaotic and unready in those days following Calais so Archie was impressed to see an imposing figure standing outside the Mansion as he arrived fifteen minutes early for his appointment.

"Travers, happy to meet you," he said, "I like a man who's early; this way, we'll talk in the grounds."

They stood in the garden of the Mansion, closely cut perfect soft grass, interspersed with gravel paths leading to numerous outbuildings, tennis courts, and a small lake. Huge mature trees that looked hundreds of years old dominated the view, it was an idyllic setting.

The Major-General, Colin McVean Gubbins, described the types of staff he hoped to have available soon and asked Archie what he wanted. He asked for four researchers, four analysts, one manager, and one leader. Archie also asked for an even mixture of males and females, rich and poor, well-educated would be useful, common sense would do. As many atheists as you can find, and no *'conshies'* please, he insisted.

"You won't get any males, they're mostly *'conshies,'* I'll see about atheists," said Gubbins.

"The decisions we make will kill people, and we'll break all God's laws while we're doing it."

"Calais taught you that?"

"Calais? A piece of cake compared to Ypres, the Somme, Arras and St. Quentin, sir, and I never took a scratch either. Well, I took the skin off my knees, that was all."

"You've done your research on me, I'll have to watch out for you. Duncan told you?"

"No, sir, an old comrade of yours, William Perry, said he met you briefly, typical Billy, he wouldn't say too much about the war, only that you were in hospital together."

"Billy Perry, that's a name to remember, is he okay?"

"He's fine, sir, he's sort of teaching me things."

"I hear you're dangerous enough already, but I'll say no more, Billy can tell you more if he wants to. Tell him I need good men to train others. Just that, he'll know what I mean.

"The back-room staff are all training at the moment, come back next week; Friday. I'll get you twenty to look at, interview, whatever you like, pick the ten you want, that's the best I can do. If they're not what you want, make them into it, we don't have much time."

"Good enough, sir."

"We need to keep in touch, you'll have a lot of latitude in how you act and you can be sure I'll be asking for your assistance. I've heard a bit about you, I'm intrigued as to how you know so much aged only twenty?"

"I'm twenty-two, sir."

"Of course, you are. You were born in Aberdeen weren't you?"

"Yes, sir, near enough. I don't remember it."

"Will you go back?"

"I try not to look back, sir."

They walked a little in the grounds, Archie explained about books, history, its lessons and his ties to Conner, the British Library.

"Somehow, we bring out the best in each other," Archie said, "he knows what I don't and vice versa."

"I hear you've got your own little Blitzkrieg unit, local boys?"

"Men we know and those they trust."

"Yes, use them wisely. When it comes down to a dirty job, you might want to use a Pole or a Czech, their motivation makes ours seem half-hearted. God alone knows what they'll do to Jerry if they get close enough. It'll come to that you know, suicide missions, you'll get used to it. Speak to me if you need any specialists.

"The Poles are damn smart as well, they've done work on the German codes you wouldn't believe or understand for that matter."

They spoke a little about Caesar and Guderian.

"What about Hitler then?" Gubbins asked.

"I've been thinking about that. Leave him where he is, he's more likely to hinder the army than help them, believes his own propaganda, deep down, he's not that intelligent, and he's lazy. Leave him to get in the way."

"Ha, you're not wrong, I was at a strategy meeting two days ago, took them six hours to reach the same conclusion! One last thing, we're running a few experiments overseas at the moment, I'll get someone to brief you on them. When they're done, if any of them get back anyway, I want your assessment. I also want your input on prisoner debriefs and surveillance, you've got something there. We are making this up as we go."

Archie gradually felt the fine hairs on the back of his neck rise, not as a warning, excitement perhaps. He knew he'd had part of this conversation before, with someone else, Caesar perhaps. He had the strongest feeling he was being watched; scrutinised or analysed, no, he was being studied, that was it. He turned around to face the main Mansion and saw a face at a window. He managed a fleeting glimpse but didn't have time to tell if it was male or female before the face disappeared behind a curtain.

"I'll save you one small building here, use it, Whitehall won't be safe much longer. Also, I'll say this now and get it over with. No-one will ever know what really happens on this site, small pieces might emerge in maybe fifty years, Cabinet papers and the like.

"Perhaps, some of the intelligence we gather and how we did it may become obvious to future generations. What we did or didn't do with that intelligence needs to remain secret forever. As you say, we'll break all God's laws, so we won't be shouting that from the rooftops. We're not doing any of this for accolades anyway, if no-one remembers me, or you for that matter, then we've done our jobs properly. Anything you need, speak to Jimmy Mackay. Goodbye Travers," he said and began to walk away.

"One last thing, sir," Archie said, "have you considered writing some false reports now, call them Top Secret. Then when they do come out in fifty years, it still obscures what we really did."

"I like your thinking, Travers, stay close," Gubbins nodded and left.

Archie breathed a sigh of relief, Gubbins had just tested him, and he hoped he had passed. Archie continued looking at the window, he'd missed something, and that annoyed him.

### Thursday 6ᵗʰ June 1940 – Morning – Colchester

Conner made a quick phone call then drove to Colchester. He knew a phone call or a piece of paper wouldn't work this time. He was aware of the harsh reputation of the Colchester glasshouse, and if he could bluff his way out of Calais, he could get Nipper out of there. After passing through the outer security gate he went straight to the cell blockhouse, asking for the officer in charge and introducing himself as Nipper's Commanding Officer and his legal representative. He was surprised to hear Nipper already had a legal representative, had been court marshalled and sentenced to two years. He said he was here to set up the appeal and needed to see his man immediately.

He could see the Lieutenant was flustered so he explained he was a busy man, had driven all the way from London and needed to see him immediately.

A Sergeant showed him into the gloomy, grimy, urine smelling building and took him to Nipper's cell.

"Nice to see you, sir," said a battered and bruised Nipper, "I've had worse," he added, seeing Duncan's aghast look.

"What have you been up to young man?"

"Well, sir, after we scarpered from Jerry, I met up with old Tarrian when I was running along the beach. We didn't know what was ahead of us so we turned back towards Wissant. There was already a few Jerrys there too so we had a bit of a ruck. When that was done, we nicked a boat, rowed north and got picked up by the Navy, ended up in Folkestone.

"To cut a long story short, I gave meself a bit of leave. I made it back to the Smoke easy enough. I didn't have any money or gear, so I borrowed some from someone who didn't want to lend me any, and he grassed me up.

"The redcaps was a bit rough with me, so I took a dislike to them right off. When I was up before the beak, I sort of hit him."

"Did you have to hit him?"

"He called me a coward, sir, I wasn't havin' that, I know I'm a bad lad, but I ain't that."

Nipper tried to stand up, half way up, he grimaced and couldn't.

"They gave me a bloody good hiding, sir," he explained, "mostly in places you can't see. I did ask for it, mind you, I was a bit cheeky. I can't stop meself sometimes, and I did hit back an' all, I should of just took it."

"How many of them?"

"Four, sir."

"How old are you, Nipper, really?

"Eighteen, sir!"

"How old are you, really?"

"Nearly sixteen."

"We're leaving now, come on, son."

Duncan rapped on the cell door, which opened, he almost carried Nipper out of the cell on his left shoulder.

"You can't take him out of the cell, sir," said the Sergeant.

"This says I can," said Duncan indicating the pistol in his right hand. The Sergeant pulled back, his face a mixture of shock and cowardice.

"The Lieutenant and I will sort this out in the office, thank you, Sergeant," Duncan said sharply.

In the Lieutenant's office, the Sergeant and a couple of Guards, he'd called for as reinforcements, stood ready to intervene. Duncan began to talk in the calm and unanswerable way he'd perfected.

"Listen carefully, Lieutenant and do not say a word. This is a fifteen-year-old boy who could not legally join the army, understand, he cannot, therefore, be subject to army law. He cannot legally be court marshalled and cannot be imprisoned here, would you like me to quote the legal precedents? Right! I am taking him out of here now, and you are going to carry him to my car for me. The alternative is, every man in this stinking hole will be prosecuted for the beatings he's taken. You will be locked

189

up and dismissed from service in disgrace, I will also make damn sure you all get what he got. Or we can just walk out quietly now? What's it to be, gentlemen?"

The Lieutenant helped Nipper to the car, not saying a word. Duncan drove out of the barracks, a month ago he couldn't have done that, after Calais it was easy.

They were halfway back to London before he spoke to Nipper.

"Would you like me to kill a couple of them for you?" he said laughing, not sure if he was joking or not.

"No, you're alright, sir, I was lucky."

"Lucky?"

"I don't think my arsehole would've lasted two years in there!

They just hadn't finished softening me up yet, that was next."

Conner took Nipper to their office in central London while he decided who should look after him. To his surprise Miss Battle said she'd take him home with her, she was a retired schoolteacher who knew what the boy needed, anyone could see he's only fifteen!

"That bit of fluff on your top lip doesn't make you a man you know. I'll get you washed, fed and smarten you up a bit," she said.

Nipper looked slightly more scared than he had in the glasshouse!

Miss Battle was a voluntary reservist, allocated duties that would free up someone younger for more important work. She looked about ninety Conner thought, in fact, she was a spritely 65-year old, who wanted to stay active.

"The young people of today don't know they're born," she would say, usually followed by, "now, the last war, that was a proper one."

\*

### Friday 7th June 1940 – London

Archie moved into his flat on Friday the 7th of June. He'd enjoyed the Savoy enormously, he felt like a millionaire on holiday; but when he'd seen the *'small'* flat Conner offered

190

him, he couldn't wait to be there. Conner explained several times, money was no object, and every penny had already been earned. Finally, Archie resolved to enjoy it while it lasted and to make plans in case it didn't, of course.

Before he left the Savoy and despite what Billy had told him, he did give him a personal tip.

"Anything you need, anytime," Billy had whispered.

"I'm sure we'll meet again," Archie had said.

Billy explained carefully to Archie that he was certainly not a criminal.

"I do know some of them, and sometimes I carry things I know nothing about from one criminal to another. That can't be a crime, can it? So, anything you need, son, you see me, alright?"

Archie did pass on Gubbins message and goodwill to him, but Billy just said he was well past all that now.

Archie also made sure he gave a tip and a smile to Grace, the pretty waitress. He had spoken to her a little, a smile and even a minor flirt, any more might have tested her innocence. Victoria was using up all his energy, and he knew he'd visit the Savoy again.

*

## Monday 10th June 1940 – Whitehall

A week after they'd submitted their paper to the mysterious Mr Bracken, the Ministry of Information summoned them to an office in Whitehall.

The doorman showed them into a small unoccupied meeting room. A middle-aged, bespectacled man came in and sat down. He looked like a school teacher, maybe a headmaster thought Archie. He pulled out a piece of paper with handwritten notes.

"Well chaps," Brendan Bracken said, reading from the paper.

"Mr Churchill is very keen on the covert tape recording of POWs, he's asked that it be tried on the Luftwaffe first, we have a few of those. We don't have many officers yet and no high rankers. A country house is being converted as we speak. You're forbidden to talk of it again of course, and you'll receive no credit.

"The propaganda items are all approved. Some were already planned, and I am personally grateful for your new and innovative suggestions. I had thought I had a fertile imagination until I read your paper!" he said looking up at them.

"The item in relation to the East End would need perfect timing and execution and is judged unworthy of official approval, verbal or written, is that clear?"

"Yes," they said.

"The Lights of Perverted Science, a briefing will be provided for you, it will be top secret. You will not disclose anything you are told or guess, even to me.

"You have the lead role on that, any target is an authorised target, to turn or terminate as you suggested. You have free rein on that. There are also a small number of German Jews in the Pioneer Corps you might wish to consider using.

"Weapon delivery systems, rockets, no individual is to be harmed, that issue is to be dealt with elsewhere. Do nothing on it.

"Cyphers, a raid is being planned, you'll be consulted and will accompany the raid, you won't lead on the raid, but you'll lead on the procurement of significant items. We are leaving some resources on the continent we'll use later. Mr Churchill loves the filming idea by the way.

"I agree with you on any invasion of the islands. It won't happen, nevertheless we see it as a battle we can win so we'll be seen to be winning defiantly against all the odds etcetera. The Americans will love that, stay away from them for the time being, please. That's in hand at the highest level, and we'll let you know when we need you.

"The stay-behinds are in hand, we have more than enough veterans of the first war, who'll remain behind enemy lines if Jerry does successfully land. Gubbins is personally taking charge of all that, there'll be nothing in writing, not ever.

"Keep the ideas and analysis coming in through the

usual channel. You'll have access to all the incoming intelligence you've asked for, make sure you liaise effectively before any action, we don't want our chaps shooting each other, well not unless it's absolutely necessary anyway.

"Travers, we'd like you to expand on your idea for grading intelligence and protecting sources, we like the pragmatism involved. It's something the red tape brigade will want to disagree on for a year. We need something to put in front of them and order them to do it. Design your process, trial it in your own team from start to finish, put it all on paper and then it'll go directly to the Cabinet through me.

"Funding, you'll receive a proper budget eventually, a modest one, it'll pay essential staff and equipment costs. It won't be enough, so you'll have to scrounge or steal the rest, and don't get caught. Any questions? No? Good, we won't meet again, I'll have a more public role. I'm afraid I won't be able to consort with the likes of you, or you with the likes of me for that matter."

He then took his notes and set them alight with a match, dropping them into an empty metal wastepaper bin.

"I've always wanted to do that," he said smiling.

He got up to leave, shaking their hands.

"Winston wants to see you both, you'll hear from him when he has time."

*

"What did you think of that then?" asked Conner.

"The strangest thing, every word he said was the complete truth, *he* was the lie. That accent wasn't right was it, he's hiding an Irish accent, he just isn't who he says he is. Who is he? It wasn't Caesar was it?"

"I'm not sure even he knows anymore, he's been in character for so long. We'll need him, and he'll need us, we can trust him, mutually assured destruction it's called."

"And he told us to do the East End job, didn't he?"

"Yes, he did."

## Chapter 15

### Friday 14th June 1940 - Bletchley Park

On 14th June 1940, Conner and Archie met at Bletchley Park to select their boffins. Gubbins had allocated them a large one storey brick building near the Mansion. Archie didn't think any of the available wooden huts were big enough for all the paperwork he needed to retain. It was a substantial building, and he refused to call it a hut. Hut seemed so common a term, building sounded classier.

He also knew there was no Hut Thirteen due to superstition, so he proudly named it Building Thirteen. It had plenty of room, a small kitchen, and its own toilet. It also had a separate room, without windows, for private, secret matters, Archie liked that idea, he could use that.

"We'll be bad luck for Jerry," said Archie, "and anyone else who gets in our way."

They scanned the candidate's personal files, sifting out four males who were conscientious objectors, then a couple of females who had children. Someone with a home to go to wasn't what they needed, you might not be clocking off at five, they needed people to arrive early and stay late. Archie didn't want individuals with a life outside the team, the team was going to be their life.

They invited the 14 remaining candidates into their building, made them a cup of tea, gave them biscuits and had a chat with them. After half an hour, Conner asked if anyone didn't fancy working for him and Archie; four walked out.

"Well, I think we have our team then," said Conner. "You've all been training together for several weeks. I want you all to write down the name of your manager on one piece of paper and the name of your leader on another. There're pens and paper over there."

A few candidates raised their eyebrows, and Archie noticed there were plenty of excited smiles too.

One wag, Mary Driver aged about twenty-five and who

sounded a little bit posh, spoke up.

"Can I vote for myself, sir?"

"Yes you may, excellent question by the way," smiled Conner.

A few minutes later Conner examined and sorted the pieces of paper into three piles.

"Well, ladies, we have Sergeant Driver unanimously declared to be your leader. The Manager will be Corporal Samms with six votes and Corporal Peebles with four votes will be your Deputy. You have the Government you deserve, make the most of it."

"Archie looked at the smiling faces, Conner had done it again, he had a team, a real team, instantly.

"He asked the three *'electeds'* to stay behind, letting the others go for the weekend, he handed out a list of tasks and a timetable for completion. He explained it carefully, then shook their hands and gave them the weekend off too.

All three stayed late, then came in on Saturday and Sunday too. They wanted to have as much as possible ready for Monday.

Archie provided most ideas for the list and timetable, but he didn't mind in the slightest when Conner presented it more eloquently than he could. He knew he'd be involved closely in the day-to-day intelligence work of the team, that's what he needed.

He needed the intelligence to be tightly focussed and purposeful, not collected and stored so it could gather dust.

Will it win the war?

Will it shorten the war?

Will it make the Americans join in?

Will it kill Germans?

He still wanted to kill something, though.

He'd already set a few priority tasks for the researchers which might prove fruitful, and his capacity for patience was improving.

## Saturday 15<sup>th</sup> June 1940 – Hevlyn Mansions – Victoria – London

The following day, Saturday, the 15<sup>th</sup> of June 1940, Conner was taking Archie back to the Savoy, this time with dinner suits. The suit fitted perfectly, but the high collar of the shirt and the tie, which Conner had bowed for him, was uncomfortable.

"It feels like a dog collar or something. It's choking me, I used to want to be a priest when I was younger. I think I made the right career choice, though," he said. "Can't I just wear dress uniform or something?"

"No, tonight we are not mere soldiers, we are connoisseurs of classical violin. We are having an evening off, and I don't mean just from work, I also include horizontal exercise, I swear you broke that bed you know."

"It had a dodgy leg before I even saw it, and that loose floorboard didn't help."

"You were on top of a charming young lady at the time."

"She was on top if I remember right, but Victoria is most definitely a charming young lady. You know her, don't you?"

"How do you mean?"

"Know, as in you knew her before I met her, as in you knew she'd be at the club that night, and as in you knew she'd leave with me."

"Yes, okay you're right as usual, you don't mind do you?"

"I have never minded anything less in my entire life."

"How did you know?"

"She's a very competent liar, I'm just a little bit better, that's all. She knows things intuitively about me that I hardly know myself. There were just a couple of half things that only you could know, half slipped out."

"And how do you feel about her?" he asked, fishing for an answer rather than asking the question.

"It won't last, it can't, but I've never felt more alive in my life."

"Let us live then, come on, we mustn't be late."

They got a taxi to the Savoy.

*'Mr Jascha Heifetz'* said a small sign outside the lounge that announced that evening's entertainment. A solo violinist accompanied by a pianist. The room was full, a room that Teddy could never have entered, Archie strode in confidently. After a few weeks of talking posh, it became his habitual voice, even with Nipper and Smudger. He managed to stay in character for longer spells, he was still learning, and this evening would be a test.

The music sounded classical, not unpleasant, just not to Archie's taste. He applauded politely and was glad they'd sat at the back of the audience.

One particular piece of music intrigued him, only lasting a couple of minutes, it was poignantly sad and haunting. He just couldn't get it out of his head. At one point, the violinist plucked the strings instead of bowing them, and he'd never heard of that before. The music somehow reminded him of death, the chin rest and the wood of the instrument shone like the wood on his Mauser and jack-knife.

Conner said it was from something called the Threepenny Opera, but Opera held no appeal for Archie, and he dismissed the thought of it.

The room cleared, Archie noticed a tighter group of people remaining on the far side. At least two were plain-clothes policemen, the others were mostly army in civvies, their bearing just stood out a mile. One was 'Tiny' Ironside, William Edmund Ironside, Commander-in-Chief of the Home Forces, Churchill's chosen man. 'Tiny' was six foot four, about 18 stone and had played rugby for Scotland. Another was Anthony Eden, the Secretary of State for War, and beyond them was Winston Churchill.

Churchill was circulating and taking some of the military types to one side, one at a time, shaking hands and nodding, patting them on the shoulder, and probably choking them with his cigar smoke.

Archie watched, fascinated and dumbstruck, after a

couple of minutes with each man, Churchill disengaged from the others and approached Archie.

"You're on now, stay where you are, don't move," Conner said, then he left and Churchill continued towards Archie.

Churchill shook his hand, *Winston Churchill* shook *his* hand.

"Very pleased to meet you, young man, I've heard you were at Calais?"

"Yes, sir, I was lucky, though."

"Nonsense, I've seen the film of you taking out two Panzers, you make your own luck in this life, you're well aware of that, you prove it by being here tonight."

"Just don't ask me to do it again, well not this week, sir."

Churchill laughed. "Oh No, young man we'll be asking much more of you than that, the fighting is the easy part, keep the ideas coming and put them into practice. You'll be sorely tested in the years to come, and you won't get an ounce of credit."

"Why is that, sir?" he asked, intrigued.

"You don't exist, of course, hardly anyone in this room exists, this meeting never took place, and my diary shows that I went to a dinner then a recital."

Archie didn't say anything.

"I am especially pleased to have met you, though," Churchill continued. "The decision not to relieve Calais was mine you know, and mine alone. It helps me somewhat to look you in the eye and say that. It had to be done, and I'll do it again when it's needed. I will confess privately to you, it made me physically sick that night. I heard the bark of the black dog approaching me.

"It was great fortune that those few souls managed to escape, and an act of divine providence that it was you and young Duncan who lived to fight another day. It gave me hope, at a time when it was in short supply."

"May I ask a question, sir?"

"You may, you've earned it, my boy."

"Souls and divine providence? Is there a God? It's just,

198

in Calais there was no evidence of him, plenty of the other chap's work, no sign of any God at all. I grew up believing in one, but I just can't anymore."

"That's a big question which needs a big answer. I have a few moments, and you deserve your answer.

"There is no God, never has been, although there may be, one day, should perverted science allow it. Politicians and Kings have known that, in every age and culture, certainly from the Greeks and Romans onwards. Admitting such an inconvenient truth to the populace you ask to vote or fight for you is the insurmountable issue, no matter what the age.

"Therefore, whilst I have become, with age and also maturity, certain of God's absence, it does no harm to ensure that should he indeed exist, that he is, at the very least, on my side. The act needs to be performed for appearance sake if naught else.

"Have you nothing to say?" he added when Archie remained silent.

"It's the right answer, sir, and I'm grateful for your honesty with me."

"Of course, you realise if you repeat what I have said I will most certainly have you shot."

Archie smiled, and Churchill laughed slapping him on the shoulder.

"I must be going, there is much to do and so little time, I think we shall meet again. There is a darkness in you, young man, I can see it in your eyes, we'll need more darkness before these deeds are done. I shall make use of it as I shall make use of you. I do not apologise for that, but I will offer the best advice I can. A famous American once said, 'Black care never sits behind a rider whose pace is fast enough."

"Theodore Roosevelt."

"Yes, well read, young man, and do you know what he meant."

"I do now, sir."

"Good, keep busy then and know this too. I can also see

the smallest spark of light in you; you do not see it yet. Do try to survive, the deeds will not take forever, although it may seem so to a young man. When this is done, we shall still need excellent liars."

There was a pause, as long as the deepest inhalation of cigar the great man could take, followed by an equally long exhalation, considerately taken to one side of Archie.

None of the carefully prepared ripostes from imagined conversations would do in reality; so all Archie did was ask one final question.

"And that small spark, sir?"

"You do not lie to yourself, the rarest of qualities in the best of liars, use that, Lieutenant Travers, use that to survive, we both shall."

Churchill left to join his entourage and prepared to leave. Archie looked up, everyone was watching him.

Conner came back to him.

"Well, what did he say?"

"Nothing and everything, I'm not sure."

"You've just spent ten minutes talking to the most eloquent man ever to exist in the English-speaking world, and you're not sure what he said? The whole room was transfixed by those ten minutes. You made him laugh and nod, you're a lowly Lieutenant of reputedly low birth and the leader of the free world spoke to *you* instead of them!"

"He said I had a darkness in me. Did you tell him that?"

"I didn't, of course, I didn't. I have spoken to him briefly, a couple of times, with Bracken just after I got back from Calais. You must just be unusually dark today, we'll have to work on that, Archie old boy."

"People just keep telling me that."

*

Three days later a large envelope arrived at Bletchley Park for Archie.

The outer envelope contained a smaller unsealed one, which held a perfect golden vellum sheet of parchment with a printed heading and footnote, showing it came from 10 Downing Street.

It read:-

*'What the bearer of this note does, he does in my name. Winston Leonard Spencer-Churchill. First Lord of the Treasury, Prime Minister of the United Kingdom and Northern Ireland.'*

A smaller note read, *'Use it wisely'*.

*

**Thursday 20 June 1940 - 0136 am - North West France**

The Westland Lysander Mark 3 light aircraft flew low over fields in Northern France. The two passengers didn't speak during the journey, they were under orders not to. Cramped, as they were in a space meant for one man, neither woman knew who the other was. After they had landed, they would never meet again. If they didn't know, they couldn't tell.

Rebecca knew they'd left RAF Tangmere in West Sussex earlier. No one had told her that, she'd worked it out herself, the journey time and direction told her they'd just flown over St. Malo and were coming down to land.

She had been Rebecca Rochford, from Hertford, twenty-four years old, she looked younger and would easily pass for eighteen or twenty. Her skin was flawless, she'd never smoked or drank, ever. She was five foot two and slim, petite even. She was a well-co-ordinated, passable athlete and performed well in most physical exercises. She was stronger, physically and mentally, than she looked, she had hidden depth and knew it. Somehow, whenever she needed a particular quality, she found enough of it to deal with whatever arose.

She had no idea if she was attractive to men or not, usually wearing little or no make-up and plain, even tomboyish, clothes most of the time.

The Directorate of Military Intelligence had recruited her while she was studying Physics and Astronomy at St. Hilda's College, Oxford, where she'd made precisely not one friend.

She knew the rougher side of life of course. She'd seen competitive behaviour and bullying at school. Drinking and

201

sex at college, boys with girls, girls and girls, boys and boys. She'd seen swearing, stealing and plenty of bullying during her training and as part of life in the Military. It just didn't affect her, she was never personally involved in any of it; it went into boxes to stay there or until needed. She'd never sworn or hit anyone for real, although the physical training for ExCo Number 1 had taken her necessarily close to it.

She was Middle English by any definition, and she hadn't been rich, her father had been a French teacher and her mother, French. She'd simply travelled through life with nothing especially good or bad happening to her. She expected to go to France, look at military targets, remember them and come back.

She'd made no friends in the DMI either, and they'd selected her for special duties immediately. They had warned her in great detail of what lay ahead, she just didn't regard it as a warning, just more information; she said yes. In France, the last burden she needed was anyone or anything waiting for her in England.

It was her mind that made her stand out, she had an astonishing memory and eye for detail, not a photographic memory. Experts had tested her and said it resembled *'eidetic memory'* or *'hyperthymesia,'* she knew it was neither, it was just her.

She had an exceptional memory for detail, she couldn't look at a page of text and remember it after only a few seconds glance. She performed no circus tricks. What she could do was look at any scene for several seconds and take a detailed mental picture. She made associations in her mind which matched those pictures and remembered them for a long time, months rather than years. She achieved this by compartmentalising her mind, she had boxes in her brain, she could put subjects into boxes and recall them exactly later, usually only once, though. She could also put them in boxes to forget them; that was useful too.

Today, she wasn't Rebecca Rochford of Experimental

Company Number 1; she was Maria Secondigny; Rebecca was in a box.

The plane landed effortlessly at the end of a short grass runway or a flat field, she couldn't tell. Two cars were waiting, they left the Lysander with just the small essential luggage they had.

"Rennes," said the first driver, she nodded, got in the first car and it drove off. They didn't go to Rennes, they went straight to St. Nazaire, where the driver, who never spoke, dropped her behind the railway station. Northern and Western France were in complete chaos, and she was there to take advantage of that chaos. The last British troops had left two days ago and some Polish the day before, timed correctly, she'd be there before the Germans arrived and settled in.

One hour after she arrived, she approached a taxi-driver who took her to a large hotel on the seafront, dropping her off with her suitcase outside the main entrance. She went into the hotel, Le Gourguillon, introducing herself as Maria Secondigny, she was expected and welcomed as the new waitress who was to start work there the next day. Her French was flawless, she'd been born there and was thoroughly familiar with the area having spent holidays there as a child. Maria had been born in Toulouse, at least according to the genuinely issued, but false papers she held. The organisation she belonged to, didn't officially exist yet, they'd planned her cover for six months, and it was flawless.

Only one person in St. Nazaire would know she wasn't Maria, even they didn't know her true identity. She didn't know who her contact was, she had to wait and watch. She had equipment near St. Nazaire that she, and only she, could find and use effectively. For the moment, she was a French waitress, although fluent in German, that was another secret she'd keep.

Her room was in the attic and tiny, so she didn't have to share, and she'd welcome the privacy. There was barely room to stand up. However, the small skylight gave a view of the docks and port entrances. She had to wait, listen, watch, and be patient.

*

## June 1940 – Bletchley Park

Archie and Conner had planned to spend at least a month at Bletchley Park. However, when they knew the specialist training for the team was scheduled to start on the 1st of July, Conner suggested Archie attend, and he agreed.

"We can't ask the men to do something we can't do ourselves or one of us at least," he said.

The training lasted eight weeks, it was the hardest exercise Archie had ever done. He'd learned new skills he intended to use and also had ideas for improving the training. He was the best shot in the group, although he only used the Mauser and the fresh ammunition Billy had obtained for him. He wasn't the best in any other discipline, but he'd held his own and knew he'd done well enough to earn the men's respect.

He'd spent time with Spud and Smudger at the beginning of the course, then realised he was stepping on their toes with the lads. He gradually drew back from the men, giving them the space they needed to be ordinary enlisted men. He just didn't belong with them any longer, he could live with that although he felt a pang of guilt. Archie Travers had been chosen by a road, and there was no turning him from his destination.

Spencer Ward, the RAMC Corporal from the Gulzar, had joined the training halfway through. He'd manfully tried everything and wasn't great, but he was brave and had stamina. He'd save lives instead of taking them, though, which was what they needed. The stronger lads took the mickey a little, they gave him the nickname 'Hospital', he didn't mind.

Archie was glad to see Tarrian and shake his hand and exceptionally happy to see Nipper. Despite his actual age, he really did have nowhere better to go and no real family now, except the men around him. Spud and Smudger had chosen well, and he hoped he didn't kill too many of them too soon. He was certain he'd have to kill some of them.

At the end of the training, he had the right number of killers, with the right number of ways to kill, available to him. He could use that, and he needed to test that capacity sooner rather than later.

*

## Summer 1940 – England

The War progressed as he'd expected; in June, July and August, the Battle of Britain was in full flow.

Archie had some inside knowledge the public didn't, he could tell the RAF were coping effectively with the attacks. He knew the Germans couldn't get air superiority, operating from the distance they had to cover. Luftwaffe fighters could only fly over a target in England for a few minutes before their fuel would run low, we could be above home ground for two hours. Even if they did by some miracle get air superiority, a fleet of barges would be no match for the world's biggest Navy. That thin strip of water would defeat Hitler just as it had dumbfounded the Romans, the Spanish, and the French. It occurred to Archie that the Vikings had been more successful invaders, a brutal smash-and-grab robbery was a workable plan. He wondered where he might get a couple of Vikings?

The training ended on Friday the 23rd of August as planned, and Archie gave most of the men a week's leave. He still itched to do something concrete and the time was ripe.

"It would be a pity to acquire skills and not practice them," he told Conner when he met him at Victoria Station on Friday evening.

"I think I may well have found the right place and time," Conner said.

They headed for the East End.

## Chapter 16

### Friday 24<sup>th</sup> August 1940 – The East End of London

Late on Friday night, Conner drove Archie to the East End of London, the blackout made it difficult until your eyes became used to the darkness. The thin strips of light from the blackout-compliant headlights should ensure they didn't run over any pedestrians, there were few people on the streets so late in the night, anyway. The further east they went the more bomb damage they saw, all legitimate targets, of course.

They drove past the Tower of London and St. Katherine's Docks, which brought back a painful and unwelcome memory for Archie. He needed to rid his mind of that shameful, embarrassing act. He needed to take it from his head and throw it away.

Conner drove them to the location in East Ham he'd scouted a few weeks before, a terrace of recently emptied houses, deserted by their occupants, near an empty warehouse. They had been earmarked for demolition, making way for better and more modern dock capacity. They were unsafe for human habitation anyway. The paperwork regarding that status had recently disappeared.

They met with Nipper, Smudger, Spud and his old schoolmate Begley, who had driven there in two separate trucks. They unloaded their heavy cargo into the house in pitch darkness while Conner kept watch and Archie worked with Begley and a torchlight.

Begley had, unsurprisingly, been the best man with explosives during training. He'd shown the trainers a few tricks and stolen quantities of the best stuff while he was there. Nipper had helped him. When he kept his mouth shut for long enough, he could almost disappear.

Begley was, by appearance, stark-raving mad. As soon as he first looked at you with his overlarge bulbous eyes that never blinked and then smiled at you showing his well-gapped teeth, you knew he had to be mad. He looked like a grey frog wearing someone else's false teeth, no wonder he'd been rejected for service almost on sight. The criminal record wouldn't have helped, but all trace of that had also mysteriously disappeared a few weeks ago, Conner was a thorough man.

Begley was only truly at peace when handling explosives, explosive devices or anything dangerous; absurdly, it calmed him down. As long as there was a war on, Begley was extremely useful, and fortunately, he also did whatever Spud asked him to. Spud had watched his back at school.

They emptied the trucks, Begley did his work, Archie watched him then they all went home and waited.

The following day the Luftwaffe air raids Conner's intelligence intercepts predicted, had taken place, when and where he'd expected them. There had been damage across the Greater London area, mostly from stray or poorly aimed bombs. Casualties were few, and no more than usual over the previous weeks. One particular set of houses, however, had suffered extreme damage. Filming would later show the civilian bodies, including two young children, being removed from the wrecked houses. The film was shown to an outraged nation, and crucially to Churchill's indecisive Coalition Cabinet.

No one could possibly suspect those small shattered bodies had been dead and frozen for weeks, who would believe such a tall tale?

There were some graves in North London where the coffins were empty, apart from the carefully measured lead weights Conner had placed there.

On the night of Sunday 25th of August 1940, over 70 Armstrong Whitworth Whitleys, Handley Page Hampdens and Vickers Wellingtons of the Royal Air Force bombed Berlin in retaliation for those civilian casualties.

The gloves were fully off in the bombing war, time would tell who had the bigger fists in the illegal bare-knuckle contest to follow.

Guderian had said *'Man schlägt jemanden mit der Faust*

*und nicht mit gespreizten Fingern.'* 'You hit somebody with your fist and not with your fingers spread.'

He was right, of course, however, Granny Schicklgruber was now about to experience it first-hand.

Anything that slows them down, anything.

*

## Friday 13<sup>th</sup> September 1940 – St. Nazaire

Maria Secondigny had known something was wrong, soon after her arrival. She had one liaison point, and they should have made personal contact within two weeks. She concluded her contact had been, at the least, compromised and unable to safely make contact. More likely they were captured and dead, yet hadn't betrayed her directly or she'd already be dead. She certainly wasn't under observation. Generally, people paid her no attention, so she'd notice even the slightest.

Maria Secondigny had therefore stayed, waited, listened, watched and methodically remembered for nearly three months. The summer was warm and pleasant, the hotel was busy, with German officers. They were boorish and disrespectful, but Maria was polite and servile, so she could listen to their unguarded and overconfident conversations. She also had to go outside to complete her mission, making sure she kept to busy streets in the daytime and never after dark.

Her first decision had been made for her, she'd continue and finish her observations, then leave. The next decision, how long to stay, wasn't complicated. She hadn't been betrayed. Therefore, all logic dictated she wouldn't be. The Analysts in DMI had calculated that six weeks was the optimum time to remain, increasing the information gained while lowering the risk of capture, the perfect balance of the two. Six weeks wouldn't take her to the next full moon, though, eight weeks would, but that might not be long enough to do all the work she could. She saw things which wouldn't be visible from the air or sea. Six weeks might be the ideal time, but she was twice as competent as the other females she'd encountered in

## Friday 13th September 1940 – St. Nazaire

training. She decided, based on pure cold logic, that she'd stay for twelve weeks.

Towards the end of her time there she chose to expand her observations. It was a calculated decision, she felt no risk of discovery, so she took it readily. She began to take longer walks along the seafront, she took the ferry across the river and walked along the coast. She memorised the places of interest, mostly gun emplacements and also suitable sites for more. That side of the coast also gave an excellent view of the U-Boat pens under construction and the enormous dry dock.

She arranged to borrow a bike and took to riding around town, then the coast a little, then the country a little. Then, finally, when it seemed just normal she intended to go for a longer ride north to the Petite Ile Jaquet. She knew it well, knew exactly where the old den was. She'd played there as a child during summer holidays, among the lines of centuries-old waterways that crisscrossed the empty land north of St. Nazaire.

On what would be her last walk, Maria Secondigny walked calmly back to the hotel. She'd enjoyed the view of the sea and memorised the outlines of the German Navy Vessels she'd seen. She kept her gaze to the pavement as she walked, not too fast or slow. She wore no make-up, everyday clothes, loose trousers, a plain headscarf and tightly double knotted laced stout boots. It was ten to five, and she'd just reach her work on time.

"Where are you going lovely?" said a German soldier.

Remembering she could speak no German, she walked on ignoring him, keeping her eyes to the ground.

"I asked you a question! Woman!" he shouted now, "papers, show me your papers, papier."

She had to show him her papers now, she stopped, kept her gaze downwards and showed him her papers. She became aware of the menacing presence of another German soldier behind her and the absence of bystanders. Two people crossed the road to avoid the scene, another man, walking towards her, turned around and walked the other way. She was alone.

"Your papers are in order, but I can't see your face, you have to look at me, show me your face, woman. Visage!"

She had to raise her face.

"A pretty little face," he said, giving a quick nod to the man behind her. He grabbed her shoulders tightly, spinning her off her feet and round into the alleyway to her left.

She knew what they wanted, she just didn't understand why. With her training and practiced strength, she could overpower one of them and maybe two with the element of surprise. However, showing that skilled training here would betray her fatally.

She wouldn't let herself be raped, would she? Her first time couldn't be rape surely? She had to resist, just the right degree, enough, hope for the best and see what she could make happen. The second soldier held her in an iron grip and braced himself against a wall, in a backyard, unseen from the main road.

The first soldier took his helmet off.

"Yes, I know you, you work in the Gourguillion, where all the officers go. I bet you let the officers fuck you, don't you, you French bitch. I bet you let them fuck you up the arse, don't you?"

He leant towards her, pulled her jacket open, grasping her breasts through her blouse. He undid the blouse clumsily and pulled down her bra to expose her breasts, squeezing them roughly and pressing the nipples hard between his thumb and finger.

"Oh yes, I bet you like it up the shithole, don't you, bitch!"

"No! No! Please, I'm a virgin, please, no!" she made herself cry in French, it might help.

He reached down to undo the tight belt from her trousers, and undid the top of her waistband, trying to pull them down. She kept moving her legs, writhing forcefully. He couldn't get the trousers off over the boots, and the tight knots in the laces dumbfounded his clumsy hands.

"Let me take them off, it will be better for you," he said, slapping her face, hard.

"No! No! Please, no!

"Hurry up, Gottlieb," said the second one.

"Put the bitch on her knees then," he insisted, and the other pulled her down to her knees, skinning them on the damp stone floor of the yard.

Gottlieb pulled out his stiff cock, it did look small even to her inexperienced eye, she didn't laugh, although she wanted to. The other German grabbed the front of her throat and squeezed roughly upwards to her chin, forcing her mouth open while grasping one breast tightly with his other hand.

Gottlieb held a knife to her eyes threateningly. He grabbed the back of her head with a handful of hair and fucked her mouth, roughly, choking her. The knife and the choking prevented her from biting his cock, he managed five thrusts before he came, keeping his cock fully in her mouth, while he drained his balls into her throat. He withdrew, she spat and retched, gagging tears flowing down her face.

The second German laughed.

"My turn," he said, and the two rapists exchanged places.

The second German did the same, his cock was bigger, and he lasted longer, making her vomit on his trousers and boots. His semen ran into her throat as he held the final thrust as far inside her as he could manage, before pulling it out. He slapped her face for fouling his clean boots, then took her headscarf which had fallen off and used it to wipe them clean. Then he stuffed it in her mouth and spat in her face, wiping his hands clean on her hair and shoulders. Gottlieb still had his cock in his hand, watching as she slumped forward, vomiting again and crying, on her knees. He emptied his bladder onto her downturned head, spat on her and they left, slapping each other on the back.

"Next time, we'll fuck you in the arse, French bitch. You'll split her hole next time, Gerolf, you lucky bastard," said Gottlieb.

Maria vomited again then stood up, pulling her knickers and trousers back into place and did the same with her bra and blouse. She found a puddle, a depression in the solid concrete, containing fresh rain from that afternoon. She washed her mouth out in the puddle, rinsed the urine and vomit from her hair and wiped the worst of it from her clothing.

She became aware of a lace curtain moving in a window opposite her, it was a grey-haired old lady watching, she must have seen everything from her window. Maria looked up, the old woman held her gaze for one second, let the curtain fall back into place and turned away from her window.

Maria rinsed the headscarf in the water and wrung it out, replacing it on her head, composed herself and walked to the hotel. She'd be late for work.

*

## Friday 13th September 1940 – Hevlyn Mansions – London

It was fifteen minutes to three in the afternoon in Hevlyn Mansions. Archie was angry, someone had taken one of his ideas for obtaining German coding equipment and devised their own plan, and it had received initial approval. He was angry because he had the idea first and wanted to see it through first. Secondly, he was pleased the plan was too risky to work, there were far too many uncontrollable factors. Thirdly, the proposal was from some flash chancer called Fleming, who wanted to be a famous hero after the war. Worse than that, the plan might just work by some freak chance, and he was jealous in advance. *'Operation Ruthless'*, indeed, any idiot knew you gave a plan as dull a name as possible, unless of course, you were just a flash chancer looking to be flash.

He based his much more practical plan on personal experience of combat. It was safer and needed a measure of patience so *'Ruthless'* might work before his plan had a chance. He couldn't complain, though, he didn't exist, and he wasn't doing this to be famous, anyway. He wanted his worth to come from inside him, not the flattery of knaves.

He hadn't seen Victoria for a while, about four weeks, and he didn't think he would see her again, the relationship had run its course. It was glorious and life affirming, it was a business arrangement, although the sex had been real, some things you just couldn't fake. Conner explained that to him when he'd asked for details.

He had experienced other liaisons, since and during Victoria, usually starting at the club, and other times elsewhere. His inhibitions had disappeared at possibly the best time in the 20th Century. In London in 1940, young people were having as much fun as they could, while they could. A young, handsome officer with money and his own flat to return to, had no difficulty finding short-term partners. He also had considerable catching up to do, so he did, keen to cram in as much experience as he could manage, with as little complication as possible.

He liked women, nearly all of them in fact, tall, short, blonde, brunette, single, married, slim or curvy. He had a distinct preference for petite and had found nothing as desirable as Victoria, but he had fun searching. Regrettably, there had been no meeting of minds, no deep connection, and nothing lasted more than a few encounters.

He was better at sex now, he thought proudly, and a quick learner. He was becoming a good teacher too, and he'd been reliably and consistently told he was well-endowed, perfectly sized in fact. He also knew what women talked about when discussing men. Women liked sex as much as men, and that was just fine by him.

Should he feel that proud, was that just arrogance? He considered that thought and decided if he were rubbish at sex and didn't care, that would be shameful. So surely he was allowed to be proud of the opposite, based on reliable witnesses, obviously.

Yes, I've spent enough time agonising over my flaws, I'll be proud of the better points.

Tonight was different, though, he'd arranged to see Grace. He'd take her for a meal at a small, not too posh restaurant and treat her like a lady, instead of a maid. He'd enjoy that, and he'd see what would happen.

At five to three, he stood up to start getting ready. Then suddenly, he sensed the steaming smell of fresh piss rising from Corp's body as he robbed it, and tasted it in his mouth. He went to the kitchen sink and washed his mouth out, spitting furiously, gagging, and almost vomiting. The kitchen sink became a ditch in Calais, only this time he *had* killed Mike, Spotter, and Corp. He couldn't recall whether he'd really done it or not, had he just invented his story? To cover his real guilt?

No, he was certain he hadn't killed them, he would have, though, and what was the difference?

He stopped spitting, and the smell and taste were gone, but there was still something wrong. He splashed more water on his face, yes, something was wrong, and he knew he needed to fix it. No, that wasn't it. There was a wrong, and he needed to right it.

He'd do some good to balance the bad, that would work, wouldn't it?

Archie collected Grace from her terraced house in North London and took her to the restaurant he had in mind. They had a nice time, she'd watched enough rich people eat to know how to do so herself. They talked and got on well, it was nice. After the meal, he drove her home and walked her to her front door, before ten o'clock, as she'd asked.

"Would you like to go to the cinema next week?" he asked.

"Yes that would be lovely," she answered.

He kissed her on the forehead and squeezed her hand, intending no more than that, she stretched up towards him and gave him the slightest peck on the lips.

"I told my dad you'd be a perfect gentleman, he wasn't so sure and said you'd better be."

"Sorry, your dad knows me?"

"Billy's my dad you silly man, I thought you knew, it never occurred to me to mention it. You didn't ask me out to talk about my dad did you?"

"No."

"Telephone me about the cinema, next Friday would be best for me, it's my day off."

"Yes definitely."

*

### Saturday 14ᵗʰ September 1940 - London

The following day, Saturday, Archie asked Conner if he minded him going to Bletchley Park for the weekend, he had some thinking to do and needed no distractions. Conner readily agreed, so Archie packed what he needed and drove there, thinking and reflecting carefully on the journey.

He'd wasted a little too much time recently. He needed to keep moving, he needed to act, to stay sharp.

When Archie left on Saturday morning, Conner made one brief phone call and waited. Victoria arrived at two in the afternoon and stayed until two on Sunday afternoon. She didn't talk about Archie, Conner did, she gave him the advice and the comfort he needed. She was all things to all men, and she knew Conner well. When she was gone, Conner felt alone and wondered for the first time if he knew Victoria at all.

As she left his apartment and hailed a taxi, she wondered if Conner would ever get what he really wanted.

On reaching Building Thirteen on Saturday afternoon, Archie wasn't surprised to see Driver there, still working. He insisted she should go home for the rest of the weekend. He told her there was no point being so tired you made mistakes and made sure she knew how pleased he and Conner were with her.

He sat in their room. The room Conner and Archie had set aside for private talks, it had no windows, just a light, one desk and two chairs, no pens, no paper, and no evidence.

He made a mug of tea in the kitchen, drank it then

stared into space for two hours. He left the room and looked in the filing cabinets, finding what he was looking for. He read, then replaced the files in the drawers, he could remember what he needed to.

He went out to his car, collected some of his luggage and lay down on the rough canvas camp bed he'd brought with him, and slept in the windowless room. He slept easily enough, he still had remnants of that skill. He woke early, at five o'clock, washed in the small kitchen and, unable to sleep more, put on his running gear and went for a long run. He was hungry and thirsty, but doing without would do him no harm. He hadn't wanted for anything since he got back from France and he needed to remember that feeling of want, he needed that frame of mind again.

He ran around the grounds on a circular route, meaning to go at a steady pace until he could go no further. He meant to punish himself.

After ninety minutes, he stopped, exhausted and sat on a bench under a tree on the grass in front of the Mansion. To his surprise, another chap in running gear, sweaty and breathing heavily sat next to him and offered him some water.

"Thank you," Archie said.

"You're Travers aren't you?"

"Yes, Archie," he said, "and you are?"

"Turing, Alan, a boffin you'd call me, I hear you asked for all atheists in your hut, caused a bit of a stir, everyone thinks the worst of you and Captain Duncan now. Trained killers looking for targets. Funniest thing; we're not allowed to discuss work at all, but everyone still likes a bit of scandal to gossip about instead."

"Conner told me about you, Alan, I'm not allowed to know what you do or how you do it. He'd read your paper on the thinking machine. A mind made of metal, fuses, and little light bulbs. He tried to explain it to me, however, beyond seeing some science fiction, HG Wells, metal human from the Planet X, I'm afraid it's not the way my mind works."

"That's an excellent analogy, you're just a hundred years early."

"A hundred years?"

"Fifty perhaps, you need a good war to provide the environment where science can flourish, not too big a war of course, or we all kill each other."

"Okay, I was sort of hoping for some hand-held superweapon and a bulletproof suit of armour in one of these buildings."

"Heisenberg is who you need by the way."

"Sorry?"

"He's not a Nazi, he's the one you'll turn to our side or stop altogether."

"Are you certain?"

"Yes, I don't say anything unless I'm certain."

"I'll bear that in mind then, thank you, Alan."

"You were in Calais weren't you?" Alan asked hesitantly.

"Yes."

"May I ask a question?"

"You've earned it."

"You've killed?"

"Yes."

"How many?"

"Including or excluding fellow members of the BEF?"

"Excluding."

"I lost count."

"No, I just need to know roughly?"

"About forty."

"What did it feel like?"

Archie thought for a while, casting his mind back to the utter disregard he had for Mike, Spotter, and Corp.

"It felt like I was an animal... killing other animals. Survival of the fittest, more Darwin than Deity inspired. If there was any God left in me, then Calais flushed it out. If there is one, I'm definitely going to Hell now, it'll be warm, and I'll know people."

"I'll probably see you there, then. God doesn't like

people like me."

"Well, he can fuck right off then."

"Yes, he can, can't he?"

"You want to know if I enjoyed it, but you're too polite to ask, so I'll tell you. I honestly don't know. I certainly enjoyed being alive when it was over."

Just then, Archie saw Gubbins come out of the Mansion and walk towards them.

"Travers, the very man, come inside, I may have a small job just for you," he said waving to him.

Archie got up to leave, then turned round to Turing.

"Listen, if you ever need a corner cutting, you know where I am. Only those people with no imagination stick to the rules, and we can't win by sticking to the rules. I found that out in Calais too."

Alan Turing nodded and smiled.

Archie went inside with Gubbins.

"Listen, old boy, can you stay around for a couple of days, you could be the ideal man for something, damn lucky you're here, will you help?"

"Yes, sir, whatever it is," he replied, although it did spoil some of his plans, Gubbins wasn't a man to say no to. He knew now he was one of the Heads of Special Operations Executive, had won the Military Cross in the Great War; and he was asking Archie Travers politely if he'd help him!

He'd do it for nothing, and if a man of Gubbins calibre ended up owing Archie a favour, it would be a significant achievement.

*

Obliged to stay at Bletchley Park for a few days, Archie used the time to review the effectiveness of their small team. He managed a few more short conversations with Alan although he didn't broach the subject of code-breaking, Gubbins had been clear on that, yet forgiving in other ways.

They'd identified the use of sophisticated Luftwaffe bomber guidance systems from one short message that was just a set of numbers.

They were cross-matching related messages which had links but had been transmitted from and to different locations, weeks apart.

There were other similar successes, and he felt a sense of great satisfaction that a few people in a small team were punching above their weight, had saved lives and taken them as well.

Most of all, he felt they were sorting the gold from the dross of intelligence and occasionally making some gold from dross. Intelligence Alchemy, he called it. The team were good people, worth taking risks for, worth looking after, worth standing next to in a tight spot, and he felt a little better.

They'd compiled all available intelligence on Nazi Special Weapons Programmes and dug into every possible antecedence of the principal characters, in particular, any links to the Allies. More work was required there, and he needed a plan, his best, a long-term one. He needed Conner for that, and he also knew they needed more expertise than they jointly had, he needed another boffin.

*

## Monday 16th September 1940 – Bletchley Park

After another early morning run with Alan, he made everyone's tea that Monday morning and no one questioned where on earth he'd bought the biscuits and the one pound tin of Cadbury's Roses. Billy Perry, of course.

At midday, he reported to Gubbins again, he definitely needed Archie.

## Chapter 17

### Friday 13<sup>th</sup> September 1940 – St. Nazaire

Maria Secondigny changed her clothes in her room, everything had changed forever.

She had to think and plan, but she also had to work that evening. It was midnight before she sat alone in her room, her mask hadn't slipped, not for one second.

She planned carefully and in detail.

*Maria waited a week, she'd finished her work for the evening, she washed, put on makeup, a skirt and blouse, bare legs and heels. She walked boldly along the seafront near the same spot as the previous week. She'd seen Gottlieb before, from a distance, patrolling this area. She saw him again and walked towards him brazenly. He saw her and stopped, she continued walking towards him, then stood right in front of him. She looked apprehensive, just not in the way Gottlieb thought.*

*"You want more?" he said.*

*She walked into the alley, and he followed her, looking over his shoulder.*

*He pushed her roughly against the wall and kissed her. His tongue probing inside her mouth, she kissed him back, his hands lifted her skirt and pulled at her knickers, ripping them off, she reached for his crotch and undid his trousers. He dropped them to his ankles, she stroked his cock with her left hand.*

*"Oh yes, I'm going to fuck your shit hole this time you bitch," he said then stuck his tongue deeper into her mouth.*

*She bit his tongue hard and deep at the same instant as the small sharp kitchen knife severed his carotid artery. He couldn't talk or scream, he could only splutter and choke as his life bled out of him.*

*She stopped biting his tongue, his blood now in her mouth and let him fall to the ground. She looked at him, spat on him, returning his blood to where it belonged and reached down, severed his cock and stuffed it into his bloody*

220

*mouth. She washed her hands in the puddle, rinsed her mouth out and...* woke up.

A tempting plan, but it won't work, she thought, Gerolf knows where I live and work, they'll know who did it. Unless I can get both at once, unlikely and even if I did, they'd shoot ten peasants for each dead German, they'd done worse in Poland. They'd know soon she wasn't going to dare to report them, then they'd come back, and it would be worse.

*'I will not be subordinate to any man. I will be no man's slave.'*

No, she had to leave, and it would have to be the next day, Saturday the 14th September 1940.

Maria alone knew where the emergency radio was buried with weapons and other essentials.

She got up early, 0530, dressed and quietly took the bike from the yard then rode north-west. As ever, she wore her ordinary clothes, blouse, warm jacket, hard-wearing trousers and her usual stout walking shoes. A small parcel in the basket of the bike held sandwiches, a drink, an apple and a small sharp knife for the apple.

The bicycle ride into the country north of St. Nazaire would have been pleasant in other circumstances. Several miles into scrub and marshland was a flat and comfortable ride. She cycled past the area of the den three times before she stopped to check her tyres, there was nothing and no one around, she was 100% certain of that. She pulled her bike into the trees and along a small trail hidden from the road, barely wide enough for her to push the bike.

She found the den, just off the path, overgrown now, but after pushing through some brush, the flat dry outline of the den was still there.

She found the first stash straight away, a thin layer of earth covering a plank of wood under which she knew was a radio. It had been left there by British Military Intelligence, among the retreating Allies, months before. She knew what was there, it had been left there specifically for her, in a hiding place of her choosing.

Okay, she told herself, think, think, what should it look like, what should it feel like, the earth didn't look recently disturbed, some grass was sprouting on top of it. There were no footprints, no flat grass or broken twigs, touch nothing until you're sure. Nothing was wrong, nothing was wrong, no, wait, wait and listen. She could hear nothing, don't touch it, come back next week, be patient. Something must be wrong, it's been three months, it's now or never, do something.

She left the earth and plank as it was, then went further into the trees to the bank of the nearest waterway crisscrossing the land.

She sat on the bank and listened and looked, hearing nothing. The first stash was just the spare radio equipment. Okay, the second stash first then, she decided and reached into the water, found the thick rope, pulling it towards her, making sure there was no splash. The sealed, wet and muddy package came slowly to the surface. She checked the knot in the rope, yes, she'd tied that knot herself in England. She opened the bag and the seals, the container was, as designed, completely waterproof. She took the rucksack with the second smaller radio transmitter and placed it carefully to one side. She checked the pistol and put it next to the rucksack. She ignored the Sten gun and looked at the knife she now held. She gripped it firmly by the leather bound handle with her right hand, much bigger than the apple knife, much better for her purpose. She thought of Gottlieb. Her contact had betrayed her somehow, she knew that. She could only guess how little time she had left.

She heard a rifle click twice behind her.

She put on her best, sweetest smile and turned around. The German started to return her smile, but never achieved it. In one flowing movement, she pushed his rifle to the left with her left hand while her right hand thrust the knife upwards into his ribcage. As in her training, she pushed and twisted the blade deeper. His rifle did fire, missing wildly, then he still punched, scratched, bit, kicked and kneed her as she tried to smother, choke, and stab him all at once.

Her knife was long, razor sharp and needle pointed, almost a short sword in her small hands, and it was the difference in her favour. That, and the fact that when a man first sees a woman, his first thought is whether he wants to fuck her or not. That thought cost this German his life, she knew her smile had cost him his life. The knowledge that he was only about 18 years old was only just registering in her mind as she washed his blood from her hands and her knife. She didn't care about the blood, she only cared if her trigger finger was slippery. She collected the rest of her equipment and ran north as fast as she could, knowing the air would dry the water, she needed to be as far north as possible by nightfall. She could slow down later, not yet, not until she heard birdsong.

The absence of birdsong by the den was the clue she'd missed, she was lucky and still angry with herself. Someone had already disturbed the birds, the German.

They must have found the first radio and kept it under surveillance. She must have been betrayed but why only one guard? Maybe they'd dropped their surveillance level when she'd stayed twelve weeks instead of six? She'd never know, it didn't matter, running mattered, nothing else. Someone must have heard that gunshot.

She clicked one of her teeth with her tongue to check it was still firmly in place and the poison capsule still safely inside. She ignored the blood in her mouth, the scratches on her face, and the black eye she knew was coming. She wished he hadn't kneed her in the groin, though, that hurt the most, the pig.

Maria slowed to a steady pace on narrow paths between the waterways. She knew the area well, so she was aware there were no roads here, only narrow footpaths, no vehicle could chase her. If she kept up a steady pace, then nothing should catch her, that radio had better work first time, though.

She waited until night, at precisely 2100, she cranked

the radio's battery into life and turned it on, it sounded okay, the lights and noise were normal. She tapped her personal identification code and her emergency message, it took less than thirty seconds to send, reducing the time in which any listener could detect the signal. She knew the Germans would have at least two radio detector vans, to get a cross-referenced signal to pinpoint the origin of any radio transmission. They wouldn't understand the message, but they would know it was an agent.

Typical radio protocol and encrypting messages used up a dangerous amount of time. The emergency pickup signal took less time, but she still had to wait for a reply. She waited a full ten minutes, and the positive response came, *'Dinner is not ready yet,'* which meant *'chosen spot chosen time.'*

The timing of her radio signal on the night before the full moon was pre-planned, her idea and she'd devised the one-off code she'd use.

She packed up everything and set off, it wasn't possible to detect and trace the direction of such a short message in such a short space of time. Although no British expertise could have, the Germans were extremely efficient and had plenty of practice in Poland and Czechoslovakia so she couldn't afford to take chances. The radio was cumbersome and slowed her progress, she shouldn't need it again, but without it, she had just one chance of rescue. With it, she had another quarter of a chance, ridiculously poor odds, but she'd been taught to maximise every possible advantage.

She resumed her running at a slow jogging pace. Her eyes adjusted to the dark, there was moonlight and only light cloud. She could keep up a steady pace and not take huge risks with her footing.

She slowed down to a walk and continued until nearly midnight when she reached the channel of the Neuve waterway, running south-west to north-east and then turned south. She was lucky, she found the small waterlogged area easily and waded across it. It was waist deep in places, then shallower as she came to the small island she remembered. It was fifty feet across, and she found the dry middle, huddling into as small a space as she could, in the dense foliage.

She was soaking wet from the waist downwards and took off her boots, socks and trousers, wringing them out now in the hope they'd be drier in the morning. She checked her groin, sore and tender to the touch in the most vulnerable of places. If she saw another German, he was getting a full Sten clip, right in the cock, she decided. She tried to sleep, they'd pick her up in 24 hours, luckily it was a warm night, she just had to be patient.

She knew no man or dog could follow her trail in all this space and water, she didn't fear capture that night, the pickup was where everything could go wrong.

She slept poorly, the sunlight woke her early, she waited and listened, trying to rest as much as possible for the ordeal ahead. She heard nothing all day that wasn't natural. She waited until her watch said six o'clock, then she ate and drank, the sandwiches were a bit stale now, but she'd need the strength tonight or never. She checked and cleaned her Sten. She heard a buzzing in the distance and couldn't tell if it was dragonflies or wasps.

She waited again until nine o'clock, dressed and packed. Still keeping low, she waded into the water again, only knee-deep now, going north, due north. After twenty yards in the water, there was much drier going, and she made better time. A mile and a half later she came to the main canal, 'Canal de Breca', running east to west, broad and straight.

A converted Lysander could easily land on its flat calm water, it ran for miles with only flooded fields, water, and swamp on either side. They'd told her it was a straightforward task. Yes, in full daylight in a friendly country with help on the ground she didn't have. She'd just have to do her best.

She had four small canisters of paraffin, each with a wick she could light. She'd have to move fast to get the rectangle of fires in place quickly enough to signal the plane.

She set down her equipment in a flat space in the grass, south of the canal and placed one canister next to it. When she heard the plane, she'd light the canisters in a rectangle which would frame the canal as a short runway. Four lights, a rectangle, a runway, child's play.

She waited, and at the expected time she heard the engine noise of the Lysander approaching and following the line of the canal, west to east.

She lit the first light and waded across the canal. The damp wick on the second one wouldn't light so she unscrewed the top, pouring the contents onto the grass and lit that instead.

She ran west, the third one burned okay, the fourth didn't and she had to light the grass again. Damn, you'd see that for miles, she thought, but she had no choice, and there shouldn't be anyone for miles. She ran back to her equipment.

The Lysander's engine noise changed, and it positioned itself for the landing run. As it approached the water, a strong bright headlight came on above its centre, lighting up the canal beautifully. The water was calm and just wide enough for the plane's adapted landing gear, its floats and wheels making it amphibian.

A different buzzing noise broke into the rhythmic sound of the Lysander engine, it was coming up the canal too. A small boat with an outboard motor and its own searchlight. Dazzled by the light, she couldn't see exactly what it was, and ran towards it regardless, the Sten cocked and ready. In her hurry and carelessly, she slipped, going over on her ankle and falling. She stayed behind the blazing grass, it might blind any approaching eyes to her, and waited.

A small flat boat with an outboard motor came into view, lit up by the blaze, four men on board, two with weapons drawn. She emptied the full Sten clip into the boat, it swerved towards the bank nearest her and hit it, collapsing into the water with loud noises of splashing and drowning. She replaced the clip and emptied the second into the men, boat, and water. Her ammunition exhausted, she dropped the Sten, pulling out her pistol and knife, listening, there was nothing except bubbling from the canal now.

She started to run to the Lysander, but couldn't, it felt like a break, not a twist in her ankle. She limped, hopped and stumbled forward, still alert, she could see the Lysander lights ahead, well past the fires she'd lit, and it had landed safely.

She stumbled on, hardly able to see, the blaze had made her lose her night vision. She was nearly level with the Lysander when she stumbled headlong into a German leaving the undergrowth. Her pistol dropped from her hand with the force of the collision. Unluckily for him, her reactions were quicker, the plane had been the focus of his attention. He still gripped his rifle, but she was faster with the knife. She pushed him over onto his back and plunged it down into his chest, using both hands, once, twice, three, four times then a fifth. She drew breath, panted heavily and tried to listen at the same time. Not hearing anything other than the engine noise, she looked at the dead German, he looked a bit like Gerolf, Gottlieb's friend, in the dim light. She opened his belt and pulled down his trousers, he did have a big cock, albeit soft? She took it in her hand, pulled it towards her, sliced it off, shoved it in his dead mouth and spat in his face.

Not bothering to wipe her face or hands, she hopped and waded the short distance to the Lysander, dragging herself clumsily and painfully up the small, built-in ladder.

"Go! Go!" she shouted.

The pilot revved the engine immediately, taking off within fifty yards and turning sharp left and left again for the coast. He waited until they were flying low over the Atlantic and heading on his route to the south-west coast of England before he dared say a word.

"Are you okay, Miss?" the pilot said.

"No, I am not fucking okay," she said, swearing properly for the first time in her life.

"I'm covered in German blood, I've broken my fucking ankle, I've got bruised ribs, a black eye, a split lip and one of them kicked me in the groin yesterday. It's fucking painful, alright," she said weeping.

"And did you really slice that German's… "

"Yes, I did, I really fucking hate Germans, and him, well I just didn't like his face."

"Perfectly alright Miss, perfectly alright, I'm not too keen on them myself as it happens. There's a small bottle of dark rum for you in the back."

"Thank you."

She took a sip of alcohol for the first time in her life, it was disgusting.

She drank all of it.

*

### Tuesday 17th of September 1940 – 0600 – Bletchley Park

Rebecca Rochford woke up gradually, half upright in a hospital bed, but not in a hospital. She smelt of hospital, yet the room didn't. Her hands felt a crisp cotton nightdress, she'd been washed, and felt her ankle was in plaster. One of her eyes was swollen, and half closed, but she could still see okay. Her bottom lip was scaly, cracked and she felt a cut in the corner of her mouth. Her throat was dry in an unfamiliar way, and she had a thick, dull headache she'd never experienced before. She remembered the dark rum, is this a hangover, she wondered?

She twisted in the bed for comfort and found her groin was still tender.

She pushed herself more upright and saw a jug of water with a glass.

"Let me get that, you'll still be giddy after the anaesthetic," said a man's voice, as she made a terrible mess of the task.

"I'll hold it for you," he said, putting it to her lips, "take sips at first, you've been out of it for about twelve hours. That's it, slowly.

"It's six in the morning on Tuesday the 17th of September 1940, you're in an intelligence building in Bletchley Park. Your ankle was a straightforward break, they've set it without any operation so it'll be six to eight weeks with the cast on. You'll walk okay, maybe not run as well as you used to. You'll never parachute again, and they'll try and take you off active service now and give you some desk job you'll hate."

"Sorry?" she said.

"I've just been reading your personal file, it says never lie to this woman, she'll see it from a mile off. So I thought I'd start off on the right foot. You look like shit too, by the way!"

She laughed warmly, and in a way that was unfamiliar to her.

"It says you have no sense of humour either, so some of it's wrong then, that's a relief."

"Why?"

"Some of your file is a bit scary."

"Good, those bits are probably true. Why are you here then?"

"I'm to debrief you, as soon as possible."

"I know that, I mean why you?"

"They're worried about you and want to make sure you get it all off your chest."

"And how will you do that?"

"I can tell when someone's lying."

"How can you do that?"

"I'm the world's biggest liar."

She laughed again, giggled even.

"You're not that big."

"The best, then?"

"Can we start straight away?"

"I thought you'd want to, the tape recorder's ready. I've got the sheets of drawing paper and pencils you asked for, I had to steal some from a boffin, nice chap, Alan, he won't mind."

"When did I ask for paper and pencils?"

"You talk in your sleep, has no one ever told you?"

"No," she said, realising why that was.

"You're very lucid. Do you want to talk or draw first?"

"Both, I think."

"Oh, one more thing before we start."

"What?"

"My name's Archie, and I'm definitely not German."

"Okay, I see, you have excellent sources," she laughed.

"The very best."

They talked, and she drew for two hours, he asked few questions and only open ones, it was like talking to an encyclopaedia or a machine, unusual, yet hugely practical and useful. He knew St. Nazaire would be strategically vital and why. Plans and actions formed in his mind as she spoke.

He made her stop for a short break and to let her eat a light meal, which he sent for. He just drank tea.

"You're a talented artist," he said, admiring the intricately detailed pencil sketches she'd produced effortlessly while talking. They were somehow three-dimensional, an effect produced by subtly changing the pressure on the pencil. She had masses of detail, from pencil outlines of vessels to detailed scenes of dock areas and German military installations, some were like photographs. She could have made a living just doing that.

"I've never seen anything like it, how long have you been drawing like this?"

"About two hours, I had no idea I could do it until you told me."

Archie stayed silent, as impressed as he'd ever been in his short life and trying not to show it.

She never got tired and never made other than complete sense, he had to insist she stopped for breaks and food. At midnight, he had to ask her if he could take a break, she said, not yet, so he carried on until six in the morning when she finally said she was finished.

He let her sleep and went for a proper badly needed rest, he went to the private room in his building and closed the door. He needed to sleep, but resolved not to let Rebecca wake up alone, so he set his travel alarm clock for only 6 hours later.

He went straight to her room when he woke, she was wide awake and talking to the medical officer and a nurse, who were taking her pulse, temperature, blood pressure and the like.

When they left, he took a seat by her bed and asked her if there was anything she needed to say, now the tape recorder was gone?

"Okay," she said, "now we're finished, you need to tell me what I lied about."

"You're sure?"

"Yes."

"On the 13th of September, give or take, probably Friday the 13th, something unspeakably evil happened, to you. Physically and emotionally, rape, I think, more than one German was involved, you survived, you think you're okay, but you're not."

"I have no idea how you did that, oh you are sharp, Archie, very sharp indeed. I'm impressed, I don't get impressed," she added.

She then told him exactly what happened in every detail, in a dispassionate, almost detached way.

He felt nauseous and somehow guilty, as she spoke, and knew it could have been worse. Guilty? How could he have taken care of her? He didn't even know her. He was glad she was here safely, and yet he still felt an overwhelming need to kill those two Germans.

He stopped talking and listening. Emotion filled his mind, a vague, distant memory, a scent, an absence, he couldn't pin it down. He searched for it, yearning for it, then it faded.

"What are you thinking?" she asked. "You've been miles away for twenty minutes."

He paid her the compliment of telling her exactly what

he'd been thinking.

"Please don't worry about me, that happened to Maria, not me, it's gone now."

He genuinely thought she was telling the truth. She genuinely thought she was telling the truth.

"You have to tell me how you knew?" she said.

"You spoke differently, English but almost another accent, not French, though. You hesitated, you don't hesitate, just for a second you were deciding which lie to tell. You adjusted your gown to make sure you were fully covered, you hadn't done that before. Your face didn't match the words. You had darkness, death, murder even, in your eyes when you got to that part, and you shouldn't have. You have death in your eyes now, too. People tell me I have that, I can never see it. I can see it in you, though."

When he saw she wasn't going to say more, he got up to leave.

"I have to go now, we have to work on what you've given us straight away."

He handed her a card with his name and number.

"I need, we need, the best people, you have something I've never seen before, and I need it. I need to use it. Use you, in fact. Keep the card, call me when you're on your feet again. Think about it for seven days before you call. You have to be sure."

"Promise me you'll never lie to me," she said.

"I wouldn't dare."

"Before you go, you have to tell me something I don't know about you. It has to be the worst thing."

Her direct insistence and lack of inhibition, with someone she'd just met, unsettled him. He had to think quickly, and he tried something bland.

"I can seem like one, but sometimes I'm not a nice person, I have seen and done evil, pure bloody evil, and I mean to do it again."

"I already know that, Archie, that's not enough, you're not the only one with good sources. You have to give me details, a reason to say no."

"God, you are one pushy person!"

"There is no God, come on, young man, I need the detail."

"Okay, okay," he said. She was relentless.

He told her the story of Mad Mike, all the details, just as he'd told Conner.

She looked at him, fixed him straight in the eyes, it was only then he saw how big her brown eyes were and how huge her pupils had become.

"Well, any self-respecting deity would condemn you, but Darwin would be proud. That is the worst thing you've done or would have done. It's not the worst thing you'll ever do, you're already planning to do worse, I can see the death in your eyes now."

She was right.

Archie said goodbye, walked to the door and opened it, pausing to look back at her, as she smiled. Her hair a mess, her black eye half closed, her split lip swollen and crooked, her small frame dwarfed by the cast on her ankle. Despite all of that, he'd never seen anyone look less like a victim in all his life. He knew that look, and she didn't have a trace of it. He'd been a victim, but that was about to change.

\*

She called the next day, Thursday the 19th September at three in the afternoon, the telephonist put her through after a short delay.

"Hello, Travers speaking."

"Archie, it's Rebecca."

"Yes, have you made a decision already?"

"Do I get to kill more Germans?"

"As many as you like."

"When can I start?"

## Chapter 18

### Wednesday the 18th September 1940 - England

Before Archie left Rebecca at Bletchley Park, he handed the tapes and drawings personally to Gubbins.

"She's the only one who came back, isn't she?" he said.

"So far, yes, we'd given up on her, to be honest. We've scrapped nearly everything in France and started again from scratch. She'll get no thanks either. If we praise what she did, then we have to admit how much we failed elsewhere."

"Vichy?"

"We think so, De Gaulle may be a royal pain in the arse, but his contacts remain the most reliable we have in France. There was bound to be collaboration, we just didn't expect so much, so soon."

"I suppose blowing up some of their Navy in Mers-el-Kebir in July didn't help?"

"Had to be done, we gave them enough warning, shame they should break off Diplomatic Relations. We'll have to go through the Americans now, that brings the Americans closer to us, though. The French will hate us now for a hundred years, even if we win the bloody war for them. We just had to show the world our determination to win, and there's always a price in war."

"Always, sir."

"If she agrees to join your team, you look after her, is that clear?"

"With my life, sir. I promise."

Archie left Bletchley Park at four in the afternoon, he didn't go straight home, he drove north instead.

He hadn't seen his family in Wallingford for years now, he'd received one letter, but hadn't answered. Keeping in touch with his past was unnecessary, they didn't know where, or who he was now.

*'Look forward, not back, bury the past.'*

Today was different, officially Archie Austin had been

missing in action in Northern France since May 1940. Large numbers were missing, most were long dead, a precious few were Prisoners of War. Telling the Red Cross who they had in captivity wasn't a priority for the German Army.

Archie stopped the car on the outskirts of Wallingford and waited until dark when he changed clothing. He put on his old Private's uniform, old boots included. He didn't want to risk anyone witnessing the change of identity. He took his old backpack from the car boot and checked its contents. He was hungry and tired, he'd only eaten a few snacks since he'd left London on Saturday. The old uniform was uncomfortable to wear, its rough cloth and poor fit returned to his mind. It still smelt musty, mothballs mixed with blood, gunpowder and death.

He waited until ten o'clock and pitch-dark in the blackout. He knew he'd have no difficulty finding the house, even without street lighting. He drove further on and found the house, parking around a quiet corner nearby, a Private wouldn't have his own car. He checked his watch, the luminous hands of Dolf's watch reminding him of his capacity for mercy. He waited briefly next to the car, letting his eyes gain their full night vision. He'd prepared what he wanted to say carefully, and he'd imagined the conversation a hundred times, he was as ready as he could possibly be.

He walked around the corner, found the house he wanted, checked around him again, and walked up the short path to the front door. He knocked firmly and confidently on the door then took a few steps backwards. A tall male with a familiar face opened the door.

Archie raised his silenced Luger pistol and shot him in the head, not quite between the eyes, although satisfyingly close. He turned around and walked to his car, he didn't hurry, he just went deliberately at his normal pace. He could hear a raised female voice, but it wasn't alarmed yet.

*'You should punish in the same manner those who commit crimes with those who accuse falsely.'*

Archie had read that, Thucydides again, he had time for that thought now, such was his progress since Calais.

The car started first time, and he drove straight from the side street turning left, away from the house, heading for the main road south. He didn't plan to stop for an hour, until he reached the quiet spot where he could remove the false number plates and change clothes.

Archie was a little disappointed, he'd prepared many words to say to Mr Kline, yet when he saw him, he needed to kill him more than he needed him to know who was doing it. Any conversation might have delayed him or identified him later.

The following day, the police would just see a dead man of Irish birth and German ancestry, who had changed his name from Klein to Kline. They would examine him and find a recently manufactured German bullet from a silenced Luger and an expertly made hole in his forehead. Special Branch would investigate a killing involving those characteristics. What could they conclude, other than Kline being complicit in fifth column treason that had gone wrong for him? There was no other evidence, nothing traceable, nothing proved or disproved, just suspicion, just one word would be enough; liar. Kline was a liar, let's see how his family liked that, his stuck-up bitch of a wife and his wanker of a son.

The killing felt satisfying and was well worth the long wait.

It was easy to check local records and find Kline still teaching, at the Grammar now. Too old for military service, he'd moved house to a smarter property. Archie knew his spineless turd of a son had moved to Ireland, to live with relatives as soon as war broke out.

Archie knew many Irish people living in England had joined the forces, and more came from Ireland so they could sign up. The Irish didn't like Churchill, and the dislike seemed mutual, but did the Irish like Hitler any better? That son wouldn't just walk back into England after the war ended. Any friends he did have, would return from active service and shun the coward, let's see how he coped with having no friends.

Establishing a usual routine for Kline had been easy, he rarely went out in term time, and never late at night. Archie would knock on his door and if he answered he'd kill him, not his most expert, detailed plan, but it worked.

He drove south for one hour and pulled into a layby he'd scouted earlier. He changed into his Lieutenant's uniform, replaced the Luger in his pack, storing it and his old uniform in a bag in the boot. He drank deeply from his old water bottle, poured some of it over his hands then splashed it on his face. As he drove, the scent of Calais remained in his nose.

He arrived back at Hevlyn Mansions early, just catching Conner before he left for the day, he told him briefly about Rebecca, explaining his delay and saying they'd talk more in the evening.

Archie went upstairs and wolfed a couple of slices of toast and butter with a mug of strong tea while he ran his bath. He soaked in the tub, washed and scrubbed his body thoroughly, paying close attention to his hands and nails, determined to remove a thin layer of skin, and he did begin to relax at last. As soon as he was dry, he went to bed and slept.

The telephone ringing woke him at three in the afternoon.

"Hello, Travers speaking."

"Archie, it's Rebecca."

He was Archie again.

Archie told Rebecca to take a complete break of at least a week, just live a normal life, eat, sleep, read a book and call again in a week.

When he put the phone down, he washed his hands and face again, shaved, brushed his teeth and put on his full uniform. He needed a long talk with Conner, over a meal would be best, the Savoy perhaps.

Before he left, he rang Mary Driver at Bletchley Park to tell her about Rebecca.

"She's already here, brandishing your card and asking politely for something to read," Driver said.

Archie laughed out loud.

"I think we'd better let her read whatever she wants, she just can't take anything out of the building."

"Oh, she knows that. She's arranged to be brought over and collected every day, she has a wheelchair too."

"Just make her as welcome as you can. I'll get back as soon as possible."

"The welcome isn't a problem. She's making everyone a cup of tea while I was to phone you, we like her a lot already, and we'll look after her. It's just, she already knows exactly what she wants to read."

"That's the trouble with some of these exceptionally intelligent people, they're not daft, are they? I'll get the detail later when we meet up, and thank you again, Mary, I don't know what we'd do without you."

Conner and Archie had dinner at the Savoy that night, the usual menu, their usual corner table, discreet. Fortunately, Grace wasn't on restaurant duty that evening. Billy nodded to acknowledge them when they arrived, Archie wondered what that nod meant this time. He gave Conner the rest of the detail on Rebecca, then talked about Grace and his planned next date with her.

"So you spent an evening with a lovely young lady, and you didn't even try to get in her knickers?"

"Yes."

"And what was that like, then?"

"It was nice."

"Just nice?"

"Yes, and nice was just nice, that's all."

"Is it love then?"

"No, it's just nice, that's all. She's nice and makes me want to be nice."

"And the problem is?"

"I'm not a nice person."

"People say you are."

"Who?"

"The team at Bletchley for a start, they loved the tea and biscuits, you're always nice to them, they always say so."

"I'm just pretending, though."

"And if you pretend to be nice for long enough, forever perhaps, then you'd be nice all the time."

"There's a difference between pretending to be nice and being nice."

"What if nobody notices you're pretending?"

"*I'd* still know."

"And you can't lie to yourself?"

"Exactly. I think so, anyway."

"So, the crux of the matter is you need to do something not nice every so often, so you can manage to keep up the nice act most of the time."

"That's it, how do you work these things out so well?"

"I've been practicing a lot longer than you have."

"I need to do some more evil. Honi Soit Qui Mal y Pense."

"So do the men, all that training and they're itching to go."

"*Claymore*?" Archie asked, referring to his own plan for getting intelligence on German Coding equipment.

"Not till the spring now."

"*Ruthless*?"

"It'll never happen, too stupid."

"What then?"

"We need to go to the Metropole and volunteer for something."

"Yes, Gubbins owes me a favour now, and I've half of an idea for half a plan."

"Even better; let's talk then leave SOE with me," said Conner.

*

### Saturday 21st September 1940 - London

That Friday evening, Archie took Grace on a chaste and nice visit to the cinema. Arthur Askey in 'Charley's (Big-Hearted) Aunt'.

The next day, he left London early and arrived at Bletchley Park by midday. As expected, he found Mary and Rebecca still in their building. Mary gave Archie a briefing on the week's team output, then asked if it was okay if she left for the weekend, Rebecca had exhausted her with questions.

Rebecca was on crutches already and hopping around desks. Her lips were better but still split, she had a little colour in her face, and her hair was a dreadful mess. The black eye had turned a dark yellow, the swelling had gone, and he could see now that her left eye was just slightly smaller than her right. The bruising on her cheek looked worse, it had spread, and the scratches were scabbing over. She was similar height and build to Grace, there was no likeness, though.

"Can we sit in the room?" she said.

"Of course, we can."

"It seems like the right thing to do."

"I'll just be one minute," said Archie and went to the kitchen to wash his hands, drying them with a clean towel on the way back to the room. He sat opposite her and took a jar of Vaseline from his pocket, dipped his finger inside and used it gently on her lips. She looked at him, surprised and puzzled, unsure what to say or do. When he finished, he put the jar in her open palm and closed her hand around it.

"I've read most of the nuclear fission intelligence, I did that first," she said.

"I would have asked if you'd given me a chance, but I don't think you're going to give me many."

"Have you read the report on the heavy water and the French scientists leaving Bordeaux?"

"Yes, Wild Jack, and the Navy report on the recovery of items from the coast."

"There's something missing!" they said simultaneously and laughed.

"What do you think it is?" she said.

"I think we should look for ourselves, together, when

you're better."

"You did say I could kill more Germans."

"I did."

Satisfied with that answer for the moment she changed subjects, she was like a machine.

"Alan is correct, Heisenberg is the one to get close to," she said.

Heisenberg was one of the leading German Scientists researching nuclear fission. He was no Nazi, but importantly, he had already proven to be too useful a scientist to sideline.

"I can't figure out how they haven't just shot him or locked him up or something?" she added.

"Apparently, his mum knows Himmler's mum."

"You've got to be joking?"

"No, seriously, it's in an old file, they go hiking together. Another thing, just my opinion, not sure where it comes from, maybe the whole uncertainty principle, I think he's grasped the basics of excellent lying."

"Which are?"

"In his case, keep your lies as close to the truth as possible and as flattering to the listener as you can credibly manage. It's an art form."

"Lies they would want to hear?"

"The best kind."

"Do I still look like shit?" she asked suddenly.

"No, not at all," he said without thinking, she still did.

"The best kind, definitely the best kind. I'll let you off with that one. I'll only let you off with the best kind of lie. Remember that. Remember you promised not to lie to me."

"Bloody Hell, woman, here I am, the world's best liar and you won't let me do my job."

"I have to test you now and again, that's only fair."

"Okay."

"Right, let me look you in the eyes."

She looked at him again, grabbed the back of his head and pulled his face uncomfortably close to hers, she was breathing his air. The pupils in her brown eyes were huge in the dim light of the room, her eyelashes were exceptionally long, he hadn't noticed that before.

"Mmmm, it's definitely gone hasn't it?"

"What?"

"The murder in your eyes, it's gone."

"So has yours, what of it?"

"Mine was older and fading, yours was fresh and growing. You've killed since we last met, haven't you?"

Archie had felt the question coming. There was no point in lying to Rebecca or Conner, but they had to ask the right questions first.

"Yes, on Wednesday night."

"Who was it?"

"An old enemy."

"What did he do to become your enemy?" she pressed him relentlessly.

"He took the life of someone, who was once very dear to me."

"How did you kill him?"

"Bullet between the eyes, near enough anyway."

"Was he a German?"

"German father, Irish mother."

"German enough then?"

"Enough for my purpose, yes."

"No more questions, for now," she said, experiencing a new feeling, a mixture of guilt and shame perhaps, she thought, is that what guilt feels like?

"I apologise, I won't test you like that again, Archie. I thought it would be fun, but it wasn't, was it?"

In the silence, before he replied she tried to recall the last time she'd apologised, sincerely, to anyone. She couldn't.

"It was okay, not exactly fun, did I pass the test, though?"

"Oh yes, you are definitely the world's best liar. Now, what do we do about Heisenberg, and how do I get the females in your team to stop trying to do something with my bloody hair?"

## Wednesday 16th October 1940 - Bletchley Park

Rebecca finally walked into Building Thirteen in Bletchley Park without the cast on her ankle. She was wearing the full tailor-made Lieutenant's uniform Archie had arranged for her. She looked different in a skirt, almost female. No, she had a female shape, but she still didn't look female, she walked like a man.

"Archie, in the room now!" she demanded as soon as she came in.

"Of course," he said, noticing badly disguised, but good-natured sniggering from his team.

"Tell me about your girlfriend, Archie," she snapped at him.

"What do you want to know?" was his bemused reply.

"Something that'll distract your bloody team from my hairstyle, I don't know, the sort of thing a normal girl would want to know."

"There's no point arguing is there?"

"None."

"Okay, her name is Grace, she's twenty-one, I've known her for about four months, she's a waitress, very pretty and very nice."

"Nice! I can't say nice! Even I know what nice means, you don't tell her she's nice, do you?"

"Oh for goodness sake, what's wrong with using the word nice?"

"Nice means boring, dull, ordinary, you idiot."

"What's a good word for nice then?"

"There isn't one, idiot."

"She brings out the best in me then."

"Oh, that's no good either. Your best is no use to anyone, your worst is what makes you useful, idiot."

"Just make something up then."

"Oh, just let me have some saucy detail then," she said exasperatedly.

"There isn't any."

"So you're sleeping with someone else, several

243

someone else's probably."

"What? How the hell do you do that?"

"Men who aren't getting any sex have a certain look of despondency about them, I've never seen that look in you, the opposite, in fact. Women can smell sexual success on a man, it's a chemical messenger phenomenon. There's lots of work about it, Adolf Butenandt won the Nobel Prize for Chemistry in 1939 for his work on the subject. Think of it as a caveman thing. That should help an idiot like you. Of course, he couldn't accept the prize, being a good German, but that doesn't make him a bad chemist."

"Could you slow down a bit please, my feeble male brain can't keep up with you," he said, hoping she wouldn't realise it wasn't a joke. "So, assuming you're correct, which I don't necessarily admit at this stage of the interrogation, you're saying Grace should notice, well she doesn't, so your theory's out the window. Theoretically."

"No, idiot, she either pretends she doesn't or perhaps she's too naïve to notice, or know what it means. She could be one of the few who don't respond, she doesn't sound at all like me, though?"

"You're still not helping me at all."

"I'm not trying to help you, I'm just providing you with information, it's up to you to analyse it and form your own conclusions. You need to plan better, don't you?"

"Oh bloody hell, I do ask for it, don't I?

"Yes."

"Just make something up then, it'll probably be accurate anyway."

*

Archie took Grace out a few more times, and it remained only nice. Teddy had planned to marry a virgin, then Archie had met Victoria. He had other needs he hadn't identified exactly, but it wasn't Grace, he'd thought it might be, it just wasn't.

Breaking up with Grace was stomach wrenching, and Archie felt guilty, and cruel. He timed it to coincide with his team going on a couple of long, unspecified dangerous trips. The excuse of being unfair to Grace, he might never return, etcetera, was too true a lie not to use.

*'Always make your lies as close to the truth as possible.'*

Rebecca had made him hone that skill.

Archie resolved not to look for love or anything remotely like it. If he still didn't know who he was, how could he know who he was looking for?

He was glad he'd left Grace intact for whoever she did marry, Billy was capable of giving Archie a hard slap.

He spent more time in Bletchley after that. Gubbins had requisitioned a small stately home near Bletchley for their operational team. It had outhouses and stables they converted into workshops and weapons storage. Its original name was Great Horewood Manor, for obvious reasons, they took down the name sign and just called it *The Manor*.

*

### Autumn 1940 – England

Conner took Archie to see a cottage nearby which he'd rented for them; he knew they'd need space away from the men and vice versa. He drove away from the site at Bletchley Park and took the main road south, Watling Street. After a couple of miles, he turned left onto a tarmacked country lane, barely wide enough for two cars.

On the left, after two miles, they saw a large disused brick barn with a hayloft, the shutters swinging open in the light wind that day. Immediately following that, they crossed a small bridge and turned left onto a gravel track leading to a dead end with thick hedgerows on the left and straight ahead. The cottage stood on the right, set slightly back from the track.

Conner parked on the right just after the building, where the previous occupant had laid down more gravel, allowing a car to reverse and return to the road. The stream on the left of the track wound around the cottage in a 90-degree angle, bordering it on two sides. The third side was heavily wooded, with mature tightly packed trees. The fourth side leading to the tarmacked road was a small patch of rough grassy wasteland.

The Cottage had a small garden. Its overgrown hedge and old stone flags between shrubs, which needed a little weeding, gave it some character.

The three-bedroomed former farmhouse originally had four bedrooms, the two smaller rooms had been converted into one large bedroom. Conner told Archie to take that room.

The downstairs was one big lounge, an open fireplace and dining area then a large kitchen. The kitchen had a huge larder with steps leading down to a small cellar, serving as a coal and wood store with a wide thin window, which looked into the garden from ground level.

The overall result was a quiet, private place where the only sounds you could hear were the streams gentle bubbling and birdsong.

Archie felt it would be a little shady during summer months, but the pleasing variations of green on trees and hedges outweighed that. It felt like a small sheltered island of peace in a world of chaos and danger, and with the right people inside, a home.

"I like it, it's quiet, I like quiet now," Archie said. It's still a palace to me, he thought.

"Gubbins found it for us, he wants a favour, though, from you again," said Conner.

Rebecca initially preferred to stay on site at Bletchley, there was a boffins club she belonged to. He and Conner frequented local pubs and clubs and found not inconsiderable comfort in casual sex. A reputation as a well-endowed, raffish ladies' man did Archie no harm and gave no false promises he'd have to break. He stayed well clear of his own team, though.

After he'd broken up with Grace, he discussed it at length with Conner. Conner just listened and let Archie talk himself out until there was nothing left to say. Articulating your thoughts to someone else helped make better sense of them, especially with someone like Conner.

*

The following night, after not eating for twenty-four hours, Archie went for a short drive into the East End of London. He took a short walk in his old Private's uniform with Dolf's jack-knife in his old kit bag.

*

Two days later he read a story in the Times, page 7 no less, and no more than a few lines. The Police had found the body of Norah Baker, Norah the knife, a known prostitute, with her throat cut. She was discovered under a railway arch near The Brown Bear public-house and close to Leman Street Police Station. They made links to other crimes in the area, and historical crimes. Police were pursuing inquiries relating to Norah's known underworld connections, and her fondness for robbery at knifepoint and fraud. The harsh, convenient truth was, in the autumn of 1940, no one cared about Norah Baker. Neither did Archie, not now anyway.

Her death was more satisfying than Kline's, it had taken more time to track her down, and he'd planned it methodically. The chloroform had subdued her while he'd dragged her to the railway arch, tied her up and gagged her. He'd made sure she had time to wake and know who was going to kill her, and why. He'd made the cut a quick one, he kept the knife razor sharp. He pinned her down roughly, looking her in the eye as she died, the blood running out of her neck onto the dirty concrete. The smell reminded him of Calais, piss, and Mad Mike, although not a drop of blood went on him this time.

Kline had been too easy, too distant, impersonal, and the light hadn't been good enough to see any fear on his face. He'd never killed close up, and he knew he'd have to. He needed to be certain he could do it when he needed. If he could kill a woman, even if it was just a worthless example like Norah, close up, in cold blood then he could knife a German Sentry.

He had considered mutilating the body or opening her up like the Ripper would have. When it came to it, he felt no need. He didn't regret that. It would have been gratuitously sick. He classed what he'd done, as legitimate practice for what he'd have to do later, in the service of his country. He wiped the blade of the knife clean on her skirt and spat in her face.

He was the fittest, Norah was the lowest, and she hadn't survived.

He left her, in complete calm and walked casually back to his car. He found he was whistling that violin tune again, it popped into his head occasionally. He should look up that Threepenny Opera tune. Still, one more piece of Teddy was gone, safely out of his mind, he'd be Archie again when he'd changed clothing.

Archie hadn't known her full antecedence until he'd read it in the paper, it intrigued him. That wasn't why he'd killed her.

*

## Autumn 1940 – Bletchley Park

Gubbins latest favour was easy enough, and Archie readily agreed to help design part of a training course for the Directorate of Military Intelligence, specifically on Intelligence Interrogation techniques. Gubbins had asked him to help, he said it needed a fresh mind and Churchill had recommended him.

The teachers were working from a manual written in 1914.

Archie was to teach people to recognise if someone was lying. Then get them to tell the truth. Then know for certain that they had. There were many straightforward tell-tale signs, body language, eye contact, hesitation, asking the same question twice at different times, check if they remembered which lie they'd already told. Be pleasant, not nasty, speak as a friend, not an enemy, offer them something rather than threaten them, persuade not punish. Find something adverse about them, something they don't know you know. Then give them a chance to tell you the truth about it, they might take it.

All basic common sense, sadly none of it was in the manual.

He reluctantly agreed to help give the first lesson to make sure the teacher understood what he meant, and to see what questions the trainees asked.

Archie didn't want to be a teacher! He knew how to do stuff, not how to teach others.

He entered the classroom of twenty, bloody hell, they all looked posh. He looked at the attendance list, he was right, mostly double-barrelled names a few titles, mostly junior and one flash chancer. He guessed that most had opted for DMI to avoid coming under fire elsewhere. Jimmy McKay was the only one he recognised, he, at least, was SOE.

*'Sod it, I'll just go straight for the throat.'*

"Good morning, I'm Archie Travers, it's been a while since I've been in a room so full of fine gentlemen."

"How many people here are ready to kill as many Germans as it takes to win this war?"

They all put their hands up.

"How many of you would be happy if someone else did all that killing for you?"

One hand went up. Jimmy McKay.

"Well done Jimmy, you're the only honest man in the room. Lesson one; don't worry too much about spotting the liar. Try learning to spot the truth teller, it'll save you a lot of time."

The session lasted for two hours, it should have taken one, there were some big liars in that room.

Finally, he told them the story of how he first met Rodolf Von Rundstedt and had to decide if he wanted to hit him. Starting from his walk along the railway line past the old pillbox. He told them to imagine what they would have done with the tools he had.

"You can speak German. You have a Lee Enfield rifle and bullets. An empty Luger. French and British troops are present, none speaks any German. The Germans have massacred ninety percent of your company the previous day, some with a bullet in the back after they'd surrendered. You have ten bars of chocolate and two hundred cigarettes. You have ten minutes."

He gave everyone a chance to say their bit, then cut them off as soon as they made a mistake.

"Sorry, you're dead. Next," he said.

No one got it remotely right, they were all dead, and he never told them the answer. He was sure he'd given them enough clues.

"I'll leave the full answer with the Professor here, in a sealed envelope, he'll know it, and he'll only open the envelope when someone gets it exactly right. He'll tell you how many parts out of the ten needed that you've guessed correctly.

"One last question," he said, "what was the first lie I told you today?"

Jimmy spoke up, "Can I have a guess?"

"By all means."

"Just after you said good morning, you called us fine gentlemen, you really think we're a bunch of posh boys who got lucky?"

"You're sharp Jimmy, I'll have to watch out for you. Yes, that was a lie, the best kind of lie, one you wanted to hear."

Archie paused, taking in the disapproval of the trainees. He wasn't sure he should be enjoying this so much. If they couldn't handle a little humility and desire for self-improvement, then they wouldn't last five minutes with any Jerry officer.

"But it wasn't the first lie I told you, I didn't even tell you my real name," he said, noticed some smiles and laughter then left. Some of them were worth teaching.

"You made some enemies there, they won't forget that," Jimmy told him later.

"Stuff them, Jimmy, I've got a lot worse than that to come."

## Chapter 19

### Saturday 2nd November 1940 - 2200 - French Coast off Bordeaux

Archie, his Chosen Men, and Rebecca were sweaty and claustrophobic aboard the submarine, HMS Triton, off the west coast of France near Bordeaux. No full moon, this time, there would be complete darkness.

Conner was in Switzerland by now.

Archie was in charge tonight. He'd personally briefed each man six days before, in England, and they were eager for action. Some after Calais or Dunkirk, Begley and Ben Dempsey because they'd not yet worn their uniforms in earnest. Archie gave each man what he called an individual walkthrough of their part of the mission, at night, in the Manor grounds. Then he made them do it blindfold at midday. He played the sound of waves lapping on a beach through a loudspeaker and made additional soft noises, he asked them to identify. A footstep on gravel, the clicking of a weapon being cocked, even the sound of a cough or half a word in German. He made sounds all around them and asked them to point where they came from. They thought he was bonkers, but did it anyway.

The Chosen Men met Rebecca for the first time at the briefings, they knew she'd done the same training as them, they knew who she'd killed in France and how she'd done it. Her story grew more savage with each retelling, but it never approached the whole truth, that was for her and Archie alone. Her usual detachment from emotion still took some getting used to, she was still one step aside from the group, any group in fact.

The Chosen Men looked at her, standing next to Archie and then Smudger, and stood in absolute awe of her achievements. Each man privately resolved to throw themselves in front of a bullet to protect her. They never discussed it, it was a potentially deadly decision, a mistake, contrary to mission orders, it remained a hard fact nevertheless.

Rebecca was there because Archie said she needed to be, she knew this part of France well. She'd never been to La Jenny herself, but she'd memorised the maps, aerial photographs and guidebooks he had the team find for her. If anyone checked, her knowledge was clearly vital to the mission. In fact, she was there because he'd promised her she could kill some Germans, and he wouldn't deny her the chance, ever.

They weren't going there intending to kill Germans, though, the plan was not to attract attention until after they'd left. They probably wouldn't see a single soul during their mission. They were there to destroy 85 litres of heavy water, deuterium oxide, the last remaining quantity in France.

'Wild Jack,' whose reports Rebecca and Archie had read, was Charles Henry George Howard, the 20th Earl of Suffolk and 13th Earl of Berkshire. Jack had smuggled French Nuclear Scientists out of France, together with most of their heavy water stores, via Bordeaux. The French had hidden further stores of heavy water and other high-value items near the coast. 'Wild Jack' had already successfully recovered some items. This last stash was too bulky to smuggle out clandestinely, so they were going to destroy it, regardless of any small risk of radiation contamination.

"Christ, he's too mad even for us, let him blow himself up," Conner had said when Archie had suggested involving him.

Conner and Archie had met with Special Operations Executive at their Metropole Hotel headquarters near Trafalgar Square. The presence of that priceless heavy water had persuaded SOE to sponsor the raid and give it priority. Gubbins was happy to let their ready-made team handle it.

"And if it works, I'll owe you another favour, Travers," he'd said. Archie liked Gubbins a lot now, he was a hard taskmaster, which suited Archie, and he'd added him to his still short list of role models alongside Caesar and

Churchill.

The presence of other high-value items intrigued Archie and Rebecca most.

The submarine headed for a quiet part of coastline near Bordeaux, Arcachon Bay. There was no real security presence here, there was nothing to guard. They might encounter a random patrol when they reached the coastline and the beach, but at midnight, in winter, only outrageous ill fortune or appalling weather could impede them.

The team left the submarine at midnight in three semi-rigid rubber dinghies. Archie, Rebecca, Spud, Begley and Nipper in the first, the others split evenly in the other two.

Smudger was in the second boat with Davey *'Siggy'* Stubbs, Stuart *'Bestie'* Buddy and *'Hospital'* Ward, the medic.

*'Taffy'* Tarrian led the third with The Dempsey brothers, and Joseph *'Moley'* Mowles.

They paddled slowly and noiselessly ashore, beaching on the long sandbar they knew was there. Tarrian had reluctantly agreed to stay and guard the dinghies. Three went left, and the rest went right, taking up guarding positions, north and south along the beach. Archie's boatload went straight ahead, Spud on point, Nipper, and Begley at the rear, all thoroughly well-armed. Begley's large backpack being the most dangerous item of all.

Archie and Rebecca were in the middle, Archie carried his Mauser over his shoulder for comfort, he shouldn't need it. Rebecca had a Thompson sub-machine gun over her shoulder, more to her taste than the Sten. She'd also borrowed Archie's silenced Luger and held it in her hand. Archie had strapped her ankle carefully and tightly with crepe bandages, underneath a specially designed and fitted pair of boots, extra small size, her feet were tiny, he discovered. She'd said she was fine and wasn't lying, he could tell, but he wasn't taking any chances.

After only about two hundred yards straight inland they found the solitary building they wanted, a substantial holiday home, in the middle of nowhere and, as expected, empty and lifeless.

Archie sent Spud and Begley to search inside the house and upstairs to make sure it was empty. Nipper scouted around outside, then kept watch on the small track that led inland.

Archie and Rebecca found the shutters of the cellar entrance at the rear of the house. He used an enormous custom-made pair of bolt cutters about four feet long to slice the padlock holding the shutters closed. They went down the cellar stairs, using torches strapped to their heads, and closed the shutters behind them. They moved the assorted camping equipment, garden tools, and crates out of the way then removed the old tarpaulin, uncovering the large black drums that could only contain their target. Rebecca took the small Geiger counter from her pack, it produced the confirming crackle, and the red needle swept up the dial.

"That's it, and it looks like it's all here as expected," she said.

Archie meanwhile was carefully moving the metal barrels away from the wall, to reveal two heavy brown leather briefcases, he placed them on top of the barrels.

"There's no sign of any leakage," Rebecca said before moving her head torch away from the barrels and towards the briefcases.

"Now, let's see what Father Christmas has brought you, have you been good?"

"Certainly not!" he said.

In the torchlight, Archie identified only the thick folders of research papers he expected, in the first case. The second contained the same, although it had a smaller pouch at the front, he opened it and pulled out two small, yet heavy, black cloth bags, he undid the drawstrings to reveal a large number of...

"Diamonds!" Rebecca said.

"I really don't recollect being that good?" Archie said. He took the first bag, tied the drawstring in a tight knot and stuffed it down the left inside front of Rebecca's tunic, then put the second bag on the right.

"What are you doing?" she asked.

"Following orders, I'll explain later."

"That should be interesting."

Archie sealed the briefcases, and they went outside to find Begley and Spud waiting for them.

"Any problems?" he asked.

"None," said Spud.

"There're seven barrels in there, I want them all blown to smithereens please, Begley. Take the entire house and nearby trees too, we want Jerry to know we've landed here and worry about it. One hour from now, at 0130 please."

"My pleasure, sir."

Half an hour later they were safely back on board the submarine. Archie handed the briefcases to the *'Tube Alloys'* Liaison Officer. *'Tube Alloys'* was the cover name for the British nuclear weapons development team, only Rebecca and Archie knew that.

The Captain waited until the scheduled detonation time and, watching through the periscope, saw a massive explosion and fire erupt.

"Mission accomplished, gentlemen and lady," he said.

"May I have a look please Captain?" Rebecca asked.

"Quickly please," he said loudly.

Rebecca looked, satisfied with what she saw, then stepped back from the scope.

"Dive!" ordered the Captain.

"That's a shame," she said to the Captain.

"Pardon me?" he asked.

"Well, we didn't get to kill any Germans, did we. You couldn't find me a ship to torpedo could you?"

"No, I could not, young lady."

\*

At 0500, Archie woke Rebecca in her quarters.

"The Captain wants to see you," he said.

She returned to the control room, the Captain was looking into the periscope, he didn't look round.

"Go over there and stand by Able Seaman Brown, place your hand on his," he said.

Brown's hand was on a brass lever, and she gripped it carefully and apprehensively.

"Fire One," the Captain shouted, her hand moved with Brown's and then he moved her hand and his to another lever.

"Fire Two."

"Dive. Standard evasive movements please, gentlemen."

Five minutes later the Captain checked the periscope again, then invited Rebecca to look.

"Quick as you can, please," he said quietly.

She looked, he saw her smile, pulled her back gently and then said.

"Down periscope, dive, dive, head for home."

He relaxed and looked at Rebecca, smiling.

"It was only an armed freighter I'm afraid, going down quickly, we won't outstay our welcome. On its way out of St. Nazaire, between fifty and seventy-five on board. Some U-boats will go hungry and thirsty without those supplies. Good enough?"

"Yes, thank you, Captain."

She and Archie walked back to her quarters.

"How did you persuade him to do that?" she asked.

"He was allowed a target of opportunity on the return journey, and I told him where you spent your summer holidays this year."

"Thank you, Archie," she nodded at him grabbing her chest with her hands.

"Here I am, the most valuable tits in the world and at least fifty more Germans off my list, what more could a girl want? My ankle's killing me, by the way."

"Let's have a look then, at the ankle, obviously."

*

Conner had used his genuine Swiss Passport to enter Monaco on his private yacht. All official records showed he had lived permanently in Monaco for more than ten years. Money could still buy anything in Monaco.

He entered Vichy France from Monaco and travelled to Switzerland by chauffeured car. Relations between the Vichy regime and Prince Louis 2nd of Monaco were cordial, at least in part because of his connection with Marshall Phillippe Petain, the puppet head of Vichy France. Prince Louis was trying to remain neutral in the War. It wouldn't last, Conner knew, but it would last long enough for his present purpose.

When needed, Conner occasionally became the wealthy son of a Swiss Banker. Other than being a Swiss Banker, it was the safest occupation in Europe.

His elderly guardian and principal mentor, Monsieur Alexandre De Cyrene sat in the rear of the chauffeured car for this trip. As far as Conner knew, Alex was a Swiss Citizen, a close friend of his parents who had raised Conner as his own, with care, purpose and drive, although without love. He was also the owner of a highly regarded Swiss Bank; Conner wasn't sure how you could own a bank that contained everyone else's money. Untypically for such a ruthless antecedence, Alex was a righteous if solitary man.

"You have been raised for a purpose, Constantine, to lead and direct, you are to affect history at a crucial time. Few are given that burden, few can bear it."

When someone told you that, even aged only five, it did catch your attention. When someone with the intellect and quality of Mr De Cyrene told you something like that, all you could do was follow their lead. You could only follow the lead you were given, and his was the best.

Although Conner enjoyed leisure and luxury in plenty, it was always well earned by application and ability. He had no reservations about his life, everything he'd ever done had been what he'd wanted to do. He had no family and not even Alex could buy him that, but he had Archie now, and he hoped the maladjusted Rebecca would grow closer. He was pleased with his two teams, Bletchley, and the Chosen Men, he'd found a brother and perhaps a sister, and his two teams could be his children.

Conner had met Heisenberg before, June 1939 in the

United States, Conner had been Swiss then too. His father's bank had sponsored Heisenberg's trip there and funded a summer home for his family in Southern Bavaria. Alex always briefed him thoroughly and so intensely, it left him with a headache and a dull sensation of his brain being full. He'd tried to persuade Heisenberg to emigrate to the United States, the bank was offering funding for a prestigious professorship as bait. Conner also met Albert Einstein and Leo Szilard while there.

Genius was always in short supply, and a genius was usually short of money, they all needed the leisure time and financial security, which gave them time to think.

Professional rivalry and jealousy were as rife in academic circles, as in any power group.

Sadly, an unpleasant measure of charlatanism was also present. Many geniuses couldn't tie their shoelaces or buy a loaf of bread. Some were unaccountably lazy, one extraordinarily creative thought exhausting them for a month. Some produced their best ideas when poor and hungry, fame and fortune then rotted their brains.

In September 1940, Conner's agenda was to speak as the son of an old friend in neutral Switzerland. A friend, concerned by the war, its implications for business and the safety to enjoy the fruits of such business. Heisenberg accepted the bait of a luxury holiday in Switzerland for his family.

A private dinner invitation to the Dolder Grand Hotel in Zurich would catch the attention of a Prince, it worked effortlessly on Werner Heisenberg.

Over a dinner, of several courses and just the right amount of the best wine, Conner learned what he needed to know.

Interdepartmental rivalry within the Nazi Party was hampering the development of nuclear energy as a power source and a weapon. Funding was uncertain, and there was no longer enough expertise in Germany, deprived of the Jewish intellect that had fled to the United States and England. Heisenberg had been close to emigration but feared the deadly retribution on all of his relatives if he gave his expertise elsewhere. Now, he chose to stay close to any research to affect it for "the benefit of the whole world" he'd said.

Constantine agreed wholeheartedly with everything Heisenberg said. Then he told him that, as always, his father and his bank would willingly aid his scientific aims in any possible way. He knew he could contact him personally through the bank. The bank was strictly neutral, of course, and happily conducted business with many nationalities, the English, for example.

Heisenberg bemoaned the funding allocated to conventional rocketry, *that* was the imminent danger to the world, not nuclear fission.

Chillingly, he spoke of the SS.

"Reinhard Heydrich will remain an implacable enemy of mine until his dying day, and perhaps even his death would be dangerous to me and many others. He is mad, quite mad, like many others, no sane scientist should ever allow his genius to fall into the hands of a madman. I say this not for me and not for you, Constantine, nor just for our time, but forever. I can deduce and correctly conclude that this Nazi regime won't last forever, yet I can also conclude that there will be other Nazis, other evil ideologies. I have faith in a God which I combine with science. There will be madmen who'll use religion as an excuse to fuel their madness. Their desire for power, their need to be the fittest and therefore to survive at the expense of others."

Constantine thought long and hard, even through his own headache, after he'd poured Heisenberg into his chauffeur's careful hands for return to his family.

Heisenberg was a rare human being, a scientific genius, a believer in a God, thankfully a mature and benign one who didn't interfere overmuch, yet having enough common sense to survive. His survival and informative presence in Germany was imperative to the Allies, officially or otherwise. Conner, Archie, and Rebecca would have to make sure he survived.

Conner decided that one good facet of war, was that charlatanism became more self-defeating, charlatans died more often in war than peace. Reality worked more often in war, fakery didn't, war was a form of natural selection, unaffected by modern civilised principles and protective, but counterproductive benevolence. Humankind needed an occasional war to weed out the inferior in the upper echelons of power. That's why it was perfectly acceptable and proper for Archie or Churchill to prosper in war. They were born for it, they didn't start it, but they'd see it finished.

Conner was acutely conscious that Darwin and Hitler would approve of those ideas, it made the fact no less true.

*

## Wednesday 6th November 1940 - Bletchley Park

On her return from Operation Claudius, the Bordeaux explosions, Rebecca was worried, which was downright unusual for her. When you had no emotional intelligence, you didn't worry what others thought of you, and you didn't worry what you thought of others. You certainly didn't worry about someone you'd never met.

She knew from other team members that Archie had finished with Grace. She reasoned quite logically that it was a direct consequence of her conversation with him. She'd taken it too far again, she'd asked too many questions, and she'd killed Grace for him, she'd broken the spell for him.

At the time she'd been certain she was just providing information to him, he'd taken it as more. No, it was his responsibility, not hers, absolutely. No, that was her own guilt and shame again, trying to rationalise and excuse her behaviour. No wonder she had no friends, friendships were complicated, best not to have any. Stay detached she told herself.

Her trouble was, she felt a sense of belonging in the team, in both teams. Her life was turning into a difficult struggle not to get closer to people. The fact that she didn't know exactly how to get involved, helped her to keep the distance she needed. The attitude of people towards her had changed since she'd returned from France, and she'd also felt a distinct difference in her attitude to others. War was making changes to everyone, and it was leading her, slowly and clumsily, towards caring about people. Just when death was closer than ever. Great timing, she thought then withdrew back into her shell.

The BB Club, for Big Boffins, was an outlet for her, though. It was a small exclusive group of the brightest people at Bletchley Park, who couldn't discuss their current work, but could discuss any other great scientific issues. There was no emotion there, only intellect, mostly speculative and theoretical. She was interested in nuclear fission, not in the sense that it might produce limitless energy or hugely powerful explosive power, only what it meant in respect of cosmology.

That evening it was Rebecca's turn to set the question.

"We agree the Universe is continually expanding. All matter is held together by gravity, that's why there are spherical planets. It should be shrinking, imploding surely?

"There must have been a single, vastly powerful, gravity defying expansion, an explosion, from a single point and it's still happening now.

"If the Universe is expanding, what is it expanding into?

"If it started in a single place, how did all the matter currently in the Universe fit into that single place?

"It would have to be a big place, as big as the Universe surely, and that doesn't make sense.

"Unless all the matter was compressed into a smaller space, a stupidly tiny space, and where did all that matter come from?"

The BBs loved that, theoretical speculation, genius for its own sake. She, on the other hand, desperately wanted to do something with her knowledge, she wanted to go there, see it, do it, she wanted to go to other planets, other stars. She certainly wasn't made for this planet, she needed another one.

"We may have to have a long think about that one, Rebecca?" Alan said.

*

Archie worked closely with Rebecca and Mary Driver on the intelligence categorising system. Archie instinctively recognised what was important and what wasn't. He could identify links between disparate pieces of intelligence. He could tell speculation from reasoned deduction.

The list of his investigative skills was lengthy.

The list of what he couldn't do was shorter, he couldn't explain his instinctive skills to anyone else, except Rebecca, and she worked with Mary, producing what they called a grading matrix. That matrix should enable most competent clerks to correctly identify reliable and priority intelligence. There was no shortage of information needing conversion into useful intelligence. They couldn't take action on all of it, they barely had enough people to read it. The complete system ensured they would consistently identify and act on the most relevant, reliable and urgent intelligence.

Archie and Conner had given the evaluation reports and results to Bracken on the 1st of November.

"Leave this with me," he'd said, "Winston will love this."

Archie bought chocolates and biscuits then gave them to Rebecca to hand over from herself, he also mischievously asked her to work with Mary Driver on a Christmas party for the teams. She couldn't say no, *he'd* backed *her* into a corner for once, he liked that.

*

**Thursday 8th November 1940 – Whitehall**

Archie brought Rebecca down to Whitehall with him, he'd found out Grace had left the Savoy and had joined the Women's Royal Air Force. He was, therefore, able to book Rebecca into the Savoy and make sure she had the break and luxury she deserved, but in which she never indulged. He asked Billy to look after her, knowing he couldn't possibly think there was any link between Rebecca and the break up with Grace. Billy thanked him for ending it with Grace and for acting like a gentleman.

"She deserves better than you and I," Billy said, "as for being a gentleman, you knew I'd kill you didn't you?"

"I knew you'd try. You're right, she deserves better, than me anyway," Archie said.

Billy laughed. "I'll look after Miss Rochford, don't you worry."

*

Archie spent some time with Rebecca, making her feel welcome and trying to be nice, without ever mentioning the word, obviously. Their time together was productive in terms of ideas and planning for Operations Claymore and Rapier, but Conner's return from Switzerland would still be welcome.

When not talking exclusively about work, she was different, though. Here was Archie, being a perfect gentlemen, dinners, theatre, cinema, sightseeing, everything he could think of, and the woman remained implacably grumpy and almost monosyllabic. She'd been fine on the journey back from France, but on their return, she'd suddenly become a misery; he'd rather she just took the mickey out of him like she usually did.

He was just about to give up and throw her in the Thames when purely by accident while passing a hat shop, she dragged him in.  It was cold, and he did need a winter hat for when he was wearing civvies. She found the hats hilarious, which to be fair, so did he. She laughed least at a grey fedora trilby, not too big or too small, so he bought that one.

After that, she spotted a beautifully aged, high back leather chair in a second-hand furniture store they were passing, and insisted he buy it for the flat.

"You have your thinking cap, now you need a thinking chair," she said, thankfully her usual slightly weird self, once more.

*

Having calmed Rebecca down enough to feel safe

leaving her alone, he decided to undertake another act of penance. He had money of his own now and the comfort of an officer's uniform and voice, he forced himself to undertake a duty he dreaded.

He drove to an address in Pinner, a pleasant suburb of outer London and parked outside, going over what he needed to say. He nearly chickened out, then just grabbed his briefcase, left the car and knocked on the door.

The widow of Gerald *'Jezz'* Hastings answered the door. She was late twenties and attractive, well dressed and made up but looked very tired.

"Mrs Hastings?"

"Yes," she smiled at him.

"Good morning I'm Lieutenant Travers."

"Have you finally found him?"

"No, I'm afraid not."

*'Oh bloody hell, she doesn't know yet.'*

"You'd best come in then," she said.

They sat in a tidy living room.

"Well, what is it?" she said.

"I understand you know your husband was declared missing in action in Calais."

He was just guessing now, he'd told the War Office about the death more than six months ago.

"Yes, and I've heard nothing since."

"Well, I'm afraid I have bad news for you. Your husband was killed in action in the Battle of Calais."

"How do you know? How do you know now and not back then? You're all bloody useless, bloody officers, you're all the same, bloody useless he said in his letters, bloody useless."

"I was there when he died, Mrs Hastings."

"Hiding no doubt, while the men did the fighting."

"No, I was just a Private then."

"He never mentioned no Travers, and you're no Private, you're too posh."

"I was a stray from another unit, and he helped me, I knew him for less than a day. He died bravely, trying to save an officer's life, and I shot the German, who killed him, that's all."

"I suppose you want a medal then?"

"No, it's just, I thought you'd know he was dead by now."

"And how come you took so long to get round here then?"

This just wasn't going to plan at all.

"You've just come to ease your conscience that's all, you're all the same."

Archie started to take the envelope of money he'd prepared, from his briefcase.

"He was a teacher you know, he was in a reserved occupation. He wouldn't stay at home, said he couldn't let young men he'd taught go, and then stay behind safe at home.  He should have been an officer, not you, you'd be dead not him."

"Mrs Hastings, some of the surviving men have had a collection for him, and we'd like you to take this."

"I don't want your bloody money, blood money," she said throwing the money back at him.

"I want my husband back."

"I think I should leave now, Mrs Hastings."

"Yes, run away, like you did in Calais."

Archie did leave, attempting to retain some dignity but failing, as she screamed down the garden path at him.

He drove around the corner and parked the car.  The money was still there on her floor, five hundred pounds. He'd told her the truth. Truth was overrated, and she hadn't believed it anyway.

"I am never doing that again as long as I live," he said to the rear-view mirror, as he searched his eyes for something he might have missed.

## Chapter 20

## Christmas 1940 – Spring 1941

After the hat and chair day, Rebecca had become calm and cheerful enough for Archie to resume his search for meaningless, distracting casual sex in London. He went to the club and other places, experiencing some transient success, half hoping to see Victoria and half not, relying on her comfort would be a pleasant, but backward step for him.

Conner had briefed him and Rebecca on his meeting with Heisenberg, Archie was impressed, as he'd expected to be. Rebecca was astonished, just beginning to recognise the depth of Conner's abilities.

As they sat talking in their private room at Bletchley Park, Rebecca asked if she could talk about camouflage.

Of course, they said.

"Ours is rubbish!"

"What do you mean, we wore black for the Bordeaux job, it was dark, and we wore black?" Archie said.

"You mean you didn't notice how easily we saw the others when we returned to the dinghies?"

"Bloody hell, you're right, I noticed and was pleased to see them, what an idiot."

"There were black human shapes against a different kind of black, we need to break up the outlines, use different shades and colours and add some textures as well. The same materials reflect or show up uniformly. It's a bit like the drawings I can do and make them look three-dimensional," she said.

"You're a bloody genius."

"I didn't know I could do it until you told me, if you hadn't sat next to me waiting for me to wake, if you hadn't… "

Conner spoke to fill the silence.

"There's a chap I'm aware of, an artistic type, Roland Penrose, he's doing some work on this for the Home Guard.

You should see him, he'll be pleased to help."

"Yes, Rebecca and I can go together," said Archie.

"He's a Quaker Conscientious Objector."

"You go on your own Rebecca, you'll be fine," Archie ended.

*

Archie's idea to get Rebecca and Mary to organise a Christmas Party proved a master stroke. Rebecca accomplished some almost normal human behaviour, she still refused to let Mary do anything with her hair, there was no female behaviour, although human was a definite step forward.

The venue for the joint team Christmas party was the Manor. It was five miles from Bletchley Park and had seven large bedrooms. Some Chosen Men shared rooms, and it was still a distinct improvement on their former barracks. It sat in a couple of acres, down a long driveway and gave the privacy and security the team needed. It provided a broad area for target practice, and Begley had taken over the small stables as his workshop. The team had grown used to Begley, but they still didn't want his gear in the house. Only Spud and Nipper were allowed in there, given no one else wanted to go inside, it presented no problem. Archie planned to install an obstacle course and a small gymnasium.

It had a large reception and dining room, a huge kitchen and a library filled with old books. The ladies wisely insisted on preparing the food and Spud and Bestie, as bakers, insisted on helping.

The food wasn't great, there was lots of French bread, English cheese, some real Turkey meat, from Billy, and a vast number of hot roasted potatoes fried to a crisp with hot lard.

Archie and Conner provided all the drink, two barrels of beer and two dozen bottles of wine, the Savoy Cellar had revealed some of its secrets.

Conner drank only one glass of wine and Archie only half a glass, topping his up with water. He couldn't afford to relax in front of either team. He'd begun trying to always stay in full control, mind, mood, and voice. He couldn't risk his true self coming to the surface so publicly.

Archie noticed Spud and Mary Driver getting on well, and could tell today wasn't the first time. He hoped that would develop into an affair.

Tarrian, as a rugby-playing Welshman, could have downed two barrels on his own, he wasn't drinking today. He was making his way down to London later to see his wife and their baby. She was pregnant while he was in France, gave birth when he returned and was pregnant again. He was as proud of his son as any man could possibly be, and he hoped for a little sister next time.

"Funny, we'd been trying for a while, and nothing happened then bingo two at once," he'd proudly said to Archie.

I'm so glad I didn't kill him too, Archie thought.

Archie couldn't see any other potential liaisons, although they were all having a cracking time, dancing, singing and playing party games, charades and the like.

Spud got up, called for silence and sang *'Molly Malone'* in a deep baritone, every time he said *'Sweet Molly Malone'* he looked at Mary. The lyrics weren't entirely suitable, the sentiment and warmth in the singing were.

Archie was happy to see them enjoying themselves, he'd use them when he needed to, he knew that, but this false niceness would provide some balance to the using.

Even Begley calmed down a little, once you got used to him looking like a madman all the time, you could recognise that he behaved reasonably most of the time. He and Nipper became best mates, Begley teaching Nipper about explosives; they were from the same wrong side of the same wrong street.

Nipper had settled into the team well, after his hard time in Colchester. Joe Dempsey had spoken to Archie about Colchester and had said he and Ben would look after him. They knew the reputation of the North London children's home Nipper had grown up in, Colchester with kids, he said, but wouldn't explain further. Archie knew what that meant.

Conner had provided presents for everybody, Swiss watches, male and female, not suspiciously expensive, certainly better than any of them owned already.

"I just wanted to make sure you're all on time," he said in the self-deprecating tone he tried to use sometimes; it never worked, the man just oozed class.

There were crackers too, home-made ones, the work of Rebecca and Mary Driver, they assured everyone. The bangs and sparks were unusually loud and bright, and Begley did look suspiciously pleased. Then, when Rebecca insisted on giving Archie one particular cracker, he made sure she pulled it with him.

At least I'll take the madwoman with me, he thought.

He was relieved by the usual small explosion, then saw the joke typed on a small piece of paper and read it out.

*Q: Why do they bury Germans 20 feet underground?*

*A: Because deep down they're really nice.*

Everyone groaned.

"Isn't it funny then?" she said.

"No, it's funny. It's just that some jokes are meant to be groaned at," Archie said, then spent the next half-hour trying to explain that to her, while she drank more wine.

Nipper stood up and demanded silence.

"Thank you for my best Christmas ever," then flopped down into a chair, asleep before he hit it.

"I told the idiot, he was too young to drink," said Begley and then made sure he was sleeping okay and wouldn't puke.

The party finished, earlier than planned, the drink had run out. Archie drove Conner and a tipsy, giggly Rebecca to their cottage. They let her sleep on the sofa with a bucket nearby, just in case, while they talked about life, the universe and the meaning of it all. Archie had a couple of glasses of wine while relaxed at home with Conner, confident Rebecca was safe and wouldn't vomit or need to go to hospital with alcohol poisoning.

Conner, Archie, and Rebecca decided to work on Christmas Day, to make sure the others had that day off.

Conner insisted they all stay at the cottage and prepared the spare bedroom for Rebecca. They checked into Building Thirteen, and nothing was happening, perhaps all sides were having the day off.

That evening, they ate a frugal meal and shared one bottle of wine between the three of them.

"Brothers!" said Conner to Archie as he clinked his glass.

"And a sister," said Archie as he clinked Rebecca's.

"Family," she said smiling, genuinely and with a gentle warmth he hadn't seen in her before.

They listened to the BBC, talked and showed Rebecca how to play pontoon and gamble for pennies, she was good at it! Archie swore she was counting the cards in her head.

*

## Tuesday 4th March 1941 – 0400 - Operation Claymore – Lofoten Islands

After two more months of training, waiting and more training, it was finally 0400 hours on the 4th March 1941. Conner personally received confirmation of the signal from the submarine 'Sunfish'. The Captain confirmed sighting the German Armed Trawler 'Krebs' at its expected anchorage off the coast of the Lofoten Islands in the Norwegian Sea.

Conner already knew *'Force Rebel'* of Operation *'Claymore'* was proceeding as planned, for their attack on four small ports in the Islands. They would attack any enemy troops and shipping they encountered in the ports and the Fish Oil Production Facilities located there. The Fish Oil was exported to Germany for conversion into Glycerine and used to produce high explosives. The British Force would, as Archie and Conner had outlined to Bracken months ago, overwhelm the inferior force there. They would take prisoners, blow up selected targets, destroy shipping and film everything as a great propaganda coup for the Ministry of Information; only if it all went to plan of course.

The lesser-known purpose of the mission; *'Rapier'* would remain Ultra Secret and perhaps would never be wholly or accurately revealed, those who would undertake it, never existed.

This part of the mission would remain hidden from everyone in *'Force Rebel'*, only Conner's team and a few people on board, their small converted Minesweeper with its crew of entirely SOE operatives, would know some of it.

The code-breakers at Bletchley Park had identified 'Krebs" as a trawler that acted clandestinely as a weather forecasting and reporting vessel. They'd recognised it signalled its vital information to the U-Boats plaguing British Shipping in the Atlantic. They could only decipher the code infrequently and slowly, usually too late to take any effective action. What they and Conner's team did know for certain was that this small, poorly armed vessel contained a working Enigma Machine and Code Books. If such material were captured, it would be invaluable to the war effort. It had to be done carefully, secretly and there could be no witnesses.

Conner had spoken to each man individually, explaining exactly what that meant.

"For the duration of Operation Rapier, this unit will take no prisoners; that is my precise order and my absolute responsibility," he'd said. "Any man not willing to accept that order may leave the team now."

They all agreed to stay without a second's hesitation.

The vessel would sink with all hands during a purely coincidental and credible raid on the nearby Lofoten Islands. That way the secrecy might just hold long enough to make a significant and effective contribution to the War in the Atlantic.

At 0530, the Chosen Men and Rebecca boarded the same three dinghies they'd used in France. This time, they were equipped with small outboard motors, they might need a quicker getaway. They still planned to use only the muffled paddling they'd so carefully practiced.

They all wore dark clothing, an experimental camouflage for this operation only. Black, dark brown, dark rock, dark blues and with fuzzy velvet patches sewn on randomly. In daylight it looked ridiculous, in this particular light, it didn't look like anything.

The 'Krebs' lay near a rocky outcrop that provided safe anchorage for the night, the outcrop also provided great cover for three approaching dinghies. They paddled closer, keeping the rock between them and the trawler, steering to the right of the rock. Conner, in the lead boat, paused briefly at the point where he could just begin to see the bow of the trawler. It was before dawn, maybe fifteen minutes, enough time to approach unseen and unheard. They expected a maximum of two guards on deck, probably only one, in this place, at this time. He half expected to see or hear distant sounds of attack from far behind the trawler, but that would only provide another distraction for its crew. With a fracas going on ahead of them they could attack from the rear.

The Chosen Men needed to move fast, none of the other ships knew they were there. They had no radio contact with their own ship, and the targets for the Royal Navy vessels were a safe distance from this anchorage. They needed to be clear, well before any ship spotted the trawler.

Conner motioned forward with his right hand, and the boats closed the distance between them and the trawler. The sea remained calm, no waves just smooth ripples, and he could see the 'Krebs' was about the same size as the 'Gulzar.'

They could hear no sound from onboard, and at 0610, each boat feather touched the starboard side of the trawler. One dinghy at the bow, the stern, and the middle. One man from each dinghy attached a specially designed short and wide ladder to the side of the trawler. The sides of the ladder were shaped like question marks, with thick rubber on the curves, to prevent any scratching noises. Archie had designed them, his originality had impressed the SOE boffins, he'd stolen the idea from Julius Caesar.

As planned, Rebecca was the first one to climb up, armed with Archie's silenced Luger. She weighed the least, would rock the boat least and make less noise than any man. It was a purely practical decision, and she made not a single sound as her blackened face peered over the edge, ladder in one gloved hand, Luger in the other. She saw one guard, standing and looking out to sea. She fired two seconds later, and they heard the muffled sound of a body falling onto the deck. In training, she'd proven to be as accurate a pistol shot under pressure as any man. The slim handle of the Luger fitted her small hand as if they'd been made for each other.

Nipper was next on board at the bow, a silenced pistol in his hand too.

Spud was next at the stern.

They all climbed noiselessly on board with their soft rubber soled boots, the middle group approached the wheelhouse, seeing just one man inside, asleep, Archie signalled for Rebecca to target the sleeper. Then, seeing the prow and stern teams were ready to move, Thompson sub-machine guns in their hands, he gave the signal.

Rebecca fired one shot through the head of the lazy guard. Archie burst straight into the wheelhouse, forcing open the door to the Captain's cabin, firing his Thompson with deliberately short and focussed bursts. He wanted to kill any man he saw but not damage any machines or papers. They couldn't give the Germans any chance to dispose of or damage the machine and codebooks.

Outside his vision, the firefight was confusing, it lasted about ten seconds, stopped and then started again for one brief burst, and one single shot then stopped.

"It's Christmas again," he shouted to Rebecca, "in here please," he added, already sealing up the first Enigma Machine.

"Seal and bag the second one with the code books, I'll take this."

"Machines first, people second," she added, smiling and

pleased with herself.

Archie smiled too, his flowing adrenaline allowed him the luxury of a little smugness. He cradled the precious machine up the narrow steps from the Captain's quarters that had doubled as the radio and code room. The Captain's, and one other naked male body lay riddled with his bullets on the bunk.

He handed the machine down to Conner on the dinghy.

"I'll get the other one," he said.

"There's another?" Conner said.

"Yes, we've hit the jackpot today," Archie said, beaming with pride.

The smile disappeared when he turned round and saw Joe and Ben Dempsey arguing in front of a group of prisoners at the stern of the trawler.

From the corner of his eye to the right, he could see Nipper, Smudger and others coming from the bow quarters. Ahead, he could see Tarrian in the wheelhouse, helping Rebecca with her two bundles.

Archie lost his temper, he didn't even try not to, adrenaline was flowing, and he walked over to the Dempsey's.

"What the fuck's going on here!" he shouted. "Where's Spud?"

"He's copped it, sir and Bestie too, they're down below," said Ben, looking daggers at his brother, Joe.

"Spud's dead and these bastards are alive?" said Archie taking his Thompson from off his shoulder and cocking it.

"Look at them, they're just kids," said Joe, stepping between Archie and the Germans.

"I fucking told you to shoot quickly and not to look at faces and not at the eyes. I told you, it would be more difficult later, I fucking told you, have I got to do your job for you?"

Ben looked at Archie, with pleading in his eyes, not pleading for the Germans, he was pleading with Archie not to kill Joe.

Archie took a deep breath, "I'm a bit busy at the

moment, just fucking guard them then, you stupid cunt."

"Ben, give me a hand with this stuff," he said waving Ben towards the wheelhouse and turned his back on Joe and the Germans. I'll give Ben one chance to get Joe to do his job, he thought.

As they reached the wheelhouse, he turned around, just in time to scream.

"Down!"

He'd seen the flash of a ship opening fire in the distance. There was nothing nearby worth shooting at, so the 'Krebs' was the target. Three agonising slow motion seconds later the stern of the trawler blew apart, spraying thick wooden splinters outwards in all directions. The shockwave blew Ben on top of Archie, and they fell to the deck. Archie's head was ringing, he was intact and vaguely aware of some Germans being dead, some blown overboard, some taking the chance, even with wounds, to jump into the sea. He knew he'd seen Joe blown into bits.

Another shell hit the trawler amidships, thankfully on the other side of the wheelhouse.

The wheelhouse! Rebecca!

He pushed Ben off him and went up the six steps to the shattered wheelhouse. He ducked and flinched again as some smaller explosions sparked and flamed from the trawler itself. Probably just some ammo exploding, but he barely had enough time to register that, when another explosion ripped into the ship. This time, it hit below the water line. To his right, he could see Smudger, bare-chested and frantically waving the biggest shirt you've ever seen. Archie couldn't see clearly for the dust and tears in his eyes, I hope that's a clean white shirt.

Ben splashed water on his face and shook him.

"You alright, sir? Sir! You alright?" he said.

Archie shook the water from his face and opened his eyes fully.

Straight ahead, he saw the impossibly huge pupils, belonging to the eyes of Rebecca Rochford staring at him with an intensity that almost made him weep.

275

"Yes, I'm fine now. Well, no, I'm not fine, I'm alive, and that'll have to do for now. Have they stopped firing?" he half coughed the words out.

"Yes, it's our Navy an' all, sir, our own bastard Navy. Sorry Ma'am," he said to Rebecca.

"That's all right Ben, a good morning just got really shitty," Rebecca said.

Archie stood up and could now see Rebecca more clearly, holding tightly on to two sacks, clasping them safely between her arms knees and chest as she crouched. Crouched beneath the massive dead frame of Tarrian, his back and rear stabbed to death by a hundred pieces of shrapnel, glass, and wood.

Smudger appeared behind Rebecca and peeled Tarrian's dead body off her back. She just stayed on her knees not moving for a second or two then said.

"He just grabbed me and held me, you shouted to get down, and I just stood there looking, he grabbed me, turned me away from the sound and sheltered me."

"He never made a better tackle then, Ma'am," said Smudger, lifting her and the bundles up in his huge arms.

"I'll get her in the dinghy, Archie, don't you worry, you sort yourself out."

Conner came back on the trawler.

"Ben, Begley, with me, the rest of you get the cargo back to the ship, leave this mess to Archie and me."

Conner could see a smaller boat was approaching from the Navy vessel, one of the destroyers, he couldn't tell which. They were stopping to pick up the wounded and fleeing German swimmers.

He noticed the trawler was drifting from its anchorage and beginning to list.

"There's two dead below, Spud and Bestie, Tarrian in the wheelhouse, Joe's gone now, is everyone else okay?" asked Archie.

"Four dead, yes," said Conner, "the rest just a few scratches."

The Navy boat approached, "Archie, Ben, stand back,

leave all the talking to me, Begley make sure something sinks this tub forever and don't shoot at the Navy either, any of you!"

Conner spoke to the Captain and officers who boarded the trawler in his usual calm aristocratic manner. He handed the Major a sealed envelope which he opened and read. They listened intently, nodding, clearly about to do everything he told them.

Archie and Ben sat on the wreckage, half looking at the mess that used to be Joe and some German ratings.

"What happened below, Ben?"

"Spud and Bestie went first and copped it from behind when they were firing ahead. Joe and me took them lot, and by the time we looked up, those young lads were on their knees begging. I raised mine, then he held me back, he's my big brother, I've always done what he said, always. He was wrong this time, dead wrong. We ain't got time to be nice."

"I'm sorry I called him a cunt."

"Well, he was actin' like one, d'you think Jerry would 'ave looked at Nipper and let him go. No chance. You're right, you've got to shoot first and think later, much later. I don't know what I'm gonna tell me mum, not a flamin' clue."

"Tell her he died trying to save the lives of others and killing Jerrys, that's true enough."

"Will you talk to her with me, sir?"

"Yes, I will if you want me to, Ben."

"Thank you, sir, and who's gonna tell Sergeant Driver and Spud's mum, they was sweet on each other, really sweet. What a bloody mess."

"And we won this one, what's a defeat going to feel like?"

"We'll just have to make sure we don't have one."

"Right chaps, we're off, the rest is down to the Navy," said Conner, "and Begley, don't blow anything up, the Navy want to do it."

"Oh, sir, it was gonna go up a treat!"

*

The journey back to the Faroe Islands took less than a day and a half, at full speed with excellent spring weather. Archie was grateful for that, Rebecca refused to go down below, saying she felt claustrophobic. Conner and Archie wrapped her up in a duffle coat and blankets and gave her hot soup and tea. Archie had a mind full of evil thoughts he needed to sort out, that would have to wait. There were times when you couldn't leave someone on their own, and he stayed by her side for the whole journey. Luckily they could access a toilet from the deck, he couldn't persuade her to wash, though, so they remained black faced.

All she would say was, "I killed him. That was my fault, I should have moved, I should have moved quicker, I should have done something."

A plane took the three of them, and the prized German equipment, from the Faroes directly to Croydon aerodrome. The remaining Chosen Men would go home more slowly, and they'd have a week's leave when they returned. A car took Conner and the equipment straight to Bletchley Park, he'd claimed to have slept on the boat, Archie knew he'd have been writing letters and reports.

Another car took Archie and Rebecca straight to Hevlyn Mansions. Rebecca grew even more withdrawn on the journey, but Archie knew her better now.

Once in his flat, he sat her in the thinking chair. The main area of the flat was open plan, kitchen then living space as you entered, with two bedrooms and a bathroom leading off that space to face the rear.

"This is a great chair, I told you, almost a throne, Caesar would have liked this chair," he said. Where did that come from he wondered?

He took her boots off and undid the tight crepe bandages from the weak ankle.

"How does it feel?"

"Okay," she said.

"Wait there," he said and began to run a hot bath for her.

While the tub was filling, he returned with a tin basin full of hot soapy water and a towel. He washed her feet gently and moved the weak ankle from side to side in a circular motion, testing it for any sign of harm.

"It's fine, I'm sure," she said.

"In the bath then, there's fresh towels and a robe. And don't forget to wash your face, you look like shit, you know!" he shouted after her as she shut the bathroom door.

He took off his own boots, his jacket, loosened his shirt then washed his face and hands in the kitchen sink while the kettle boiled for a pot of tea.

Rebecca came into the living room, wearing his robe. He gave her a cup of tea, steered her into the bedroom and laid her on his bed. He tightened the robe around her and carefully tucked her in, she could barely keep her eyes open. He looked at her asleep briefly, then turned off the light and returned to the chair.

After drinking his tea while it was at the perfect temperature, he went to the bathroom, stripped and got in the still warm, dirty bathwater. He brushed his teeth with the still moist toothbrush and used the mouthwash, washing his hands again, trying to get the smell of murder from them, and the taste of it from his mouth. The rest of his clothes were in the bedroom, so he put on the same trousers and shirt, rather than disturb her. It was cold in the room at nearly midnight, so he lit the gas fire, turned the thinking chair to face the hearth and put off the lights.

He sat in the chair for two hours, deep in thought and unable to sleep, tired as he was. He balanced the feeling of loss in his mind against what he'd gained since that fateful and fatal truck journey with Conner and some good men. He knew he'd gained more than he'd lost, but it would take time for that knowledge to develop into anything that made him feel better. He had time to think and plan, he still had more to do, and he was somebody now.

He heard the bedroom door open, there was no other sound, not even the faintest of bare footsteps on the polished wooden floor. Rebecca just seemed to float around the chair next to him, she wasn't wearing the robe, just one of his best white cotton shirts, warm, sturdy and soft. She didn't say a word, just sat on his lap and curled her knees up like some elfin spiritual presence, it felt like she had no weight at all. He cradled her in his arms and held her as close as he dared. Her scent entranced him, she wore no perfume, but she smelt new, fresh and clean, somehow. It had been some time since he'd felt clean.

They didn't say a word, as if they knew they were engaged in a spell that talking might break. He'd never felt less lonely in all his life, never felt more like he belonged somewhere, in a time and a place that was unique and meant for him and him alone.

It was half an hour later, two thirty on the wall clock when she spoke.

"Before I went to St. Nazaire, I asked Gubbins if you could debrief me when I got back."

"It was you I saw at the window, studying me."

"Yes, you had something I hadn't seen before."

"What was that?"

"I don't know, I'm still trying to work it out," she said snuggling even deeper into his lap.

"Krebs is the German word for the constellation of Cancer, the crab you know," she said.

"The Egyptians called it Scarabaeus, the Scarab, their sacred emblem of immortality," he said.

"Its centre is 6,523 light years away, that's 6,523 years travelling at the speed of light, that's 186,000 miles per second. Immortality would be useful, even if you hurried. Can we live forever and will you take me there?"

"Yes, of course," he said.

"You promised not to lie to me!"

"Are we dead yet?"

"No?"

"So far so good, then."

They went to sleep only minutes later, he in the chair and she in his lap. Two hours later Archie woke, then carefully and gently carried her to the bed. She didn't wake fully, and when he lay flat on his back exhausted, she snuggled towards him again, wrapping her arms and legs around him. He hugged her gently in return, and they remained asleep, or sleepy, just like that until the following afternoon.

They only slept; that was all they needed, that and the simple presence of the other.

Archie was disconcerted by his constant, unprompted, untouched, unfulfilled erection and wondered why that was happening. Rebecca experienced the delicious warm feeling of silky moisture, tingling inside her vagina for the first time in her life and wondered what on earth it was.

The End

The story continues in Book Two – The Flattery of Knaves.

Other titles by Richard A. McDonald are available on Amazon in paperback and Kindle formats.

If you have enjoyed this novel, please feel free to put a review on Amazon. If you haven't, please give it to someone else who might.

For more information search for Richard-A-McDonald on Facebook.
https://www.facebook.com/profile.php?id=100012231016546

18172000R00168

Printed in Great Britain
by Amazon